Praise for *My Champion*

"Ms. Campbell's debut novel propels readers into the fourteenth century with vivid descriptions and details of the life of the commoner. The nonstop action, strong plot, and fascinating characters draw you deeply into the story. As the first in a trilogy about the de Ware brothers, *My Champion* will have readers clamoring fo...

—...antic Times

"Sparkles with h... ...g characters. A deli... ...utcliffe

"Well-written, w... ...n, *My Champion* is a sexy, light-hear... ...tory." —Rexanne Becnel

"From the first vivid word, Glynnis Campbell immerses the reader deep in medieval England, creating characters rich with texture and emotion and a vibrant story of uncommon loyalty, betrayal, and a love destined against all odds."

—Amy J. Fetzer

MY HERO

GLYNNIS CAMPBELL

JOVE BOOKS, NEW YORK

This is a work of fiction. Names, characters, places, and incidents either are the product of the author's imagination or are used fictitiously, and any resemblance to actual persons, living or dead, business establishments, events, or locales is entirely coincidental.

MY HERO

A Jove Book / published by arrangement with
the author

PRINTING HISTORY
Jove edition / July 2002

Copyright © 2002 by Glynnis Campbell
Cover art by Griesbach & Martucci

Visit our website at
www.penguinputnam.com

ISBN: 0-515-13333-7

A JOVE BOOK®
Jove Books are published by The Berkley Publishing Group,
a division of Penguin Putnam Inc.,
375 Hudson Street, New York, New York 10014.
JOVE and the "J" design
are trademarks belonging to Penguin Putnam Inc.

PRINTED IN THE UNITED STATES OF AMERICA

10 9 8 7 6 5 4 3 2 1

To my mom . . .
For open arms and healing hands—
Haven for my spirit,
Champion of my dreams,
Hero of my heart

With undimming gratitude and admiration
for Helen and Cindy
and my lovely sisters at OCC/RWA

Prologue

Summer 1329

"I SHALL *NEVER* MARRY SUCH A CREATURE AS A BOY!" Cynthia le Wyte hissed to herself, slamming the heavy garden gate behind her, narrowly missing the embroidered edge of her best surcoat.

She'd had about all an eleven-year-old girl could endure of those de Ware lads. How she wished she'd stayed home with her little sisters. If Duncan de Ware wasn't taunting her with verses about her unfortunate orange hair, his brother Holden was nigh lopping off her locks with wild swings of his ever-present sword. Bless Lady Alyce for lending her the key to the privy garden this morn, else she'd be dodging the blows of the de Ware knaves yet.

She leaned back against the warped oak door and tucked the key into the deep velvet pocket of her surcoat, listening for sounds of pursuit. To her relief, none came.

Satisfied that she was no longer the fox to their hounds, she stepped forward to survey her sanctuary. And fell instantly in love.

"Oh!"

Before her stretched the garden of an enchantress. Graceful willows and fruit trees sprang from beds of fragrant mint—apples, warden pears, plums, damsons, cherries. Delicate blossoms, some as white as frost, some blushing pink, permeated the warm air with a heady perfume that dizzied her.

In a sunny spot, kitchen herbs and vegetables thrived—rows of radishes and neeps, parsley, peas and cabbage, fennel and thyme, garlic, pasterniks, sage and rosemary.

Colorful primroses nestled at the foot of tall stalks of purple iris. Violets and borage ran riot over a patch of wet earth along the west wall, and marigolds popped their bright faces up amidst sprawls of lavender and heliotrope. Row after row of lilies and daffodils marched at the north border of the garden, interrupted by an occasional daisy poking its head through their ranks.

Cautiously, she tiptoed forward. After all, she didn't wish to tread upon some spell dropped on the garden floor by a scurrying elf. Carefully, she scanned the foliage. At any moment, she imagined, a woodland sprite might peep out from behind a cluster of cowslip. Or perhaps a tiny fairy would fly, struggling, into a spider's dewy web.

Feeling as fey as her surroundings, she impulsively slipped the soft boots and woolen stockings from her feet and let her bare toes revel in the carpet of damp grass.

Instantly the past two days of impeccably good behavior and obligatory curtseys her father's diplomatic visits always entailed seemed a small price to pay for this—the discovery of the long-lost Magical Garden of Castle de Ware.

Cynthia lightly brushed her foot over a cluster of daisies, letting the delicate petals tickle her arch. Her giggle startled a sparrow from a willow branch. She took a deep breath, drinking in the combined scent of the flowers and herbs and trees as if it were an enchanter's potion.

Then she spied the roses.

A cascade of fat blossoms sprawled over the old stone wall. Some of the blooms were a deep, velvety red, some as smooth and white as fresh cream, and some the most delicate shade of pink she'd ever seen. A garland of them ran along the garden wall, spilling down in long tendrils like the jewel-studded hair of a princess.

She sighed reverently, letting her gaze lilt from flower to flower like a butterfly.

She wanted them. She *wanted* them.

Her own mother's garden was so drab, so practical, full of herbs to flavor pottage and heal the sick. How much lovelier the le Wyte castle would be with roses like that tumbling over the wattle fences. And, she thought slyly, how simple a matter to snip a few cuttings. . . .

She frowned and gave her head a firm shake. One didn't steal plants. Not from one's host.

Still . . .

The bushes were well established, the wood at their bases gnarled with years of survival. And Cynthia knew just how to take cuttings of branches to make new plants without harming the old. Surely no one would miss a stem here and there. . . .

She tucked her bottom lip between her teeth.

Nobody seemed to be about. Her father had been engaged all morning in some sort of holdings inspection with Lord James de Ware. Lady Alyce no doubt still sat in her solar, working on the tedious embroidery she'd tried to convince Cynthia was fascinating. The elder de Ware boys were likely battling it out in the tiltyard by now, and the younger had made himself as scarce as a bee in winter. Cynthia had been left to fend for herself.

Those roses were breathtaking. If she was very careful . . .

Pursing her lips in determination, she pulled forth the small eating dagger from her belt and crept stealthily forward.

Garth de Ware studied the young assassin sneaking up on the roses. He screwed up his forehead, annoyed.

He'd come to his favorite spot in the garden, the willow bower, to study his Latin. With his two older brothers sparring today—in the lists, in the great hall, in the courtyard, and anywhere else there was room to draw two blades—quiet was a precious commodity. Here, amidst the *flora,* he'd expected to review the intricacies of Latin conjugation in *pax.*

At least he'd *thought* he'd find peace.

Until the garden gate creaked open at the hands of that skinny waif with orange hair—the le Wyte brat.

He glowered before he could temper his mutinous thoughts. Damn her eyes! He had no wish to be interrupted by a little girl who'd want him to take her hawking or riding or some such nonsense. He sat very still in his shade-dappled shelter, guarding his privacy like a grouse protecting eggs, and watched as the small murderer violated the serenity of the garden.

Actually, he had to concede, quirking up a reluctant corner of his mouth as she padded obliviously by his hiding place, the brat wasn't so bad. She'd come with her father two days past, and in that time, she'd never once asked him to entertain her. That, to a boy of fifteen summers, was a great blessing in itself.

Now if she'd been a few years older and a great deal comelier, his brothers would have leaped to do her bidding. A pretty young face often caused temporary madness and heated rivalry between the two of them.

This lass, however, had surely spent no more than ten years upon the earth. And from the little he'd seen of her, she looked as far from a minstrel's ideal as a partridge was from a falcon. A lady was supposed to be as pale as alabaster, fair-haired, demure, sweet, and fragile. Little Cynthia le Wyte was none of those. She was sturdy and freckled. Her hair was an outrageous shade of orange. Her feet were as bare as a peasant's. And the way she gripped that dagger in her fist as she crept close was anything but delicate.

Still, he supposed, cocking an eyebrow, there *was* some quality about her—something earthy, something honest— that made her, well, interesting.

She paused to smile then.

And Garth's world stopped.

That smile lit up her whole face, as if the sun shone for her alone, as if neither freckles nor orange hair could prevent her from expressing the sheer beauty of the moment. For one brief slice of time, she possessed an inner radiance as captivating as a rainbow. And in that magical instant, Garth caught a glimpse of the woman she would become.

There was life in her eyes. And vibrancy. And mischief.

Her smile was thoroughly engaging, as pure as a spring stream. He wondered what it would be like to drink from that stream.

Wonder made his heart flutter, the same wonder he felt when the odd little brown bulbs in his mother's garden surprised him by miraculously blooming into rare and splendid flowers.

He settled back then and watched in charmed amusement as the blossom slayer went to work. She patiently sawed at the rose branches, carefully avoiding the thorns, her tongue anchored to the corner of her lip in concentration. Then she tucked the foot-long pieces gingerly into her surcoat pocket. Once, the nearby chirp of a sparrow made her start in alarm, dropping her dagger. And after that, from time to time, she'd look furtively over her shoulder. Yet she never noticed him sitting motionless beneath the bower.

Her stealth was pointless, of course. His mother wouldn't have minded her transgression in the least. Lady Alyce gave often and willingly of her roses, which were known and prized as far away as two days' ride from the castle. Had this little fugitive but asked, his mother would have gladly loaded her skirts with cuttings.

The girl moved on to the deep red rosebush, the one whose dropped petals always reminded Garth of spilled blood. As if she'd heard his thoughts, she chanced to prick her finger on one of its nasty thorns. But the brave lass made no outcry, only wincing and popping her stubby finger into her mouth to suck on the tiny wound.

Then she paused for a moment, slowly lifting her head, and her face took on a dreamy cast. He knew at once she'd caught the scent of his mother's prize, the white-blossomed bush against the wall. The tiny flowers were in full bloom, and their sweet fragrance never failed to seduce visitors to the garden unfamiliar with the exotic plant.

Unfortunately, as he'd learned from countless summers past, those flowers also seduced honeybees. It was one of the reasons his mother had procured the bush in the first place. Bees in the garden, she said, helped the flowers to produce more abundantly.

But they also stung the naive.

Of course, the little girl squatting beneath the roses would know nothing about the white-flowered bush. She'd likely reach out for a cluster of blooms and stuff her hand directly into a throng of crawling bees.

He couldn't let that happen. Not to a lady. De Ware men protected ladies.

Dropping his book onto the grass, he hopped to his feet. Emerging from the curtain of willow branches, he quickly commanded, "Move away!"

The girl gasped loudly, clearly horrified. She leaped up, scattering the rose cuttings, and swung around, her eyes as wide as silver coins.

He scowled. He hadn't meant to scare her. Not *that* much.

She chattered breathlessly, flushing scarlet and backing away. "I meant no harm, my lord. I swear it. I only—"

"Move away!" This time his harsh command was intentional, for dozens of bees squirmed mere inches from her shoulder. Still the lass seemed unaware of the little yellow firebrands. She stood frozen in his regard like a hart under a hunter's bolt. "Now!"

Cynthia stumbled back from the lordly voice, utterly abashed. Her heart beat so hard she feared it would escape her breast. Dear God, Lord James de Ware's son had caught her stealing!

The boy raised his hand, and she thought for a mad moment that he intended to clout her for her crime. She cringed backward into the jasmine. A pleasant cloud of fragrance instantly surrounded her. A branch tickled her neck. She lifted one quivering hand to brush it aside. Then, striking as unexpectedly as summer lightning, a sharp pain lanced across her shoulder, then upon her neck, then beneath her ear. She shrieked—stunned, betrayed.

"There!" the boy said pitilessly, shaking his head and swaggering near. "You see? That plant is teeming with honeybees. I warned you to move away."

He pulled her none too gently by the arm away from the bush, glaring at her with eyes as hard as jade.

She peered up at him, mortified, in pain, but too proud to weep. Sainted Mary, what would the lord's son do with her?

She wasn't sure what terrified her more—the bee stings or being caught thieving roses.

She'd never been stung by a bee before. Once, when her family had visited a particularly filthy manor house, she'd awakened covered with flea bites. Her mother had known exactly what poultice of herbs would ease the itch. But these were no flea bites. They felt like sharp needles of fire. And her mother wasn't here. Heavy with child, Lady Elayne had remained at home.

Suddenly, she was scared. Some people swelled up horribly from bee attacks. Some people died. Her mother had taught her the remedy for stings, but Cynthia couldn't for the life of her remember it.

She knotted her fingers together, afraid to touch the spots that pulsed with fiery pain.

"I'm wounded," she said in a strangled whisper.

One corner of Garth's mouth twitched. "I assure you, it's not so grave as that." He shook his head in amusement, but his green eyes softened at once to the color of pine boughs.

For a moment she was pacified. Almost.

Until he drew his dagger.

Then she gasped and clapped a hand to her mouth.

"Come," he urged, ignoring her response and grasping her by the wrist. "Let me see."

"Nay." She tugged back in resistance, drawing in an uneasy breath. Why couldn't her mother have come? she despaired. This barbarian was after her with a knife!

"What ails you, lass?" he challenged, raising a brow. "You're not afraid, are you?"

Her gaze lingered on the gleaming silver blade he wielded. Aye, she was afraid. She was petrified.

Then she looked into Garth's eyes. They were thoroughly gentle now, the hue of mist over the spring heath. A hint of humor glimmered in them. But so did compassion.

Garth de Ware wouldn't harm her. She was suddenly as certain of that as she was that the sun would rise each morn. No one with eyes that kind could inflict hurt.

She lifted her chin a notch. "I'm not afraid," she decided.

He chuckled. Then he tenderly brushed aside her unruly mop of hair, frowning down at her neck. She wondered what horrible boil had formed there. As he raised his dagger, she trembled in spite of herself.

"The honeybees must have thought you some rare new flower," he murmured cheerfully, "with that bright hair of yours." He laid the sharp blade flat along her neck. It was still warm from the sheath.

She held her breath and shut her eyes as he lightly scraped across her throat with the honed edge of the knife.

"That's one," he said triumphantly, showing her a tiny black barb finer than a piece of silk thread.

She blinked in surprise. How insignificant the stinger looked. And yet it had caused far more pain than Garth's great dagger.

He then turned her toward the sunlight, tipping her head to one side to locate the second wound lower on her neck. Her fear began to ease under his ministrations. His fingers, trailing across her throat, felt as gentle as her mother's. And despite his scowl of concentration, a tender wisdom shone in his eyes. Mayhaps, she thought, he was not so knavish as his brothers.

Garth could feel young Cynthia staring at him, unsure whether to give him her trust. Though the lass put on a brave face, she quivered like a snared dove beneath his hands.

"I'll wager you've not seen a shrub like that before," he murmured, hoping to ease her fears with conversation.

Her eyes flicked briefly over the bush. "The jas . . . jasmine?"

He coaxed the tiny black barb between his thumbnail and his dagger. Slowly, he drew the stinger out. "You know its name?"

He stopped his ministrations and turned to her. Their heads were inches apart. She was really rather comely despite her strange coloring, he decided. Her large, pale blue eyes seemed luminous against her sun-kissed skin. And that orange hair was . . . intriguing.

"My . . . my mother taught me the flowers' names," she faltered, turning a pretty shade of pink.

Garth nodded and returned to his labor. A faint grin lurked at the corners of his mouth. She'd blushed. Actually, all the little girls he knew did that when he looked at them. His mother said it was the de Ware curse. She said Garth would break many hearts on the road to manhood. Whatever that meant.

"Forgive my coarse touch, my lady," he said with an apologetic smile as he placed a hand on the embroidered neckline of her surcoat. He'd heard his brother Duncan use those words with wenches many a time. He wasn't entirely sure of their meaning either, but the ladies seemed to like hearing them.

Cynthia swallowed. Garth's touch was anything but coarse. In sooth, his fingers felt like warm silk against her flesh as he slipped her surcoat and underdress the merest bit off her shoulder. Her skin tingled oddly.

"Perhaps then you also know that fruit?" he asked, nodding to a white blossomed tree.

She blinked languidly at the tree, then shook her head.

"That," he announced, "is an apricot. My grandfather brought it back from the Holy Land. He fought in the Crusades."

Cynthia nodded, only half-listening to Garth's words. She was far too enrapt by the touch of his large hands, firm and warm and delicate on her neck, and the twinkle in his proud eyes—gray-green, penetrating eyes with thick, gently curved lashes—to pay much heed to what he said. Something about the noble slant of his nose, the dark, masculine down along his upper lip, the strong, square angle of his jaw, had a most curious effect on her. The blood rushed feverishly to her cheeks, leaving her skin strangely sensitive.

"This is the last one," he said.

Cynthia blinked, trying to remember his conversation. "The last . . . apricot tree?"

He flashed her a one-sided smile. "Nay. The last barb."

"Oh."

Cynthia's heart drummed like the feet of a captive rabbit as Garth bent near. Moisture formed along her upper lip. What was wrong with her? she wondered. Mayhaps the bee stings had poisoned her, made her feverish.

"It must be buried deep. I cannot see the barb." He narrowed his eyes and cocked his head this way and that at her shoulder, trying to catch some glint off the stinger, that would disclose its position. Twice he lifted his dagger. Twice he brought it down.

"Perhaps there *is* no barb," Cynthia said stridently. She didn't know how much more of this nerve-stretching intimacy she could endure.

"Nay, it's but swollen to the size of my father's silver medallion." He frowned. "If I could but feel . . ."

Cynthia raised her brows. Feel what? What did he intend? He'd sheathed his dagger and was looking furtively about like a naughty child about to steal a tart.

Without warning, he clutched her by the shoulders and lowered his head to the bee sting. Cynthia's breath caught in her throat. His soft brown curls brushed past her cheek like a caress. His lips pressed wetly, warmly against the flesh of her shoulder, just like a kiss. She trembled at the shock of his embrace as she felt him nibble there. For one tense moment, she didn't breathe. Then he abruptly lifted his head and spat to the side.

"Ha!" he exclaimed in victory. "It's done."

Cynthia gaped at him with glazed eyes. She felt suddenly dizzy and weak. Part of it was relief—the ordeal was over. But part of it was a skin-tingling, toe-curling sensation, the birth of a desire so overpowering it threatened to dissolve her very bones.

Then Garth stood tall, blocking the sun with his broad shoulders, and issued a stern warning. "Now stay away from that plant, little moppet. It's always fraught with bees."

Cynthia's lids felt curiously heavy. She sighed wistfully. With the sun behind him, haloing his magnificent head, Garth de Ware looked heroic. And so he was. He'd come to her rescue, like a knight to a lady. Her shoulder burned deliciously where his lips had seared her flesh. She swore she'd never wash the spot again.

Glowing with the birth of this new emotion, she pressed one hand modestly to her bosom and curtseyed in her most formal fashion.

"I will never forget the great service you have done me,

Sir Garth," she said breathlessly. "You are a most brave and courteous knight."

Of course, she knew he wasn't truly a knight. Not yet. But she noticed he didn't correct her. In sooth, he looked rather pleased with the title. He flashed her another of those charming, crooked smiles and, retrieving his book, nodded to her in farewell.

She stared steadfastly, unwilling to forgo one glimpse of her newfound champion.

As he closed the gate after him, he called wryly over his shoulder, "Don't forget the cuttings you dropped, little thief. You'd best not leave any evidence strewn about."

Cynthia glanced down at the damning slips of roses. How insignificant they seemed now. When she looked up again, her hero had disappeared.

She smiled dreamily at the garden gate. Then she wrapped her arms about her and twirled once in delight.

"Perhaps I *will* marry after all," she declared to her flowery audience. Sweeping up her boots and stockings with a graceful flourish, she gave the garden a knowing grin. "Garth de Ware," she whispered, "someday you will be mine."

Fate, however, had a cruel habit of interfering with the best-laid plans. That very evening, Cynthia's mother lost the boy growing in her womb and fell deathly ill. Cynthia and her father were summoned home before the sun had even broken through the pall of night. By the time they returned, it was over. Lady Elayne was dead. Cynthia was the new mistress of le Wyte. All her childish dreams were abandoned, and her precious cuttings, forgotten in her pocket, withered and died.

1

QUIET REIGNED IN THE DIM BEDCHAMBER, SAVE FOR OLD Elspeth's soft weeping and the ironically healthy crackle of fire on the hearth. Outside, a punishing rain pelted the sod, but heavy tapestries hung at the windows, dampening its sound.

The life force was almost gone from the man in the bed. Cynthia could feel it in the weakening of his grip. It was too late. None of her healing powers would save her dear husband. She placed trembling hands upon his clammy forehead, hands she'd used time and again to comfort him, hands through which God sometimes performed miracles. But this time, when she closed her eyes, she saw clearly the image of the black snake.

Death.

It was inevitable. Lord John was not a young man. He'd known he was dying for weeks. But for Cynthia, seeing that dark, incontrovertible image in her mind's eye . . .

John had already spoken his farewells to the others. The Abbot had performed last rites. Roger, John's steward and dearest friend, stood sentry at the footpost of the bed like a loyal hound, iron gray and ramrod straight. Elspeth knotted her fist in the bedhangings beside Roger, dabbing at her bleary eyes with the corner of her apron. All that remained was for John to bid adieu to his wife.

Cynthia bit back a sob and clasped his cool fingers again. He frowned, and she leaned forward to catch his faint whisper, his final bidding. His words barely stirred the wayward curl that had fallen from her coif, but that made them no less offensive. She drew back sharply.

"Nay," she protested, grief burning her throat. "I cannot."

His face contorted with disappointment, and it was all Cynthia could do to keep from dissolving in tears. But she swore she wouldn't cry. She wouldn't make this moment any more difficult for him.

"Please, Cynthia." His voice was as weak as wind through a cracked door.

She clamped her bottom lip between her teeth, determined to remain strong. How could she do it? How could she keep such an impossible promise? "All right," she managed to choke out, "I swear." She squeezed his hand in reassurance.

He smiled faintly. And then he was gone.

The frail, gnarled fingers grew limp in her grasp. His old eyes glazed over with the dull patina of death. One final breath rattled out between his lips, and his body sank into the feather pallet.

Now long-stemmed tears welled in Cynthia's eyes, threatening to spill over. It was no matter that his death had been coming for months. No matter that he'd lived a long, rewarding life. Her husband, the kind and gentle man who'd given her the last two years of that precious life, was gone. And there had been naught she could do about it.

She let John's wrist drop gently upon his chest and reached across to close the lids over his eyes.

Forever.

Behind her, Elspeth gulped out a single sob, then buried her face in Roger's thick surcoat, muffling the rest.

Out of habit, Cynthia pulled the furs up to John's neck and tucked them in around him. Then she gazed once more at his rugged, wrinkled face. Remarkably, there lingered at the corners of his slack mouth the vestiges of a smile.

Suddenly she was transported to the past spring, when

they'd walked hand in hand through a meadow thick with new daffodils, the air fresh and sweet with a recent shower. What had he said to her then? That she was his salvation. That she'd taken his weed patch of a life and filled it with flowers. His smile had been so full of joy and so sincere that she was moved to prove her affection for him at once, spreading her mantle and coupling with him among the daffodils.

The seasons came and went, days spent in light and laughter. All told, God gave them but a score of months together. Still, this was how she'd remember John always—smiling as he had on that spring day.

She closed her eyes and waited for the hollow ache in her throat to subside. John wouldn't want her weeping over him. His dying command proved that. And after all, he was at peace now. His long suffering was over. With that small consolation, she managed to swallow her sorrow. She kissed first his pale forehead, then his papery cheek in farewell.

The abrupt bark of the dour Abbot clearing his throat encroached upon her private ritual. She flinched, startled. She'd almost forgotten *he* was there. In sooth, she wished him gone. In her vulnerable state, the last person she wanted to deal with was the ghoulish Abbot.

Reluctantly she faced him, suppressing a shiver. Today, he looked even more like a messenger of death, his black robes contrasting starkly with his sickly pallor, his sharp-boned face and sunken cheeks skeletal.

"He is with God now, child," he intoned soberly, folding his spidery fingers before him in a semblance of humility.

Child. How the word grated on her ears. Only the Abbot could make the endearment sound like an insult.

He'd never liked her. He'd made that clear from the beginning. And she made no pretense of affection for him. But for the sake of John, to whom the Abbot appeared singularly devoted, she kept her opinions to herself. She endured the man's condescension, his hypocritical patronizing, his interminable Sabbath sermons on the inferiority of the female gender, and his resolute blindness to the fact that Cynthia was a grown woman, capable of her own thoughts and decisions.

Soon it would be over. Now that John was . . . gone, she needn't put up with the Abbot's affectations of fatherly concern. He'd not be at Wendeville long. John had bequeathed him a holding at one of his neighboring estates. In a matter of days, the Abbot would be out of her life.

In the meantime, she dared not let him witness a hint of the disabling loss she felt with John's passing. It would only fuel his criticism of her. She straightened her spine and did her best to level him with a cool glance.

"Please see to the blessing and entombment at once, Abbot. Then if you'll pack your things . . ."

The Abbot stabbed her with a sharp, disapproving glare. Then, as quickly, he judiciously lowered his eyes, snuffing out their dark fury. "Of course. As you wish." He steepled his fingers thoughtfully beneath his chin. "But, child, what about kinfolk who may want to see him before . . . ?"

"John had no kinfolk, save me." She narrowed her eyes. "I'm sure you knew that."

He did. And as far as he was concerned, a wife of less than two years could hardly be called kin either. His blood boiled as he thought of all that Wendeville wealth in the hands of a child. Why, she hadn't even the look of a proper grieving widow. She should be wailing like her old nursemaid, wringing her hands, turning helplessly to the church, to *him,* for comfort, for guidance.

Instead, her cheek was conspicuously dry, almost as if she were . . . relieved? The golden flicker of the fire danced across her young, luminous face and seemed to turn her disheveled hair to flame, the devil's fire. Aye, she most definitely looked relieved, like a great weight had been lifted from her shoulders, as surely as the old man's soul had been lifted from his body.

This wasn't how it should be. The wench was too much in control, too aloof. And far too clever for his taste. Lord John's body was scarcely cold, and already she planned to evict *him,* the servant of God who'd neglected his own monasteries to remain steadfastly by the dying man's side. She'd find a formidable foe if she thought it would be easy.

He had no intention of leaving her alone with the vast Wendeville fortune. One way or another, he'd receive his due.

He twisted his fingers in wordless irritation, resisting the urge to strangle the wayward wench into accord. But he knew ire was not the answer. Anger was never shrewd. Nay, he must be meek. After all, it was the meek who inherited . . .

"Abbot?"

"Perhaps you act in haste, child." He fixed a bland, sympathetic expression on his face and looked down his nose at her. "It's a harsh trial, losing a husband, and you so young. Wait a day or two. Allow me to offer you spiritual . . . comfort."

To his consternation, she actually winced at his words. "I find comfort in the peaceful manner of his passing, Abbot," she said, unpinning the dried rose spray from her surcoat and placing it upon Lord John's silent breast. "Would that all men could die so happy as my John."

His nostrils flared. John Wendeville had certainly been that. Happy beyond reason. Happier than any mortal man deserved. The wench had coddled him like an infant. He frowned at the array of various scented oils and potions by Lord John's bedside, medicines she'd concocted for his ills. It turned his stomach to imagine Cynthia's hands applying their devil's ointments to the old man's wrinkled skin. After all, the church believed in the sufferings of the body. His own scarred back attested to the fact that pain was the avenue for delivery from the sins of humanity. Why should the old man be spared the discomfort of his own dying?

He sulked as he watched Lady Cynthia blow out a candle at the head of the bed. Damn the heathen wench! And damn John for wedding her. She'd ruined his plans. All the years he'd spent romancing the old goat as if he were a suitor, all the forced smiles and exchanged pleasantries, all the patience as the childless lord's life dragged on and on and on . . . All were wiped away now, all because of the harlot before him. Cynthia le Wyte had come to seduce the lord's wealth away, using the one weapon the church couldn't employ.

She'd *slept* with the wrinkled prune.

He closed his eyes to slits, unable to blot out the repugnant vision that came to mind of young Cynthia mounting the wasted old man in eager ecstasy. He turned away in disgust, letting the dim light obscure the enraged veins sticking out from his neck.

He'd have to control that rage if he wanted a scrap of his reward. It might be too late to save the inheritance, but there was still a chance to wheedle a healthy stipend from the bereaved widow.

Bereaved? The idea almost made him laugh. Unlike her sniveling maid, the cold Cynthia hadn't shed a single tear for her husband. And she clearly bore *him* no love. Nay, squeezing blood from an apple would be easier than wresting a penny from Lady Cynthia.

If only the wench had died with John . . . He clenched his fingers together, imagining the feel of her soft, supple neck between his hands as he choked the life from her.

". . . a simple, private ceremony. Abbot?" Cynthia said. "Abbot?"

The Abbot jerked his head up, startled. Cynthia could see his thoughts were elsewhere. Probably thinking up ways to salvage her recalcitrant soul. She sighed and looked one last time at John's restful face.

Would that all men could die so happy.

Her husband *had* been happy. For two years, Cynthia had stayed by his side, a faithful wife, an adored companion, even an enthusiastic lover. That he survived an entire year after the physician tucked him into his deathbed was likely due more to her doses of affection than the foxglove and wormwood she painstakingly administered to him for his failing heart. She'd devoted herself to pleasing him—preparing his favorite foods, regaling him with snatches of song, letting him win at chess . . . occasionally.

Gently, she leaned forward and blew out the last beeswax candle beside the bed. A wisp of smoke rose upward, flirting with the mustard brocade bedhangings.

Aye, theirs had been a marriage of convenience. Neither of them had deluded themselves about that. Cynthia's father was land-poor, widowed, and sonless, with an eldest daugh-

ter whose countenance could only be described as hale at
best. When the wealthy but feeble Lord John Wendeville offered for Cynthia's hand, le Wyte hastily arranged for her
sacrifice to the heirless lord in order to increase the family
fortune.

Cynthia was never bitter. She knew full well, and accepted, that marriage was a political arrangement. She'd
hardened herself to circumstance long years ago, upon her
mother's death. At eighteen, she'd realized she was no great
beauty. Nor did she possess the kind of holdings to tempt a
suitor. Therefore, she entered into the union with pragmatic
grace, if not enthusiasm.

And Lord John was quite pleasant, as it turned out. He
was patient and kind, sweet and generous. He dressed her in
velvet, showered her with emeralds, put up with her impertinent old nursemaid, even allowed her to fulfill her dream of
owning a pleasure garden, from which she picked him daily
bouquets.

John knew he was dying. He simply wanted companion-
ship in his final years.

Cynthia gave him far more than that. She was a wife in
every sense of the word, surprising him with a devotion he
swore rejuvenated him. It delighted her to see him weep in
gratitude as she pleasured him with unwavering patience.
And it was not for lack of trying that she never conceived an
heir for him.

In their months together, as Cynthia's garden flourished
beneath her loving hands, so did her husband. That he'd die
soon did not curtail her care of him. He was like the annuals
she set out each spring. She nurtured them, coaxed the beds
to blossom in joyous profusion, then accepted their withering
and dying. It was an accustomed cycle. And it was a matter
of pride with Cynthia that not once in the old man's short life
with her did she falter in her tending of him.

That care, to the Abbot's quite vocal consternation, in-
cluded the use of a great many potions and poultices concocted from the massive herb garden she'd planted in the
castle courtyard.

In sooth, the Abbot scowled even now at the mazer of
ground herbs with which she'd liberally dosed John's wine

for the past two days to relieve him of pain. No doubt the Abbot thought she'd poisoned her own husband with what he referred to as devil's medicine.

It was no matter. That "devil's medicine" had cured many a vassal and servant in John's household. Her knowledge of herbs and the gift of healing she'd acquired at the time of her first blood had convinced even the folk of the surrounding villages to trust in her miracles. Besides, she cared little what the Abbot thought. He'd be gone by week's end.

"Lord John recognized your . . . loyalty and service, Abbot," she said, trying to keep the edge from her voice. "He has been quite generous."

"Oh?" His casual tone belied the interest in his piercing black gaze.

"He bade me tell you he has bequeathed you the holding at Charing and the fields surrounding."

The Abbot blinked. "Charing?"

"Aye."

"How kind." His voice broke. His chin trembled.

Cynthia felt a twinge of remorse. Perhaps she'd been too hasty, too judgmental. Perhaps the Abbot wasn't as unfeeling as he seemed. Perhaps he *was* touched after all by the loss of his benefactor, no matter how he despised *her*. She tried to think of some small word of consolation. But staring at the pasty, somber man looming in deathly dark robes before her, her mind came up empty.

"After the ceremony," she said as gently as possible, "I'll send along two servants to help you get settled at Charing."

In the awkward silence that ensued, she retreated from the shadowy chamber with Roger and Elspeth, closing the door with finality on both the Abbot and a chapter of her life.

The Abbot stared at the closed door, stunned. His chest constricted. He could scarcely draw breath.

Charing. Lord John had left him Charing. Why, the Charing property didn't represent a twentieth of the old man's wealth. It was a travesty, a slap in the face. After all he'd endured, the sacrifices he'd made, this was his reward—a moldering castle on the barren land adjoining Wendeville. The niggardly tribute left a bitter taste in his mouth, like a moldy bone tossed to a faithful hound.

Rage snaked its way through his veins, heating his blood as he gazed down at the chilling body laid out so peacefully upon the pallet.

He'd been cheated. There was no other word for it. He'd been betrayed by the old fool's incorrigible lust for his lascivious young wife. How many times had he warned Lord John about the danger of lechery? How many Sabbaths had he spoken, within the walls of Wendeville's own chapel, of that deadly sin?

But his word had been ignored. The very word of God had gone unheeded. Disgust twisted the Abbot's mouth. Fury sharpened his vision. He coiled the fingers of one hand into a bony fist. Then, with a strangled oath, calling upon the wrath of God for penitence, he drove that fist with all the rancor of a cuckholded husband into Lord John's lifeless, sin-riddled groin, again and again, each blow punctuated by the name of the old man's transgression.

Cynthia!

By the time he was sated, sweat beaded his brow. He gasped for breath. His knuckles throbbed with pain.

But pain was an old friend. And that old friend soothed him, clarifying his thoughts. He carefully wiped the moisture from his face with the corner of his sleeve and smoothed the cope over his cassock.

He knew what he had to do now. Lady Cynthia Wendeville may have sent him packing, but it wasn't the last of his influence she'd feel. There were always others he could use as instruments for his work.

He had at least a year. No widow would dare marry before at least that token period of grief. Until then, Wendeville's coffers would be safe enough.

Slipping a spy into the servants' ranks would be child's play. His world teemed with the repentant—lost sheep who'd lay down their lives to do his bidding, who'd gladly sell an influential shepherd like him their very souls.

As a parting gesture of concern for the bereaved Wendeville household, and to protect his investment, he'd even help

Lady Cynthia select a new chaplain. He'd find her a humble cleric from the poorest monastery in the land, a man of little ambition, a man who believed in the blessedness of poverty—in short, a man who'd not interfere with his own aspirations to wealth and power. Oh aye, he'd find a chaplain for Wendeville. In sooth, he already knew just the person for the position.

2

APRIL

GARTH DE WARE GASPED AS THE WANTON WOMAN RODE HIM mercilessly. She was exquisite. Her long, black hair fell forward, lashing his bare ribs. Her eyes glittered like emeralds. Her fingernails raked his shoulders, and her sleek, round buttocks pounded down upon him as relentlessly as the tide. He felt every glorious inch of the swell of his manhood as it strove upward to shelter in the warm recesses of her flesh.

Lord, he thought, his body straining with divine sensations, this was heaven.

She leaned over him, thrusting voluptuous breasts forward which he happily caught in his cupped hands. They were so soft, so delicate, he feared he might hurt them. Then she bent to him, shoved aside his hair, and lapped voraciously at his ear, and it was all he could do to keep from bruising her in his eagerness. She eased a nipple between his lips, and he suckled like a pup, gasping at the sweet honey of her skin.

Tension stretched his body until he felt like a bowstring ready to snap. Her nipple popped from his mouth, and he tossed his head feverishly back and forth.

"Mariana . . . ," he moaned, his breath coming shallow and rapid. "Ah, Mariana . . ."

Suddenly, he woke. No woman rose above him, only the pale ceiling. The dawning sun sketched leafy patterns across the bare plaster. For several seconds, he was disoriented. Then the truth blinded him with crashing clarity.

The dream. It had returned to haunt him.

He groaned and squeezed his eyes shut. His bunched cassock was soaked with sweat, and an all too familiar, craving ache gripped him between his thighs.

Ah, God, he despaired—his body mocked him yet again. Here he lay, a man of the church, stiff as a lance and sworn to chastity.

He let a cold, somber mask fall reflexively over his face like the visor on a close helm, concealing the rapt ecstasy of the dream, blotting it out of existence.

He refused to lower his eyes, refused to acknowledge that betraying part of his body. Certainly he'd not defile himself by seeking relief, even though as nigh as he was to bursting, he could probably have found it with a single stroke of his hand. Nay, he was a monk, he told himself grimly, and if it was God's will that he continue to endure this wretched dream, then perhaps it was meant as a test of faith.

So he clenched his teeth, stared gravely at the ceiling, and waited for the fiery longing to subside. He tried to forget Lady Mariana's bewitching form, tried to think only of her cruel honesty and her mocking laughter. He forced himself to remember how much she'd hurt him.

Unlike his older brothers, he'd come late to wenching. Holden and Duncan had probably sampled the charms of a score or more damsels each by the time they were twenty. Garth's virginity had always been a source of bemusement for them.

Part of Garth's reluctance to pursue carnal pleasures was that he was fated for religious pursuits. A young man with two older brothers as brilliant and worthy as his had little hope of securing a profitable position in the church. Since his skill with his studies exceeded that with the blade, particularly when compared to his illustrious siblings, his destiny seemed clear.

Oh, he'd tasted the life of a knight, and he could wield a sword as well as most. His father had made Garth and his close friend, Robert, responsible for guarding Duncan, the heir to the de Ware estate, on his myriad adventures. And once, when Garth traveled with Holden north to the borders of Scotland, his brother even entrusted him with the holding of a castle there. Unfortunately, Garth failed miserably, outwitted by the Scots wench who eventually became Holden's bride. It was then he decided to return and keep to his pious path toward the church.

For six months he worked diligently under the scrutiny of Castle de Ware's chaplain, memorizing, studying, falling naturally into the rhythm of prayer and blessing, worship and chant. He showed promise, the chaplain informed his father, and might even aspire to the office of bishop. Garth seemed destined for greatness.

Until Lady Mariana de Martel came to live at the castle.

The orphaned daughter of a landless lord upon whom James de Ware had taken pity, she blew into Garth's life like a devastating whirlwind, steering him off course and dominating his every waking thought. She devoted herself as thoroughly and deeply to sexual pleasure as Garth did to the church, and it was only a matter of time before he was tempted by her far more fascinating religion.

She teased, taunted, tortured his untried body with seduction and denial until he was crazed with desire. The sight of her made his blood run hot, and his heart raced if she so much as brushed his arm in passing.

One torrid August night, Mariana called him to her bedside, wailing and writhing under the influence of devilish nightmares. She sent away her maid and bade him bolt the door. A half dozen times that night she called upon his young, virile body to exorcise the demons of her dreams. By the time dawn broke and Garth stumbled back to his own chamber, he was dazed and exhausted.

Rather than easing Garth's infatuation, however, she'd only piqued it. He turned his face from the church and began to worship Mariana, devoting himself completely to pleasuring her. He decided at last that he'd not be content until he made her his wife.

But Mariana had other plans. She'd grown bored of him. He no longer seemed to be able to satisfy her endless cravings. She avoided him, made excuses, left him waiting in an empty bed.

Garth was young and inexperienced, and love was blind. Like a knight facing the quintain for the first time, he never saw the blow coming.

He could remember, word for word, everything she said as he lay naked, drained, trembling with fatigue and shame-faced rage. It pained him too much to recall those words now. But after she was through with him, after she shredded every scrap of his newfound masculinity from him as easily as his linen undergarments, he was filled with such self-loathing and humiliation that he could scarcely draw breath.

He would never, he vowed, shame himself with a woman again.

And so he threw himself wholeheartedly into the church. He withdrew beneath a cassock so thick that Eros's arrow couldn't pierce the wool. To his parents' dismay, he moved out of the castle and humbled himself to the level of a simple monk at a poor monastery. There, he embraced his new life with the zeal of an ascetic. And he never looked back at the life he'd once led.

Until the dreams came to taunt him, forcing him to re-member, nay, to *relive* his past.

He sighed heavily. The pressure in his loins had abated now. All that remained was disgrace. And for that, he must confess to the prior. Contrition for his sin, the sin of lust, was the only way to rid himself of it once and for all.

He folded back the rough wool blanket and sat up, raking his fingers through his mussed hair and forcing his bare feet with intentional cruelty onto the cold stone floor. The back of his cassock stuck to him. The damp wool itched against his skin, but he refused to allow himself the comfort of scratching. Quickly he laced on his sandals and crossed himself, muttering a hasty prayer that he wasn't late for Sabbath Mass.

• • •

Prior Thomas padded across his office, stroking his freshly shaved chin with one hand, patting his growing stomach with the other.

"I see," he murmured uncomfortably.

Thomas wondered how long this would take, and more to the point, how soon he could eat. God forgive him, but this was part of a prior's occupation he truly detested—passing judgment on men who were in sooth no more flawed than he.

And naturally, God had seen fit, in some kind of penitential jest, to send him Garth de Ware today. Brother Garth came to him at least once a fortnight with some or other imagined sin for which he felt he owed contrition.

This week it was lust.

The prior rubbed his hand over his face. By the morose look in Garth's eyes, he knew he wouldn't be able to explain that any normal, warm-blooded male of his age naturally felt the stirrings of the body. Nor, he feared, would Garth be content with a stern lecture. Nay, Garth was one of those rare, irritating fanatics who insisted on harsh self-punishment. Something had happened in Garth's past to make him believe he was unworthy, and nothing on heaven or earth could convince him otherwise. Thank God the prior had locked away the monastery scourge, else Garth would doubtless insist on a daily flogging.

Garth stared up at him expectantly, and though the youth knelt humbly enough before him, Prior Thomas had to remind himself that the young man was in sooth his underling. Garth de Ware's steady, noble gaze marked him as the son of a lord. His countenance was anything but humble. It was the face of a man born to power, a face that commanded respect, led armies, and doled out justice.

Or had once.

When Garth had first come to the monastery, though his spirit seemed somehow lost, his body was strong and fit. He'd been a striking youth. Now, apathy had ruined the lad's appetite and, in the prior's opinion, left him too spare. Garth's was by nature a warrior's body, not fashioned for the inertia of a monk's life, no matter how readily his mind adapted. The lad was literally wasting away.

Thomas ran a palm over his own round belly and expelled

a weary puff of air. Above all, the prior liked order—lengths of wool that made exactly two cassocks, jongleur's verses with happy endings, just enough of last year's wine to last till the new barrels were ready, all loose ends tied. Such things were incontrovertible proof that God was in his heaven. Garth de Ware? He was an anomaly, a reminder that perhaps all was not right with the world.

What had brought him to God's fold, the prior couldn't guess. It was the one subject Garth would never broach. But it was apparent the young man simply didn't belong here. His own parents said as much, inquiring frequently after Garth in the hopes he'd change his mind about the monastery.

It wasn't that Garth wasn't fit for the church. He certainly possessed the fear of God, love of Christ, and devotion to mankind required of a man of the cloth. But with his keen intellect and noble ties, he was better suited to the position of castle chaplain or abbot or even bishop, some office requiring frequent contact with the secular world.

The prior feared the seclusion of the monastery was slowly draining the life from Garth de Ware.

Still, Garth did as he was told, and Lord James de Ware supplied the monks with a generous annual oblation. Prior Thomas supposed it was none of his affair whether the young man's calling was true or not.

He cleared his throat and tried his best to mold the cheery crinkles of his bald forehead into stern furrows. He'd have to choose his words carefully. Garth would indubitably castrate himself if he thought it a seemly punishment for the sin of lust. It truly was a shame the lad was not of the *in seculo* clergy, a parish priest or chaplain or friar who worked "in the world," for though the church officially frowned on such a thing, a goodly number of such men possessed concubines, wives, and even offspring. Clearly, *they* never grappled with the sin of lust.

"You say you cried out her name?" he asked, steepling his fingers importantly.

The young man's gaze hardened. His cheeks flushed with shame, but he faced the prior bravely. "Aye, Father."

"So your tongue shares the blame of your sin?"

"Aye."

The prior nodded, pacing thoughtfully. "Then it is fitting that your tongue bear the punishment." He clasped his hands before him. "I will have your vow of silence for . . . a fortnight."

He let his gaze slide over Garth's face, gauging the severity of the sentence. It was oft difficult to tell how much chastisement the lad felt he deserved.

Thankfully, Garth lowered his eyes in acceptance. His humiliation over, he pressed a holy kiss to the prior's ring and silently excused himself from the office.

After he'd gone, Prior Thomas heaved a relieved sigh and clapped the matter from his hands. He'd made the right decision, and, he thought rather selfishly, he'd earned several days' respite from the youth's self-reproaching tongue.

As it turned out, his timing couldn't have been better. By week's end, an eminent visitor would arrive at the monastery, a man who would change Garth's life forever. And because he was sworn to silence, there wasn't a blessed thing the young man could say about it.

The late morning rays of Friday's sun slanted down in wide diagonal bars between the columns of the monastery's inner courtyard, alternately casting Garth in light and shadow as he walked the long, open hallway, beating the dust from his cassock.

What had happened to make the prior call him to his office so urgently? He'd been halfway through copying the third verse of Psalms when Brother Michael summoned him.

He hoped it wasn't bad tidings. It was difficult being away from his family. He seldom saw them more than twice a year. His father was not a young man anymore. His mother always seemed tinier and more fragile than he remembered. His brother Duncan's wife was expecting their second child. A hundred unpleasant things could have happened.

Bracing himself for the worst, he scratched at the prior's door. Prior Thomas swung the portal wide almost before Garth had lowered his hand. A broad smile wreathed the old man's face. Not bad news then. Garth offered up a silent prayer of thanks.

Then he spotted the visitor.

Garth had had the dubious pleasure of meeting the distinguished Abbot only once before, but it was hard to forget the man. He was as gaunt and terrifying as the tortured saints featured in Bible illuminations. And though the Abbot wore a mask of long-suffering humility, the controlled voracity tarnishing his lowered eyes told a different tale. The man was well aware of his own immense power.

"Garth, come in, come in," the prior said, ushering him in hastily. "The Abbot graces us with his presence." He added in a whispered aside, "Don't worry. I told him about your vow."

Garth felt shame stain his cheek. The Abbot was the last person he would want to know about his sin. Such an elevated man of the cloth bore no sympathy for human weakness, particularly lust. It had probably been years since the Abbot's skinny stick was aroused by anything. If ever.

Mortified by his own sacrilegious thoughts, Garth hung his head and knelt before the Abbot. He dutifully bent to kiss the Abbot's ring, repressing a shiver. The man's hands were as bony as a month-old corpse's and as cold.

"Garth," Prior Thomas continued when Garth had risen again, "the Abbot brings wonderful news."

The Abbot smiled blandly. Garth suspected he'd smile like that even if he brought news of Christ's second coming.

Prior Thomas rubbed his pudgy hands together briskly enough to start a fire. "A marvelous opportunity has arisen. It seems Castle Wendeville has need of a resident chaplain." He winked and confided, "'Tis the keep where the Abbot himself has served on many a Sabbath." The priest rocked up on his toes. "But since the Abbot has his own holding now . . . well." He could barely contain his excitement. "Of course, 'twill require some responsibility—the delivery of sermons, translating books and so forth, blessings, burials, all the ecclesiastical duties for a noble household of modest size. And, well . . ." He steepled his hands before him.

"I believe you would be perfect for the position," the Abbot intoned, "*Father* Garth."

Garth's breath caught in his throat. Unreasoning panic drummed its heels at his heart. *Father Garth.* Nay! He didn't want to be Father Garth. He *never* wanted to be Father Garth.

He was *Brother* Garth, lowly monk, humble servant. And wholly content as he was.

"Isn't it marvelous?" the prior beamed.

Garth met his eyes, but couldn't return Thomas's smile.

Nay, he thought. Monastery life was safe, uncomplicated, serene. For four years he'd lived happily here, isolated from the evils of the world beyond his cell. It was simple. It was quiet. He liked that isolation, the tranquility. He liked surrendering all care, all control, to the prior. He liked his methodical, placid existence. He could spend weeks in the scriptorium, coming out only for prayer and meals, and never speak to another soul. Which suited him perfectly.

"I'm sure you'll make a fine chaplain, my lad," Prior Thomas assured him.

The most Garth could summon up was a sickly smile.

Lord, he didn't want to leave.

Why had the prior chosen to oust him? He'd caused no ripples on the monastery's calm sea. He'd made no enemies. He followed the rules as piously as he could, and when he couldn't, he did penance for his sins. What in heaven's name had he done to deserve eviction from the only haven he knew?

By the rood, he'd give his left arm to have his voice now. Why? he wanted to ask them, though he knew full well one never questioned the will of God, nor that of the Abbot. At least not aloud.

But the moment the Abbot swung away to pick up a document from the table, Garth clenched his jaw, narrowed his eyes, and glared hard at Prior Thomas, trying to make him understand, willing him to change his mind, sending him a silent threat.

Prior Thomas must have been overwhelmed by the presence of his superior. The old man's faintly gratified expression never faltered, even in the wake of Garth's most menacing stare.

The prior clapped him on the shoulder. "We shall be sorry to see you go." He didn't look sorry in the least. In sooth, he looked inordinately pleased with himself. "When would you like *Father Garth* to begin?" he asked the Abbot.

Garth snapped his gaze toward the prior. Never, he thought. Never.

The Abbot scanned him from head to toe dismissively. "He can't have many possessions to pack, and I'm certain you can find others to take over his responsibilities. As you can imagine, I'm a busy man. See that he is ready to leave on the morrow."

Garth's heart dropped. He suddenly longed to put his fist through the plaster of the prior's wall. In the space of a moment, the neatly packed cart of his life had been utterly overturned.

He felt betrayed. Exiled. Damned. And only in the most private confessional of his soul did he admit the emotion underlying all the others—terror.

But despite his reluctance and in accordance with the Abbot's wishes, after a long and sleepless night, he bade a bitter and silent farewell to the indifferent stones of the monastery walls, leaving forever his life of serenity.

The sun winked its mocking eye behind a bank of grim clouds as Garth trudged behind the Abbot's cart to Castle Wendeville with all the fervor of a prisoner to his execution. He had no desire to ride. Nay, he'd rather huff like a winded warhorse and blister his heels on the rough road. It was only fitting, he thought, that his body should suffer as much pain as his spirit.

3

CYNTHIA SHIVERED AS SHE PLACED FIRST ONE BARE FOOT, then the other, atop the winter-packed soil of the garden.

The sun peered over the gray horizon, tentatively nudging the world awake like a late-arriving husband afraid to incur his wife's wrath. The dark trunks of the apples and willows in the orchard released eery wraiths of steam that wisped into the air as if to escape their earthly prisons. Mist made a soft carpet across the sward, and the faint crackling of ice-covered grasses thawing in the sun's caress peppered the silence.

Was today the day? Every morn since John's death, she'd completed the spring ritual, coming to the garden at dawn to kick off her boots, press her toes into the cool mulch, and wait for the familiar sensations. But winter seemed exceptionally stubborn this year, dragging on and on without the merest stirring of life beneath the soil.

She cleared her thoughts and waited.

Nothing.

She wiggled her toes.

Nothing.

She closed her eyes.

Nothing but cold, hard ground. Still. Silent.

Perhaps spring would never come, she thought dismally. She sighed and bent down to retrieve her boots.

Then, just as her fingers brushed the soft leather, it began. A gentle humming. Faint. Distant.

The soles of her feet tingled and grew warm, as if the earth squirmed slowly awake beneath her. Like the roots of a tree sucking water from the soil, her veins began to absorb the warmth. The pleasant vibration wound its lazy way up through her ankles and calves and thighs. Then it gained momentum, circling her hips and waist, flowing upward to a liquid pulse in her breast and throat, coursing powerfully now along her arms to emanate from the very tips of her fingers, filling her head with sound and heat and light.

She smiled. It was time. The earth beckoned her.

It was time to plant.

The energy resonated behind her eyes, at the base of her neck, in the restless stretch of sinew along her spine, like the embrace of an old friend.

She squatted down, crumbling handfuls of soil between her winter-pale knuckles and breathing deep the damp, rich odor of earth. And for the first time in weeks, she felt promise.

John had bid her be happy after his death. The dear man couldn't bear to think of her suffering. And she'd done her best to fulfill his wishes, short of keeping the promise she'd made at the end, the one that worried at her like a diseased tooth. Aye, she'd smothered her own cares these past weeks, busying herself with the troubles of the castle folk, setting bones, relieving aches, birthing babes. But it was difficult, lying like a dormant bulb beneath the cheerless, barren soil of widowhood.

At last this morn the sun broke through the winter's pall, and with it came the assurance of new life, new beginnings. Inhaling a fresh breath of spring, she could almost feel the flower of her soul reaching upward to be born.

Heedless of her velvet surcoat, she knelt in the mud and carefully brushed aside the carpet of straw mounded up over last year's roses.

"Oh, la!" Elspeth shrieked in dismay as she came plowing across the damp ground of the garden toward Cynthia. "What happened to the lovely lady I dressed this morn?" Her wim-

ple flapped about her old apple-cheeked face like a flounder-
ing dove pasted to her head.

Cynthia grinned. She was happier than a miser with a pile
of coins, kneeling here before the skeletons of rosebushes
that had survived the cruel winter.

"Why, ye're covered from head to heels!" Elspeth
scolded, rushing forward to scrub at Cynthia's forehead with
a corner of her apron.

Cynthia wrinkled her nose and ducked away from the
pointless scouring. "Look, Elspeth. The roses."

"Is that what they are?" Elspeth asked, pausing in her
labors to cast them a critical gaze. "Those scrawny sticks?"

"Wench!" Cynthia shot out a grimy hand and playfully
swatted her maid. "You'll be raving over the beauties by
June, and you know it."

"Aye," Elspeth conceded with a wink. "Ye do have a way
with sticks."

Cynthia rocked back on her haunches and rubbed the
aching small of her back. Her joints complained like the rusty
hinges of an abandoned garden gate. "I've been too long in-
doors, El."

"Well, ye take care not to work too hard. And don't ye
burn yer fair skin."

"I'll try, Elspeth," she promised half-heartedly, scrabbling
in the loose soil and discarding a stone.

Cynthia always worked too hard the first day. And she always felt the effects of the sun the second. But the ache was
part of a familiar cycle, necessary as a rite of passage, and
she welcomed the soft burn that pressed its heavy hand even
now upon her shoulder.

"Yer body's not so forgivin' as 'twas when ye were a
young thing," Elspeth said, kicking the stone closer to the
growing pile, "and ye have to bear in mind ye're a widow
now." She nudged the soil nonchalantly with her toe. "If ye'd
only pay a little mind to yer appearance, there's a world o'
fine men out there. . . ."

"Elspeth," Cynthia warned. She planted her fists on her
hips. For two short years of marriage she'd had a reprieve
from Elspeth's nagging. Now it looked like the mother hen
had come home to roost. But Cynthia was older and wiser.

She knew what marriage was like, and, despite her vow to John, the vow she tried to ignore every waking moment, she didn't intend to rush into it again. "I've already *had* my husband," she said with a levity she didn't feel. She dusted her palms together. "Besides, you know how I feel about appearances."

"Aye," Elspeth sniffed. "But ye're too young to stay alone the rest of yer life. And if ye'd only pay as much heed to yer *own* appearance as ye do to the garden's, ye'd have the gentlemen fallin' at yer feet."

"I don't want gentlemen falling at my feet. Any man who'd love a lady solely for her fair face . . ."

"Isn't a man worth havin'," Elspeth recited. "I know."

Cynthia nodded succinctly. She'd never fooled herself about her looks. She knew she was far from beautiful. Oh, she supposed she'd had the potential for beauty. She'd been born with milky-white skin, and, according to Elspeth, her azurine eyes had made Cynthia the infant look as ethereal as an angel. She had straight, even features, and her bone structure was bred of generations of handsome Norman ancestors.

But then her hair had grown in, hair the color of a Seville orange, a startling, undesirable shade that made people shake their heads in sympathy.

After that, she supposed her lack of concern for her looks drove her further and further from the troubadour's ideal. Instead of worrying about attracting a mate, she cultivated her affection for the outdoors. Day after day, three-quarters of the year, she'd toil in the garden, often from dawn to dusk. Consequently, by the end of summer, her skin was always as brown as a peasant's. No amount of wheedling or cajoling from Elspeth could entice her to stay out of the sun. Her nose was commonly sprinkled with freckles, her large hands callused from hard work, and, like a flower, Elspeth told her, all that extra sunshine had made her grow beyond what was common, for she was exceptionally tall for a woman.

Frankly, Cynthia didn't care.

"You see this rosebush?" she said. "It's all brown and barren and ugly, aye?" She tapped her forehead with a finger. "But the wise gardener knows that the beauty lies within the plant."

"Aye," Elspeth grumbled, rolling her eyes. "And the wise gentleman knows there's beauty in the homeliest of wenches."

"Exactly."

Elspeth crossed her arms and screwed her face into a disapproving pout. "Well, ye'll have to find a very wise man, then, and one with good sight, to even *see* there's a lady under all that muck!" Then she muttered a soft curse, and Cynthia saw moisture beginning to fill the old woman's eyes despite her cantankerous words.

"Oh, Elspeth . . . El," she said gently, laying a comforting hand on her shoulder, "don't you see? I've *had* my husband. I've had a marriage. I've had a man to love and—"

"Nay, m'lady," Elspeth said, her chin quivering. "Ye've had a man to fetch for, to wait upon hand and foot, to feed and clothe and help to the garderobe, to care for like a wee babe. But, m'lady, ye've not had a man to love."

Cynthia withdrew her hand. The words hung in the air between them, stark, raw, powerful. She swallowed.

It wasn't true. It wasn't true at all, she thought, lowering her eyes. Was it? John had shared all of his dreams, his laughter, his tears with her. How could she not love him? Of course she'd loved him. He was her husband.

But when Cynthia would have protested Elspeth's allegation, she saw that the maid had already fled toward the keep. She sighed, wiping her forehead with her grimy sleeve, staring down at the ugly rose twigs.

Had she loved John? There had been warmth between them, and understanding, and a sweetness that tugged at her heart. But had she truly loved him? Or was the ache in her breast a yearning for something she'd never known?

Sometimes, deep within her, she was certain there had to be more between a man and a woman—something powerful, something wondrous. She felt the fire of it in her body sometimes, dancing just beyond her reach, taunting her. Always she smothered the vague longing, relegating it to the place she'd left all her childhood fancies. But she couldn't suppress the feelings forever. Not when spring blew through her soul, and she felt like a bud aching to burst into bloom.

She gazed out through the open door of the walled garden

to the moisture-hazed orchard beyond. The smell of freshly turned earth was strong, the clarity of the sparrows' songs astonishing. On such a perfect day, she should be content. But suddenly she was as restless as a cat in the north wind. Her gaze rambled across the distant expanse of pale green sod, over tufts of weeds and bare patches, until it caught on a spot of vivid yellow at the far end of the orchard. Shielding her eyes with her forearm, she looked closer. Then she blinked.

It couldn't be. Not the daffodils. Not yet.

She scrambled to her feet, dusted the dirt as best she could from her surcoat, and set out through the trees.

It was likely some lady's mislaid scarf or perhaps a piece of knightly trapping, she reasoned. Certainly not the daffodils. It was far too early for daffodils. But despite all rhyme and reason, as she neared she could see, sure enough, a patch of the yellow blooms had miraculously sprung up through the frost-hardened ground to poke a defiant tongue out at winter.

Daffodils.

In the very spot where she and John . . .

Her throat closed. Slowly, her eyes filled with tears. And in that vulnerable moment, as spring filled the world, drifting even to the deepest shade of the orchard, the terrible truth smothered her.

John had known all along she didn't love him.

He'd known.

Why else would he have exacted that terrible promise from her? Why would he have chosen those words? *Swear to me you'll marry again,* he'd said. *Swear to me you'll marry . . . for love.*

Hot tears spilled over her cheek. A choking agony cut off her breath. All at once, she felt John's loss like a heavy rock pressing upon her chest.

Ah, God, he'd known.

Deep sorrow squeezed her heart. Guilt crushed her. She collapsed to her knees on the wet grass and buried her face in her hands. Then she wept—for John, for herself, for her blindness and his benevolence. Grief denied for too long rained upon her soul like the first shower of spring upon scorched earth, stunning her, consuming her, drowning her.

Weeks and months of sorrow poured out, and it was a long while before the well of healing tears ran dry. But eventually her sobs subsided, leaving only a telltale hitch now and then to remind her of the storm's passage. That and the daffodils, still cheerfully waving, merrily oblivious to her outburst.

How beautiful they were. There were enough to make a small bouquet. And, she thought, a tenuous smile trembling upon her lips, she knew just the place for them. She wiped her eyes, then carefully cut the tender stems with her dagger.

What was past was past, she decided as she collected the blooms in the fold of her soiled apron. Whatever wrongs she'd committed, John *had* gone to his grave a happy man. She had to believe that. Besides, he'd never have stood for her blubbering days on end over him, not with the sun so warm, not with daffodils in bloom.

As for the promise . . . If she never found the strength to honor it, if she never found the will to diminish John's memory by replacing her affection for him with some faint imitation of devotion for another, well, at least John would be none the wiser. And if, at her life's end, she didn't fulfill that promise, it was between her and God what would happen with her immortal soul. Nay, she never intended to marry another.

Her apron full, Cynthia made her way toward Wendeville's chapel. She felt less like the lady of the castle and more like a pauper bringing a gift to the king as she walked across the sward in bare feet, the yellow blossoms cradled against her belly. And that feeling was only magnified by the impressive appearance of the chapel itself.

No matter how frequently she visited, the chapel never failed to fill her with awe. It was holy and quiet and serene—the oldest part of the castle. The afternoon sun streamed through the brilliant stained glass, leaving designs like bright fallen petals on the cool gray stone floor.

The new addition at the chancel of the chapel still startled her. The great stone tomb dominating the nave bore a carved effigy of Lord John Wendeville, the way he supposedly looked as a young man. But Cynthia saw only a stranger's face when she gazed upon the reclining figure. The man was attired as a knight with a lion crouching at his feet, his hands pressed together in prayer. Atop these hands, hands that little resembled her late husband's, she tenderly placed the daffodils.

"I've brought flowers, John," she whispered, and still her voice seemed a shout in the death-quiet chapel. "The garden will be lovely this year. The long winter didn't harm the roses at all."

She carefully separated the blossoms, arranging them in a spray atop the tomb, then relegated her soiled apron to the floor.

"And I heard the first cuckoo today. It made me think of that song. How did it go?"

She bent her head over her hands to think, close enough for a bee traveling upon one of the daffodils to flit onto the bright blossom of her hair.

Then she began to hum softly, a song about a rude cuckoo who stole a robin's supper, throwing in the words where she could remember them.

The bee meandered across her orange tresses in search of nectar. It staggered twice, fell to a lower curl, then lost its grasp completely and tumbled onto her shoulder.

Cynthia struggled through the last verse, then tossed her head back for the familiar refrain.

The dazed bee, annoyed and confused in the tangle of her hair, floundered onto its back. When it squirmed aright, it stung her for all it was worth.

The song ended on a shriek. Cynthia clapped one hand to her shoulder and one to her mouth, amazed not only by the sharp pain, but by the loudness of her own voice as it reverberated within the chapel walls. She jumped back, scattering the flowers over the edge of the effigy, and winced as her fingers brushed away the half-dead insect. It buzzed in an ineffectual circle on the floor, and she frowned down at it.

"A bee!" she said in wonder. It was scarcely spring. What was a bee doing . . .

A strange vibration tugged at the nape of her neck. Some long lost incident pushed upward at the crust of memory to be reborn. In all her years of gardening, she'd only been stung once before, long ago. But there was no forgetting that pain.

Suddenly, it was as clear to her as if it had happened yesterday—the de Ware garden, the roses, the honeybees . . . the boy.

All at once, the chapel door exploded inward.

She whipped round. Her heart tripped. The door struck and bounced off the plaster wall.

A tall, chestnut-haired stranger loomed in the doorway, his dark robe swirling about him, his shoulders squared with primed power, his hands clenched as if ready to do battle. His chest heaved with exertion, and he glared at her with fierce green eyes that seemed to condemn her.

Dust motes scattered riotously in the shock of sunlight, but she couldn't move, couldn't breathe. The man's chest rose and fell once, twice, and still she stood riveted to the spot by his gaze.

Finally a familiar figure shattered the moment, gliding forward past the man, his black cassock rippling like inky shadows swallowing up the light. "Are you ill, child?"

"Oh!" she exhaled, placing one hand at her bosom to assuage her panic.

The Abbot peered down his nose at her. "I hope we didn't startle you."

Of course he'd startled her. Half to death. But if she knew the Abbot, frightening her was likely his intent. In sooth, she gleaned some satisfaction from the likelihood that her sudden shriek had aged *him* another ten years.

"I hope *I* didn't . . ." The words caught in her throat as her gaze flickered again over the man accompanying the Abbot. Sweet Mary, he wore the cassock of a holy man, but he looked like no friar she'd ever seen. "Startle *you*."

She tore her eyes away long enough to see the Abbot smile with thin affection. "Naught that you do could ever startle me, child."

Ordinarily she'd snap back a clever retort, but today she wasn't interested in dueling with the Abbot. Nay, she was far more intrigued by his companion—the towering, grim-faced, broad-shouldered man of the cloth who continued to challenge her with a stare that had now become curiously colored by awe.

"I've brought a chaplain for Wendeville," the Abbot

droned, glancing down at the bee still spiraling on the flag-stones beside her bare feet. "Apparently not a moment too soon, if *vermin* are already infesting the chapel." Cynthia spared the Abbot a glimpse, getting the distinct impression he wasn't just referring to the bee. "Lady Cynthia," he said, nodding with false deference, "may I present Father Garth."

Garth.

She looked closer.

It couldn't be, she thought. It was mere coincidence. The bee made her remember the boy in the garden, and here was another with his name. Garth was a common enough name. Surely it was someone else. And yet . . .

"Garth?" Her pulse pounded erratically at her temples. It was childish, this sudden excitement. But the man before her had gray-green eyes and hair the hue of walnuts . . . and suddenly she wished with all her heart, childish or no, that it *was* that boy. Aye, it was naive, a memory from a girlhood filled with faeries and foolish dreams, and she was a woman grown. But she couldn't recall a time when she'd been happier, that halcyon time before her mother had died. Garth de Ware was a part of that life. *Please,* she prayed with uncharacteristic whimsy, *let it be him.*

Garth had never felt more awkward in his life. Blessed Mary—he'd thought he'd left his warrior ways behind him.

The lady's scream had started it all. His heart had plummeted at the sound, and for the first time in four years, his hand had whipped around to his left hip, seeking his sword. Finding nothing but cassock.

As unnerved by his own instinctive response as he was by the shriek, he nonetheless burst into the chapel like a knight bent on vengeance.

Then he froze. And almost broke his vow of silence. For before him, bathed in the ethereal light of the sun-washed chapel, stood the most fey and wondrous creature he'd ever beheld. A wave of paralyzing heat assaulted him. The breath caught in his chest, and his heart tripped like a newborn lamb.

The devil had taken a pleasing shape. There was no other explanation for such beauty. The woman was nearly as tall as he, but as statuesque and well proportioned as the pagan sculptures he'd seen long ago in Rome. Her skin was smooth and vibrant, like the flesh of an apricot, and a delicate sprinkle of freckles frolicked across her nose and cheeks. Her lips were sensual, as inviting as a cherry tart, and her eyes were an ethereal shade of blue matched only by a clear English sky. Most striking, however, was the shock of unbound orange hair that curled riotously about her face, framing it like a storm-tossed halo. It reminded him of marigolds and sunlight and long-abandoned summers of childhood innocence.

Her sideless surcoat, where it wasn't smudged with dirt, was the color of Highland pines. Beneath, a soft gray kirtle hugged her lovely form, and the sight of the delicious curves it revealed made Garth's nostrils quiver like a steed's sensing danger.

Mother of God, he despaired silently, *what comes to test me now?* Surely this was some jest. The Abbot couldn't be serious. He'd have to be mad to place a man burdened by the sin of lust in the household of temptation herself.

The woman's gaze swept him from head to toe, settling at last on his face, searching his eyes for . . . something. "Is it possible," she said, her breathy voice drizzling over his nerves like honey, "that your surname is de Ware?"

He stiffened. She'd heard of him.

"Indeed," the Abbot said coolly. "You're acquainted with his family then?"

From beneath his brows, Garth could see her face light up with pleasure. It made him melt inside.

"It's been some time," she breathed. "But I'm so pleased to see you again, Garth." She warmly inclined her head and extended her hand. It was a capable hand, strong and genuine, a little soiled, but unfettered by jewelry or guile. "My father was Lord Harold le Wyte?" she prompted.

Panic seized him as he stared at her hand. He knew without touching her that that hand was as warm as fresh-baked bread. He suppressed the desire to take it, greeting her with safe, stony silence instead.

As far as Lord Harold Le Wyte, he neither remembered her father nor wished to remember *her.* If he *had* known her, it was from a time he'd put under lock and key long ago, and he didn't intend to pry open that box. Ever.

Her pretty smile faltered. Her hand hung in empty space.

"Oh, I should mention," the Abbot said. "Father Garth is under a vow of silence."

The smile congealed on her face. She awkwardly withdrew her hand. Garth felt a twinge of remorse, but he'd never been more grateful for a penance in his life. He couldn't have forced words past his lips if his soul depended on it.

"I understand." She didn't look as if she understood at all. In sooth, she looked rather offended, as if he'd taken the vow just to spite her.

"It's a temporary penance," the Abbot added, "just a sennight more."

"Ah." Her glance flickered over him, inspecting him rather too thoroughly.

"I'm certain, Lady Cynthia, you'll be pleased with Father Garth. He is known to be a fine scribe, as well as an expert on sin and the moral life."

Garth winced at the Abbot's subtle barb.

"I'm so glad you found him, Abbot," the lady said.

He was doomed. That wistful longing flirting about her eyes would surely be his undoing. Her very presence rattled his composure and did unspeakable things to his loins. And—God have mercy—short of castration, there was no way out of the hell his life was about to become.

4

W HAT TRIFLING PLEASANTRIES THE ABBOT AND THE woman exchanged, God only knew. Garth was too be-deviled by the chaos in his brain to pay them any heed. But all too soon, the Abbot began to speak of leaving.

"I regret my haste," the man said without a hint of regret, "but I trust you shall see Father Garth settled? I must away to Charing before nightfall."

Garth stiffened. Was the Abbot abandoning him, then?

Aye. Indeed. With little more than a curt nod and a sweep of his somber robes, the Abbot managed to make the hastiest escape from Wendeville since Lot fled Sodom.

The chapel door closed behind his swirling cope with an ominous thud, like the portal of a prison.

Garth clenched his fists repeatedly, sorely tempted to rush headlong after the Abbot. But that was a coward's way out. And he was no coward. He was a de Ware. Still, left alone with a woman for the first time in four years, he floundered as uncomfortably as a fish thrown from the river. He knotted his fingers in the coarse fabric of his cassock and stared at the well-worn flagstones.

Cynthia broke the ponderous silence, gently clearing her throat. "The chaplain's chamber is rather modest, I'm afraid."

Her voice sounded as rich and lush as her hair, and her eyes shone like opals. "The chapel is the oldest part of the castle."

Garth wheeled abruptly away. He might not be able to flee this temptress, but he certainly couldn't be expected to carry on conversation with her, considering his vows, and he definitely wasn't going to look into her big blue eyes again.

Instead he pretended to make a thorough inspection of the chapel's stained-glass windows, though for all he noticed, they could have depicted either the Last Supper or the Feast of Valhalla.

Her hospitality was apparently undimmed by his disregard. "It's lovely, isn't it?" she crooned. "The glass came from Sussex."

She came up behind him in a soft rustle of skirts. Close enough that he could smell the fresh earth on her. Close enough that he could feel her warmth at his back. He clenched his jaw, studying the narthex window intently enough to crack the glass.

"John had it commissioned when we were first wed," she told him. "It was his gift . . ."

She broke off, and something in her voice surprised him. Something caught at his heart and stilled his breath.

Sorrow.

He'd forgotten. She'd just lost her husband.

"His gift to me," she finished quietly.

Garth lowered his eyes from the window and let a sigh ease from him. Lady Cynthia was in grief. In sooth, when the Abbot told him that Lord John had been old and feeble, he'd assumed there was no love lost between the decrepit lord and his young bride of two years. He could see now he was wrong. Cynthia had cared for her husband.

As he turned toward her, she smiled brokenly and wiped at her nose with the back of one dirty hand, leaving a streak where a tear had fallen. His heart softened at once. And he knew, as impetuous as it was, he could no more refrain from consoling her than a sparrow could refrain from singing. Lending comfort was as natural to him as breathing.

He reached out for her as he would to a child, cupping her cheek in one palm, brushing his thumb carefully across the smear to erase it. A wave of guilt washed over him. Compassion was the church's daily bread. How could he have been so selfish, so caught up in his own troubles that he failed to notice her grief?

But as soon as their gazes converged, Garth's fatherly instincts vanished. The innocent gesture suddenly seemed perilous. His hand burned with forbidden fire where it touched her cheek. Her skin was velvety and inviting, as smooth and warm as a fresh-laid egg. He could feel the racing pulse of her blood beneath his fingertip at her throat. And as he watched, her eyes grew veiled with some unnameable yearning and her lips trembled apart. His nostrils flared, and for one mad moment, as the sun drenched them both in a stained-glass sea, he feared he might lower his head to kiss those lips.

But an intruder shattered the moment, barging in through the chapel door. The two of them parted as quickly as torn parchment, and Garth lowered his regard at once, praying he didn't look as mortified as he felt.

"My lady," the newcomer, an elderly gentleman, said, inclining his head. By the jangle of keys at his belt, Garth guessed he was the castle steward.

"Roger!" She sounded strangely breathless. "Come in. Meet our new chaplain."

"Father." The man gave him a cursory glance from head to toe, then dismissed him. "Begging your pardon, my lady, but there's been an accident."

"Accident?" She straightened.

Garth's eyes fastened on the steward, suddenly alert.

"It's Will, my lady. He fell from his mount in the lists. He's howling something fierce. I think his arm is broken."

Garth set his mouth. He'd never broken a bone, but he'd watched the physician at Castle de Ware set his brothers' numerous times. It wasn't a pleasant sight.

"Go and fetch my bag, Roger," Lady Cynthia said, pulling her hair back and tying it up with a leather thong she dug from her pocket. "And find me wood and linen for a splint."

Garth stared at her, astonished. Certainly she didn't intend to treat the lad herself. Setting bones required a strong back. And a strong stomach. It was not work for a woman.

"This may take a while," she explained, a small furrow of

worry creasing her brow. "Please make yourself welcome. I shall return anon."

And before he could incline his head to acknowledge her, she whirled and was off in a whisper of velvet.

All his priestly instincts told him to remain in the chapel. It was where a man of God belonged, after all. This was Lady Cynthia's castle, and if she was in the habit of playing physician, what business was it of his to interfere? If she could endure the gruesome sight of a fractured bone, if she had the strength to wrench a man's arm half out of its socket while the wretch thrashed about, if she could turn a deaf ear while he screamed in agony . . .

With a self-mocking grimace, he bolted out the door after her.

He could hear the boy halfway across the yard, his low bellows of pain cracked by the unfortunate yelps of youth. Four of his companions huddled over him, shifting anxiously from foot to foot, but when Lady Cynthia arrived, they made way for her.

"What happened?" she asked the squires.

They all replied at once, but the gist of it was that the boy had been thrown or fell or leaped from his horse and landed on the hard-packed sod of the list. She knelt beside the victim.

"Can you sit up?"

The boy gasped in pain, but his friends managed to right him.

"We'll have to remove your . . ." she began, halting as Garth caught up to her and seized her shoulder.

He hunkered down between Cynthia and the youth and unfastened the lad's swordbelt and the buckles of his breastplate. They slipped off easily enough, but the mail hauberk beneath would be difficult. Beckoning with his hand, he summoned two of the squires forward to support Will's broken arm. While the lad clenched his teeth against the torment, Garth slipped the heavy chain mail off his good arm and over the top of his head. Then, as the boys carefully lowered Will's arm, he guided the hauberk off the injured limb. The brave lad made no outcry, but beads of sweat stood out on his forehead, and he shivered in his tunic.

"Thank you," Cynthia murmured as he dropped the chain mail to the ground. "Now, Will," she said, "let's find out where the injury is."

She pressed her thumbs along the boy's arm, working her way up under his sleeve. Halfway up his forearm, he gasped sharply, and she halted.

"All right. I can feel a break. Just rest for a moment. Roger will be along with my medicines soon." Then she sat back on her heels, closed her eyes, and began rubbing her hands together as if warming them by a fire.

Garth scowled. What was she doing? The boy was in pain. The steward might not arrive for another quarter of an hour. The longer the delay, the more difficult it would be to snap the arm back into place. Something should be done. Now.

He watched the lady for a moment more as she bowed her head over her hands as if in prayer. Then he made the decision. He wiped his palms on his cassock and handed the boy his swordbelt, directing him wordlessly to clamp it between his teeth. The lad screwed his eyes shut and bit down hard.

Garth blew out a sharp breath. He'd watched the physician at de Ware set bones a dozen times or more. How difficult could it be? The trick, he remembered, was distraction.

While Cynthia continued with her meditative ritual, Garth braced his foot against the boy's upper arm and adjusted his hand about the boy's wrist, preparing to pull it. But just before he yanked, he raised his left hand and clouted the lad smartly across the face.

Gasping in shock from the blow, Will had no time to yelp as Garth hauled hard on his arm. In the wink of an eye, the bone popped back into place.

Garth's satisfied smile lasted exactly two heartbeats before a female fist cracked it from his face and he rocked backward onto the sward.

Cynthia couldn't believe she'd hit him. But then she couldn't believe what he'd done. Priests were supposed to comfort the sick, not pummel them. And if she'd knocked Father Garth onto the ground with the full force of the power she'd summoned for healing, it was no less than he deserved.

"What the devil do you think you're doing?" she cried as he stared at her in stupefaction.

With a groan of frustration, she turned her attention to poor Will, who lay as pale as linen on the cold ground. She shook her hands. There was still a vestige of energy remaining in her fingertips, but it felt scattered. She'd wasted most of it on that punch, and she knew her knuckles would be bruised on the morrow. In sooth, she doubted she could harness the power now at all.

"Are you all right, Will?" she asked, bending near.

The boy's eyes were glazed as he looked at her.

"He hit me," he mumbled, spitting the leather belt from his mouth. "That priest hit me."

"And how is your arm?"

Will frowned. "It hurts. Why did he hit me?"

Cynthia pursed her lips. She wanted to know that as well. She eased her thumbs tenderly along Will's forearm, feeling for the separation, and discovered to her astonishment that the bone was set perfectly. Apparently, Garth had been lucky.

"We'll splint it properly when Roger arrives," she told the boy with a forced smile of reassurance.

Then she let her gaze slide over Garth, unable to hide her disillusionment. She had many questions, and she cursed the vow that would allow him to answer none of them. Then again, she doubted she'd like his answers. No priestly humility resided in his eyes now. He scowled harshly, wiping a trickle of blood from the corner of his lip with the back of his hand, and she thought she'd never seen a man of God look so unlikely to turn the other cheek.

Roger loped across the yard just then, bearing linen, several faggots of wood, and her satchel of herbs. She'd had neither time nor energy to summon a vision to guide her in Will's treatment, but she knew she could rely on myrtle, bruisewort, and feverfew to expedite the knitting of the boy's bones. And, she thought peevishly, Will could probably use a rosemary infusion for the nasty bruise the chaplain had given him.

As for Garth, she supposed she ought to swab his cut as well. Perhaps she would. Later. When she wasn't so angry with him.

But Garth didn't leave her that choice. As soon as Roger arrived, he came to his feet, beat the dust out of his cassock, turned on his heel, and left her to her healing arts.

Only much later, after she'd sent Will off with his arm successfully splinted, dabbed extract of mint upon her own bee sting, and begun to gather up her medicines, did Cynthia wonder again at Garth's cruelty.

What had become of the chivalrous hero with the gentle touch in that long-ago garden? Had the years changed him so much? If this was what the church had taught him, if this was his version of holy works, then she intended to have a long talk with him. In sooth, the fact that he couldn't argue with her might prove rather favorable.

She hefted up the bag of bottles and strode across the sward, still in her bare feet.

Why had Garth clouted a defenseless lad? What earthly purpose could striking a boy who was already in agony serve?

Halfway across the yard, she halted so suddenly that her satchel of bottles clattered against her thigh.

Of course.

She'd believed it was sheer luck that Garth had managed to set the bone properly. But was it?

Mayhap he'd known precisely what he was doing. Mayhap he'd simply taken matters into his own hands. From what she'd glimpsed in the moment before she struck him, Garth had known to brace Will's upper arm and to pull true. As far as punching the boy . . .

A flush of shame washed over her like warm rain, and suddenly she knew the truth. Garth *had* meant well. He'd done exactly the right thing. And—curse her misguided assumptions—she'd struck him for it. Guilt made her knuckles throb all the worse.

Swallowing the soured taste of impotent self-righteousness, she straightened her shoulders and glanced apprehensively toward the chapel. She had to apologize. She'd acted without thought. And she'd completely misunderstood him.

Knowing it would be no easier later, she trudged toward the chapel and sheepishly opened the door.

He was there, kneeling before the altar, his head bent in

prayer, the glass-filtered sunlight staining his dull cassock in blocks of cobalt and scarlet and gold.

She gulped. Though the castle was hers by rights of ownership, she felt as if the chapel was *his* sanctuary, and she didn't wish to intrude on his prayers. Perhaps she should steal away.

But she hesitated a moment too long, and when he rose and turned, he saw her. He'd apparently not heard her come in, for his eyes widened and his mouth parted in surprise. Then a shadow fell across his face as if a cloud had gone across the sun.

"I . . . I'm sorry if I disturbed you," she said, feeling suddenly clumsy. "I came to, well . . ."

Wariness crept into his dark gaze.

She took a deep breath and faced him squarely. "I came to apologize."

His expression didn't change, but then, what did she expect? She had clouted him with all the force of her healing power, flattened him with her fist. He no doubt thought her a bully.

Biting the corner of her lip, she moved down the aisle toward him. He straightened like a stalked deer, ready to bolt.

"You were distracting him, weren't you? You struck him so he'd not notice the greater pain of his arm."

She could tell by the lowering of his tensed shoulders that she was right.

"And it worked. In sooth, I've not seen a bone setting done so quickly."

If he didn't smile at the compliment, at least he lost a portion of his scowl.

"So . . ." She lowered her eyes to the floor. "I thank you for the assistance, and I'm sorry I . . ." She ventured a glance up at him. His lip had stopped bleeding, but it was puffed out where she'd hit him. "I . . ." She dug busily in her satchel and pulled out the bottle of rosemary infusion and a clean linen rag. "This should help the bruising." She stepped toward him, and he stiffened. Dear Lord, she thought, was the poor man affrighted of her now? "Do not fret," she assured him. "It is painless."

He stood his ground then, but she sensed he was tempted to flee.

She wet the cloth and stood before him. Strange, though she was tall, still she had to look up to meet his eyes. She fastened her gaze on his mouth. It was beautiful. His jaw was swarthy with faint stubble, and in contrast, his lips looked soft. They were not too full, not too spare, with an intriguing curve that promised roguish smiles. She couldn't believe she'd damaged that mouth with her fist.

Blinking back her wayward thoughts, she dabbed efficiently at the cut. He winced once, then stilled for her ministrations.

Mingling with the aroma of rosemary, Garth's own scent intruded upon her senses, a spicy fragrance like the holy incense in smoke-filled cathedrals. It was oddly soothing, and suddenly she grew aware of her own earthy odor. She wanted to explain to him that she'd been in the garden all morning, that that was the reason for her bare feet and soiled dress and the smell of dirt that clung to her. But for once, she wisely kept her thoughts to herself. There was no delicate way to excuse her appearance, and, she thought honestly, no real reason. This was who she was, and if he couldn't see past her flaws . . .

His fingers clamping about her wrist startled her from her thoughts. Apparently he'd had enough of her rosemary. But it wasn't exactly annoyance she glimpsed in his gaze. Nay, something feral flared in his eyes, threatening her and sending her a warning all at once, like a well-fed wolf nonetheless fighting his instinct to hunt. It took her breath away.

And, contrary to her usual stubbornness, for once she heeded his unspoken threat.

Her hand slipped easily from his grasp.

"I'll have Roger see to your chamber at once," she said, fidgeting with the rag and stoppering the bottle. "Give you the day to settle in."

She wheeled and hurried away, tarrying only long enough to gather her satchel and toss an invitation over her shoulder.

"I shall look for you at dinner then."

And even after she closed the door behind her, even after

she'd put half a furlong between them, still her heart beat wildly like that of a mouse sprung from the talons of a hawk.

Garth's mouth throbbed, not in pain, but with the memory of her touch. He raised the back of his hand to his lips, willing away the sensation.

He should never have let her near, the goddess with her laughing eyes and her sensual mouth, her summery fragrance and her healing caress.

In sooth, it was remarkable to him that her touch could be so gentle, for she'd certainly nearly cracked his teeth with her fist.

When she'd come in, he'd been praying for understanding, that somehow Will and Lady Cynthia would comprehend his intent and learn why he'd done what he'd done, as, under his vow, he couldn't enlighten them himself. Now the last thing he wanted was for Cynthia to read his mind.

Vile thoughts resided there, thoughts that had him desiring her company, responding to her touch, craving her succulent mouth.

He closed his eyes against the visions.

Lord, to what purgatory had the Abbot sent him?

Unfortunately, the tale of Lady Cynthia's blow of vengeance upon the new chaplain was too juicy a tidbit for the gossips to ignore. By the time Roger the steward had directed him to his quarters, gifting him with an ivory comb and a polished steel mirror to add to his meager possessions, rumors were running rampant about the castle.

As soon as Garth set foot outside his chamber, a flock of servants scattered like panicked hens from his door. When he strode into the great hall, men nodded cautiously and women whispered behind their hands. The instant he entered the armory, the knights grew silent. In the kitchen, the cauldron of pottage suddenly required the close inspection of the cook and all the serving lads. The bustling courtyard quieted when Garth made his way along the armorer's shed and the mews and the swine's pen. Even the squires busied themselves with brushing the horses when he ducked into the stables. And everywhere, giggling children followed him, nervously poking and prodding each other while he suffered their unguarded scrutiny.

He supposed he was rich fodder for their jokes. After all, everyone had heard of his renowned brothers, Duncan and Holden. They were two of the finest knights in Christendom. Surely the castle folk expected Garth to be no less. It must pique their morbid curiosity to see a de Ware reduced to the level of a lowly friar. And no doubt his vow of silence and the unfortunate incident in the lists had fueled the fire of their musings.

Whatever their intent, they'd succeeded in destroying his peace and shredding his dignity. He wanted nothing more than to crawl away like a wounded animal, to return to the chapel, to his quarters. But he was a de Ware, and his blood refused to let him turn tail like a coward. He supposed he'd just have to armor himself against their friendly onslaught.

In the meantime, he needed to find a place of temporary refuge, where he could escape the haranguing mob, if only briefly, and order his thoughts.

He ducked into the tiny room he had sought out. Alone at last. He spread the burgundy velvet curtain closed behind him and leaned back against the cold stone wall, heaving a sigh of relief. Then he smirked. It was utterly absurd that the only peace he could secure in the vast Wendeville estate was in a garderobe.

He shivered in the drafty chamber and loosened the cord around his cassock, idly wondering how long he could remain sequestered here before someone suspected him of an ailment of the bowels. He bunched up the voluminous robe, revealing his linen undergarments, deftly untied the points with one hand, and freed his full staff to aim a stream of piss down into the dark, dank hole.

How he'd survive the day, let alone the weeks and months to come, he didn't know. Isolation had become a way of life for him, his religion a comfort. Being thrust into the laity again so abruptly with its chaos and disorder and . . . and temptations was like yanking a hapless bat into the blinding sunlight. He wondered if he'd ever grow accustomed again to the glare of the secular world.

He hitched up his leggings, giving his quarterstaff one last shake, then tied the points. He smoothed down his cassock, then, knotting the cord, he blew out a resigned breath and reluctantly shouldered the garderobe curtain aside.

"Ah-ha!"

Garth's heart vaulted into his throat. A plump old bird of a woman in russet skirts charged forward, startling him so that if he hadn't just finished relieving himself, he would surely have done so on the spot.

"There ye are!"

The wench had the round, wrinkled face of a shriveled apple, but her brown eyes sparked animatedly. She glanced quickly about for witnesses, then smacked a small but efficient palm in the middle of his chest and shoved him back into the garderobe, snapping the curtain closed after her.

Garth staggered back, resisting the urge to make the sign of the cross against the lunatic woman. She gave no quarter, blatantly inspecting him from head to toe like a farmer sizing up a plowhorse.

"I'm Elspeth," she finally announced, drawing herself up proudly to her full height, which brought the top of her stiff-wimpled head to the middle of his chest. "Lady Cynthia's maid. Have been since she was a babe in swaddlin'."

Garth blinked. Had the daft woman barged into the garderobe just to introduce herself? He slipped his gaze uneasily toward the curtain.

"Pah! No one's seen us," she assured him. "I need to talk to ye in private." She winked without smiling. "Can ye think of a more private place?"

He wished he had.

She measured him with a glare once more, like a mother sparrow with its feathers all afluff, about to scold the crows from her nest. "So ye're the new chaplain." She nodded toward his face. "That where she cuffed ye?"

He raised a finger self-consciously to his lip.

"Hmmph." Then she shrugged. "Well, it appears she's put ye in yer place, then. At least ye've got a little more life in ye than the whey-faced cadaver we had before." The woman certainly minced no words. "But I'm here to give ye a warnin'."

Garth didn't like the sound of that. He had just enough nobility left in him that the tone of an impertinent servant tweaked his ear. He straightened and folded his arms sternly across his chest.

"Now don't be gettin' yer cassock in a twist," she said, wagging a finger at him. "'Tis about Lady Cynthia."

He uncrossed his arms.

"Heed me well, lad," she commanded with unrelenting insolence. She poked at his chest, apparently unintimidated by the fact that he outweighed her at least two and a half times over. "I'd tell ye of a vow I made to Lord John, Lady Cynthia's husband, God rest his soul." She paused to make the sign of the cross.

Garth absently followed suit.

She lowered her voice. "On his deathbed, he made me swear to find her . . . a husband . . . within the year."

Garth frowned.

"Now I know it goes against the custom of grievin' and all," she continued, "and I'm sure the Abbot wouldn't approve, but 'tis a promise made on the man's deathbed. Mark ye well, 'tis not as if my Cynthia didn't have a care for John. Nay, she was with him till the end, wipin' his forehead and . . . and holdin' his hand . . ." The woman's eyes watered over, and her chin quivered.

At a loss, Garth dug in his pouch for a linen square and awkwardly handed it to her.

"Bless ye," she squeaked. Then she blew her nose soundly, crumpled the linen into a ball, and handed it back to him.

He chivalrously cached the thing.

She sniffed and lifted her chin, plucky once more. "He said 'twas to be a man of her heart. After all, Lady Cynthia spent two of her young years carin' for an old soldier with one greave in the grave. And he wouldn't see her do it again, do ye hear? Nor will I. Not while she's still hale enough to snare a fine young buck." She dusted her hands together as if to say that was that.

Garth stared hard at the woman. Why was she telling him all this? Surely Lady Cynthia's romantic affairs had naught to do with him, even if the maidservant's frank words somehow sawed at him against the grain. He was a man of the cloth, concerned with matters of the soul. What did he know of matters of the heart?

"So here's the crux of it," she confided. "I'll do everythin' in my power to bring Lady Cynthia the pick o' the litter. She deserves no less. But a year's not much time. So I say we dispense with the grievin' and get on with the gaiety. I've already put word out there'll be dancin' and singin' in the castle again within the sennight." She pursed her lips and narrowed her eyes at him. "This is what I'd have from ye. 'Tis plain. Swear me an oath that ye'll not plague m'lady with undue remorse. No sermons on grief or chastity or honorin' her husband's memory. Nothin' to harden her heart or stand in the way of her courtin'." She clucked her tongue. "Lord knows ye men of God like to burden a body with sin at every turn, but I'm askin' ye this once to forbear." She waved an impatient hand at him. "Aye, I know all about yer vow o' silence, but ye can nod yer head as well as any man. And I'll have yer nod on it right now."

Garth bristled at the old woman's demanding tone. Lord, the conniving wench possessed no sense of propriety. Never had he encountered such unabashed candor in a mere servant. It was outrageous. And yet he found himself willing to overlook her faults, for curiously enough, this chittering bird of a maid had just offered him a glimpse of salvation.

Oh aye, he'd swear that oath. On the Holy Scriptures, if need be. In sooth, he'd be only too glad to expedite Lady Cynthia's quest for a new husband. The sooner she was wed, the better. Anything to remove temptation.

He nodded his assent and, for the first time since he'd arrived at Wendeville, he felt like smiling. Perhaps, he dared to hope, God hadn't deserted him after all.

5

CYNTHIA TWISTED HER FINGERS IN THE LINEN NAPKIN. The sounds in the great hall reverberated in her ears as if she heard them for the first time. Daggers scraped across pewter platters. Wine gurgled into cups and down gullets. The hounds whuffed softly from their corner, eager for the tidbits children would bring them later. Kitchen lads brought forth steaming bowls of pottage and loaves of fragrant wastel, adroitly dodging the maidservants hefting flagons of wine. And everyone spoke at once.

Thanks to Elspeth, the castle gossip had turned around again. The incident at the lists had been declared an unfortunate accident, a mishap caused when the chaplain drew too near Cynthia's exertions. And if young Will and his friends knew a different story, they held their tongues. Their world was rife with fighting and maidens and honor, after all, and they cared not for rumor.

Still, all was utter pandemonium in the hall, as usual. In sooth, Cynthia suspected strangers could dine for weeks at Wendeville and never be spotted. Except that she knew everyone in her own household and the nearby village. She'd mended them all at one time or another.

Nay, only one stranger dined before her tonight, the humblest of priests, yet she agonized over every detail as if she entertained the king. Would he like the rue wine? Did he find his bench comfortable enough? Was there a draft in the hall?

Already, he'd made a bad choice of tables. He'd managed to sequester himself between the two quarreling Campbell cousins, and there he was stuck, picking morosely at his capon while the raucous lads jostled him mercilessly. He looked exceedingly uncomfortable, no doubt unnerved by both the boys' familiarity and the cacophony of the hall—knights bragging, maids giggling, hounds barking. She bit her lip. Wendeville Castle was a far cry from a monastery.

"M'lady?" Elspeth appeared at her side, bearing a flask of wine. She settled in beside Cynthia and filled their cups. "Will has joined us, d'ye see?" She nodded toward the youth. "Weak as a lamb, but hungry as a wolf."

"Mm."

"The way the maids are fawnin' over him, fightin' for the honor of hand-feedin' the boy, *all* the lads'll be breakin' their arms over the next sennight."

Cynthia gave her a brief smile, but wasn't truly listening. Her eyes and her thoughts were elsewhere. Heaven help her, she hadn't drawn a decent breath from the instant Garth had come crashing into the chapel, bringing with him a flood of long-lost memories. And the way he'd made her feel when he'd sent her away with the unspoken warning in his fiery eyes . . .

She had so many questions. How had he fared—he and his family? Did his mother's garden thrive? Were his brothers as bloodthirsty as ever? And, more than anything, she longed to know—what had steered a man of such honor and chivalry toward the church?

She watched Garth break a loaf of wastel between strong, nimble fingers, then ran her fingertip pensively around the cool lip of her chalice, making a game of mentally bidding him look at her. He did, surreptitiously, over the rim of his cup, searing her with his gaze before shifting his eyes anxiously away.

Cynthia's heart fluttered in her breast. Lord, what ailed her? She hadn't even touched her wine yet, and already she felt light-headed. She lowered her eyes, swirling the burgundy liquid around in her chalice.

"So what do you think?" she murmured to Elspeth, not daring to lift her eyes.

"Of the wine?"

"Of our new chaplain." She took a long drink.

Elspeth paused to give Garth a stern appraisal. "A mite too quiet, a mite too thin . . ."

Cynthia stole another glance at him just as his tongue flicked out to lick the corner of his lip. She shouldn't have. The sight made her stomach quiver.

"And," Elspeth added, "a mite too handsome for his own good."

Cynthia choked on her wine.

"Too much rue in the wine?" Elspeth asked, her face pinched in concern.

Cynthia shook her head, burying a cough in her linen napkin.

"O' course," Elspeth allowed, "he's quiet 'cause he's under a vow o' silence. And he's thin 'cause we've yet to fatten him up on Cook's fine suppers. As for bein' handsome . . ."

Cynthia slid her gaze toward Garth again. Lord, he *was* that. Even the way he tucked a morsel of capon into his mouth, chewing with sensual patience . . . She gave Elspeth a weak smile. Her voice came out in a strained whisper. "I hardly think a man can be faulted for his looks."

Elspeth snapped her gaze back to Cynthia, who set aside her wine, too edgy to drink.

She only toyed with her food as well, and by the serving of the third course, she wondered if she'd ever regain her appetite. It was only nerves, she told herself. She hadn't seen the de Wares since she was a child, and she wanted to impress Garth, that was all. It could be nothing else. After all, Garth was a priest now. He commanded a certain deference. And while the Bible did not expressly forbid friendships between men of the cloth and noblewomen, the church certainly did not encourage them. Moreover, Garth had come from a monastery, where the doctrine was much more stringent. After four years, he was probably completely unused to the company of women. Perhaps that was why he seemed so . . . restless.

But it had not always been so. Once he'd been quite another person.

"Elspeth," she said, running a thumbnail over the grapes carved into her pewter chalice, "did I ever tell you about my noble champion in the enchanted garden?"

Without risking another glance at Garth, she recounted the whole tale—the jasmine, the swarm of bees, and her gallant hero with the smoky green eyes that were mocking and kind all at once. Elspeth hung on her every word.

Afterward, the maid leaned forward expectantly. "Is it true, m'lady? And did ye . . . did ye *love* him?"

"I don't know. I was only a child. But at the time, I surely wished to marry him."

Elspeth seemed like to burst with excitement. "Well, tell me, lass. Whatever became o' the lad?"

Cynthia almost wished she hadn't shared the tale, for it certainly didn't have a happy ending. She picked a crumb from her lap.

"He's here, Elspeth," she whispered.

"Here?" Elspeth scanned the great hall, her eyes aglow. "In the castle?"

"Aye." She flashed Elspeth a bittersweet smile. "I'd forgotten all about him. It was the day my lady mother died, you see. But then the bee sting today reminded me—"

"Bee sting?"

"Aye," she said, frowning thoughtfully at her trencher. "I was stung by a bee in the chapel. And when I turned round, there he was."

"The bee?"

"Nay," she replied, chuckling. "The boy from the garden."

"In the chapel?"

"Aye." She peered at Garth over her chalice's edge. She would never forget how he'd looked storming in through the chapel door, all dark and wild and full of vengeance.

"But how did he come to be here, m'lady?" Elspeth asked.

"Hmm?" Garth's hand looked massive as he wrapped it around his cup of wine. Massive but gentle. She wondered if it was rough or smooth. "Oh. The Abbot brought him." She took a small sip of her wine. It might have been goat piss, for all the attention she paid its flavor.

Elspeth took a long drink, then screwed up her forehead in puzzlement. "But, m'lady, the Abbot brought only . . ." Her eyes widened. It was her turn to gag on the wine.

Cynthia gave her maidservant a few hearty whacks on the back that seemed only to aggravate her condition before Elspeth waved her away.

The old woman spoke again after a moment, strangling the words under her breath. "Not our new chaplain?"

"El?" Cynthia frowned. What the devil was wrong with Elspeth? "Are you all right, El?"

"Nay!" Elspeth hissed, setting the wine cup down so hard on the table it splattered onto the white linen. She whispered frantically into Cynthia's ear. "Don't ye even think of it, lass! Are ye daft?"

"Think of what, Elspeth?"

"He's not the same lad at all, m'lady. For St. Agnes's sake," she murmured, crossing herself, "the man's a priest, not some child's knight-errant. Choose another, lass. Don't be settin' yer eye on a man o' the cloth."

"Why, Elspeth!" Cynthia gasped, truly shocked. "What gave you the idea . . . I told you before . . " She glanced uneasily about and lowered her voice. "I'm not looking to wed. Anyone." She lifted her cup to her lips, staring down at its quivering contents. The wine reflected the candlelight like a polished carnelian, and for just an instant, she wondered if she was telling the truth. "Besides, only a fool would try to tempt a man from the church. One might as well court the devil."

"Aye, that's right!" Elspeth chimed in all too emphatically. Then she muttered under her breath, "Seducin' a man o' God, well, 'tis like flirtin' with Lucifer himself."

Though Lucifer couldn't be half as handsome, Cynthia thought, immediately washing down that blasphemy with another swallow of wine.

But aye, Elspeth was right. Garth de Ware belonged to the church. And besides, he was a man grown now. There was no telling what he'd grown into. He'd sprung up tall, that was certain, and his features had ripened well into masculine maturity. The faint stubble of a shaved beard shadowed his chin. His dark tawny hair, though shorter, still curled carelessly about his face, but now it served to soften the hard edges of his jaw and cheekbones, lending him a reckless air. His mouth was yet wide and expressive. And his eyes, when they weren't lowered beneath heavy brows, shone like polished jade, just as they had in that garden long ago.

But Garth was no longer the lad from the garden. As a youth, his eyes had sparkled in conspiracy, and his jaunty one-sided grin had promised a lifetime of adventure. Little of that daring remained in him now. His spirit seemed suppressed, humbled. And yet, there was something unnatural about that submissiveness. In sooth, he looked about as docile as an exotic lion from the East, stolen from its wild land to be tamed.

Surely Garth de Ware was not a man to be tamed. His monk's robes were an ill fit. And he certainly didn't belong shut up behind monastery walls. Nay, he was like a field of wild heather someone had witlessly trimmed into a box hedge. Or maybe, she reconsidered, he was more like twining ivy that—

Elspeth shrieked suddenly, interrupting Cynthia's analogies. "'Ware, ye shandy fool!" She sprang up from the table. "Pah! Addlepated simpkin!" she added for good measure.

Cynthia followed her gaze. Alton, the cockiest of the kitchen lads, swaggered across the flagstones on his way to the high table, wrestling with an over-large platter of roast meat and vegetables perched precariously atop one skinny shoulder. As they all watched in horror, the roast slid to and fro from one end of the plate to the other, dripping juice down the lad's arm each time the platter tipped. Grinning obliviously, the boy tottered about on his bandy legs to compensate for the shift in weight. But disaster was inevitable. He finally slipped on the rushes, and the platter flipped with amazing acrobatics, loosing its burden everywhere.

Turnips splashed in a wide swath, half among the rushes, half across the high table. Drippings sprayed through the air like foul rain. Onions splattered to the floor. The roast bowled forward across the white linen tablecloth, leaving a trail of juice and knocking aside a row of chalices on its determined journey toward Cynthia's lap.

In the blink of an eye, Garth leaped up and over his table, dagger in hand. Before Cynthia could even draw breath to gasp, he lunged forward across the high table like a charging boar. His dagger rose high, then plunged down with a powerful thud, stabbing the rogue roast, pinning the meat clear through to the wood planking.

A hush of awe dropped instantly over the hall. Not a hound stirred. Even the Campbell lads halted their bickering. All eyes flew to the chaplain clutching the knife with bloodless knuckles like some Viking berserker.

The furrow between his brows deepened as he stared at his own hand, evidently as dumbfounded as the rest by his spontaneous, absurd feat of heroics.

Cynthia didn't know whether to laugh or applaud. She'd never been saved from a roast before. What a boyish, charming, ridiculously chivalrous gesture. But she could do neither. Not when Garth slowly lifted his eyes across the table to hers, drawing her into his gaze. She hadn't noticed before how deep a green his eyes were. As deep as a Highland forest. As deep as the North Sea. Jesu, she could lose her way in those eyes.

"Oh, m'lady!" Alton barged into her reverie, stumbling forward. "Forgive me!" His swagger gone, he doffed his cap and twisted it in his hands, looking as pitiful as a pup who'd mistakenly bitten his master's hand. "I didn't mean to . . ."

Cynthia waved away his apology. "No harm done."

The boy bobbed twice, then shoved his cap back down over his shaggy head and squatted to attend to the mess.

Garth's grip loosened upon the dagger, but before he could withdraw, Cynthia impulsively reached for him. His hand was wonderfully warm and large. And smooth. It was smooth.

"Thank you, Father," she murmured. Lord, she could feel his pulse beneath her thumb. For one insane moment, her face flooded with heat. She longed to press his fingers against her lips, to see how his skin would feel against her mouth. An emotion flickered in Garth's eyes, visible for but an instant, an emotion akin to hunger, and an irrational thrill coursed through her veins. But then his hand stiffened. Reluctantly, she let go.

He clenched his hands once and relaxed, reminding her of a knight about to do mortal battle. Then he turned from her and crouched to help Alton.

Cynthia folded her napkin beside her trencher. Her heart fluttered like a moth around a flame, the way it did when she was about to do something of which the Abbot wouldn't approve. And indeed she was.

She couldn't very well let Garth grovel in the garbage-strewn rushes at her feet, could she? Not the new chaplain of Wendeville. Especially after she'd welcomed him with a fist the last time they met. At least that was the reason she gave herself as she rose from the bench and humbled herself to join him on the floor.

The castle folk were accustomed enough to Cynthia's odd habits that seeing their lady scoop refuse from the floor did not amaze them in the least. Soon enough, the hall grew noisy again.

Garth knelt less than a foot away. As he stretched forward for a wayward onion, the sleeve of his coarse garment rasped against the hem of her velvet kirtle. He wouldn't meet her eyes, and he kept his lips closed in a sober line as he labored. But she could feel waves of strong emotion coming off of him like heat from an autumn hearth.

Garth clenched his teeth against the breeze of elusive perfume that assaulted his senses as he reached past Lady Cynthia for a stray turnip. Surely God was testing him; it was all he could imagine. Else why torture him so, forcing him to such painful intimacy with this paragon of womankind? And before so many witnesses?

He shuddered at his own idiocy. Why in God's name he'd leaped across the table to save Lady Cynthia from a slab of meat he didn't know. It was possibly the most foolish feat he'd ever undertaken. But he'd done it without thought, on pure instinct. And now he'd unwittingly put himself in the worst possible place—directly in temptation's path.

Silently cursing himself for a bigger fool than Lot's wife,

he nonetheless hazarded a glance at the woman working beside him. And wished he'd been turned to salt. By candlelight, she was more beautiful than the portrait of the Madonna in the de Ware family chapel. A golden glow seemed to enshrine her radiant face. Her downcast eyes were as silvery as moonlight on an October pool. Even the wisps of her hair, escaping from her wimple like naughty children out to play, curled perfectly upon her cheek. Sweet Mary—she wreaked utter havoc with his senses.

He sincerely prayed his cassock was sufficiently loose to hide the evidence of his lust. For that was all it was, he was sure. Lust. It had been weeks since he'd seen a woman, months since he'd been this close to one. Close enough to detect the soft, clean scent of her skin. Close enough to feel the disturbing brush of her garments as she turned.

She touched his forearm. "Fear not," she murmured, glancing at the castle folk surrounding them. "You'll grow accustomed to Wendeville's . . . chaos."

He'd never grow accustomed to it, not if she was a part of it. Was his apprehension so obvious, then? What else could she divine in his face? Fear? Confusion? Desire? He stared at the fingers still resting on his bare arm. They didn't belong there. He was a man of God. She had no license to touch him.

And yet nothing had ever felt so right. Her hands were as warm as a dove's breast. They were hands of comfort. Hands made for toiling lovingly in the garden and patting away a child's fears. Hands unafraid of soil or spilled turnips or . . . or the sanctity of a priest's flesh.

His long scrutiny finally convinced her to release him. He let out a relieved breath, unaware he'd been holding it. Then he deposited the last of the vegetables onto the platter and strode back to his bench before she could touch him again, before she could beguile him.

Aye, Lady Cynthia was more beautiful than Eve. But he was no Adam to be tempted by a woman's wiles. He'd be damned if he'd let this one undo the four years he'd spent forgetting his sordid past.

The candle flickered in the draft sneaking through the half-open shutters of Garth's new quarters, making light dance across the parchment on which he labored. Despite the darkness outside and the dimness within, he scribed the letters flawlessly, with a steadiness of hand that belied the turmoil brewing in his mind.

Lady Cynthia had ruined his supper. It was bad enough to be denied the monastic silence he was accustomed to while dining. Worse that he'd chosen a seat between two brawling striplings. But the wench had had the effrontery to stare at him the whole while, as if she'd never seen a man eat. And then the whole episode with the roast . . .

A spot of ink smudged off to the side of the letter he'd just completed, and he grimaced, wiping it away swiftly with a linen rag.

Pah! She was only a woman, he argued with himself. It had simply been so long since he'd had any contact with one, it had temporarily muddled his brain. After his recent nightmares, it was only natural he'd feel threatened by the presence of a woman, any woman.

But was she just any woman? According to Lady Cynthia, they'd met before, and in sooth, some image of her danced at the edges of his memory. But like the elusive stars glimmering beyond his window, recollection kept skipping just out of reach.

His hand faltered around the curve of a letter, and he painstakingly retraced it to cover the flaw.

He should set the wench aright now, distance himself from her. Better he should risk offending her than lead them both into sin through familiarity. Besides, he reasoned, he had nothing to give her, nothing to give any woman. Mariana had assured him of that. Nay, he was not deserving of a woman's affections. He was only fit for the church.

He flinched almost imperceptibly, but enough to make a jog in the straight line he was scribing. Mentally cursing, he swabbed it away, then on impulse wiped over the whole line, leaving an ugly smudge across the page.

He blew the candle out, slumped in his chair, and stared at the glittering stars that taunted him from the heavens. Damn his fickle heart. He'd found a suitable niche in the church. Why then was he so discontent to stay in it?

•   •   •

Cynthia poked at the embers in her chamber's hearth, sprinkling dried sweet basil over the smoldering wood and watching it catch fire in small, fragrant bursts. The flames warmed her cheek like a blush, and she stared into them, unable to think of anything but Garth de Ware.

Garth with his impossibly broad shoulders. Garth with his thick, oak-colored hair and finely sculpted features. Garth with his fathomless green eyes that could scorch metal with a glare.

A sad smile crossed her face. His eyes hadn't always been like that. Once they'd gazed at her with tenderness and warmth.

She stepped back from the flames now, which had begun to make her eyes tear with their heat. She settled herself onto the velvet bench, perching her bare feet up at the edge of the hearth, and blew on the ashen tip of the willow poker till it glowed.

What had thrust Garth de Ware toward the church? In her experience, men of the cloth were either simple—wrinkled of face and twinkly of eyes—or corrupt, like the Abbot. Men of passion, like Garth, usually found their calling elsewhere.

Priesthood was obviously contrary to his nature. She'd seen him lunge halfway across the hall after that roast. He possessed the instincts of a knight, of a warrior, and the act had been as innate to him as walking. How taxing it must be to repress his emotions, emotions she could sense bubbling inside him like a keg of ale about to explode. How he must have to battle to subdue his inherent power of command—common to nobles, notorious to de Wares. And what torture it must be to force his body to quiet toil when his muscles demanded more challenging labor.

Why? What had driven him down that path? What had wrenched all will to thrive and grow from him, like weeds choking an abandoned garden? Whatever the catalyst, according to the Abbot, Garth had sought sanctuary at the monastery four years ago. From what she could see, the church had been less a sanctuary than a siren calling to him, enclosing him in comforting arms and pulling him down beneath the waters of human struggle to his spiritual death. He'd not lifted his eyes to the secular light of day since.

It was truly a shame, for *this* world, and not the spiritual, was the one in which they lived and breathed, the world of nature and passion and the life force the Lord had created for them. For Cynthia, to deny the corporeal world was an offense to God.

Of course, she did not expect Garth to pull himself from the embrace of the church—to do so would be blasphemy. But Cynthia knew men of faith who lived full and happy lives, who even wed and had children, to the delight of their parishioners. Surely Garth de Ware was more suited to such a life. He deserved something beyond the austere existence of spiritual poverty he'd endured over the last four years.

She sighed. Four years! Perhaps it was too late to save him.

And yet, she'd used those very words a hundred times upon finding some pathetic, ailing plant she was tempted to nurse back to health. No amount of common sense had ever kept her from trying to salvage one before. And the more hopeless the task, the more determined she grew.

She supposed a man was no different. With proper care, by gently weeding the defenses from around Garth's tender roots, he could be redeemed.

Aye, she thought, shifting upright on the seat. It was suddenly clear. She could rescue him. *She* could redeem his lost spirit. Fate had brought Garth de Ware to Wendeville, and now she knew why. He was her destiny. Once, in a long-ago garden, he'd been her knight in shining armor, bringing hope to a young girl's heart. This was her chance at long last to return the favor.

A pinecone sizzled on the fire, and with the long stick she poked it into the heart of the flames, where the sap bubbled and snapped. A smile lingered on her lips, but despite her newfound conviction, she couldn't help but imagine she might be playing with fire where Garth was concerned, too.

6

THE SUN BLAZED HIGH OVERHEAD, HOTTER THAN HADES, as Garth steered the rickety wheelbarrow across Wendeville's broad courtyard to the garden for the thirty-second time. Runlets of sweat trickled down his neck and along his ribs. The wool cassock itched about his waist. A sharp pebble had lodged itself between his foot and what was left of his sandal. And his breath cut into his lungs like a dagger.

But the pain was good. The pain helped him to focus. On his new surroundings. His responsibilities. God's plan. Anything but the long legs splayed in the garden muck before him.

Lady Cynthia had bloused a fair portion of her surcoat above her belt, effectively exposing far too much of those legs. Her sleeves were pushed up to her elbows, and she let her bare white toes burrow in the mud as she turned the earth with a spade.

He tried to think of anything, anything else at all, as she leaned far forward to pluck a weed from the ground, all bottom and skirt and delicious ankles. Then she turned, ambling forward to meet him. A smudge of dirt decorated the bridge of her nose, childlike, and it was all he could do to resist wiping it away. Instead, he forced his attention to bracing the wheelbarrow in the mud to remove the plants from it.

He wished God had granted him an extra Sabbath this week. Normally it was a chaplain's busiest day. But yesterday, Garth's vow of silence had offered him a blessed reprieve from preaching, and so he'd spent the Sabbath mostly in his quarters, recopying scripture, saying his devotions, suppressing impious thoughts. When he found it necessary to leave that sanctuary, he guarded his privacy as much as possible, moving surreptitiously through the halls like a monastery mouse. That way, at least, there was only supper to contend with, when the sound of Cynthia's throaty laughter and her impertinent stare all but destroyed his appetite.

Today, however, he found himself in the midst of the Wendeville hive. Since he had no voice to serve her, Lady Cynthia had decided she'd put Garth's back to good use instead. Already he could feel the pull of muscles unused for years, one in particular he didn't want to think about. In sooth, however, if not for the sin of pride, he would have congratulated himself. He thought he'd managed to control his reactions to Lady Cynthia rather admirably, given the circumstances.

He lifted two herb seedlings from the wheelbarrow. One fell over as he set them in the dirt.

Aye, he'd almost completely ignored his body's feckless stirrings.

Thyme. Rosemary. One by one he pitched them to the ground. Borage. Mint.

If only, he wished, pressing his lips together tightly as he discarded the plants, she wouldn't sway so when she walked.

"Please, Garth," she said, startling him.

He turned to her with thinly cloaked panic. Why couldn't she address him as Father or Chaplain like everyone else? She was far too near. And her hand was on his sleeve again. Lord, he could smell the sweet fragrance of her hair. Coriander today. Nay, anise. And where she touched his arm, her fingers felt like hot lead.

"The plants are delicate," she murmured diplomatically. "Please try to be gentle with them."

He swallowed heavily. Her voice soughed like wind through a sycamore grove. He tensed his jaw, nodded once, and resumed unloading the cuttings more carefully. How could he have been so stupid? Of course the plants were delicate. He'd been hurling them about like catapult missiles. Her presence was obviously distracting him from all else.

Garth's company had apparently driven all the wits from Cynthia. She couldn't recall which seedling she'd intended to plant next. This close, she saw the flecks of blue in his green eyes, heard the breath rasp faintly through his nose, felt its gentle breeze on her face. She could discern the shadow of the beard he'd scraped this morning and the light sheen of sweat atop his lip. She could smell his skin. Jesu, but it did strange things to her senses. She gave her muddled head a mental shake.

She'd missed him yesterday. Intending to begin the healing of his soul, she'd instead spent the first half of the day scouring the castle for any sign of him, and the second entertaining a pair of bachelor brothers Elspeth had diverted from a passing pilgrimage.

One brother was deadly dull, and the other had an annoying habit of reciting his own health history in excruciating detail. By the end of dinner, she knew every ailment the man had ever endured or might endure. In sooth, to Elspeth's horror, Cynthia used the information to rid herself of the pair. When he complained of recurring digestive upset, she prescribed spurge. The man, mortified by the herb's swift effects on the contents of his stomach, declined to stay another night. Thankfully, he took his boring brother with him.

Today, she had both time and Garth to herself. For all the good it was doing. Her heart hadn't beat steadily since morning, when she'd found him kneeling in prayer at the altar, haloed in magnificent rainbow-colored sunbeams. Nor did the sun shining now in undiluted, buttery splendor on his rich mane help matters. Lord, he *was* beautiful, and her hand still tingled from the touch she'd stolen of his muscled forearm. She swallowed hard. She had to think of something to say be-

fore this ridiculous obsession with his physical attributes
made her forget her debt to him and paralyzed her good intentions forever.

She cleared her throat. There was an awkward moment as
they both tried to take the same parsley start from the wheelbarrow, but he snatched his hand back at once, surrendering
it readily to her.

Her fingers trembled as she set the plant upon the ground.
She felt feverish. Perhaps it was the sun. Tugging the flask
from her hip, she took a long drink of watered wine, then
turned to offer Garth a sip.

He glanced at it. The tip of his tongue wet his lower lip.
For a moment he looked as if he'd like nothing more. But
then a bland mask descended over his features, and he glared
into the distance with something akin to cool dismissal. It
was as if all the humanity suddenly drained from his face. He
declined the drink.

She shivered reflexively as he breezed past her with all
the chill of the north wind. He might not be able to speak, she
thought, but his expression spoke volumes. Aye, his emotions
were as apparent on his face as the freckles were on hers, and
at the moment, his gaze was most challenging.

She sighed. Perhaps he was angry with her. Or perhaps he
was just hot. The poor man was probably unused to the outdoors, closeted in a monastery scriptorium all day. She supposed she should excuse him to the great hall for proper rest
and refreshment.

She should, but she didn't want to. She wanted to know
what had become of Sir Garth de Ware, slayer of bees, de-
fender of young ladies.

"You really don't remember me?" she blurted out before
prudence could stop her.

He halted, a seedling clutched in each fist.

"I mean, it's difficult to imagine." She shrugged. "I'm a
bit uncommon, after all. Who could possibly forget little
Cynthia le Wyte's freckled face and orange hair?" She giggled, picking nervously at the parsley. "Though I suppose it
has been a number of years. . . ."

She was chattering, and she knew it. And Garth couldn't
very well answer her, with his silly vow of silence. But he

didn't have to glare at her like that. She blushed and dropped her gaze. "Of course, I'm aware I'm no great beauty and . . ." Lord, she was embarrassing herself, pruning the poor parsley to death, and growing more irritated by the moment. "Perhaps not even very memorable, but . . ."

Garth didn't look like he was going to help her out of the hole she was digging for herself any time soon. She tossed the ruined parsley back into the wheelbarrow and planted her hands on her hips. "God's wounds! Just how many ladies have you met with hair the color of a marigold?" she snapped.

"M'lady!"

Across the courtyard scurried the new girl, Mary. Cynthia mouthed a soundless curse at the maidservant's poor timing.

"And even if you *don't* remember . . ." she muttered.

"Lady Cynthia!" the maid cried.

"You could at least be chivalrous about it and . . ."

"M'lady! Come quickly!"

"And . . . well . . . at least *pretend* you remember," she finished, adjusting her belt and whisking out the folds of her skirts.

"M'lady," Mary gasped out, skidding to a stop before her.

"What!" she barked.

The maid jumped in surprise, her brown eyes wide. "Elspeth says to come quick." The lass glanced briefly at Garth, clearly awed by his priestly station.

"What's happened?"

"'Tis a gentleman arrived from Tewksbury, m'lady. He says he's eaten yew berries, and he's ailin' somethin' fierce."

"Yew berries?" She doubted it. No one with a tongue in his head could stomach enough of the nasty fruit to grow ill from it. Still, she couldn't very well ignore the plea of a man who might well die at her gates. Muttering a mild oath, heedless of her bare feet and the muddy skirts flapping about her knees, she stalked off toward the keep. Saving Garth's soul would have to wait for another time.

At supper, Garth cursed the vow of silence that kept him from grumbling into his pottage. If that foppish lout with his long golden curls and scarlet surcoat, leaning precariously close to Lady Cynthia, had truly consumed yew berries, he'd eat his cassock. The oaf sat at the high table, giggling and flapping his hands about like a startled chicken, jabbering on and on about Lady Cynthia's miracle cures. And while Garth imagined the dolt might indeed be witless enough to eat such unappetizing fare, he suspected the man was in sooth more cunning than stupid.

Nay, Sir Scarlet, or whatever his name was, knew how to attract the attentions of an unwary woman. As Garth's own brothers had told him many a time, the swiftest way to win a lady's heart was to affect a need for her. And so the rascal had demonstrated his need by feigning illness.

By the looks of things at the high table, his plan had succeeded. Not only had he garnered himself a spot adjacent to Lady Cynthia, but he had Elspeth tittering over his every word as if it were the most entertaining drivel she'd ever heard.

Garth stabbed his bread into his pottage. Doubtless this was just the sort of cur Elspeth had in mind for the next lord of Wendeville. He ground the sopping morsel between his teeth and cast a dark look toward the boor leaning far too closely to Cynthia for decency.

Then he plunged the remainder of his loaf into the trencher, his appetite vanished. He wiped his fingers on his napkin and dropped it to the table with a sigh. He supposed his opinion meant nothing. After all, it was of no consequence to him if Cynthia took up with an unprincipled knave.

Still he suffered through the evening, questioning what kind of God could loose such a wily fox upon what was surely Wendeville's most innocent dove.

Thankfully, Sir Scarlet disappeared the next morn before sunrise, apparently without a word to Lady Cynthia. Garth wondered if the villain's swift flight could be traced to the mysterious depositing of mice in his pallet, and he prayed for the soul of such mischief's perpetrator long and hard.

Rain prevented any work out of doors, and for that, Garth was thankful. It was difficult enough being closeted with Lady Cynthia in the candlelit keep, admiring her as she tended to skinned knees and burned custard and bruised feelings with equal compassion. But watching her labor in the dazzling light of day, her loose hair gleaming like copper, her bare limbs drinking the sunshine and reflecting it back, her eyes laughing with joy, would have been sheer torture.

Meanwhile, Elspeth, true to her word, managed to unearth yet another marriageable noble despite the foul weather. By noon, a pathetic twig of a youth sat shivering by the fire, his lips blue, his knees knocking. If he was all of eighteen years, Garth would have been surprised. His voice still cracked when he spoke, judging from what few words he could squeak past his rattling teeth, and Garth could count the sparse whiskers on his chin.

Lady Cynthia was kind to the lad as well, bringing him a warm posset and blankets, and Garth endured an uncharacteristic twinge of envy. At the drafty monastery, one's faith was considered enough to warm one's bones. He could recall sleepless nights, shuddering beneath his thin wool coverlet while icicles formed on the sill, certain that his lack of holy fervor was to blame for his suffering.

"Father?"

Garth felt a tug on his cassock and peered down. A small freckle-faced boy frowned up at him.

"My mother says ye can't talk to me, but that's all right, 'cause ye can still talk to God, and my mother says ye can talk to God without even moving your lips, and I need ye to talk to God for me, because my father is in his cups and says he doesn't have time to tinker with a damn toy, and my mother is a lass and doesn't know the first thing about such matters, and so could ye please speak to God about fixing my dragon?"

Garth's mouth twitched, and he fought to keep a smile from his face at the boy's long-winded discourse. The little lad cradled a broken wooden toy in his arms, its paint faded, its edges worn smooth. Garth furrowed his brow and held his hands out for the thing. The boy solemnly handed it over.

Except for the fierce teeth painted on the face and the notches along the back, it was difficult to tell what manner of beast it was. The tip of the tail had cracked off, the tugging string was frayed, and the two wheels that propelled the toy had popped off when the axle apparently went missing. It would take far more than prayer to piece the thing back together.

But there was little else to do, and the labor would take his mind off of the spoiled boy by the fire, who yawned contentedly while Cynthia tucked yet another fur about him.

The materials were easy enough to gather. He found seasoned pine in the woodpile, a piece of rope in the stable, and, on a whim, fetched his quill and ink from his quarters.

By the time he returned to the great hall with the little lad in tow, Cynthia's charge had grown as drowsy as a cat who'd found a bucket of cream, and he wondered disgustedly if the youth perhaps expected her to rock him to sleep.

With a self-disparaging sigh, he chose a spot on the farthest side of the fire to work and sat cross-legged in the rushes. The little boy crouched beside him on the floor, watching in sober silence.

He replaced the string first, separating strands of the rope and twisting them into twine to knot about the beast's neck. Next he took out his dagger and carved a stick of pine into cotters and a dowel for the axle. He replaced the wheels and drilled small holes in the axle with the point of his knife for the cotters to keep the wheels in place.

As he worked, the boy crept closer and closer until he leaned upon Garth's thigh. Garth smiled. After four years in a monastery, he'd forgotten how delightful children were, so trusting, so expressive, so unpretentious.

The lines defining the dragon's features were badly dulled, but Garth could make them out well enough to trace over them with his quill, and this operation the boy watched with hushed reverence. Inspired by the lad's awe, Garth even added his own touches, a few scales here, a delineated flank there, claws upon the wheels, and the boy seemed highly pleased by these additions.

Sadly, there was nothing he could do about the cracked tail. He turned it in his hand and looked at the boy, remembering his own childhood, his own toys. The de Ware boys had each possessed their own wheeled knight on horseback, and they'd engaged in the fiercest warfare. But it seemed to

Garth that his brothers rather enjoyed nicking bits and pieces off of one another's knights, as if reveling in their wounds and glorying in their battle scars; something, he thought in amusement, they'd never outgrown.

Sudden inspiration took hold. This dragon would boast the most gruesome wound ever. Holding the maimed beast and its severed tail on his lap, he picked up his dagger and carefully pressed the edge of the blade against his thumb. He made the smallest cut, no more than a thorn prick, but a feminine gasp of horror startled him.

"What the devil . . ." Cynthia demanded.

A drop of blood dripped onto his cassock before he could smear the rest along the edges of the dragon's wound.

The rest of Cynthia's question was obliterated by a shriek of wind that rushed in the opening door, fluttering the fire, and bringing with it an ominous crack of thunder and one rain-drenched, irate noblewoman.

The lad Cynthia had been tending leaped up suddenly as if his hair was afire, and the woman barreled forward with neither introduction nor fear.

"There ye are, ye good-for-naught half-wit!"

Even Cynthia backed away from the woman's acrimonious onslaught.

"Where can he have gone, I'm wonderin'." The woman shook herself like a wet dog as she charged forward, spattering the rushes with raindrops. "Where's my darlin' son while his bride's a-waitin' on the chapel steps, all teary and shiverin'?" She beat hard at her sodden skirts, making mist. "While his father's trippin' over his words to find somethin' to say to her poor parents?" She seized the boy by the arm, and he yelped like a beat hound. "While the priest is goin' on and on to pass the time, sermonizin' on Commandments even Moses never heard of!"

Garth ducked his head in a desperate attempt to contain his laughter.

" 'Oh,' says your cousin, drunk as a fish, 'he's gone to find him a *real* wife instead o' the child he's betrothed to.' " With that, the woman seized her son by the ear and dragged him toward the door, unconcerned with the gaping spectators. "A *real* wife? Ha! Ye'd not know what to do with a real wife."

With that, she charged back out into the stormy afternoon, slamming the door behind her, leaving a silence broken only by the crackling of the fire.

Cynthia hardly knew what to say. Whatever had just transpired, it didn't bode well for the lad. Where had Elspeth come by the boy anyway? She turned to ask that very thing, but her maidservant slipped quickly into the kitchen, her cheeks flaming.

"Well." She gathered the blankets the boy had shed in his haste, shaking the rushes from them, and the rest of the castle folk returned to their duties. Meanwhile, Garth sat with one hand clamped firmly about his jaw, studiously examining the toy he held on his lap. She looked closer at his profile. If she didn't know better, she'd swear that crinkle at the corner of his eye was not concentration but amusement.

Incredulous, she faced him, crossing her arms. "Do you find this humorous?"

He wouldn't meet her gaze, but the corner of his lip twitched then, and she saw that indeed he was thoroughly entertained. She supposed it *was* amusing. The boy's eyes had popped like to leave their sockets when he'd seen his mother coming for him. And she'd looked as angry as a drenched hen.

"Look, my lady." Little Dylan jumped up, the toy in his hands. "The Father fixed it. He put on scales and claws and a terrible frown, and look!" He held the toy up to her face, too close. She reared her head back and glimpsed the bright red edge staining the wood. Dylan whispered loudly in awe. "It's blood, my lady, *real* blood."

Cynthia pressed her hand to her bosom. Dear God, that wasn't . . .

She glanced at Garth. He was looking at her now, and the residue of laughter still sparkled in his eyes. She lowered her gaze to his thumb, which he clutched against a wad of linen. She gulped. What kind of man would pierce his own flesh just to please a child?

And Dylan was beyond pleased. She never understood why little boys loved gore so dearly, but the dragon with the grisly wound and real priest's blood would probably be Dylan's proudest possession for years to come.

"You'll need comfrey for that," she told Garth.

He frowned and shrugged. She supposed being a de Ware, he was accustomed to bumps and bruises and cuts. But he was a member of her household now, and she wouldn't have anyone under her care suffer infection. Tousling Dylan's hair, she strode off to fetch her bag of medicines.

When she returned moments later, Dylan was gone, probably off terrorizing all the little girls in the keep. Garth was crouched near the fire, staring into the flames. She paused in the shadows of the entryway to watch him.

His eyes reflected the fire's flicker, and she could see calm contentment there. He'd enjoyed working on Dylan's toy, she knew. She'd been watching him then, too, though she pretended to be preoccupied with their wayward guest. The Abbot had said Garth was a talented scribe, but the dragon's snarling fangs and curving claws had been the result of far more than a steady hand. Nay, Garth possessed singular imagination and artistry. Dylan had been fascinated with the priest's labors as well, leaning so close and with such fervent interest that Cynthia feared the intrepid lad might actually climb onto his lap.

Garth didn't seem annoyed in the least. He looked perfectly at ease with the little boy's grubby hand planted on his thigh and his freckled face pressed close. But then Cynthia supposed Garth was accustomed to children. He probably had nieces and nephews of his own. How sad it must have been for him to be away from them, locked in a monastery with nothing but grown men.

Garth stirred the fire with one of the leftover pieces of wood he'd brought, and the flames licked up, suffusing his face with a golden glow. How beautiful he was, she thought yet again, his chiseled features etched in warm relief by the firelight, his hair catching the color in shades of amber and bronze. As he stooped before the hearth, his wide back and shoulders strained against the coarse wool of his cassock, leaving no doubt that he was both a man and a de Ware. And yet there was something boyish about the way he sat poking at the fire. She could envision another, smaller version of him crouched beside this grown Garth, a little boy of his own with tousled hair and wide green eyes, and the thought made her smile.

So lost was she in her musing that she was astonished to find Garth staring at her. The pleasure was gone from his eyes, replaced by something cool and unapproachable. For one instant, she was tempted to creep back up the stairs to her chamber. But she was not a timorous mouse to be daunted by a dark look, even if it saddened her to know it was the sight of her that had erased the smile from his face.

So she marched forward, pulling out the tincture of comfrey and chattering to fill the ungainly silence.

"Has it stopped bleeding yet? I can't imagine what you were thinking." She seized his wrist, despite a mild show of resistance from him, and inspected the cut. It was wide but not very deep. "You know, I'm certain little Dylan would have been just as content with madder ink." She didn't believe that. The boy was obviously thrilled with his sanguineous treasure. But as a healer, she certainly couldn't condone such mayhem.

She wet a small linen pad with the borage and supported his hand as she swabbed gently across the cut. His flesh was warm from the fire, his palm wide and smooth, so unlike the scarred hands of the peasants and knights she usually tended to or the wrinkled paw of her departed husband. Garth's fingers were long and supple, his hand well muscled, and, to Cynthia's utter mortification, she began to imagine how that hand would feel upon her own body, tracing her hip, fondling her ankle, caressing her breast. She swallowed hard.

A prominent vein ran across the back of Garth's hand, and Cynthia felt the pulse there quicken, almost as if he read her thoughts. She dared not look at him, certain her eyes betrayed her wayward mind.

"It was kind of you to repair his toy," she murmured, tossing the soiled pad into the fire, but loath to return his hand, "especially at so great a price." She chewed the corner of her lip, then blurted out, "In sooth, you are so good with children, I believe you might one day make a fine father."

Garth pulled his hand away at that, withdrawing it into

the sleeve of his cassock faster than a startled turtle, and Cynthia knew she'd said exactly the wrong thing. Before she could explain or apologize or soothe his ruffled feathers, he wheeled away, gathered his tools, and exited the great hall.

7

DESPITE HER RASH COMMENT, CYNTHIA'S OPINIONS about Garth's paternal nature were only reinforced the next morn.

She'd ventured along the wall walk during a brief respite in the downpour to enjoy a breath of rain-washed air. The clouds, while still concealing the blue sky, had broken momentarily like soldiers regrouping for battle. The trees drooped with their drizzly burden, and the sod lay black with moisture. As she let her eye course along the far gray horizon and the nearer knolls, she spied two figures walking along the edge of the forest.

Garth's dark cassock camouflaged him against the trees, but the tiny golden-haired girl in the blue kirtle stood out like a flower amongst the grass. Cynthia narrowed her eyes. The lass was the armorer's daughter, and she appeared to carry something in her cupped hands. They stopped beside a massive old oak tree and Garth motioned to the girl. She nodded. Garth then knelt on the wet ground and began digging with a hand spade.

When the hole was about a foot deep, Garth held his hands out to accept the girl's burden. Cynthia gasped in empathy when she realized what it was. For weeks now, the child had been nursing a sick old dove in the mews. The bird must have finally succumbed.

Carefully, Garth placed the animal in the ground, then made the sign of the cross over the grave. The little girl knelt beside him, and they prayed together over clasped hands. But when he began to scoop dirt over the hole, Cynthia could hear the child's mewl of protest. He stopped, then pointed to the sky. No doubt he was explaining wordlessly that the rain would get the poor dove wet if she weren't covered properly. After that, the lass allowed him to finish covering the grave and even pressed the soil firm with her own hands.

The deed finished, she threw herself at Garth, burying her face in his cassock to weep. For a moment, Garth seemed alarmed. Then he wrapped his arms about the lass, patting her back and stroking her hair.

Cynthia bit her lip and felt her eyes go all watery. What a comfort the priest must be to the child, who'd lost her mother a year ago. Cynthia remembered her own mother's passing, how in the first months she'd missed her tender embraces and gentle words. Even now, it seemed a long while since someone had held her like that, drying her tears, smoothing her hair. . . .

Dear Heaven, he'd seen her. He stared at her over the girl's golden head, his expression too distant to read, but his eyes clearly locked with hers. She blushed, aware she'd been spying on him, intruding upon a private moment. She should go, she knew, but his gaze had frozen her to the spot.

She looked away first. She had to. Elspeth, with her usual unfortunate timing, marched up at that moment, nearly frightening her off the precipice of the wall walk.

"Ah, here ye are, my lady!"

"El!" She tripped and made a grab for the embrasure, casting a quick embarrassed glance toward Garth.

"'Tis slick with rain out here," Elspeth scolded. "Why don't ye come in and dry yerself? Lord William and his retinue should arrive anon, and ye must—"

"Who?" She rounded on her maid, scowling. "Elspeth, we've had visitors every day. What have you done? Sent a herald forth with news that the Holy Grail resides at Wendeville?"

Elspeth giggled rather too enthusiastically. "Oh, my lady!

The Holy Grail indeed! Lord William's retinue is just passing
by. Surely ye won't deny them shelter from the storm."

Cynthia lowered her brows. Of course she'd take them in.
It was the hospitable thing to do. But she couldn't shake the
notion that crafty Elspeth was up to something.

A fat drop of rain splashed on her cheek, and a flash of
lightning across the purpling clouds warned of the storm's return. She cast one final glance over her shoulder as the downpour began. Garth had scooped up the little girl in his arms.
Shielding her with his body, he strode briskly across the grass
to return her to the shelter of the keep.

As it turned out, their visitors that afternoon were pleasant company indeed. Lord William was cordial and polite,
neither too humble nor overbold. The rain had done naught
to dampen his good nature or his handsome countenance, and
Cynthia instantly liked the man.

His knights, near a score in all, were honorable and
chivalrous, and Cynthia watched several of Wendeville's
wenches swoon and giggle in turns over the fine young men.

At supper, she shared a trencher with William. His manners were impeccable and his conversation interesting. He
was fair of face and strong of bone, and his rust-colored hair
flowed like molten copper to his wide shoulders. His brown
eyes lit up when he spoke of hawking, his favorite pastime,
and sparkled fondly when he recalled taking his youngest
nephew riding for the first time.

After the meal, William's men goaded him into strum-
ming his lute, and Cynthia was amazed by his skill and the
playful timbre of his voice as he sang a madrigal about the
pleasures of spring. Watching the bobbing heads and listening to the laughter about her, Cynthia wondered if mayhap
the castle folk had suffered from the dearth of company Lord
John's illness had afforded. In sooth, all of Wendeville
seemed to enjoy the respite from grief that the presence of
their cheery visitors afforded.

Then Cynthia spied Garth. While everyone about him
banged heartily on the trestle table in rhythm with the music,
he sat scowling, his arms crossed over his chest.

What was wrong with him? Did he disapprove of the
tune? True, it was not the somber plainsong of the monastery

to which he was accustomed, but surely he didn't condemn
them for a bit of lighthearted music. Sweet Mary, the song
wasn't even lewd, as madrigals oft could be. She stared at
him until she caught his eye, then lifted her brows in askance.

As if surprised by his own posture, he unfolded his arms
and let his face relax. He didn't exactly smile, but a sort of
resignation settled over his features. She wished she knew his
thoughts. What an enigma Garth de Ware was, she decided,
and she grinned at him in spite of his dour countenance.

Garth tapped his fingers restlessly atop the table. He was glad
Lady Cynthia was having a good time. Truly he was. The
poor woman had lost her husband, after all. She deserved a
little frivolity in her life. And if that frivolity came in the
form of a handsome nobleman who sang like a nightingale
and now danced apparently like he was born to it, what concern was it of his?

Garth held his breath as the gentleman appropriated Cynthia's hand and led her about in a circle with the rest of the
dancers. She looked so beautiful, so alive, so . . . happy.

In sooth, Garth couldn't fault the man at all. Lord William
was neither overbearing nor timid. He appeared to be well
versed in the gentle arts, but by the breadth of his shoulders,
Garth could see he was no mediocre warrior. And he could
dance.

Garth, too, could dance. He'd been forced to learn alongside his brothers. Their mother never allowed the de Ware
boys to indulge in the more violent sport of swordplay unless
they practiced the courtly graces in equal measure. And if it
weren't for the fact that for the last four years, Garth had
been a monk, forbidden to engage in such exhibitions, he'd
prove it.

The air rushed out of him on an exasperated sigh. What
the devil was he thinking? Not yet one sennight in the secular world and already he felt the pricking of the sin of pride.
What did it matter if he could dance? He was a priest, that
was all. His legs were for kneeling in the worship of God.
Anything else would be vanity. Perhaps it was good that he
was under a vow of silence, after all. In sooth, he might be
well advised to maintain that vow another fortnight.

He was staring into his flagon of wine, considering the merits of extending his vow to a lifetime of silence, when Cynthia jostled his elbow. Startled, he turned to catch her gaze, full force. Dear Heaven, she was breathtaking. Her face, framed by stray tendrils of her fiery hair, was flushed with delight. Her skin was misted with exertion, her cheeks rosy, her lips curved into a coy smile.

An intense longing bloomed inside him like wine warming his belly. His heart seemed to pulse to the beat of the timbrel, his lungs to breathe in the harmonies of the lute. He suddenly ached to join her, to join all of them, to share in their revelry, their humanity. For one terrible moment, his legs quivered in mutiny, threatening to move against his wishes.

Another dancer wheeled her away then, and the feeling passed. He swallowed back panic. How close had he come to taking that first step? To forgetting who he was, what he was? To violating his own principles?

Drawing the back of his hand across his perspiring lip, he rose on shaking legs. Measuring his pace to contradict the rhythm of the music, he made fists of his hands, steeled his jaw, and walked deliberately past the merrymakers.

He almost escaped. If he had paid heed to the weaving pattern of the dancers, he might have cleared their path. But as fate would have it, as Cynthia rounded the wheel, he stepped left, square upon her toes.

She emitted a small, muffled squeak and pitched forward suddenly, falling against him. Her hands snagged the front of his cassock, and instinctively he caught her shoulders. A dizzying wave of sweet perfume arose from her hair to tease his nostrils, and he swallowed hard as he felt the weight of her warm body pressed against his.

He should push her away, he knew, and yet something held him immobile, some hunger, some unspeakable desire, some force that dismissed all sense, all reason. She raised her head to look at him, and he saw his own need reflected in her eyes, doubling its power, intensifying his desire. Suddenly, in the midst of the great hall, there were but the two of them.

Against all wisdom, he lowered his gaze to her lips. How full they were, so tempting, parted in expectation. His thoughts careened dangerously. Damn the crowd. Damn his vows. He wanted to kiss her. Now.

And in another moment, he might have.

But that bossy little scrap of a maid of hers elbowed her way between the two of them. "Oh la! Ye've ruined the pattern now, m'lady!" She steered Cynthia from the circle, sparing him a heated glare that could have cauterized a wound.

Garth closed his eyes. He well deserved Elspeth's ire. He'd promised not to interfere with her machinations. In sooth, as soon as he was able to rein in his passions, he'd likely wish to prostrate himself before her, to bless her for interrupting a moment of sheer madness. But for the remainder of the long evening until he found safe harbor in his quarters, all he could manage was a fierce scowl and a wretched craving that kept his hands locked in fists.

Cynthia only half-listened as Lord William escorted her along the herb garden of the inner bailey in the fickle morning sunlight. Her hand rested familiarly along the top of his sleeve, and yet his arm might have been only the cushion of a chair for all the attention she paid it.

Her thoughts had whirled crazily through her brain all night, ever since that encounter with Garth de Ware, intruding even into her dreams, and come morn, she could make no more sense of them than before. She knew she should pay heed to her visitor's words, and she had, up till now, at least enough to respond with an occasional nod or smile of agreement. But Garth had appeared at the far end of the courtyard, and suddenly her ears grew deaf to Lord William's discourse.

Old Simon limped along on Garth's arm. It appeared the feeble man had misplaced his walking stick again. The poor wretch could scarcely keep his thoughts in order, much less his possessions. Cynthia wondered if she should lend assistance. She knew, as Garth did not, that Simon usually left his stick propped against the wall of the east garderobe.

"So your ears have deserted me as well."

"What?" Cynthia snapped her head around. "I'm sorry, Lord William. I . . ."

He chuckled warmly. "You've been staring at him for some time now."

She felt a flush steal up her cheek. "I don't know what you're . . ."

He clucked his tongue. "Be careful, lest you speak falsely. They don't approve of that, you know."

"Who?"

"Men of the church."

"I . . . I was watching . . . old Simon."

He patted her hand in a brotherly fashion. "I saw the way you looked at the man last night, even when he was stepping all over your feet."

Panic seized her, panic and denial. "Sir, are you suggesting . . . ?" she breathed. "He is a man of the church. I would not dream of . . ." She stopped to smooth her skirts, composing her thoughts. Sweet Mary, she wasn't dreaming of anything so blasphemous, was she? "What you saw in my eyes was naught but innocent pleasure," she explained, eager to convince herself as well.

Laughter sparkled in Lord William's russet eyes. "Pleasure? Would I could please a woman so well."

She opened her mouth in denial, but his upraised hand halted her.

"Peace, my lady. I wish you well with him."

Cynthia felt the heat rise in her cheeks. "You are mistaken. Garth de Ware is a devoted man of the cloth, not prey to . . . earthly desires in the least."

"In sooth?"

She could see he was laughing at her, and it rankled her. Last night had taken them both by surprise, that was all. After all, neither of them were accustomed to such intimacy. For Cynthia, she'd lost her husband weeks past. For Garth, it had probably been years since he'd been close to a woman. Lord William simply didn't understand.

"Then kiss me," he said.

Cynthia thought she'd heard wrong. "What did you say?"

"Kiss me."

"But I . . . scarcely know you."

"You know I wish you no ill." He leaned forward to whisper to her. "Kiss me. I'll wager your chaplain will seethe with jealousy. But if he stirs not an eyelash, then I'll yield the day and bow to your greater instincts."

"He'll not even blink," she assured him.

He stared at her a long while, a strange play of emotions crossing his features—mild lust as he gazed at her mouth, but also a bit of sadness, and a sagacity that made him look for an instant far beyond his years.

"But if he does blink, I'll waste no more time in courting you, my lady." He reached forward and toyed with a loose lock of her hair. "I'll pack up my men in sorry defeat," he said with a good-natured smile, "and wish you well."

It was nonsense. The whole conversation was absurd. By God, she'd prove she had no claim upon Garth de Ware, that he was devoid of feeling for her as well. She faced William squarely and raised her chin. "All right then. Do your worst."

He winked, sweeping one hand about her neck, the other about her back, and turning so they were in full view of the chaplain, and he kissed her. His lips were soft, his freshly shaved chin smooth, and his touch upon her throat light-fingered, undemanding. He tasted sweet, like the sugared cinnamon loaf they'd shared for breakfast. But she felt no more stirred than she had as a girl when her father gave her a quick buss on the cheek.

After a lingering moment, he released her lips. He parted from her but an inch and murmured, "Can you not feel the daggers of his eyes even now? Look you."

She peered over his shoulder and gasped. Lord, if glances could slay . . .

Garth's face had become a rigid mask of displeasure. Her heart pounded at such potent rage directed at her. Mayhap, she reasoned, he only disapproved of such public displays of affection. Or perchance he thought Lord William an unsuitable suitor.

But deep inside, a thrill of dangerous desire infused her blood, and her flesh tingled with delicious trepidation.

"You see, I've won the wager. I must say he is a fortunate man," William whispered, "to garner the attentions of so charming a lady."

Cynthia felt so breathless she could neither protest his accusation nor receive his compliment with even the simplest courtesy.

William stepped back then, bowing over her hand in polite farewell. "You would do well to tell your maid to stop seeking a suitor for her lady's heart, when it is so clearly already spoken for."

His words left her speechless. Surely he was mistaken. Perhaps her own heart beat a little faster when Garth drew near, but certainly the priest felt nothing for her, nothing beyond a false desire for her gender that their chance proximity sparked. And such moments were always fleeting, followed at once by his cool disregard and mild disdain.

Still, Lord William's words haunted her all the rest of the day, even after he and his company took gracious leave of the castle. What if Garth did feel something for her? What if his remoteness stemmed not from irritation, but from a heart too fond?

It didn't matter, she decided later, bundled snugly in her pallet against the frosty air of night. Whether he felt affection for her or not, she'd made a promise to herself, and she intended to keep it. She'd vowed to rescue Garth from spiritual death. She wouldn't abandon him now, even if it meant leaving her own heart at peril.

Once she'd compared Garth to an ailing plant. She knew now he was most like the wild ivy, that to flourish he must choose his own path, find his own footholds in the crevices of the garden wall. And it was up to her to be that strong foundation upon which he could climb. He might well cling to her affections for a time, if such was the road to his soul's freedom, but she must remain firm, unbending, resolute.

Moonlight seeped through the clouds and the crack of her shutters, heralding the storm's passing. The sun would return on the morrow, drinking up the last of winter's tears and promising renewal. Garth, too, would soon bathe in the nurturing light of restoration. She would do everything in her power to make it so.

Cynthia was a born healer, after all. It was God's gift to her. She could summon the earth's power, lay hands on a sickly man, and make him strong. Shouldn't she be able to use that gift to heal a man's spirit as well? Certainly there was no harm in the attempt. She'd always cured the infirmities of others, miraculously absorbed their ills without injury to herself. Why should afflictions of the soul be any different?

Aye, she vowed, burrowing her nose under the furs, she'd use her talents to save Garth de Ware, yet keep herself aloof from his awakening passions. She'd be more of a . . . caring sister to him. She smiled, pleased with her decision, and slipped to sleep, soothed by the simplicity of her promise, never realizing how difficult it would be to keep.

8

STARS EMBROIDERED THE BLACK VELVET SKY. GARTH'S head thrashed on the pillow, his mind clamoring with swirling, erotic visions. The woman's long hair lapped at his ribs like flames of a sensual fire. Her hands gripped his shoulders, and she sheathed him in her silkiness again and again, riding him like a charger galloping through sea foam.

She pressed forward, and he gasped at the fragile beauty of her breasts. Tenderly, he caressed the peaks, fascinated by their change as his thumb brushed across a soft brown nipple.

She bent down to him, smoothed back his hair, and whispered incoherent words of passion in his ear. He shivered and lunged upward into her, caution cast to the wind. She gave her breast to his mouth, and he sucked hungrily, groaning at its sweetness.

His body began to quiver with a tension starting in his belly, expanding outward to the top of his head and the soles of his feet. As the sensation grew out of his control, he released her breast so he wouldn't harm her. His breath came in quick gulps, and he gasped as she smiled down at him in ecstasy, her pale blue eyes languorous in the moonlight, her hair a brilliant orange corona about her lovely, freckled face.

"Cynthia . . . Cynthia . . ." he moaned, no longer master of his mind.

Garth awoke as his body burst into a violent shudder of release. His muscles strained with effort, and his seed pulsed forcefully from him like wine too long in the cask. He cried out, then threw his arm across his mouth to silence the cries, gasping into the wool of his cassock sleeve.

The pale moonlight lent a blue cast to Garth's quarters as he quaked in his sweat on the pallet. This time had been different. This time his body had betrayed him completely. He felt the sticky, wet evidence of its anarchy upon his thighs and belly.

It hadn't been Mariana this time, either. The goddess looming above him had been Lady Cynthia.

Sighing miserably, Garth peeled back the coverlet and grimaced in disgust as he beheld the sordid ruins of his cassock.

Why did God torture him like this? All he wanted was to quietly and completely devote himself to the church, to melt into the chapel walls unnoticed, like a forgotten tapestry over a drafty window. Was it too much to ask?

He pulled the cassock off and flung it into the basin. The chill breeze sobered him as it blew against his naked skin. He scrubbed the wool with a brusque vengeance, shivering with cold all the while. But even though he wrung out the garment and spread it along the hooks in the wall, beside the other he'd unfortunately washed just hours earlier, he knew neither would dry by morn. Either cassock would be as uncomfortable as a hair shirt. And as appropriate, he thought morosely.

With a silent curse, he flounced back onto his pallet and burrowed under the furs, praying none would discover the castle chaplain sleeping in sinful nakedness.

But alas, Lady Cynthia came for him before he was yet awake.

"You *do* know how to write?" The disembodied voice danced among his dreams. "Garth?"

He opened his eyes.

"I said, you *do* know how to write?" she repeated.

His heart tripped as he pushed up to his elbows. Lord, the lady had breezed into his quarters like she belonged there, all green surcoat and clinging underdress, as fresh as an April meadow. She looked at him expectantly, as if it were in sooth a decent hour.

He rubbed a hand over his eyes. It was tempting to dismiss her as part of a dream, to fall back onto his pallet and go to sleep. After all, it couldn't be far past Matins. Even if he did feel like he'd lain awake all night.

What was it she'd asked him—did he know how to write? He couldn't help grimacing at that. How could a friar not write? It was what they did all day. He nodded.

"Good. Then pray bestir yourself and dress, for there's much to be done in the privy garden."

Her gaze flicked lower for an instant, and he saw her breath catch. It was then he remembered he was naked beneath the coverlet. A hasty glance at the wall revealed the twin cassocks condemning him. His bare shoulders rose brazenly above the coverlet, but it was too late to snatch the furs up. She'd already seen him. She already knew.

To his relief, she politely made no mention of it, clearing her throat instead and throwing back the shutters at his window. "What a layabed you are, Garth. And I thought friars were accustomed to rising with the sun."

He blinked against the light and swiveled his head to look out. Blessed Mary, the storm clouds had scattered in the night, and the sun was already a full fist above the horizon.

"I've brought you something," she said, holding up a pair of sturdy leather boots. "I saw one of your sandals had worn clear through. I noticed you have rather large feet, but these should fit you."

She glanced down at his foot, which stuck out beyond the coverlet. He yanked it back beneath the furs, feeling even more violated. It was bad enough that she'd caught him without his cassock. Something as personal as the state of his clothing was not her affair. And she most definitely should not concern herself with the size of his feet.

"Please hurry," she said with irritating cheer, setting the boots upon the floor. "Time is a-wasting. And don't forget your quill and ink." Then she swept out the door like a flirtatious spring zephyr.

Much to Garth's chagrin, the boots were nearly a perfect fit. And he was grateful for them moments later as he trudged past a huge pile of malodorous earth at the west end of the outer garden.

A dozen men carted seasoned manure to the pile, and children mixed it into the wet soil with spades, when they weren't hurling it at one another like it was ammunition from a trebuchet. Chatty young girls pulled at weeds, tossing them into a wheelbarrow. Elspeth presided over the herb garden, bleating out directions to several maids for the planting.

And there, beyond the herbs, the gate to the privy garden stood wide, as inviting and foreboding as Pandora's box.

Cynthia squinted her eyes, scanning the garden for the perfect spot to plant the cowslip. Aye, she thought, plucking the seedling lovingly from the wheelbarrow, there, beside the west wall. She took a deep breath of fresh, damp garden air and began to hum.

An hour earlier, the sun had pushed up over the lavender hills like a lily blooming, the cloudless sky slowly turning the color of a robin's egg. A dainty carpet of fairy's tears had graced the sward as she made her way to the privy garden at dawn, making the day seem almost magical.

Still, none of it had left her as breathless as she'd felt creeping into Garth's chambers. For longer than she cared to admit, she'd stood in his doorway, admiring the softness that slumber brought to his face, the provocative tangle of his hair, the way his nostrils flared gently as he inhaled the rarefied air of dreams.

Then he'd stirred in his sleep, flung an arm outward, and she discovered a prurient secret. Father Garth de Ware slept unclothed. It was, if not sinful, at least wicked. And yet it wasn't indignation she felt as she let her gaze rove over the sculpted contours of his bare shoulder. Nay, she'd bitten her lip against the surge of molten wonder that seeped into her blood.

What a mystery was her chaplain, and how that mystery called to her. The longer she watched him, the more she yearned to know what lay beneath that coverlet, to throw back the furs and . . .

She'd finally had to shake herself from her own wayward thoughts. And indeed, when she at last summoned the resolve to rouse him, it had felt akin to waking a dozing dragon.

But she had more innocuous plans for Garth this morn.

His indoctrination back into the secular world had to be handled delicately, without haste. Today she intended to remind him of what simple delights existed beyond the monastery. And so she'd laden a great basket full of palatable pleasures for him, a feast for the senses. Since she was certain monastic fare consisted of ubiquitous herring and coarse cheat bread, she took great pains to pack the very best Wendeville's stores and Cook could provide. Lent had begun, but that didn't diminish the bounty of pickled eels, fresh grayling and shrimp kept cool in straw, and a loaf of very fine, white pandemayne, as well as candied orange peels, dried figs, gingerbread, and apple tarts spiced with cinnamon. She'd filled a skin with cool claret from the cellar, complete with two silver flagons.

Hopefully, as Elspeth always vowed, once a man's belly was filled, he was like clay in a woman's hands.

Overhead, a raven swooped out of the willow onto the garden wall, squawking in competition with Cynthia's soft roundelay. Undaunted, Cynthia lifted her voice in a rollicking round of "fa-la-la's." She sang out the long, loud, final note of the tune, stuck her tongue out at the bird, then turned to fetch another seedling from the wheelbarrow.

A heavy shadow fell suddenly across her, driving her heart into her throat. For an instant, she imagined the raven had transformed itself into human form. Gasping sharply, she dropped the seedling and stumbled backward, unfortunately over the rake. She tripped and toppled onto her bottom, her legs sprawling every which way.

"Jesu!" she cried, clasping a hand to her bosom. Looming over her, as dark and silent as death, stood Garth. "I didn't hear you."

Garth bit back a grin. The idea of Cynthia hearing anything over her own singing at the top of her lungs, as well as the sight of her subsequently tumbling into the dirt on her backside, was nothing short of uproarious. But when he beheld the silky lines of her exposed limbs and the sensual disarray of her curls, all humor deserted him. He froze.

"You could at least help me up," she chided, reaching out a hand.

Against his better judgment, he offered her his arm. Her fingers upon his sleeve were like a hot iron singeing through the damp wool as she pulled herself to her feet. Lord, he realized when she stood before him—a few inches forward and he could have brushed her forehead with his lips. God help him, he longed to. She smelled delightful, like cinnamon and earth and spring.

He must have been staring. She hastily lowered her eyes and disengaged herself from him.

"I'm . . . redesigning the privy garden," she explained a little breathlessly. Then she pushed the gate closed behind him. "I thought . . . I thought you could help. If you'd write down the names of the plants in their proper places . . ."

Garth clenched his jaw.

The garden was deserted. There were just the two of them. Alone. The oak door rattled behind Garth as the latch swung home. Imprisoning him.

He lowered himself stiffly to the sod bench. With clumsy fingers, he stretched the parchment over the block of wood that would serve as a desk. The sooner he accomplished the task at hand, he thought, the sooner he could flee. He hastily uncorked the bottle of ink and dipped his quill.

"If you'll make a diagram of sorts, label the trees . . ."

With a fleeting glance around the garden, he set his quill to the page.

"Those two are peaches," she said, shading her eyes and pointing to the furthest trees to the left. "Sweeter peaches you've not tasted," she confided. "Cook makes a wonderful peach tart that scarcely needs honey." She pointed at another. "And that is a hazelnut. Last Christmas it gave so abundantly, we had packets of roasted hazelnuts for all the villagers' children." She pointed again. "And over there . . ."

Garth put the quill down, finished. She looked at him quizzically. He showed her the parchment. It was admittedly the worst scribbling he'd ever done in his life. But the words were there. And the trees were labeled properly. And now he could leave.

"Ah." She blinked. "Well done." But somehow she didn't look exactly pleased. "You know your trees. Are you familiar with the shrubs as well?"

He squinted past her at the bushes lining the rock wall and began writing again. Thank the Lord he'd first learned Latin by identifying the plants in his mother's garden. There was *Ilex.* And *Jasminum.*

From the corner of his eye, he saw her reach down to pluck a weed. Then another.

Hedera.

One weed came up clutching a great ball of earth in its roots. She knocked it against her thigh to dislodge the dirt, soiling her skirt.

He scrawled "*Rosa*" onto the parchment.

She pushed her sleeves back from her wrists to her elbows to get at a patch of clover choking the daffodils. Blessed saints, the skin of her forearms looked as smooth as polished parchment.

Laurus.

Then she must have forgotten he was there. With no preamble whatsoever, she hoisted the back hem of her surcoat up through her legs and tucked it into her belt at the front like a peasant, exposing a considerable length of silky limb and even a glimpse of knee.

Mayhap, Garth thought, if he closed his eyes tightly enough, the sight of Lady Cynthia lifting her skirts and baring those long slim legs would disappear. It didn't. When he opened them again, to make matters worse, she'd kicked off her slippers, exposing creamy white toes that looked like ten of the Orient's most precious pearls dropped in the mud.

His quill dripped onto the page, spattering ink across the holly he'd just labeled.

Bent over at the waist, the wench struggled with a particularly stubborn weed, scrabbling at the dirt with her fingers, grunting with the effort. Finally, she dropped down to her knees and wrapped both hands around the tough stalk, pulling for all she was worth, to no avail.

He wheezed a troubled sigh. Lady Cynthia Wendeville should in no wise be digging in the dirt like a half-naked serf. It was improper. And unnatural. And it was driving him to madness. He'd not allow it.

He may be unable to protest with words. But there was something he could do about it.

He corked the ink bottle and set his quill aside. Shaking his head in disgust at his own folly, he snatched up a spade resting against the garden wall and motioned her back. He drove the spade deep into the soil and rocked it. The weed popped out easily.

"Thank you," she said, wiping black mud across her cheek. She made a grab for the shovel.

He compressed his lips, unwilling to surrender it.

"I'll need the spade to turn the soil," she explained.

He'd be damned if he'd let her hoist the heavy thing while he scrawled on a scrap of parchment. De Ware men didn't watch women toil. Besides, the shovel felt good in his hands, and there was no shortage of work to be done. And mayhap, he thought as a breeze wafted the sweet fragrance of her skin to him, if he kept his eyes to the loam and his hands to the shovel, they wouldn't be tempted to stray places they shouldn't.

He took the implement from her and attacked the soil with a vengeance, wishing he could excise the lust from his soul as readily as a weed from the earth. He dug and turned the soil, smashing clods with the back of the spade, casting rocks from the beds into the pile of weeds. Yard by yard, he let the shovel chew up and spit out the loam.

If only his own life were so simply turned over.

If only he could bury his corrupt past as neatly as last year's depleted soil.

If only he could be content with his lot as a priest.

By God, he decided, driving the spade hard into the earth, he would *make* himself content. He would embody the priesthood even more fully, embrace the joy of serenity, the love of simplicity, the satisfaction with poverty. He would pay even less heed to his corporeal shell, work toward a more divine existence. He would prostrate himself before beggars, give the last shred of his garments to the poor, spend half the day in prayer. He'd do whatever it took, he vowed, turning over a worm-riddled clod of dirt, to make this sinful longing go away.

Cynthia paused in her labors and leaned against the rake she'd been using. She blew at the lock of hair that had fallen out of her wimple and watched Garth curiously. The man half strangled the spade in his fists, and if there were any bulbs left beneath the soil, they'd surely been split asunder by his aggressive gouging.

Yet something about that unbridled strength aroused her. Garth's back strained against the wool of the cassock, dampening it, and his forearms bulged with each plunge of the shovel. Moisture peppered his forehead and glistened on his hands. Like a hard-driven plow horse, he chuffed through his nose. She wondered if her arms could even reach around that broad back, wondered how his heavy breathing would feel against her ear.

Swallowing hard, she forced her attention back to the rake. Mending Garth's spirit was a delicate process, and involving him in Wendeville's daily regimen was only the first step. She could ill afford to let misplaced emotions sabotage her noble intent.

She swept her arm across the sundial in the garden's midst, scattering leaves, and returned to clearing the straw from the rosebushes, concentrating on the rhythm of the rake and the task at hand. Before long, immersed in her work, she began to hum an old madrigal to herself.

She'd started on the sixth verse when she noticed that Garth had ceased working. He was staring at her most oddly. She wondered vaguely if she'd been singing out of tune. Then she remembered a rather nasty alternate set of lyrics she'd once heard to the same harmless madrigal, something vulgar about a Scotsman taking his cock and ballocks to sell at market.

Her face tightened, and she felt the blood rise in her cheeks. Her hands fidgeted on the rake.

"Do you know the tune?" she asked with brittle innocence. "It's all about a maid selling her stock at the fair." She chewed at her bottom lip. Lord, why had she chosen *that* song? "And a pretty penny she got for them, too." She could hear herself babbling, but couldn't stop. "The cock crowed for Matins every morn, and the oxen, forsooth, they were the biggest pair of bullocks . . ."

Garth's eyes widened.

Dear God—she'd done it now, offended him and dug herself into a hole big enough for a tree. Madly, she scanned the garden for another topic.

"Oh!" she exclaimed, her eyes locking onto the sundial. "Will you look at that? Noon already! You must be famished!" She dropped the rake and, to hide her embarrassment, busied herself with the contents of the food basket cached against the shaded wall. Pulling forth the linen tablecloth, she turned toward Garth. "Cook was good enough to . . ."

Before her, with bowed head, Garth knelt in the dirt. For one ludicrous instant, she imagined he worshiped at her feet. Then she realized that noon was time for prayer at the monastery. Since friars couldn't always go running to the chapel to say their devotions, they often knelt in the field.

At first, Cynthia glanced away, feeling like an intruder on his silent conversation with the Lord. But as the prayer dragged on and on, she let her eyes stray to him.

His great, muscular hands were clasped before him, and he rested his forehead on grimy knuckles. He squeezed his eyes shut in concentration, and his lips moved rapidly, though soundlessly, through Latin syllables. Now and then his nostrils would flare passionately and his forehead crease, and Cynthia bit her lip to still her wicked thoughts, thoughts that had him voicing such earnest devotions to her.

Garth only knew so many devotions. And he couldn't go on saying them all day. No matter how safe it made him feel to hide in prayer, he was going to have to face her. And it wouldn't be easy, not with the ribald lyrics to that madrigal buzzing about in his head between the words of prayer. He reluctantly made the sign of the cross and came slowly to his feet.

"I've a surprise," Cynthia offered. She squatted like a little child beside the basket of provisions.

The bridge of her nose now featured an endearing streak of mud. Wisps of her hair had slowly wormed their way out of the pristine wimple. It looked as if a wild orange cat perched atop her head, eager to escape its linen prison. He itched to tug the cloth off, to see her brilliant tresses pour down like liquid copper in the sun.

She was humming again, an innocuous roundelay this

time, as she shook a linen cloth out briskly, letting it float
down to the sod in a large square.

"Sit," she directed, doing so herself.

He hesitated, but the faint rumbling in his stomach made
his decision for him. He sank down upon the blanket, tucking the cassock austerely about his legs.

She plunked the basket down before him, grinning. He
looked at it, then at her.

"Well, take it out." She chuckled, wiggling her adorable
toes in the sunshine.

He closed his eyes quickly, turning his attention to the
bundles of food tucked into the basket. The smells were divine. Despite his misgivings, he began to feel like a child
with Christmas packages as he unwrapped fish and shrimp,
bread and preserved fruit. Soon, the tablecloth was spread
with flagons of wine and platters of food piled high enough
for a small retinue.

"I'll wager you've not tasted the like in some time," she
said with a wink.

It was true. Monastery fare was simple and monotonous.
He hadn't eaten bread this fine since he lived at Castle de
Ware. The claret trickled, deliciously cool, down his throat.
But his appetite was not as robust as it had once been. After
a small piece of grayling, half an apple tart, and a few figs,
he sat back, content to watch her finish.

It was a grave mistake.

She took a dainty bite of a tart with teeth as perfect as a
row of pearls, and golden juices trickled down her chin. Her
tongue darted out to lap them up, but a smudge remained that
begged to be licked off.

Garth averted his eyes, pretending to study a crack in the
garden wall. When his gaze was drawn inexorably back, the
smudge was thankfully gone.

"I must commend Cook on these tarts," she said. "I think
the pinch of ginger makes all the difference."

She sipped her wine, her lips a delicate blush against the
cold silver as she parted them for the jewel-red liquid. She
sampled the candied orange peels with a sigh of rapture, her
eyes rolling in undisguised ecstasy as she licked her sticky
fingers one by one.

Garth's thighs tensed. His loins tingled with all too familiar heat. Did she know what she was doing to him? She'd been a man's wife. Could she not recognize the signs of desire? His cassock could only hide so much. Lord, he had to leave. Now!

Yet he found he could no more escape than could a seafarer caught in a whirlpool.

She drained the last of her claret. A drop fell from the cup onto the top of her bosom like a single crimson tear, then trickled down, disappearing beneath the fabric of her kirtle onto her breast. Garth shuddered. He could vividly imagine caressing her there. She'd be soft, warm. And the taste of the claret upon her flesh . . .

He prayed she couldn't see the erratic rise and fall of his chest as he fought to breathe steadily. Couldn't feel the charge in the air as powerful as a summer storm. Nor detect the trembling in his arms as he handed her his empty platter.

He'd never felt so torn. Part of him longed to rest his head in the lap of this woodland nymph, to listen to her sing madrigals, to lie back, sipping claret and gazing up at the budding branches of spring like some spoiled pagan god. But part of him wanted to run headlong back to the chapel, nay, all the way back to the monastery, to shut himself in his cell and never emerge again.

In the end, he did neither. Fate took pity on him. Lady Cynthia, declaring that planting past noon was inauspicious, gathered up the remains of the feast and released him from her service.

9

Yesterday, it had been more difficult than she'd imagined for Cynthia to let Garth go, but she'd seen the cloaked desperation in his eyes. He'd been overwhelmed, perhaps by the richness of the food or the decadence of the sunlight. Like a novice gardener, she'd nearly killed him with nurturing, thinking to force his blossoming. She'd so desired to see him surrender to his earthy longings, at least kick off his boots or loosen his cassock belt and enjoy the glory of the spring day.

But Garth had lived four years behind gray monastery walls with grim monastery dictates. Change would not come overnight. And as impatient as she was for his rebirth, she knew the merit of letting things bloom in their own time.

This morn, however, was a new day, and when she arrived at sunrise, to her astonishment, Garth was already in the privy garden, stooped over a row of seedlings with a ewer of water. She swept silently across the dewy grass, slowing her pace at the archway to watch him. His back was to her, and amber glints shone in his hair as the sun softly kissed each curl in turn. The contours of his muscles, displayed in relief beneath his strained cassock, made her stomach flutter in a most inappropriate way.

Still he didn't notice her. Her heart dancing a nervous jig, she crept up behind him as quietly as she could. Then, little more than a yard away, she grinned mischievously and sang out, "Good morning, Father Garth!"

He whipped around so quickly, his eyes wide with shock, that he nearly lost his balance. She burst out laughing. The humor of the situation must have struck him as well, for before he could suppress it, he rewarded her with a sheepish smile.

Throwing *her* instantly off balance.

Until now, she'd never appreciated the full measure of Garth's allure. Nor how dangerous he was. She'd glimpsed his appeal before in small details. The way his thick, tawny hair curled deliciously down onto his neck. His shoulders, broad enough to carry the weight of the world. The idle strength in his hands, so splendid to behold. But the warmth of his smile . . . ah, that made him devastatingly handsome. His eyes crinkled delightedly at her little joke, and the curve of his mouth was curiously inviting. All at once, she was the one unable to speak.

But in the prolonged interval of silence, Garth gradually sobered. He turned his gaze from her and gestured awkwardly toward the half dozen buckets of water around him.

"Aye, good," she said, her voice breaking like a twelve-year-old lad's. "The new plants should be kept damp."

She thought perhaps she could do with a dousing of cold water herself. The sun had scarcely risen, and already her blood ran hot.

But Garth resumed working without another word, laboring tirelessly through the morning.

She should have been pleased. It was her intent, after all, to involve Garth in demanding labor to give his frustrated muscles an outlet for their restlessness. And he was doing remarkably well. Not even her servants worked so industriously. But did he have to be so damnably focused on duty? Why it irritated her, she didn't know, but Garth didn't give her a second glance all morn.

And now the air felt as fierce as dragon's breath. The sun's flames, directly overhead, steamed the earth and scorched the back of Cynthia's neck. The humid heat, along with her inexplicable pique, combined to drive her to the brink of madness. She mentally cursed the heavy wool kirtle she'd chosen. All that wool belonged on a sheep, not a person. She might very well roast in it on a day like this. Inside her boots, her toes were ready to mutiny.

Wiping her dripping forehead for the twelfth time, she decided she'd had enough. She speared the ground with her small spade and tore the wimple and veil from her head. They hit the sod with a thump like a downed pigeon. She shook loose her fiery curls and lifted them off her neck to cool it.

"Ah!" she sighed, that small change effecting a world of difference. "I'd vow I was baking in a woolen tart." She laboriously pulled the boots from her grateful feet and wriggled her toes in the moist soil. "That's better." She wiped her dirty face on her discarded wimple.

Then she glanced at Garth. Droplets of sweat had welled along his forehead and beneath his nose. Wet patches discolored the neck edges of his robe. If her surcoat was stifling, his cassock must be near suffocating.

"I'd not think you remiss," she confided, "were you wont to loosen your own trappings. You must be roasting beneath them."

Garth stiffened visibly. He looked as if he'd rather perish in his cassock than bend the rules of propriety by removing what tenuous obstacle remained between the two of them. He shook his head once, grimly, and returned to his annoying diligence.

They toiled in silence then, but for the incessant drone of insects and the papery rustle of bulbs going in the ground. The forest birds were too hot to stir or sing, and not even the suggestion of a breeze teased the still air.

Cynthia began to feel as withered as an old rose. She tucked one last bulb into the soil, then went to fetch the watered wine she'd brought. It was but a quarter gone, no thanks to Garth. He hadn't taken a swallow. She unstoppered the wineskin, took a long swig of the musky drink, then forced it into Garth's hands. He hesitated, then wiped the rim of the skin with his sleeve, as if her heathen lips might soil his holy ones, and took one modest sip.

Vexed by the heat and her scratchy kirtle and Garth's self-righteous nonsense, she bid a farewell to propriety altogether and brashly tossed off her surcoat, leaving only her clinging underdress. This she hiked up, belting it high to cool her legs. She untied the laces at the back and loosened the neck, pulling the sticky wool away from her body.

Garth had congratulated himself, thinking he'd been doing well, tolerating the lady's presence with exemplary stoicism. He'd endured the fire burning outside and within him, melding them into a discomfort he could blame entirely on the sun. It was simply his purgatory, he maintained, the suffering of the flesh that would purify him in the end.

But this—this was beyond purgatory.

Cynthia's legs, lanky and smooth, shone with sweat. From his vantage point, crouched in the mud of the garden, his gaze involuntarily traveled up their full length, from shapely ankle and muscled calf to rounded knee and smooth thigh, stopping where they disappeared beneath her bunched skirts. Her kirtle, devoid of its modest surcoat, snugly embraced her every curve. Her neck, where the hem had been pulled away, was chafed by the wool, and he had an insane longing to kiss the pink flesh there. The fire burgeoning within him had nothing to do with the sun, he knew, and it created a burning thirst in him that no drink, save that of her affections, could quench.

Yet he couldn't slake that thirst. He was a friar, he reminded himself, though even that concept fluctuated in his head like a desert mirage. Agitated, he rose abruptly to his feet and poked hard at the soil with his planting stick, willing away the image of the bare-legged goddess toiling beside him.

Alas, he stood up too quickly. The world wavered and shifted in his sight. Peripheral shadows blurred his vision. He vaguely sensed the stick falling from his nerveless fingers.

His last thought was that a de Ware never fainted.

Then his eyes rolled, and his bones turned to jelly. The horizon tilted, and everything went black.

Cynthia recognized the vacant look in Garth's eyes. Dear God, he was fainting! His eyelids fluttered as he swayed on his feet. She dropped her spade and rushed forward, catching him about the waist. For a long moment, they teetered on the brink of balance, Garth completely limp and Cynthia gritting her teeth and oozing into the soft mud beneath her heavy burden. At last, his dead weight was too much for her, and they sank to the ground in their odd embrace, Cynthia near crushed by his large, lifeless body.

She gasped for air, spluttering against the itchy brown wool of Garth's cassock. She wriggled beneath him, but he had her pinned, and all her squirming only made a bigger mess of the newly planted cowslip they'd squashed in their fall.

Suddenly, Cynthia fought the unbearable urge to giggle. How ridiculous they must look, this great bear of a man flattening her like meadow grass. Sweet Mary, she prayed, snickering helplessly, don't let Roger find me like this. That made her laugh all the more. She'd be discovered dead by her steward, suffocated by a friar, a ludicrous grin plastered on her face.

She wiggled her hands around until they were against Garth's chest, then pushed with all her might. He budged, and with a groan, she rolled him off of her onto a row of violets.

But her levity faded when she looked at Garth's unconscious face. She didn't need her divining gift to tell her he needed to get out of the sun. The bull-headed fool. He'd labored all morn in the blistering heat in those heavy robes with scarcely a swallow of drink.

She clasped his thick wrists, and shaking her head in regret, dragged him unceremoniously and with great effort across the furrows she'd just seeded, into the shade.

His face was flushed, but he no longer perspired. His skin was hot and dry. When she placed two fingers along his throat, she could feel his heart racing. Wasting no time, she untied the cord at his waist and flung open his robe. She blew cooling breaths across his face and chest and fanned him with her discarded headpiece.

He needed water. Slicing a sizable rag from the cleanest part of her surcoat, she dipped it into the watering pitcher and let a small stream trickle between his lips. Then she used the cloth to gently sponge his brow, his neck, his chest.

Eventually his heartbeat began to slow.

The danger past, Cynthia perused Garth's body at her leisure as she moved the cooling cloth over him. How different it was from her late husband's. John had been wrinkled and pale. Garth was smooth and strong, like a two-pronged buck she'd seen once in the wood. His chestnut mane was thick and shining, gloriously defying the strictures of a friar's pate. His freshly shaved jaw was strong, his neck broad, and now that his formidable chest was laid bare, she could see, high up on one breast, a jagged white scar that might have come from the slash of a sword. Though his flesh was spare, he most definitely possessed not the body of a friar, but that of a warrior.

Soft brown hair made a line from his breastbone to his navel and further, interrupted only by the top of his linen loincloth, and she felt a fleeting perverse urge to follow that furred path to its destination.

But he was rousing.

From the darkness, Garth could hear his own heart beating forcefully in his ears, feel it pounding in his hot temples. Yet a chill breeze caressed his jaw, his forehead. He drifted in and out of awareness. Before, he'd imagined he was in the privy garden, suffocating in his monk's cassock. But now it seemed as if he lay nude upon his back.

Confused, he scowled and cracked his eyes open just wide enough to see the woman staring down at him. What did she want? After an endless moment of painful disorientation, he remembered. He *was* in the garden. He'd been working when . . . His head felt weighted with lead as he lifted it to determine his condition.

Satan's claws! He was half-naked. What the devil . . . ?

His nostrils flared. He snatched up the edges of his cassock, flapping them together like the wings of an angry gyrfalcon. He ground his teeth. Damn his vow of silence! He should upbraid her soundly. He was a priest, for the love of Peter! What had possessed her to . . .

Just what *had* she done? He pierced her with his eyes.

"You fainted," she explained limply.

Which only made him angrier. De Wares, this wench

should know, did not faint. He tried to sit up, but to his chagrin, he tottered weakly, forced to settle back onto his elbows.

She fetched wine for him then, clasping the back of his head to help him drink, as if he were an invalid.

Humiliated, he shook off her patronizing hand, grabbed the wineskin from her, and took a quick gulp. Too quick.

As Cynthia bent forward toward him, her kirtle gaped at the loosened neckline. Nestled down inside the garment, perfectly revealed for his pleasure, was a lovely breast, the skin creamy and smooth, the nipple set upon the full, pale mound like a tiny and precious rosebud.

He choked on the wine, tearing his eyes away from her tempting flesh, but not before the throbbing in his loins began.

Bracing himself against the rock wall, he scowled out the archway of the garden to the field beyond. Somewhere in the distance, though he couldn't hear them, he knew the monastery bells tolled. With each imaginary ring, he mentally forced his arousal to subside, retreating into the discipline of his office.

Dispassionately, he tied the cord of his cassock, rose to his feet, and, quelling her assistance, placed the implements solemnly into the wheelbarrow. Then, without a backward glance, he wheeled it out the gateway.

Behind him, Cynthia made a noise like the sizzle of a snake.

"You. Ungrateful. Sanctimonious. Bastard."

He froze, startled by the depth of her anger.

"Is that the thanks I get for saving your life?" she demanded.

He sighed, gathering his strength, set the wheelbarrow down, and slowly turned to face her. She looked for all the world like a half-wild gypsy standing with her arms akimbo. He battled to maintain his bland expression.

"Do not look at me like that!" she hissed. "As if you were not a man, but some stuffed quintain's dummy!"

He tightened his jaw and narrowed his eyes, but in an instant reined his irritation back in again.

"Oh!" she groaned in exasperation. "The food I brought

today gone to waste, and my flowers . . . Do you know you crushed all the cowslips and most of the violets? You almost crushed *me* when you fainted!"

The woman had no idea how tenuous his control was at this moment. He was trying not to think about this beautiful, wild-eyed hellion rebuking him like an avenging angel, her skirts revealing more than they covered, one satiny shoulder exposed above the neckline of her gown. He tried not to visualize his body atop hers, as she said it had been moments ago. He tried not to imagine what she'd done with that damp cloth. He forced himself to listen only to the illusory monastery bells. Prayed they would save him from himself.

"What has happened to you?" she whispered. "You were once so full of life, so compassionate."

The wench could no more contain her thoughts than one could keep wine in a cask full of holes. Dear God, nay—were those tears brimming in her eyes? Anything but tears.

"How could the church do so much damage to a man's spirit?"

Within the stony shell of his body, Garth shuddered. Sudden fear vexed him, the fear of a man whose most secret door has been unlocked by a woman. She'd spoken the truth more eloquently than he could himself. But she'd also trespassed into his heart. And he couldn't allow that, for her own protection as well as his.

He gazed at her with schooled mercy and calmly, deliberately made the sign of the cross, blessing her errant soul.

"Don't you bless me!" she cried. She crossed her arms smartly across her chest, but a tear traced a muddy path down her cheek. "You are the one who needs saving!"

She would have stalked off then, he was sure, leaving him to find his way out of the dust of that singularly feminine alloy of fury and hurt. But a maidservant came hurtling toward them even as she turned to go.

"M'lady!" young Mary cried, nearly bowling Garth over. "'Tis Meggie, m'lady! Elspeth says her babe is comin'!"

Cynthia dropped her own worries like a hot coal. "Meggie? Dear God!"

She streaked past him, her skirts tugging free of her belt. He watched her all the way across the sward until she was swallowed up by the great gray stones of Wendeville Castle. Then he sighed.

Providence had once again been kind to him. It seemed the woman was always rushing off to see to someone's ills. To be sure, he'd owe extra prayers to the patron saints of the sick on the next Sabbath.

Staring up at the chamber he knew to be Cynthia's small infirmary, he briefly wondered if there was something he should do to help. He hoped not. He'd had about all the temptation he could endure for the day. Surely even Adam had not been so tormented by Eve. He supposed she'd manage well enough anyway. After all, birthing was a woman's affair.

A parchment of seeds had dropped from Lady Cynthia's pocket. He picked it up, brushing the dust off the letters scribed on it.

Marigolds.

His lips hardened into a grim smile.

How could he forget someone with hair the color of marigolds?

Somehow, he thought, rubbing his thumb across the word, Lady Cynthia Wendeville *was* familiar. But it must have been years since they'd met, and he wasn't about to go digging into the past. He'd sealed his old life away into a safe tomb four years back, and he was loath to call that Lazarus forth now. No matter how persistent she was.

And she *was* persistent, flitting from cajolery to reproach as easily as a sparrow from branch to branch, trying to jar his memory of the secular world. Well, whoever she was, whatever she'd meant to him in the past, that daughter of the devil had certainly shaken him to the core. He tossed the packet of seeds into the wheelbarrow and prayed that God would strike him dead if he ever forgot just how dangerous she was again.

Cynthia tossed her soiled tunic over her head as she hurried through the great hall, dropping it on the rushes.

"Leave it!" she commanded as Mary hesitated to pick it up. "You can fetch it later. I need you to come with me now."

She plunged her hands into the large basin of water beside the pantry screens. "The babe is not due till summer," she murmured mostly to herself. She scrubbed hard, leaving the water muddy, and dried off on the linen hung above the basin. "Is she in the infirmary?"

"Aye."

"Come then."

Elspeth met them halfway up the steps, her brown eyes as round and sunken as river pebbles. She looked twice her age. "Oh, m'lady," she whispered in misery, crossing herself, "Jeanne says the babe . . . the babe is dead."

Behind her, young Mary gasped.

Sorrow pierced Cynthia's heart. It was Meggie's first child, and her husband was away on pilgrimage. But such was the way of life and the will of God. There was no time for tears. She straightened. "Then we must save Meggie," she stated. "Mary, you fetch clean linen, and tell Cook we'll need a pot of the water he's boiling for stew. Elspeth, my herbs."

As Cynthia reached the top of the stairs, a weak scream issued forth from behind the closed door. Bracing herself for the worst, she took a deep breath and entered the chamber.

The young mother's eyes rolled like a frightened calf's. Her forehead was dotted with sweat. Her stomach, exposed like a silvery half-moon in the dim light, writhed with cramps. The linens at the foot of the bed were stained crimson with blood. Jeanne the midwife was beside her, holding Meggie's hand tightly, trying to comfort her, but her own face was lined with guilt and frustration.

Cynthia pressed the door closed behind her. She went to the window and slowly opened the shutters to let in more light. Then she came up beside Meggie.

"My lady," the girl gasped.

"Meggie, I'm going to see you through this," she said, speaking soothingly as she rubbed her hands together, palm to palm. "You know, don't you, lass, that the babe is not living?"

Meggie's haunted sable eyes were answer enough.

"There was naught you could do for the infant, Jeanne," Cynthia murmured to the midwife, who looked up in despair. Her hands began to tingle with heat. "But I'll need your help with the mother."

A faint scratching on the door announced a red-faced

Mary, bearing an armload of linen and a small but heavy cauldron of steaming water.

"Now, Meggie," Cynthia said, stroking the girl's forehead, "it will be over before you know it. We've got to make quick work of it so you'll begin to heal all the sooner."

Cynthia closed her eyes and rested her palms on Meggie's head, patiently letting them guide her. Blurs of color circled lazily in her mind's eye, coming slowly into focus. Images flashed past in a blaze of white light—monkshood and shepherd's purse—and, after a moment, she envisioned Meggie whole again, surrounded in a halo of healthy blue.

When the warmth in her hands subsided, she shook them like a hound shaking off water. Then she wet a linen rag and gently swabbed the blood from Meggie's thighs.

Elspeth arrived with the herbs.

"Monkshood, Elspeth," Cynthia murmured.

Jeanne gasped, her eyes wide. "Monkshood?"

Mary made the sign of the cross and looked on fearfully.

The other two women might have hesitated at her request for the deadly herb, but Cynthia knew she could rely on Elspeth. El had seen too many miracles at her hands to question her judgment.

Cynthia ignored the others and unstoppered the vial of monkshood extract. "This will make you feel very light, Meggie," she cooed, pouring the liquid generously into her palm, "almost as if you could fly."

She reached very tenderly between the girl's limp legs and smeared the extract at the spot where the infant's tiny blue head was crowning.

"I want you to tell me when you feel as if you are flying, Meggie."

There was no need for the girl to speak, for in a few moments her body relaxed, and her face took on a dreamy expression, as if she'd not a care in the world.

"We'll take the babe now," Cynthia murmured to the midwife.

Jeanne ran a hand across the girl's belly and massaged, pressing gently at first, then more firmly. Cynthia eased her fingers in around the babe's head, trying not to think about its poor, lifeless body. It was slippery, difficult work, but she managed to turn the baby and pull it forth as Jeanne pressed hard on Meggie's belly. Meggie was mercifully oblivious through the whole procedure. She scarcely knew the deed was done.

Cynthia received the afterbirth onto a thick pad of linen and handed the baby to Mary. The young maid went white.

"You stay with me," Cynthia ordered. The girl had probably never seen so horrifying a thing, but Cynthia couldn't afford to lose her help.

Mary swallowed hard, but she nodded, carrying the grisly burden away.

Cynthia applied a poultice of crushed shepherd's purse to stop the bleeding. She then insisted the midwife scrub her hands clean in the hot water and go home to rest, adding a directive to her to send the chaplain to the infirmary. She had Elspeth press a thick wad of absorbent linen between Meggie's legs while she scoured her own hands. Then she took over, covering Meggie with a thin sheet and combing the girl's hair back with her fingers till she fell asleep.

Meanwhile, Mary cowered in the corner of the chamber, and now she hissed like a frightened kitten. "She's bound to die after what you did, m'lady."

Elspeth rounded on the terrified maid, wagging an angry finger. "Lady Cynthia's healin' is held in the highest regard, whelp. There may come a day ye'll be thankful for it yerself. Until then, ye'd do well to remember yer place and hold yer tongue."

"But 'tis a witch's herb, monkshood," Mary argued.

Elspeth's voice was dangerously soft. "Then would ye be callin' Lady Cynthia a witch?"

"See that you wash your hands well, both of you," Cynthia interrupted before a fight could ensue. "Monkshood is not a witch's herb, but it can be dangerous."

She shook her head. Where anyone got the notion that an herb could be evil was beyond her. After all, hadn't God created *all* the plants? True, some of them could be poison if used in ample amounts, but they possessed no mystical powers. Herbs were simply for healing the sick and removing pain.

A tentative scratch came at the door as she scrubbed at a spot of blood on her sleeve.

"Come," she called in reply.

Garth scowled. He'd half hoped no one would hear him. He had no idea why he'd been summoned. After all, he knew naught about birthing. And he was filthy from the garden.

He pushed the door inward anyway. A de Ware never walked away from a lady in need.

The metallic odor of blood unnerved him for an instant. His eyes sought the source at once. Meggie lay atop the pallet in the midst of the chamber. The linens at the foot of the bed were streaked with scarlet, as if the pallet itself had been slashed and wounded in some gruesome battle. But though her face was as pale as plaster, as still as death, the young woman yet lived. The sheet rose and fell to the rhythm of her breathing.

The two maids tidying the chamber stared at him. He clearly didn't belong here. This was a woman's domain. Yet Cynthia motioned him in, fetching a bundle from the bed with great care.

"The babe," she said quietly, not meeting his eyes, "needs blessing. I was hoping you'd defer your vow of silence to see it done."

He frowned. The infant could scarcely be moments old. Why such urgency?

She lifted her gaze to him then, and he knew at once.

The babe was dead.

He swallowed hard. She wanted him to perform last rites.

She continued to stare at him, beseeching him with eyes burdened by sorrow, haunted by pain. And in that moment, no matter what had passed between them before, no matter that he thought her the daughter of Eve, he knew he'd do anything to take that suffering from her eyes.

He took the feather-light bundle from her into his own arms and strode to a private corner of the infirmary, whispering the words around the painful lump in his throat to save the babe's wretched soul. By the last Amen, Cynthia had gone.

He handed the babe to Mary. The women would no doubt

prepare its tiny body for burial. The mother snored softly from the pallet, her grief abandoned for the moment in the land of dreams. Elspeth blew her nose, then shoved the rag into her pocket, busying herself with gathering up the soiled linens. His work here was done.

But what of Lady Cynthia? It was his duty to comfort the living as well as bless the dead. Certainly she must be in need of comfort. After all, he'd seen how she took her duty to her household to heart. In some way, she probably felt responsible for this tragedy.

He found her in the outbuilding she'd fashioned to grow starts of tender plants. It was a cozy place, kept warm by a roof of sheepskin that let in the sun's light, and wet by a well sunk in its midst. Earthenware pots of all sizes, filled with assorted foliage, cluttered the wooden shelves. As he let himself in, warm, moist air enveloped him as if to give him welcome.

"Close the door . . . please."

Her voice came from the far corner, muffled by a forest of greenery. Then her head popped up between the fronds. Her eyes were red from crying, and he felt a sudden, inexplicable longing to cradle her against his shoulder, to let her sob her sorrow into his cassock.

"Oh. Chaplain." She self-consciously wiped at her cheeks, then gestured toward the entrance. "If you'll kindly . . ."

He secured the door.

"The babe?" she inquired.

He nodded.

"If you've come to tell me it's the will of God," she muttered, "you're wasting your breath."

He frowned, taken aback. Cynthia snipped a flowered branch from one of the plants with all the wrath of Perseus beheading Medusa. She wasn't grief-stricken. She was vexed.

"I know. He is at peace now." She snipped another branch. "His soul is in a better place." Snip. "God works in mysterious ways." Snip. Snip. "You need not preach to me. I've faced death more times than you can imagine."

She hooked the shears over a nail in the wall and gathered

the white-flowered stems into a bunch. With a swish of her wool skirts, she tried to pass.

He caught her arm. He didn't know why. It was foolish and instinctive and dangerous. Mayhap it was the vulnerability underlying her bitter words or the helpless frustration reflected in her eyes.

She gasped softly as the flowers were crushed between them. A light breeze wafted their fragrance past his nose, a fragrance vaguely familiar to him. It had been ages since he'd smelled that sweet pungence. What was it? His mother had grown this in her garden. He was sure of it, but . . .

Jasmine.

He only mouthed the word, but the air stilled as if he'd uttered an enchantment. A queer prickling traveled up his spine as he inhaled the scent.

Jasmine.

He struggled to remember. There was something about jasmine and the woman before him. He perused her face, his eyes only half-focused, and gently took the bouquet from her fingers. Faint images of lazy summer afternoons spent reading in the garden buzzed around his brain like . . .

"Bees," he murmured before he could grasp the significance of the word.

He remembered now, something . . . He looked at Cynthia directly, studied her face. She raised trembling fingers to her lips. Oh aye—he remembered her well. How could he have forgotten the orange-haired sprite that had stolen his mother's roses? The little lass leaning back against the jasmine? Her shock when she was stung by bees? He'd rescued the poor frightened girl. And she'd called him "Sir Garth."

She was a grown woman now, but he recalled all too vividly how soft and vulnerable and trusting the little girl had been as he wielded his blade to remove the barbs from her tender flesh.

"Cynthia le Wyte."

Cynthia's heart missed a beat. Garth's voice took her breath away. She didn't know what she'd expected, but it certainly wasn't the deep, resonant, rough-edged timbre so unlike his carefree childhood voice. The way he said her name sent a shiver through her very soul. Then, as if his voice weren't enough to convince her that he was the most alluring man alive, his eyes softened, and one side of his mouth drew up in that familiar quirky smile to remove all doubt.

She couldn't help but return the smile, but her heart pounded in her chest like a fuller's paddle. The feelings she'd had for him as a girl were nothing to the way she felt now. Her legs weakened beneath her, and she could feel a blush begin upon her cheek. Sweet Mary, she could forget herself in that smile of his.

But no sooner did she entertain that thought than the grin faded from Garth's face. He pressed his lips together in a thin line, and his eyes flattened. He released her arm and stared over her head toward the wall as if she were invisible.

Lord, she realized—he had broken his vow of silence.

10

GARTH CURSED SILENTLY. HOW COULD HE HAVE LET A woman come between him and his word? And with but one day more of his penance to serve? For four years he'd kept his monastic oaths, answering to the Lord with undying devotion, inflicting severe punishment upon himself for unworthy thoughts. He'd embraced chastity with such sobriety that he was often the butt of jests comparing him to his notoriously lusty brothers. All for what? To be tempted from the simplest vow by a mere woman? It was unconscionable. How could he have forgotten the harsh lesson he'd learned from Mariana?

He clenched his jaw so tightly he feared his teeth might crack. Slowly, purposefully, he pressed the jasmine back into her hands, rejecting it as thoroughly and unmistakably as he must her.

"What is it?" she asked, her face the portrait of innocence. "Your vow? It's all right. I swear I'll not tell a soul. It shall be a secret between us."

He pulled the corners of his mouth down in disgust. A secret. That was just the sort of deceit he should have expected from a woman. Sighing deeply, he closed his eyes to her, clutched his crucifix in a reassuring fist, then turned away with a measured precision that belied his state of mind.

He'd hurt her. He knew he had. And that knowledge would eventually serve as his own private hell. But for now, all he could think about was how he'd been gulled again by that most vile, most shrewd, most conniving of God's creatures. Woman.

He planted one foot in front of the other and made his way steadily toward the door.

"You know," Cynthia said crisply at his back, surprising him, "the Abbot never told me what it is you did to deserve that ridiculous vow of silence. I wonder . . ."

Garth's heart jerked against his ribs, but his feet managed to hesitate only slightly in their bid for freedom. Lord, what mischief did the woman perpetrate now? She was like a ferret burrowing at his soul. He owed her no explanation. He was not obliged to reveal his iniquities to her. Confessions were between the sinner and the church.

If only he could make it to the door before . . .

"Let me think," she said with the pensive coyness only a woman could master. "What sin might a man of the church commit?"

His fingers fumbled with, then gripped the iron handle of the door, and relief surged through him as he pulled it open. The contrasting wave of cool air struck his cheek like a sobering slap. He was safe now. He'd return to his quarters and spend the rest of the day praying for forgiveness for . . .

"It must have been a grave sin indeed to require such a grave penance."

Satan's teeth! She was following him. A quick glance told him the meddlesome wench had secured the door behind her. Worse, she looked for all the world as if she intended to dog him the rest of the day, nettling him with rude questions.

Very well, he decided. If she could dismiss propriety and common courtesy, he could do the same. He'd ignore her completely, march off as if her chatter were no more than a breeze blowing past his ear.

It worked for three long paces.

Then the chain of his crucifix broke, and the wooden cross slid from around his neck, clattering on the stones at his feet, throwing off his stride.

He whirled. To his horror, Cynthia snatched it up like a

prize, closing it in her fist before he could reach it. He glanced at his stolen goods, then clenched his teeth, as tense as a cat about to spring, sorely tempted to pry it from her hands.

Apparently unaffected by the threat sizzling in his eyes, she ran an idle finger along the worn wooden edge of the cross. "I'd venture so far as to say you must have violated one of the seven deadly sins," she guessed.

The blood left his knuckles as he tightened his fists in the folds of his cassock.

"The seven deadly sins . . . hmm . . . ," she mused.

He ceased breathing.

"Well, I don't think it was covetousness. There is little to covet in a monastery."

She tapped his cross against her lip. Lord, it was unconscionable. The cross was a priest's relic, not some trinket for her amusement. How dare she place her lips where his had pressed a thousand times. . . .

"Nor do I imagine it was envy."

He stood very still, staring at the crucifix. He wanted it very badly. But he could see in her eyes, she wasn't going to give it to him. Not yet.

"I'm certain it wasn't sloth, for I can see by your work in the garden you are not an idle man."

She'd done it now. Exceeded his tolerance for torment. Besides, she was getting perilously close to the truth.

He whipped away from her. Never mind his crucifix. It was probably defiled now anyway. He'd get another one.

In the meantime, he'd put up with no more of her taunting. He stalked off with a satisfying snap of his cassock and the longest strides he could manage.

They were apparently not long enough.

"By your fitness," she said, running to stay at his heels, "it's definitely not gluttony."

He felt as tightly wound as a catapult about to fire and as panicked as a novice about to fire it.

"Anger?" she guessed, breathless from the chase. "Mayhap. Even now . . . your fists betray you . . . clenching and unclenching like that. . . . Hmm. What about lust?"

He halted so abruptly that she collided with his back with an "oof." Involuntarily, he wrenched his head toward her.

Something in his eyes must have given him away and shocked her terribly, for she suddenly grew clumsy, fumbling with the crucifix, and he knew one instant of grim satisfaction.

"Oh!" She worried the chain while her gaze darted about like a singed moth, uncertain where to alight. "I . . . I . . . didn't . . . ," she mumbled, scarlet chagrin rising in her cheeks. "I'm so . . . sorry. I thought surely that . . . that pride was your sin."

Garth compressed his lips, thoroughly humiliated. Was that admission supposed to comfort him? Pride was the one thing he *didn't* have. Curse the wench! It was bad enough he'd made confession to Prior Thomas. But this, this was unbearable—a woman he hardly knew divining his guilt.

He could hear the gossip already, imagine her glee at spreading it. Father Garth—a monk of four years, a de Ware, sworn to chastity—lusted after womanflesh.

He bit the inside of his cheek to quell the shout of fury and shame threatening to explode from him. By God, he'd not let her see his disgrace. He'd hide it if it killed him.

He stretched himself to his full height, concealing his emotions like a knight primed for battle, confronting her with the countenance of a calm but deadly warrior. Now he could face her. With this mask, he could face the devil himself.

He refused to beg for the crucifix. If she wanted it, she could have it. She probably needed it more than he did anyway. He nodded coolly, then turned on his heel and fled to seek holier ground.

Cynthia couldn't move. She felt as though the breath had been sucked out of her, taking with it the mist over her eyes.

Lust. Lust was his offense. Not pride.

She'd been certain his sin was pride. Pride was always the vague failing for which monks were punished. Sweet Mary—if she'd known, she would never have played that cruel game with him. But she'd been frustrated by the babe's death and vexed by the aloofness in Garth's eyes, and at the time she'd wanted nothing more than to poke those cool, un-feeling orbs.

Lord, she could still see the subtle flinch at the outer edges of his eyes when she'd exposed him. He'd tried to hide it, sheathed his emotions faster than a knight shoving a sword into its scabbard, but she'd glimpsed it—the pain, the humil-iation. God, how he must hate her.

As he paced off, the fabric of his cassock slapped the air like the sail of a ship bound for frozen climes. It wasn't till he'd disappeared inside Wendeville's chapel that Cynthia leaned back against the castle wall, still clinging to the cru-cifix, and considered what had just transpired.

A million thoughts bounced about in her head. Garth de Ware had committed the sin of lust. Christ's bones! What had he done? What constituted lust to the church? Had he slept unclothed at the monastery? Had he sought his body's release at his own hands? Dear God—had he been found with a lover?

Suddenly the heat of the day seemed overwhelming. Cyn-thia fanned herself with one hand, swinging the cross idly from its chain with the other.

Garth de Ware was very much alive, she thought, a thrill of delight coursing through her body. There *was* passion there. The flame was not extinguished, though the battle to suppress it still raged within him, even after four years, driving him to take vows of silence to curb his desire.

But she'd been right. There was hope. There was a chance.

A shiver ran through her as she recalled the spicy scent of his hair and the way it curled upon his nape, the evergreen depths of his eyes, the habit he had of clenching his hands, the aura of undeniable strength and masculinity that sur-rounded him. Just knowing he was capable of suffering the pangs of desire set her heart all aflutter, and it was full night before she could banish the enticing image of Garth de Ware, his cassock cast aside with his inhibitions, from her mind.

Mary pulled her cloak tighter against the midnight chill and glanced down at her hands. Her knuckles were rubbed nearly raw from all the scrubbing she'd given them. She had no desire to be caught with traces of monkshood on her person, especially since she was going to see the holy man again tonight.

Her body thrummed eagerly. The news she brought him was a juicy bit of meat. It would please him greatly, and when he was pleased, he granted her special favors. With these favors, she knew she could make her way into heaven. After all, he was a powerful man of the church. He could save her immortal soul.

A thief like her, he'd told her, had little hope of passing through heaven's gates, even if her crime was but stealing bread for her starving baby brother. She shivered. Naught frightened Mary more than eternal damnation. But she knew if anyone could keep her from the fires of hell, it was him. So she groveled at his feet, did his bidding, catered to his every wish; this time to spy for him. He, in turn, received her worship and absolved her guilt.

The moon was bright, making ghostly shadows at the edges of the wood, as she furtively left the great hall of Wendeville Castle. The chill air reminded her of the priest's cool, quivering fingers upon her shoulders as she received him, and she closed her eyes in a silent prayer that it would be his will tonight.

The place wasn't far. But it was secret. The holy man insisted that none but she know of his presence, and Mary felt his trust like a light shining for her alone.

The crofter's cottage was dark but for a faint golden glow visible through cracks in the old timbers. She took a deep, thrilling breath. It was easy to imagine that the glow was a divine presence, that inside those walls the holy man spoke to God Himself.

Casting a quick glance about her, she pulled the door open on its oiled hinge and entered the cottage.

The priest's candle flickered eerily as he glided toward her. He looked gaunt and pale in the shifting shadows, more spirit than human, like the illuminations he'd allowed her to peek at once in his jewel-encrusted Bible. She sank to her knees in awe.

"You have news?" he demanded in the stern voice that made her shudder expectantly.

"Yes, Father."

She told him everything in a rush, certain that his time was as valuable as gold. She told him about Meggie's travail, the stillborn babe, the monkshood. When she was finished, the priest indulged her with a smile.

"You have done well, Mary, child," he praised, laying one slim hand atop her covered head. "Now let us speak of another task I wish you to perform."

Mary listened as attentively as a disciple, moved by the Abbot's helpless shrugs and frowns of concern. When he was done, after she lapped up the milk of his appeals as eagerly as a kitten, he looked into her adoring eyes with the familiar entreaty she'd waited all evening to hear.

"Do you wish to receive the Lord this night? Do you wish to receive Him through me?" he asked gently.

Mary weakly, thankfully sighed her consent.

The Abbot tugged the hood from her head and pulled his lips back in an approving smile.

She clasped her hands before her as if in prayer, and looked up at him. He closed his eyes and took a deep breath, his translucent face radiant with religious ecstasy. At last, he opened his robe to her, showing her the ungainly swelling beneath his cassock. She took glad communion there, aroused by his cries of wonder, swallowing every precious drop of the bitter offering he delivered unto her.

Much later, as she lay upon her own pallet, savoring the traces of him that lingered upon her lips, Mary fingered the amulet of angelica the holy man had placed around her neck. It would serve as protection, he'd assured her, against the evil witch that was her mistress.

Garth blew out a defeated breath, crumpling another sheet of parchment in his fist and tossing it dispiritedly to the stone floor of the chapel. Beside him, the flame atop the chunky yellow candle quavered as if fearful of its master. Garth raked a hand through his hair and stared up at the full moon dyed blue by the colored window. A small cloud passed over its face, creating a dark shadow that floated its way through the scenes of stained glass like a demon dancing among the saints.

He rubbed a tired eye with his palm. He should be abed. He knew that. But tomorrow's sermon eluded him, and the troubling war within him kept sleep just out of his grasp.

He knew all too well the name of his foe.

Cynthia le Wyte.

Curse the wench. Now that he recalled her, he couldn't exile her from his thoughts. She reminded him too clearly of the sweet days of his youth—endless hours lounging in the dappled shade of the willow with naught but larks and squirrels for company, mornings spent conquering Latin as zealously as his brothers conquered the sword, long summer afternoons scented with life and dreams and jasmine.

He'd banished himself from that world as surely as Adam had gotten himself expelled from Eden—also because of a woman. And here was another of her ilk wreaking havoc with a man's soul.

Yet he found it difficult to utter the names of Cynthia and Mariana in the same breath. They were nothing alike. Aye, Cynthia was every bit as beautiful and tempting as Mariana had been, but those were superficial things. There was something beyond that, something more profound in Cynthia that had the capacity not only to wound him more deeply, but to utterly destroy him.

Today, when she'd handed him that poor dead child, when her anguish spoke to him through her eyes, he'd seen a facet of Cynthia le Wyte he'd forgotten, something that harked back to that time in his mother's garden and compounded the confusion of his feelings.

He'd seen her vulnerable.

Which had made her all the more irresistible. All the more dangerous.

Of course, her subsequent brutality had erased all such fears from his mind. He'd never imagined such viciousness dwelled within her. The way she'd picked and poked and prodded at him until she found the chink in his armor had been nothing short of brutal.

And yet she'd seemed astonished when she'd stumbled onto his sin. In retrospect, it was clear that she'd only toyed with the embers of his iniquity, never expecting them to burst into flame. And when they had, she was more shocked than he.

In sooth, he knew in his heart she hadn't a cruel bone in her body. He'd watched her work her healing on every wretched soul who requested it over the past several days, whether their ills were real or imagined. She showed uncommon strength, generosity of spirit, true compassion.

But whatever had inspired her to pry so relentlessly into his troubled spirit didn't matter, he kept telling himself. So she'd exposed his sin. So she'd stripped him of his dignity. Humiliated him beyond bearing.

He *would* bear it. Priests bore humiliation all the time. It tested one's faith, strengthened one's spirit.

What daunted him more was thinking about the days, weeks, years to come. How could he maintain his propriety, his dignity, his sanity when she flitted about, probing at his soul, whether it be with gentle fingers or vicious claws?

Isolation had been his answer before. But it was absurd to think he could hide behind his cassock now. Nay, now he lived in a secular world, a world flawed and unordered and riddled with sin, amongst a congregation to whom, on the morrow, he was supposed to preach the word of God.

Scowling in resignation, he retrieved the rumpled parchment from the floor and attempted to smooth the wrinkles from it. It was a piece of offal, unfit for a priest addressing his flock for the first time, but it would have to do. In a few hours, the sun would lighten the sky.

Frustrated, he slammed his hand flat on the pulpit, putting the candle out of its misery, and made his way by moonlight back to his cell.

Cynthia peered through the veil of steam rising off the surface of the bath awaiting her. The first rays of the sun filtered through the arched windows of her solar and glinted off the bathwater like sparkling jewels. The ethereal haze gave the cloudless morn and the distant tree-covered dales a dreamlike quality.

But the dark hours of the morning had been more nightmare than dream. The Sabbath had begun early for Cynthia. Too restless to sleep, she'd lain awake half the night while

images of Garth committing the sin of lust slithered eroti-
cally through her brain. Thus, when Elspeth came just past
midnight to whisper that the cooper's wife had begun to
birth her child, it was little bother for Cynthia to rise and go
to her at once. By candlelight, in the hushed hours long before daybreak, Cynthia and Jeanne the midwife took turns
holding the dame's hand, mopping her brow, giving her sips
of soothing chamomile tea. While the stars yet shimmered in
the ebony sky, a healthy baby girl made her appearance.

Scarcely had Cynthia crawled back to bed when Elspeth
shook her awake again. Two young squires had eaten tainted
oysters for supper. Rubbing her grainy eyes, Cynthia trudged
downstairs.

Canine thistle helped purge the poison from the boys. She
was then obliged, upon hearing their blushing confession, to
deliver a stern lecture about the questionable merits of in-
gesting raw oysters as aphrodisiacs.

No sooner had Cynthia gone to fetch a bite from the
kitchen than yet another crisis reared its head. One of the
hounds had snapped at the groom's daughter while she slept.
The puncture, dealt to the meaty part of her hand, wasn't too
deep, for all the ocean of tears the girl wept. She probably deserved the bite anyway. Cynthia knew the lass loved to tease
the hounds with bits of meat.

While Cynthia tended the girl, her father decided he, too,
might as well avail himself of her talents for his clutched
bowels. She gave him dandelion extract.

By the time the sky lightened from indigo to apricot, Cynthia was too exhausted to sleep. She popped a morsel of stale
bread into her mouth and had servants lug a cauldron of hot
water up to her room so she could bathe.

In a short while, Garth would deliver his first sermon at
Wendeville. She didn't want to miss it, but she couldn't go to
the chapel smelling like sweat or blood or worse. She eyed
her herbs, lined up in multicolored vials upon the table.
Lavender? Cinnamon? Oil of roses? Nay, she thought. What
she wanted was in the herb cellar.

The cellar door was ajar when she arrived, and candlelight
flickered along the plaster wall. Frowning, she peered in.

"Good morn?"

The light jogged wildly, and Cynthia heard a gasp.

"Who's there?" she asked, venturing in.

There was a rustling, as of parchment. Then Mary, the new servant, stepped forward timidly.

"M'lady." She bobbed her head.

"Mary, what are you doing here?"

"Naught, m'lady." She looked as guilty as Judas. The candle trembled in her hand.

"What's that you have there?" She nodded toward the bunch of leafy stems clutched in Mary's fist.

Mary dropped the plant instantly to the earthen floor and took a step backward. "I . . ."

Cynthia scooped it up. "This is henbane, Mary." She frowned. "It's poison. What were you . . . ?"

"I . . . I've been feelin' poorly, m'lady. My belly. I thought . . ."

"Come." She motioned the girl closer.

Mary's eyes widened. She fingered the amulet about her neck.

"Don't fret. I'm not going to beat you," Cynthia said. She restored the henbane to its niche on the shelf and began rubbing her palms together. What was one more ailing soul today?

"'Tis n-naught, m'lady," Mary stammered. "'Tis gone now." She curtseyed several times as she made her crabbed way toward the cellar door. "Th-thank you, m'lady." As an afterthought, she ducked back in and snatched a piece of parchment from the shelf, a parchment, Cynthia glimpsed, filled with words scrawled in an unschooled hand. "I'll just be goin' back to the k-kitchen then." She nervously bobbled the candle into its wall sconce and scurried out the door.

Cynthia raised a brow. Her new servant was as skittish as a foal. Henbane for her belly? Cynthia shook her head. It would most decidedly end her pains, *all* of them. It was fortunate she'd caught the girl.

Cynthia shook the tingling from her hands, then scanned the shelf of herbal extracts and oils. Everything seemed to be in order. Some of the vials were stoppered with wood, others sealed with wax. A few, those rarely employed, had a layer of dust on their shoulders, and many were so oft used that several identical bottles stood like a company of soldiers, ready at her command. At last she found what she sought in a small, unremarkable amber bottle. She snatched it up and smiled to herself.

Jasmine.

The first rays of the sun shot arrow-straight beams through the stained-glass windows of the chapel, making tapestries of color on the opposite wall. Smoking spices lent a fragrant mystery to the air. Standing in the arched nave before the rows of wooden benches, Garth fingered the worn edge of his Bible as worshipers straggled in in an awed hush of whispering voices and rustling skirts.

He was still discontent with the sermon, despite struggling with it again after Matins, scrawling out long lines of discourse one moment, only to cross them all out a moment later. Aye, he'd tried to focus his thoughts. Today was the Sabbath, after all, the busiest day of a priest's week. And this would be the first sermon he'd ever deliver to his new congregation. It was important to make a good first impression. He'd ransacked his Bible looking for the right verses. He'd broken two quills writing. And he'd given himself an aching head, frowning in concentration over the ink-stained parchment.

But he hadn't counted on the freckle-faced temptress intruding upon his every thought. He'd hoped the light of day would diffuse her image.

His palm dampened the leather binding of his Bible. Even here, even now, as the congregation slowly filed in, visions of Cynthia surrounded him.

The incense was faintly reminiscent of her sweet skin. The communion wine, poured into a deep silver chalice, rivaled the scarlet of her lips. The double glow of candles in the sun shone no brighter than her hair. Even outside the confines of the chapel, through the open doors to the morning beyond, she haunted him in the delicate hue of the sky, the song of the sparrow, the gentle breath of the breeze. Her face seemed imprinted on the stands of golden oaks. Her laughter echoed in the merry call of a meadowlark.

He missed her.

That confession astonished him, for it was absurd.

The wench had torn his world asunder. She'd caused him more grief and aggravation in the past few days than he'd endured in four long years at the monastery. She'd completely mortified him. She'd unearthed a past he'd rather stay buried. She'd aroused feelings in him that no man of the cloth should ever have. There was no godly reason for him to wish to spend another moment in her company.

But he did.

In sooth, his heart skipped this morn every time skirts brushed past the chapel door.

He clenched his fist about the rolled parchment that contained the essence of his sermon. It was an inferior piece about the importance of attending chapel every Sabbath, truly a waste of breath, considering it would be spent on those already attending. But it was the best he could come up with in the lean hours on the wrong side of midnight.

He heaved a resigned sigh. His breath stirred the flame on the beeswax candles before him. He let his eyes stray to one of the stained-glass windows, where the sun's early light was just beginning to illuminate the artist's scene. It was a portrayal of the Christ as a teacher, his arms outstretched, instructing the children assembled at his feet in the ways of God. A tiny bird perched on the shoulder of one of the children, a pretty girl wearing a garland of flowers in her hair, reminding him of . . .

Cynthia.

She seemed to float through the chapel doorway, a vision of golden light, a seraph, the sun haloing her snowy veil and blanching her eyes to translucent silver.

Heads bobbed, and maids sank into cursory curtseys as she passed, coming straight down the center aisle toward him. But she spared no one a glance. She only stared at him, a soft smile playing about her lips.

"Father Garth." She knelt before him then, offering his repaired crucifix in one extended hand. "I believe you lost this."

For a moment, he was paralyzed. It was strange, her kneeling to him. She was the lady of the castle, after all.

And yet, he realized with sudden clarity, he was master

here. This was not the garden. The chapel was his domain. Here, she was the interloper.

With a new sense of authority lending him confidence, he took the cross from her and settled it around his neck, nodding his thanks. He caught a whiff of . . . Lord, the woman knew no mercy . . . jasmine, as she rose in a velvet whirl of saffron skirts to sit on the bench at the front of the chapel. He glanced again at the picture in the stained glass.

Of course. The colors sharpened in the growing light. Of course, he realized—a chaplain was a teacher first. It was a priest's duty to show the sinner the error of his ways. Lady Cynthia, more than anything, needed a teacher. It was up to him to instruct her, to look after her soul.

She didn't understand the order of things. She didn't see how noblewomen were to follow one path and men of the church quite another, how perhaps once there'd been a time when the two of them could frolic together in a summer garden, but that time was gone. Once there'd been a time for chasing dreams and thwarting bees, but now was not that time.

He crumpled the parchment in his fist and tossed it aside, his heart lighter than it had been in days. He knew exactly what to read. Thumbing through the pages of his Bible to the verses he knew well, he waited for the congregation's murmurs to subside.

"Omnia tempus habent et suis spatiis transeunt universa sub caelo," he recited. To every thing there is a season. *"Tempus nascendi et tempus moriendi, tempus plantandi et tempus evellendi quod plantatum est . . ."*

Cynthia felt her heartbeat deepen. She sat perfectly still, afraid to move, afraid to breathe, lest she break the thread of his voice. She closed her eyes. The fine hairs on the back of her neck prickled.

It wasn't the Scripture that paralyzed her. Nor the musical cadence of the Latin he spoke. She scarcely paid heed to his words. Nay, what held her riveted was the bewitching sound of Garth de Ware's voice.

She'd expected a cool, arrogant tone from him. Or well-schooled false humility. Ill-concealed gruffness. Or an even drone as bland as the mask he frequently donned. Never in her wildest imaginings did she guess he'd possess the voice of an angel.

"... *tempus flendi et tempus ridendi, tempus plangendi et tempus saltandi* ..."

Her hands trembled on her lap as she let the music fall about her ears. His voice rumbled and rolled, whispered and sang, floated like a roundelay, then pounded down like the surf.

"... *tempus spargendi lapides et tempus colligendi* ..."

All at once, she understood. The emotions he held in check, the passions he denied behind a staid face and a rigid body, were expressed in his voice as he read ... God-knew-what. Cynthia was so caught up in the beauty of the delivery that she scarcely heard a word. With all her soul, she longed to rush into Garth's arms and press her ear against his chest, to feel the power of his rumbling voice. She wanted to be enveloped in his strong, warm ...

"... *amplexandi et tempus* ..."

Her gaze darted toward him. *Amplexandi.* Didn't that mean "embrace"?

Garth didn't mean to look up. Especially not at that spot. But Cynthia's quick intake of breath distracted him. And once distracted, all was lost. The words danced before him on the page. He couldn't find his place to save his life.

"*Tempus* ... *tempus* ..."

"*Amplexandi,*" Cynthia quietly offered while the castle folk stared at him expectantly.

He stiffened, but refused to look up. Things were not progressing as well as he'd planned. True, he read the words properly, and Lady Cynthia appeared to listen with rapt attention. It was only that suddenly her attention seemed altogether too rapt. He struggled to find the phrases again, but everything looked like meaningless black scribbles on the page. Frustrated, he closed the tome with a thump, tucked it back under his arm, and cleared his throat.

"*Tempus plantandi.* A time to plant," he began, pacing, although the action felt oddly unnatural. "Our world is like a

great garden. On one hand, there are daisies and roses and
marigolds . . ."

Marigolds? Lord. Why had he said marigolds?

"Marigolds," he repeated more firmly. "On the other,
there are wheat and rye and barley. And then there are thistles and all manner of weeds that . . ."

Cynthia's eyes looked as liquid as melting icicles.

He cleared his throat. "All manner of weeds that grow
among the . . ."

Her lips were parted, and he could see the pearly rims of
her teeth.

"Among the thistles." He nervously licked his upper lip.
God, he wished she would stop interrupting him with those
vibrant eyes. Curving mouth. Lush hair.

"Aye, God created weeds," he croaked, "just as surely as
He created barley. But you wouldn't plant weeds in your barley field, would you?"

A few men in the congregation obediently shook their
heads. Cynthia, however, stared at him with a longing so
naked that he found himself strangling the Bible beneath his
arm.

"Nay," he answered. "Nay, you would not, any more than
you'd plant thistle among lilies or nettle amidst . . . jasmine."
The curse that sprang to mind was too foul to think about.
Damn her lustrous eyes! "Some plants . . ." His voice broke.
"Some plants do not belong with others." He paced across
the front of the nave, then stopped and made a grand sweep
of his arm. "Just as the gardens of the world are planted, so
is man set upon the earth in God's great garden, each in his
own time and place. A knight does not toil in the scullery, nor
does a . . . a peasant dine beside the king. A jongleur has no
place in the armory. A merchant does not labor in . . ."

Sweet Lord—Lady Cynthia looked as if she might devour
him any moment.

"In the fields," he finished, watching Elspeth, watching
the new maidservant, watching the two children shoving
each other on the back bench. Anyone but Cynthia.

He stumbled through his thoughts with as much grace and
reassurance as a novitiate, striving to ignore that radiant face,
those translucent eyes, that adoring smile. He silently prayed

for strength, focusing on the religious accoutrements that comforted him—the candles, the stained-glass windows, the Bible.

Eventually his voice grew steady. Gradually he relaxed into the familiar duties of his office. And at last he sensed he could face her again. At last he could offer his congregation the meat of his sermon. Finally he could deliver the message so crucial to her.

Alas, it was not to be. For while he continued his discourse, an unfamiliar messenger stole up the aisle to speak briefly with Lady Cynthia. And before Garth could say another word, before he could even begin to expound upon the very important lesson he had to impart, Cynthia fled in a hush of golden velvet, simultaneously relieving and disappointing him, and leaving behind the subtle fragrance of jasmine.

11

THE SATCHEL OF HERBS AND TINCTURES RATTLED ON the saddle behind Cynthia as she rode with her guard toward the village. She wished she'd been able to stay for Garth's sermon. Never had she been so moved by the sound of a man's voice. She could have listened to him all day.

But there'd been no time for delay. There'd not even been time to change out of her heavy velvet Săbbath gown. The messenger said the stomach illness had affected at least three members of the village nearby already. Time was of the essence to keep the sickness from spreading.

A hundred yards from the first house, a dirty little urchin ran up to meet her small entourage. She knew him—Little Tim atte Gate. Tear tracks muddied his cheeks, and he sniffled as he bade them hurry, for his father was sick. Unmindful of soiling her skirts, Cynthia reached down and scooped the lad up before her on the palfrey, nudging the beast to a swift pace.

Her heart pumped faster. She was facing the unknown, and others were relying on her. This ability she had to heal was a mixed blessing. Sometimes, looking into the bright eyes of a child she'd rescued from death's grasp, elation burned so fiercely within her breast that she thought she'd burst. Other times, no matter what potions and curatives she tried, no matter how long she labored beside a suffering patient, death—that heartless reaper of souls—slowly drained the life from its victim, and she inevitably languished in defeat and despondency for days.

Still, her gift brought with it a certain responsibility. If anything could be done to relieve suffering or remove pain, Cynthia felt obliged to try it. The villagers depended upon her and knew she'd drop everything to come to their sides should they need her.

"There!" the little boy cried suddenly, wiggling on her lap and pointing toward a stone hovel off the main road.

Cynthia nudged her palfrey toward the cottage while her men waited outside. The house was as stooped as an old woman and as tightly shuttered. Smoke boiled forth from a hole in the roof. Cynthia set the child down, then dismounted herself. She grabbed her bag and swept past the boy to let herself in.

The interior was oppressively hot. A cloud of smoke swirled about her when she opened the door, stinging her eyes and throat. She coughed. Where anyone got the notion that stifling heat and darkness were beneficial to a sick person she couldn't imagine. She left the door ajar and immediately ordered the bevy of children in the cottage to open the shutters.

Tim's father, Rob, lay curled on his side atop a filthy pallet. A threadbare coverlet concealed the bottom half of his body. He shivered uncontrollably. Cynthia pushed up her sleeves and commanded Nan, Rob's wife, to begin warming water over the fire. Then she set her bag down beside the bed and bent to peer closely at her patient. The stench nearly gagged her. His skin was flushed and dry, and his eyes were sunken in his head.

"How long has he been this way?"

"Two days, my lady," Nan replied.

Cynthia touched the man's forehead. It was papery and hot. By the stink, she didn't need to ask if he was having trouble holding his food. She felt both sides of his throat. His pulse was rapid, and there was swelling beneath his ears.

She closed her eyes, took a deep breath, and began

slowly rubbing her palms together. Her flesh tingled at the friction, warming until the heat was like a glowing force held between her hands. Then she placed her palms on either side of the man's head, resting her thumbs at his temples. She imagined a bright white radiance flowing down her arms, through her fingertips, and into Rob's body, warming him, soothing him, healing him. And in brief flashes behind her eyes, she received images of the herbs he needed.

When the light diminished, when the power ran its course, she withdrew her hands, shaking off the vestiges of energy that lingered, like a hound shaking off water.

"He needs something to drink," she told the wife.

Nan, her eyes full of nervous doubt, wrung her hands by the fire. "He can keep naught down, my lady."

"He must have drink," she explained. "See how dry his skin is? We must find something he can take in small sips." She opened her satchel. "I have herbs I can use, but only when he is able to take a little liquid."

She reached into her bag and drew forth a stoppered vial. Shaking it gently, she handed it to the woman.

"This is yellow dock. I want you to find a clean rag and wash his body with this. We must wipe away all traces of illness."

Yellow dock's merits were questionable, but Cynthia found it useful for keeping many a fretful relative busy while she administered more potent cures.

"You, Tim. I saw hens in the yard. Can you fetch me a fresh egg, one laid this morn?"

The boy nodded solemnly and scampered off to do as he was bid.

Cynthia whispered to Nan, "You must keep the children away from his filth. Do you understand?"

"Aye, my lady."

"He'll need warmth, but you must let the fresh air in as well."

Cynthia picked through her bag of vials and packets, setting a few aside, dismissing several immediately, finally choosing the three she'd seen in her vision.

"I'm going to leave you these. Give them to him only

after he can drink a few spoons of watered wine without vomiting. This," she said as the woman sponged her husband's forehead, "is lady's mantle. It should settle his bowels." Nan nodded. "And this is extract of roses," she continued, holding up a tiny bottle. "Mix it with a little honey, and it will work as a restorative."

The little boy marched in then, carrying the egg before him like some precious jewel. She took it and asked one of the older children for a clean cup.

Rob moaned on the bed, drawing his knees up, and Nan's brow wrinkled in worry.

"His belly pains him," Cynthia said, picking up the third packet, dried red clover. "Make a posset out of these leaves. Steep them in boiled water. Then strain the leaves and let him sip at the liquid. It should help with the pain."

The older child handed Cynthia a cup, and she cracked the egg into it, swirling it around with a piece of the shell. Then she ladled warm water from the pot on the fire over the egg, swishing it so the egg would cloud the water. When the cup was half full, she knelt by the man.

Nan's brow creased. "But, my lady, he can't have eggs! Lent has begun!"

Cynthia had expected that the woman would protest. She paused in her labors. "I know," she murmured, "but truth to tell, Nan, your husband must have nourishment. He'll die without it. I'm certain God will forgive him this one transgression. Let us only pray that your good Rob lives to pay the penance."

Nan chewed at her lip uncertainly for a moment. Then she lifted her husband's shoulders so Cynthia could tip the broth, sip by sip, into his mouth.

"Make this for him twice a day, if possible," Cynthia said quietly. "But it must be absolutely fresh. Send your children to fetch the eggs, and your neighbors will take no note of it. Keep everything tidy, and should another of your household take ill, use the same herbs."

Nan bobbed in agreement. Cynthia lowered the man's head and tucked the coverlet in around his shoulders.

"I shall visit on the morrow," she assured the woman, rising and picking up her satchel.

As she bid them farewell and mounted up again, Cynthia sucked in a deep breath of fresh air. She oft wondered how these people could live like mushrooms, huddling together in their close, dark, damp world. Were she as penniless as they, she'd choose to bed down like a wild daisy, in an open field beneath the sky.

The second family had much the same complaints as the first. It was odd, she thought. The two lived at opposite ends of the village. Sickness typically appeared like spring bulbs, clustered at first in one area, then radiating outward.

There were two victims of the illness this time, Jack Trune and his eldest son, Richard. They, too, had had the complaints for two days. She learned from Elizabeth Trune that the two men had been to market on Friday in the village of Elford.

"Did they see Rob atte Gate there, do you know?" Cynthia asked, cradling Richard's head to give him egg broth.

"Aye," Jack croaked from where he lay.

"Does Rob have the sickness?" Elizabeth asked.

"Aye."

Cynthia explained about the egg broth. Elizabeth seemed only too eager to have an excuse to forgo the restrictions of Lent. Cynthia smiled to herself. If this continued, every household in the village would be sneaking out to fetch eggs and concealing it from their neighbors.

It was early afternoon when Cynthia mounted up again for the trek home. She looked forward to a nap in the solar. It was a consequence of her gift that healing others drained her own energies.

As her horse plodded along the curving lane, a young man called out from behind her, despair cracking his voice.

"Please, my lady, if you will!"

She looked around. Here was a face she didn't recognize, a face darkly handsome, but twisted in pain. He made no effort to hide the tears streaking down his cheeks.

"They say you can heal the sick!" he cried, loping toward her.

Wasting no time, she turned her mount. "Take me there."

His shoulders dropped in relief. He beckoned her to follow.

"She's my wife," he said brokenly. "We'd just come to the village from Elford to make our home here."

"Elford?" An uneasy prickling started at the base of Cynthia's spine.

"Aye, 'tis on the other side of—"

"What are her complaints?"

The man ran a shaky hand through his grimy hair, as if the memory were almost too much to bear. "Her stomach pains her. At first, she screamed with the pain, then later . . . when she could keep no food inside . . . she only moaned. She grew fevered, trembling most horribly . . ." He began to weep anew. "She's seen visions . . . terrible visions . . . demons and . . . and . . ."

Cynthia swung down from her horse and hastened inside the cottage.

The girl on the pallet raved, thrashing about, and kicked off her coverlet. Cynthia pushed her sleeves up to her elbows and looked sternly at the young man.

"How long has she been ill?"

"Since we came," he sobbed, gazing helplessly at his bride. "Four days. Ah, God, what is to become of her? What will—"

"Listen to me," Cynthia told him stoutly, bringing his head around with a firm hand. "Are you going to mewl like a babe all day, or are you going to help your wife?"

Taken aback by her words, he slowly recovered his dignity, wiped his nose across his sleeve, and nodded. "I'll help you."

"Hold her, then."

For hours, Cynthia worked with the sick young woman, laying hands on her thrashing head, applying poultices, sponging her hot skin, slipping sips of boiled water between her lips.

At last, the worst of it passed.

Cynthia was weary to the bone. But the girl would live. And the lad had kept his word, staying by his wife's side the entire time. As Cynthia rose on wobbling legs to leave, he threw himself gratefully on his knees before her, blessing her and pressing a small silver coin into her palm. She wouldn't take it, of course. To put a price on her gift was to curse it.

In time, the sun finished its watch, and the sky blushed crimson. Cynthia was exhausted. Her eyes felt as sandy as oysters. She'd slept little last night, and she hadn't eaten all day, not wishing to partake of the peasants' meager stores. So with trembling arms she pulled herself up atop her mount and lit out for home.

Arriving at Wendeville long past supper, she let Elspeth bring her meal to the solar—pickled herring, a crust of pandemayne, a cup of ale, almond cream. All the while, Elspeth fussed over her like a cat washing its kitten. But Cynthia was too tired to eat much. The moon had not yet risen when she collapsed on her pallet in a heap of stained and crumpled velvet.

Restful slumber eluded Cynthia. Visions of moaning, retching peasants filled her dreams, row upon row of them, like plants in a ghastly garden, a vast field of stinking, sweaty bodies stretching into the distance as far as her eye could see. They gasped for breath and groaned her name, and no matter how much lady's mantle she sprinkled upon them, there wasn't enough. They were going to die if she didn't help them. Their need suffocated her. But there was nothing she could do . . . nothing. . . .

She awoke with a jolt. Her heart pummeled her ribs, and she drew in a ragged breath. She sat up, rubbing her eyes, then looked down with distaste at her rumpled gown. She'd hardly had a decent night's sleep, but a strange sense of urgency beckoned her to the village.

Dressing quickly in a gray kirtle, she scrubbed her face and tucked her hair beneath a white veil. As the sun rose, she left Wendeville with her guard, her satchel bulging with herbs, and nibbled on the sticky honey bun Elspeth had pressed into her hand to serve as breakfast.

She sensed bad tidings long before she arrived. Sickness permeated the village. She could feel it on her skin, in her soul. The pall hanging in the air was as palpable as a smothering cloak as Cynthia rode, shivering, into the noxious haze.

The village was silent except for the random cackling of

hens or the occasional bark of a dog. Wraiths of smoke escaped through the roofs of the cottages. But the sounds of the village—children playing, men hammering, mothers scolding—the sounds of life, were conspicuously absent.

Recalling her nightmare, Cynthia shuddered and wondered which household to visit first. As her horse indecisively tamped the dirt with its hooves, the shutters of a nearby hovel sprang open.

"My lady! Are ye here to heal?" cried out the pale young Scotswoman who lived inside.

"Caitlin. Aye," she said, dismounting and clasping the woman's hand. "Have you the sickness?"

"'Tis my sister. She canna eat. She canna sleep."

Cynthia went inside and laid hands on Caitlin's sister. Fortunately, the illness hadn't progressed far.

"She'll live," Cynthia told her. But she wouldn't reveal what she'd felt when she'd brushed the back of Caitlin's own hand. The sallow lass's spirit was so frail, she'd not survive the sickness if it took hold in her.

The first death came at midday. It was Edward Simon. His widow's wailing could be heard all along the lane. The fool had been ill for days, but was too proud to ask for help, preferring to die in a nest of his own filth.

Such men's misplaced dignity enraged Cynthia when its price was so high. She did what she could to comfort the woman and made her promise to seek out aid should the sickness come upon her.

After that, it was as if a reaper came through the village harvesting souls. The town leatherworker was cut down, followed shortly by his wife. Within an hour, Robert the weaver succumbed.

As the nauseating stench of sickness washed over Cynthia, her horrid dream came back to her. Never had she seen a disease claim so many so quickly. Doubt pressed in all around her, and suddenly her satchel full of herbs seemed powerless against the encroaching foe, like a child's wooden sword against a charging boar.

A tiny part of her wanted to run away, to flee all the way back to Wendeville and drop the portcullis against the grasping, needy souls. She wouldn't do it, of course. She'd never turned away from the ailing, be it man, beast, or bloom. God had given her a gift. It was both her responsibility and her honor to use it.

Her first task was to get the bodies blessed and buried before their sickness could spread. She straightened and spoke to a hale young lad who stood nearby.

"Elias, do you know the way to Charing? It's not far."

The boy nodded.

"Go there, please, and fetch the Abbot to bless the bodies."

She would have just as soon never laid eyes on the Abbot again, and it pained her to have to ask this favor of him, but she couldn't let the villagers die unshriven. She thought of sending to Wendeville for Garth, but Charing was the closest keep to the village. Elias hurried to do her bidding.

"There is naught I can do for the dead," she murmured to those who stood with her. "Take me to the living."

An hour later, Cynthia had finished with a third household. But there appeared to be more than a dozen still requiring her healing, despite the efforts of helpful neighbors who offered their aid. She heaved a shaky sigh. What if she depleted all her medicines? What if her strength dwindled to naught? She brushed back a loose lock of hair with a trembling hand. Her dream was becoming frighteningly real.

The sun had only opened half an eye over the horizon, as if deciding whether or not to rise at such an unholy hour, when Garth made his way from his quarters to the great hall. On the way, he practiced his speech, whispering the phrases with a sweep of his arm here, a fatherly frown there, determining which delivery was the most effective.

He was prepared now to finish his sermon for Cynthia, the Sabbath sermon she'd missed when she was called from the chapel. His Bible was tucked under his elbow, specific passages marked with pieces of frayed ribbon.

All God's creatures, he would tell her, had their proper places. The lion did not lie down with the lamb in this world. Neither, he'd say with an apologetic smile, should priests fraternize with noblewomen.

Steeling himself for this most important discourse, he stepped forward into the great hall. Maidservants scurried past, bearing fragrant platters of fresh bread and flasks of watered wine, breakfast for the castle denizens. A gangly boy tended the snapping fire in the midst of the hall. Hounds slumbered in one corner. A knight polished his sword in another. In front of the buttery screens, Elspeth wagged a finger at Roger the steward, who thrust his chin out stubbornly against whatever she scolded him for.

But Cynthia was nowhere in sight.

Elspeth interrupted her tirade long enough to address him. "Mornin', Father Garth. If it's Lady Cynthia ye're after, she's gone to the village."

"Again?"

"Aye, I fear so." The old maid shook her head. "'Tis a stubborn malady, this is. My lady has a sense o' these things, and this morn, when she set out . . ." Elspeth's face pinched into a worried frown. "She didn't look well, not at all."

Something in the woman's words rattled him.

"Is she in danger?" He squared his shoulders. "Is there aught I can do?"

She studied him for a moment, as if judging his worth, then waggled a finger in the air. "She might require a priest at that. If 'tis as bad as she thinks, ye may be blessin' the dead by day's end."

He nodded, then glanced ruefully down at his carefully marked Bible. He'd have to defer his sermon again. But at least he'd be of some use today, dispensing last rites and comforting those who needed the word of God.

They were tasks for which he was well suited. In some ways, he envied the dead. They had reached the pinnacle of insensate repose, uncluttered by emotion, that he strived for every day of his life. As for the living, it was satisfying to describe with assurance the peace that waited beyond death's portal, the tranquil delights that were heaven. It served to remind him that he, too, might one day be freed of the internal chaos that constituted his existence on earth.

Thus, the tool of his trade in hand and Roger's directions committed to memory, Garth set out along the east road toward the village.

"And I'm ashamed to say, lass, I succumbed to the drink ere I could put a twinkle in her eye."

Cynthia sat speechless. For some time now, she'd knelt by the old man's bedside, listening to the most preposterous confession she'd ever heard. It was that of Henry Webster, the oldest man in the village. He'd raved on and on, which was amazing for a man as sick and aged as he was, about all the sins he'd committed.

At first, she listened attentively. Poor old Henry hadn't long to live. Since the Abbot might not arrive in time, Henry said he chose to make confession to an angel. And Cynthia apparently qualified. Somehow, she managed to keep a straight face as he recounted in great detail his dubious sins, among them the ugly women he regretted courting and the years he'd wasted drinking when he could have been wenching.

It was only when she ventured a glance at his withered old face that she saw the mischief bright in his rheumy eyes.

"I can see ye doubt me, lass," he wheezed. "But I tell ye, never was a lady left me without a smile on her face."

She grinned.

"Aye, like that," he said, nodding.

"I'm thinking you're enjoying this confession a little too well," she accused.

"Did I tell ye about the time I stole a real Infidel? She was a slave girl from Araby. Full ripe she was, golden as the sun, and sweet. But 'twas thievery, just the same. The Bible says, 'Thou shalt not thieve.' " He cocked his head and screwed up his face. "Nay, maybe 'twas not thievery after all. As I remember, the wicked wench cut my purse ere I sent her on her way."

Cynthia shook her head.

"What about ye, lass? Where is your husband?"

She stifled a chuckle. Old Henry Webster looked as if

he'd be glad to bed her on the spot if only his body would allow it.

"You remember, Henry," she said. "I'm widowed."

Slowly, the lust drained from the old man's eyes, and his gaze slipped absently around the room, as if he'd wandered off to another world. A long moment later, as she was about to count him lost, he looked up at her steadily, mildly curious.

"Were ye with yer man when he died?"

"Aye," she said, swallowing hard. "He died in my arms."

Henry turned his head away so Cynthia wouldn't see the tears collecting. "'Tis a sweet way to go."

Cynthia reached out and took his hand in hers. "I'll stay with you."

She could see the old man's mouth working before he clamped it shut. He squeezed her hand gratefully with what little strength a dying man had left.

"I suppose I should be shriven properly," he sniffed. "My Margaret will be waitin' up there in heaven for me somewhere, good wife that she is, savin' me a spot."

"I've sent for the Abbot."

"Truth to tell," Henry admitted, his speech beginning to thicken, "I'm not lookin' forward to heaven."

"And why is that, Henry?" She patted his hand.

He slowly licked his lips. "There's no ale there and no harlots."

Her shoulders shook in silent mirth as a ray of sunlight arced across the pallet from the cottage's open door. Behind her, someone quietly entered, probably one of Henry's friends, but she kept her focus on the old man.

Suddenly, comforting fingers wrapped about her shoulders, and she could feel the warmth of the visitor close behind her.

"Do not weep, good woman," a voice whispered, ruffling the linen of her wimple. "Soon his soul will be at peace in heaven."

"Peace?" she said, giving Henry a conspiratorial wink. "According to Henry, he plans to wreak havoc in heaven, a-wenching all the day."

Old Henry's eyes twinkled in answer.

The hands on her shoulders hardened, then abruptly slid down her arms to wheel her about like an errant warhorse.

She gasped in surprise. He stood before her, so close she could see the gray flecks in his confused eyes, so close she could feel his outraged breath upon her cheek.

"Garth!"

12

HE LOOKED AS ASTONISHED AS SHE. "YOU." HE snatched back his hands as if she were a burning brand.

"What are you doing here?" she asked, her cheeks aglow with chagrin. Lord, what must he think of her? *A-wenching in heaven,* indeed.

He looked anxiously past her toward the old man.

She rubbed the back of her neck self-consciously. "You've . . . you've come in time to give Henry the last rites. I've already heard his confession. If you'd like, I can repeat the heart of it for . . ."

Henry dissolved into a fit of wheezing. Garth made the sign of the cross, stepping around her to the bedside, and began the benediction without delay.

Cynthia took Henry's hand again and let the Latin syllables fall on her ears like quiet bells. She couldn't help but wonder how many times Garth would repeat the blessing today for souls who'd meet less timely deaths.

"Don't forget to tell him about seducing the virgins, my lady," Henry croaked.

Garth nearly strangled on his words. "What?"

The old man's body was racked by coughing.

"He wants me to give you his confession," she explained,

trying her best to look solemn. "He seduced three virgins in a fortnight, two of them—"

"That will not be necessary! Sir, all your sins are forgiven." He genuflected. "Whatever they may be."

Cynthia bit back a smile. It was terribly endearing the way Garth's nostrils flared when he was upset.

The last rites were finished without further incident as Cynthia clasped the old man's hand, feeling his life force diminish. Upon the final "Amen," Henry's spirit left him. The hand in hers fell cool and silent.

"Farewell, old friend," she whispered, brushing a rogue tear from her eye.

It was senseless to cry, she knew. After all, Henry had lived far beyond most men's lifetimes. And, according to his confession, he'd not wanted for pleasure. Still, it wasn't easy for her, sharing the slow drain of life from a man as his spirit departed.

Watching Cynthia, Garth felt such a welling up of empathy for her that he could scarcely keep himself from enfolding her in his arms to protect her from death's shadow. She still clasped the poor man's hand. Her head was bent in sorrow, and he saw her wipe at a tear. But she'd remained by the old villager, comforting him, amusing him, giving him courage to face his own death.

"There are others," she said quietly as she finally crossed Henry's hands atop his chest and blew out the candle near his head.

"Show me," he murmured.

He followed her down the dusty lane, nodding now and then at onlookers curious about the strange priest in their village.

Cynthia spoke under her breath. "It would perhaps be best to make the blessings brief, for the hour grows late, and—"

"I'll stay all night if need be," he told her, mildly offended that she'd think otherwise, "to see that their souls are properly shriven."

"I believe you would, Garth," she said with a fleeting smile. "It's only that there are those yet living who may need your aid more."

He stopped in his tracks and looked her square in her azure eyes. Something there made him shiver. "Just how many are afflicted?"

Fear flickered over her features, then vanished, so swiftly he might have imagined it. "I haven't counted."

She led him to a cottage at the outskirts of the village, in the midst of a field. The villagers followed them, murmuring amongst themselves, keeping a respectful distance.

Garth winced when the door swung open under his arm and the nauseating stench hit him full force. He knew the smell at once. Death. The bile rose in his throat, but he choked it down. A de Ware never cowered from death.

Covering his nose and mouth with his woolen sleeve, he shouldered his way into the hovel. He scooped up the first body he found, bringing his burden outside to rest upon a soft patch of clover. Four times more he braved the interior of the cottage till the entire family lay nestled along the wattle fence of their demesne.

He began with the little girl he'd brought out last. Kneeling in the dirt, he cradled the tiny, limp body across his lap, taking care to cover her legs with her thin chemise, brushing her hair back from her face. It was a horrible task, looking upon the awful handiwork God sometimes wrought upon his innocents, a task Garth only endured because he believed it would help their poor lost souls find peace.

Cynthia's throat constricted. There was a sharp stinging in her nose that always preceded a sob. And she wasn't the only one afflicted. The villagers stood silent in awe. Garth's tenderness as he crooned a blessing to the child, soft as a lullaby, caught at her heart, sending a trickle of tears down her cheek.

"My lady!" someone hissed suddenly behind her.

She turned. It was Nan atte Gate. The poor woman's face was contorted with misery.

"'Tis Tim, my lady! My little one has it now!"

"Ah, nay." Cynthia's heart sank. Leaving Garth to his duties, she followed Nan, lugging the satchel of medicines that grew perilously light.

Inside the cottage, Tim peered up at her with sunken, heavy-lidded eyes. His face was pale and slack. He looked as if he might blow away with the breeze. She brushed her hands together.

"'Tis because of the eggs," he murmured.

She frowned. "The eggs?"

Tim nodded gravely, wincing as his stomach cramped. "Not allowed . . . at Lent. God is . . . punishin' me."

She swallowed back tears. "God wouldn't punish you like this, Tim. You're one of his favorite children."

He shook his head. "The Abbot says I'm a sinner."

"The Abbot?" She clenched her jaw against a reply she might later regret, then laid her hands gently upon the boy's forehead. "Never mind the Abbot, Tim. God knows you're a good lad."

Her palms tingled with his youthful energy, weak but still flickering. When she closed her eyes, a clear image of peppermint came to her. After a moment, she withdrew her hands and reached into her satchel for a packet of the leaves.

"Make a weak brew for him with these," she told Nan, "and sweeten it with honey if you have it. I'll come back at day's end to see how he fares." Then she brushed the lad's hair back from his eyes. "God understands, Tim. He wants you to get better. He'll forgive you for the eggs."

Tim only stared at her, and for a brief, eery moment, her own conviction was shaken. *Would* she be forgiven? It was true, she'd counseled many to break the strictures of Lent. But surely that counsel was divinely inspired. After all, her power came from God, did it not? Surely it was holy inspiration that moved her to give the villagers the egg broth.

But then, perhaps more than the egg broth ate away at her faith. There was also the matter of Father Garth.

Despite her blind certainty that she simply steered Garth toward a more harmonious path, one that suited his own passionate nature, in a small corner of her heart, she feared she contrived to steal him from the church for her own selfish satisfaction. And that, she was sure, God would never sanction.

The Abbot steepled his long fingers together and smiled grimly from the solar as he watched the peasant boy take his leave past the sagging gates of Charing.

A murrain in the village. Lady Cynthia dispensing her devil's cures. And people dying. This was good news indeed. That and the list of herbs Mary had brought him were enough to condemn the lady on the spot.

But, he considered, scraping his nail over the worn stone of the window embrasure, patience had its merits. Better not to appear too eager. There was plenty of time to settle the noose about Lady Cynthia's pale and trembling neck. Besides, sickness was such an ugly business. He'd had more than his share of it with that wretched woman's late husband. Nay, he'd wait in the dubious comfort of his crumbling keep until the time ripened.

He turned from the window and went to his desk, picking up a sharpened quill. He dipped it in ink as thick as blood, and meticulously scrawled a damning *X* upon the parchment Mary had brought him, next to the word *belladonna*. Such a pretty word for such a deadly plant, a devil's herb. There would be others, many others, that would bear the fatal *X* next to their names. But the Abbot preferred to do his work slowly and methodically, savoring each blow of the executioner's ax.

By the time Garth visited the fifth house to perform last rites, the inevitable cup of yellowish broth by the bedside had begun to look very suspicious. Finally, he asked about it.

The dead man's wife paled and wrung her hands.

"Please forgive him!" she cried. "I know 'tis Lent, but she said it might help! And it did, in sooth, for a time!"

"What? What might help?"

"The eggs!" The lady clapped a hand to her mouth, realizing she'd revealed more than she'd wanted to.

"Eggs?"

"Please forgive him," she repeated. "He was a good man. And she said he'd be forgiven."

Garth was confused. He took the woman by the shoulders. "Who said he'd be forgiven?"

The woman's face crumbled. "You mean he won't? Oh, please, Father, Father, please . . ." She began to wail.

"He will be forgiven all his sins," Garth told her, waiting for her to calm. "Now, who told you to feed him eggs?"

"Lady Cynthia, of course. She's taken care of him all along. She's a great healer, she is, and a good lady, but 'tis a grave sickness, this, and she could do naught to save my . . ."

The woman fell to sobbing again, and Garth absently patted her hand.

Jesu—was Lady Cynthia instructing the villagers to disobey the dictates of Lent? What sheer arrogance! The little fool may have unwittingly brought God's wrath down upon the villagers herself.

He extricated himself from the weeping woman's clutches. He had to absolve the dead man's soul now before she dissolved into hysterics. Setting her aside, he hastily recited the last rites.

Then, his cassock flapping with authority, he set out to determine just what was at the heart of Lady Cynthia's blasphemy.

He found her in a nearby hovel. The west-facing shutters had been thrown wide, but the sinking sun could only afford so much light. Still, when he charged in, he could make out the figure of Cynthia crouching at the foot of a straw pallet, her sleeves stained and her discarded wimple crumpled in the corner.

"What healing do you practice, lady," he demanded without preface, "that you take the Lord's commandments into your own hands?"

The other three women in the room quailed at his voice, but Cynthia didn't spare him a glance. She only barked at him to close the door.

He resisted the urge to slam it, astounded by her impertinence.

"Now," she hoarsely urged her patient.

"I . . . cannot . . . ," the woman whimpered from the pallet. "Let me . . . die."

"Nay! You've got to use every bit of your strength," Cynthia told her. "Your babe may yet live. We must save it if we can."

Garth felt the blood drain from his face. He'd burst into the cottage, burning with righteous indignation. He'd never noticed the drama unfolding in the long shadows. Now he saw what transpired. A wan peasant woman shivered on the pallet, her head lolling across a filthy pillow. Lady Cynthia worked feverishly between the woman's legs, her own face dripping with sweat, her eyes fierce, her hair hanging in damp strings about her shoulders.

Garth averted his eyes and took a mortified step back.

When he found his voice, he croaked, "What in the name of God are you doing?"

"Push!" Cynthia commanded. "I can see the babe's head."

The woman on the pallet let out a high, thin whine.

"You must cease!" Garth ordered, a sheen of sweat rising on his lip at the tortured whimper. "Can you not see how she suffers?"

One of the peasant women spoke meekly. "'Tis always the way of childbirth, Father."

"That's it. That's it," Cynthia chanted to the laboring woman as Garth glimpsed a round head crowning between bloody thighs.

The woman screamed as if she'd been knifed in the abdomen. Garth clenched his hands at the horrible sound. He would have bolted forward to give her succor had not the attending peasant women looked upon him with pure horror at his very presence here.

"Again," Cynthia urged.

"Sweet Mary, lady, let her be!" he demanded. Dear God— he knew he was about as welcome as a wolf in a lady's solar here, but it was too late to leave. He had to do something, anything, to end the suffering. "You're killing her!"

"Aye, the mother is dying," Cynthia muttered. "But the babe will survive."

"You cannot know that," he argued. "It's in God's hands."

"I do know that," she insisted, leaning forward to wrap her fingers about the baby's tiny head. "Push once more."

"Would you challenge the will of God?" he asked incredulously.

She never gave him answer, for at that moment, to his utter amazement, the child emerged, slithering out into Cynthia's hands, its reddening face screwed up with fury, its tiny fists trembling in futile rage. It let out a terrific bawl.

The women seemed neither surprised nor troubled. They immediately fell into a pattern of attending to the babe's needs, a task as familiar to their hands as that of reaping winter wheat.

But Garth could only blink in wonder at the infant. Cynthia had snatched a morsel of life from the very jaws of death. Even now, the poor mother rattled out her final breath.

Cynthia bent to close the woman's now sightless eyes with blood-spattered hands. She drew a thin sheet over the woman's face, crossed herself, and rose from the bedside.

He'd witnessed a miracle. He knew that now. And whether it came from God or some strange force of nature, Cynthia had been the instrument of that miracle.

For a long moment, her eyes locked with his. They were dark with pain, weary with fatigue, deep with mystery. And as beautiful as truth. Cynthia was truly astounding, he realized. She was courageous, compassionate, persevering . . .

And she was fainting. As he gazed on, her eyelids fluttered, and she pitched forward. His heart leaped into his throat. She collapsed almost before he could catch her.

She was no light thing, but he was strong enough to carry her into the fresh air. His pulse beating wildly, he shouldered his way past the peasant women and through the door. As he emerged, the two men of Cynthia's guard greeted him with sharp glares. One of them drew his sword.

"What have you done?" the man barked.

"Is she dead?" the other hissed.

"Nay!" Garth denied loudly, adamantly. "Nay. She lives."

Jesu—he prayed it was so. Her neck arched limply over his arm, but he could see her heart's thrumming in her throat. Breath whistled softly between her rosy lips. And surely none of the blood smudging her arms and skirts was hers.

Still he trembled with inexplicable panic. He couldn't let anything happen to Lady Cynthia. Not after what he'd seen in the cottage. Not after the way she'd pulled a new life, kicking and squalling, against all odds, into the world.

As the guards hovered at a safe distance, he knelt in the spring weeds and laid her gently on the ground. How natural she looked there, her coppery hair spilled across the dark green clover, the fingers of one hand threaded through the stems. But she was not yet ready to be laid in earth. Not if he could help it.

He lifted her head to rest upon his knee and fanned her with the hem of his cassock.

"Come, Cynthia," he urged. "Awaken."

Her lips were pale, and her breath barely stirred the tendrils of hair framing her face.

He closed his eyes and bent his head in murmured prayer. "Please, God, help her. In your infinite mercy, I pray you . . ."

Still she lay silent. He clasped her hand and brought it to his chest.

"Cynthia," he whispered, abandoning prayer and letting memories of her flow freely. "Remember the roses? How you stole cuttings from them? Remember the jasmine? And the bees?" Something warm bloomed inside him as he spoke the words, long-forgotten sensations, hopes and dreams, like a dormant bulb awakening after a long winter. "I think you'd never been stung by a bee before," he began to recall. "And yet you were so brave, laying your neck bare to my blade so I could . . ."

She stirred then, moaning softly, wrinkling her forehead. "So . . . many. So many . . ."

Giddy with relief, he squeezed her hand. "But I took care of them, didn't I?"

Her eyes opened to stare up at him. It was as if she tried to penetrate his very thoughts. "You . . . took care of them?"

"Aye," he replied, though he suspected it wasn't bees she spoke of in her confusion.

"Tim," she mumbled, making a feeble attempt to sit up. "I must take care of little Tim. He needs me."

"Nay," he said. "You're as weak as a kitten yourself. I'll see to him."

"Nay!" She clutched at the front of his cassock, dragging herself up.

He was astonished by her determination. "Then I'll at least go with you. Stay with your guard while I bless the dead woman's body. Then we'll both take care of Tim."

Happily, the guards seemed to agree with that suggestion. Garth delivered last rites to the poor mother and blessed the new babe, who gurgled quietly now in the arms of one of the peasant women. Then he quickly joined Cynthia.

Little Tim seemed as insubstantial as shadow. The small boy's translucent flesh hung on him like linen over bones, and his eyes loomed huge in his pale face. They grew even wider when Garth neared his pallet.

"Are ye come," the lad gulped, "to punish me?"

Garth was too disconcerted by the remark to answer.

"Nay, Tim," Cynthia assured the boy, pushing past him to the bed. "He's here to bless you."

"Am I goin' to die?" he asked Garth.

Garth's chest felt as if he'd been kicked. What kind of question was that for a wee lad to ask?

"Nay, of course not," Cynthia scolded. She began rubbing her hands together vigorously. "You feel better already, do you not?"

"Aye. My belly's quiet." His eyes lost their flatness for an instant. "The tea was good. Better than that egg. . . ." He broke off and glanced anxiously at Garth.

"Aye, peppermint water is tasty."

Cynthia leaned forward and placed her hands upon the boy's head, blocking Tim's view. But not his loudly whispered comments.

"My lady, I like this priest better than the Abbot. Is that a sin?"

"Nay, Tim." Garth could hear the amusement in her voice.

"I know ye said God would forgive me for the eggs," he whispered. "But I don't think the Abbot will."

"But they've given you strength," Cynthia assured him.

"I don't think the Abbot will forgive me," he insisted.

At the boy's innocent words, a slow fire began to burn inside Garth. Aye, the lad had drunk egg broth at Lent. Broken shells were yet strewn by the empty cup beside his pallet. But if what Cynthia said was true—if the broth had served to strengthen the poor waif—was it a sin?

"Tim, the Abbot . . . ," Cynthia began awkwardly, shaking her hands as if she shook off water.

"Will forgive you," Garth finished with conviction, moving beside her to touch the boy's forehead. "As God does. You see, God doesn't have enough lads like you in His church. He needs all the faithful little boys He can get." The shimmer of hope in the boy's glassy eyes almost stopped the words in his throat. "Tim, God wants you to get well."

Tim solemnly searched his face. "Then I shall," he said.

Behind him, the door creaked open.

"Lady Cynthia."

"Elias," she said.

The boy had returned from Charing. He was breathless, and his face was rosy, as if he'd run all the way.

"The Abbot . . . could not come, my lady."

Cynthia winced almost imperceptibly, then gave him a calm nod. "All right, Elias." She pulled forth a vial from her satchel. "Nan, give him this. He should be better on the morrow," she murmured to the boy's mother.

Then she began rummaging in her satchel with the pent-up fury of a storm about to break. "Could not come?" she muttered to herself. "Or *would* not?"

Garth frowned at Elias. "Did the Abbot say why he could not come?"

"Aye, my lord, er . . . Father. He said he was indis— indis—"

"Indisposed!" Cynthia snapped.

"Is the Abbot ill?" Garth asked the boy.

"Not yet," Cynthia replied, pulling the strings on her satchel tight. "And it's plain he'd like to keep it that way." With a taut smile, she bade the household farewell, promising to visit on the morrow.

Outside the hovel, preparing to leave, she gave vent to her true feelings toward the Abbot.

"Indisposed!" she said, grabbing the reins of her palfrey. "He has no time to see to the souls of the dead?" She flung her satchel over the horse's crupper. The bottles within clattered together, almost hard enough to break. "Do you know the real reason he doesn't come?" she asked venomously as Garth steadied the stirrup for her. "He wishes to avoid the murrain in the village. The selfish bastard doesn't want to risk contracting the disease himself."

Halfway up to the saddle, her limbs gave out, and she slid back down against him with a small murmur of apology.

Garth frowned. The poor lass was as helpless as an infant.

Even if she managed to mount, she'd never stay astride. She needed his support.

He eyed her horse. He hadn't mounted a beast in four years, but he'd ridden every day as a boy. It wasn't something one forgot. Sweeping his cassock behind him, he threw his leg over the saddle. The familiar feel of leather beneath his thighs brought on a rush of pleasant boyhood memories.

He hauled Cynthia up before him, and ere he even gathered the reins and nudged the horse forward, she was drifting to sleep upon his chest. A warm, fierce wave of protectiveness enveloped him as she nestled closer, mingled with more carnal feelings that troubled his mind and body, feelings for which he prayed God would forgive him.

The trio of horses rode through the strange, quiet country between dusk and twilight, in shifting shadows of purple and gold. Overhead, the stars blinked on, one by one, like shy children come out to play. The air grew chill. Garth wrapped the folds of his cassock more tightly around Cynthia, who, to his chagrin, snuggled against him as if she belonged there. The road was silent but for the squeak of leather tack, the soft rattle of the knights' chain mail, and the pervasive chirps of wakening crickets.

But a battle raged within Garth, a battle fraught with passion and self-doubt and peril. Four years of faith had been shaken today, jarred by the woman slumbering obliviously in his arms.

It was dangerous, the way Cynthia spoke out against the Abbot, countermanding the orders of the church, mandating which souls would live and which would die. Heretics had been burned for less.

He'd seen her work, watched her summon up curious energy between her hands, calling upon some mysterious force to render healing, swooning with the power of whatever demon or angel she invoked.

And yet, she'd done it all with good conscience, in good faith. It was clear she worked only for the benefit of the people. She'd worked herself half to death today.

He reached one quaking hand up to brush the curls from her cheek, and a sharp dagger of guilt jabbed at him. It wasn't only Cynthia's command over healing forces that troubled him.

For several miles, he'd tried to convince himself that what he felt for Lady Cynthia was solely protectiveness, a fatherly care for her welfare, a priest's concern for her soul.

But he knew he deluded himself. Even now, the evidence of his undeniable male craving pressed firm against her. And now he had reason to suspect that his enchantment with her was but another aspect of her formidable will, that perhaps she had bewitched him.

Thank God she was asleep. Even through his cassock, every inch of skin that bore the weight of her contact burned like heavenly fire. Her fragrance wafted up to him, fresh as meadowsweet, pure as rain. Her head rested alongside his breast, and her breath moistened the wool of his cassock and—dear God—where the robe had slipped loose from its tie, warmed the flesh over his heart.

It was a sin, he knew, to feel such desire. And yet there was naught he could do about it. Cynthia Wendeville tempted his thirsty eyes, his empty arms, his starved loins. And worst of all, she threatened his lonely soul.

13

SLEEP WAS THE LAST THING ON GARTH'S MIND AFTER they returned and he lay on his pallet, gazing up at the stars. Outside, the crickets' songs slowed as the air grew chill. From the distant wood, a nightingale's call rose.

Somewhere, in another part of the castle, Lady Cynthia slumbered. He could imagine the coppery sprawl of her hair across her pillow, the soft brush of her lashes upon her cheek, the deep rise and fall of her breast as she breathed. The moonlight would bathe her in a lullaby of silver. And she'd sleep like a child, deeply, dreamlessly, after the arduous day she'd endured.

While he lay awake, haunted by doubt, enthralled by desire.

Cynthia Wendeville was an enigma. Walking amongst those with the dread disease like a saint among sinners, she toiled with her hands and her heart and every last ounce of strength. She was an angel of mercy come to sully her hands on their ills, and she worked with no complaint, no expectation of reward, even when, by the end of the day, the villagers had drained her completely, like innocent but greedy babes suckling at her breast.

And yet, that strange ritual . . .

Was she God's instrument? Or the devil's?

His loins would have him believe the latter. Not in all his youth had lust struck him such a powerful blow. Aye, Cynthia Wendeville had bewitched him. There was no doubt in his mind. Nor in his body.

He sat up, wrenching the feather bolster from beneath his head and hurling it toward the foot of the bed. He'd find no rest tonight. Plowing a hand through his hair, he trudged to the window. The moonlight illuminated the trees in ghostly shades of white and gray and spilled like milk over the stone sill. From the wood shone a pair of glowing orbs, the slow blinking eyes of an owl on the hunt.

Then his eyes caught movement along the inner wall of the castle. He frowned, dropping back out of sight to watch.

A slight cloaked figure slipped through the shadows, a cloth sack over one shoulder, the face concealed by a hood. A young lad. Nay, a woman. Probably, he thought irritably, curling his lip, en route to some tryst or another.

In sooth, the thought didn't irritate him so much as it intrigued him. But the fact that it intrigued him made him even more irritable. While he was sorting out the convoluted knot of that logic, the figure chanced to step momentarily into a patch of light.

Every muscle in Garth's body tensed.

Clutched in the figure's distinctly feminine hand, flashing in the moonlight, was something long and sharp and silver.

Climbing out through the window was the first impulsive thing he'd done in years. Stealing across the sward in bare feet was the second. Neither choice was prudent. He snagged his cassock on the stone sill, giving anyone who happened to be watching a clear view of his naked hindquarters as he slid to the ground. And his unshod feet slipped on the cold wet grass. But he dared not lose sight of the girl.

He shadowed her, ducking into the dark twice when she turned warily at the owl's call, until she stopped in the midst of the courtyard, before the herb garden. He glanced quickly about. No one else seemed to be in the vicinity. No victims awaiting her blade.

Only when she sank into a squat before a bush of nightshade did he discern that the sharp silver implement she carried was no instrument of murder. It was a spade.

He sank back against the courtyard wall, feeling like a fool. He could see now it was Mary, Cynthia's maidservant. No doubt she'd been sent to gather herbs. It was common enough for women to plant and harvest at all hours of the night. He remembered, as a boy, his own mother sowing seed at midnight by the light of the full moon. She said it ensured a wealthier harvest.

Still, watching Mary uproot, with almost brutal force and speed, the nightshade, the hellebore, and the wormwood in turn, he had to doubt her motives. Her stealth, her wariness seemed misplaced. No one operating on the directive of the household would fear discovery.

Nay, he suspected she acted on her own. When she moved on to the monkshood, stabbing almost frantically at the ground to loose it from the soil, he crept forward to confront her.

"Mary," he whispered, trying not to startle her.

Thankfully, she didn't scream. She did gasp, however, and her eyes grew as wide as hen's eggs. Dropping the spade, she scrabbled backward in the dirt, kicking up a little furrow before her.

"What are you doing?" he demanded in a low voice.

"N-n-nothin'," she stammered.

He cocked a brow at her. "It is an offense against God to lie to a priest."

She bit her lip. Fearful tears shimmered in her eyes.

"'Tis . . . 'tis G-God's work . . . I do," she said.

"God's work?" He scowled at the uprooted plants, lying like once noble knights felled in battle. "How can this destruction be God's—"

"The plants are evil!" she hissed, gathering her knees to her chest as if they'd shield her from harm. "They're the devil's herbs! The Abbot says so! He says my mistress—" She must have realized she'd said too much. She clapped a hand over her mouth.

"What does he say about your mistress?"

"I—I . . . cannot say." Her chin quivered. "But I know my lady m-means no harm. 'Tis the plants are wicked."

He sighed. Nightshade. Hellebore. Wormwood. Monks-hood. They *were* the devil's herbs. A proper, God-fearing lady never grew such plants in her garden. They were the harvest of pagans and peasants who knew no better. Still, he didn't think Cynthia would be pleased when she discovered that her maidservant had saved her soul by gouging up half her herb garden.

He ran a weary hand over his face. If, as Mary intimated, the Abbot spoke ill of Lady Cynthia, the presence of devil's herbs in her garden would only bode her worse ill. Mayhap Mary was right.

"Give them to me," he said. "I'll dispose of them."

"Ah, bless ye, Father! Bless ye!" Mary gushed. She scrambled to her knees before him and actually lowered her lips to the hem of his robe. The gesture embarrassed him. No mortal man deserved such adulation.

He just hoped to God she didn't notice his bare feet.

"Go back to your bed, Mary," he told her, nudging her under the elbow. "And speak no more of devil's herbs."

After she scurried off, he stuffed the plants into the cloth bag and evened what soil remained as best he could. But the indentations in the earth and the gaps between the remaining bushes were as obvious as gaping holes in brown hose. And he was sure that as he trudged back to his quarters, he left a trail of damning silt along the way.

Morning brought his crime to light.

"You did what?"

"I . . ." Garth cleared his throat and met her eyes squarely. "Removed them."

At first, Cynthia was too dumbfounded to speak.

"Perhaps," he gently suggested, "you were not aware they were devil's herbs."

"Devil's herbs?" she echoed numbly.

Slowly the shock wore off as she perused the destruction before her. A tuft of mint was pressed flat into the soil. Empty sockets sank where the plants had been torn out, and mounds of earth undulated between what plants remained. It looked as if someone had let the hounds of hell loose in the garden.

Yesterday, she would have been furious. Yesterday, she

would have given Garth a scathing sermon about the sanctity of a woman's herb garden. And she would have demanded that he replace every plant.

But yesterday, she could afford the luxury of anger.

Today, she was desperate. She'd had the dream again. Sallow, skeletal victims stretching as far as the eye could see, reaching their grasping hands toward her, begging for her healing, and her satchel hopelessly empty.

She needed those herbs. Badly. She didn't care if they were sown by Lucifer himself. She needed them.

And Garth, who had stood by her yesterday, who had given his blessings to the villagers with the patience of a saint, who had cradled her in sheltering arms on the long ride home, now brazenly informed her he'd confiscated the only weapons she had to fight the killer disease.

Now she might never save the village.

To her mortification, her face crumpled as readily as a lost little child's. Her eyes grew liquid. Her chin quivered, and she dissolved into disconsolate tears. Unable to stop the loud wailing that escaped her, and humiliated at her lack of control, she buried her face in her hands and turned to flee.

"Wait!" He caught her by the arm. "Please . . . please . . . don't cry. I never meant . . ." His thumb massaged her forearm. "I'll get them back. I promise. Somehow I'll get them back."

The sincerity of his voice only made her weep all the harder. Tears streamed down her cheeks, and sobs welled up from a deep, aching place in her chest. She felt as if the weight of the world rested on her shoulders. And she was too weak to bear it.

Then his arms folded about her, dragging her against his chest, wrapping her in a protective embrace, holding her with quiet strength and reassurance. And she returned again to that refuge she'd found last night, the sweet sanctuary of his care.

She'd only been half asleep as they journeyed home by the twinkling stars. And yet she'd been unable to stir herself. Garth's arms had felt more than pleasant about her. They'd felt perfect. As if all her life, she'd waited for one man's embrace.

And now, in that man's arms again, she found completion.

The warmth of his skin penetrated the wool of his robe, enveloping her. His spicy scent soothed her like fine incense. She turned her head to place her ear against his chest, and fat teardrops slipped from her lashes onto his cassock. The soft rumble of his voice echoed there as he uttered mollifying words, and she could hear distinctly the beating of his heart. He rested his chin atop her head. Nothing had ever felt more natural to her.

As natural as when, long moments later, after her sobs had subsided into rough hiccoughs, she turned her tear-streaked face up to his and sought out his lips with her own.

He tasted like autumn. All smoke and mulled wine, ripe apples and dusky honey. His mouth was soft, warm, and yielding, the sigh of his breath so faint she could barely feel it stir. And like autumn cider, once tasted, she wanted more. She clasped the folds of his robe between her fingers and drew him down, closer, deepening the kiss. She slanted her lips across his mouth. Her nostril flared against his as they shared one fluttering breath. His fingers curled slowly against her back, and a soft moan escaped her.

At the sound, his hands stilled. He broke violently away from the kiss and pushed her firmly back by the shoulders. Though she searched his face, her eyes still heavy with desire, he would not meet her gaze. Instead, he restlessly studied the ground.

"I . . . ," he began tautly, "I'll see you get your plants back."

For one reckless instant, the last thing on her mind was her plants. She wanted Garth back. Not the cool, controlled man of the church standing before her now, but the one of passion she'd glimpsed a moment ago.

A tiny muscle flexed in his jaw. "I suggest we leave for the village immediately," he muttered, "before you forget I am a priest."

She was still vulnerable enough to be wounded. She stepped away, cut to the quick by his reprimand. Just before she wheeled toward the stables to seek her mount, she fired back, "Don't you mean before *you* remember you are a man?"

• • •

Garth watched her go in silence. She was right. Every nerve in his body cried out that, aye, he was indeed a man. His mouth burned where she'd kissed him. His eyes felt drenched in honey, heavy and slow to respond. His heart pounded in his breast. And below his cassock cord . . . ah, God—he didn't even want to think about that.

How had it happened? She'd wept. Comforting her was as natural a reaction as scooping up a fallen child. But somehow, as her sobs broke against his chest like ocean waves breaking on the shore, he was moved by emotions far stronger than mere compassion. He wanted to hold her closer. He wanted to hold her forever.

Sweet Jesu—he never should have let her kiss him.

He lifted the back of his hand to his lips with the intent of wiping away any vestiges of that kiss. But he couldn't bring himself to do it. It had been four years since he'd felt the touch of a woman's mouth. He'd forgotten how soft and sweet a kiss could be, as delicious as honey mead, as warm as summer. And yet he'd never felt a kiss so deeply as the one Cynthia bestowed. It was as if she suckled the breath from him, drew his very soul between her lips, then gave him the precious nectar of hers in exchange. And he grew drunk on that ambrosia.

It was her moan that sobered him. The small whimper of desire wrung from her throat shot a bolt of lust straight into his loins, the like he hadn't felt in years. His body responded instantly. Instantly, his options narrowed. He must either bed her or cast her away.

In sooth, he'd made the only choice he could. He was a priest, for the love of God! And, he thought as Cynthia emerged from the stables, her palfrey in tow, because of that choice, his mind would be at peace, unfettered by guilt, for the journey to the village.

But his body . . . He clenched his fists until the knuckles grew white. His body would curse him at every step.

The interior of the first cottage they visited looked as bleak to Garth as an empty ale cask, despite the small fire burning in the room. What few furnishings the two Scotswomen possessed were worn to splinters. Chinks in the daub let mist in through the wattle walls. Straw stuck out between the seams of one threadbare linen pallet. The iron pots hung beside the hearth bore deep cracks.

Cynthia was given the place of honor, a rickety chair propped near the fire. Garth stood beside a warped oak table he dared not lean upon for fear it would collapse. He wondered how Cynthia could come to hovels like this day after day and not be dragged into the mire of the peasants' misery.

"You can do no more here, Caitlin," Cynthia said. "Your sister grows well already. See how her cheeks have color now?"

"But I promised her I'd stay." The pale lass glanced ruefully at her sister, worrying her fingers so that Garth feared she'd wear them to the bone.

"And so you have," Cynthia assured her. She placed a comforting hand atop the girl's shoulder for just a moment. Then her smile grew strangely brittle, and she snatched it back. "But I fear your aunt will worry if she hears no word from you."

"I canna leave her. She is my sister. I must stay."

Cynthia nodded in apparent surrender. But as she turned, stepping past him to leave, she tugged hard, surreptitiously, on Garth's cassock, murmuring low in his ear for him to follow her. They were the first words she'd spoken to him since they'd left Wendeville in stony silence. He followed her toward the door of the cottage.

As she pretended to rummage through her satchel, she spoke under her breath. "You must tell her it's . . . it's the will of God that she go to her aunt."

He frowned. Just because he was a priest didn't mean he could arbitrarily interpret the will of God.

"Please," she whispered.

"Why not let her be?" he murmured. "She is happy enough caring for her sister. It's a grim enough place for the two of them. But alone . . ."

"She'll not be alone. A neighbor will care for her."

"Still . . ."

"Caitlin's sister will live through the illness," she said pointedly. "But if Caitlin stays, *she* will not."

Her words sent a disturbing shiver up his spine. "You cannot know that."

She regarded him with eyes as clear and certain as crystal. "I do know that."

He swallowed uncomfortably as she continued to stare at him. An eery feeling overtook him, as if he looked into the eyes of a saint. Or an enchantress. He wasn't sure which. Her gaze remained steady, her faith unwavering. Sweet Mary, he realized—she believed she *could* foresee the girl's fate. And her quiet confidence wore away at his doubt until he, too, began to believe.

"Please. You can save her life," she bade him. "It's God's will." She touched his sleeve. "Surely you, Father Garth, are the instrument of that will?"

He grimaced at the question. There was no proof it was God's will. No proof at all. And doing Cynthia's bidding was far from being God's instrument. Yet her motives were genuine. And she'd been right yesterday about the babe and its poor mother.

He sighed. Certain he was about to step into waters over his head, he nonetheless nodded his consent.

Within the hour, Caitlin was packed and on her way atop a cart bound for Fryston, two of Lady Cynthia's silver coins clasped in her fist and Garth's blessing upon her head.

As for the other villagers, most of those Cynthia had treated were improved.

Little Tim atte Gate proved to be more stalwart than Garth had expected. Gone were the dark circles around his eyes. He even had a weary smile for Garth.

The motherless baby had survived the night on goat's milk and the care of the three neighbor women, who fought over her like jealous aunts.

There were but two deaths, one elderly woman who, in sooth, might well have expired of old age, and the village tanner, who'd refused to drink Cynthia's egg broth during Lent.

Garth should have felt respect for the man. The tanner had, after all, adhered to the strictures of Lent like a good Christian, even when it meant his own earthly demise. But somehow, as Garth comforted the weeping widow and her four children, all he could feel was indignation. How could a man deprive his family of their livelihood, of his love? How could a man cast away the precious life God had granted him when the salvation for that life lay so close at hand? Aye, the observance of Lent was a covenant to be kept. But when a life hung in the balance . . .

He watched the smallest child, a tiny girl sitting listlessly against one grimy wall of the cottage, coughing. Her eyes were bright with fever, her face sallow. He glanced toward the fire. A cauldron of watery vegetable pottage bubbled on the hook. The thin gruel wasn't enough to keep one healthy man alive, let alone four children and their mother. Something had to be done.

He turned to the oldest boy. "Have you chickens?"

"Aye," the boy sniffed.

He blew out a long breath. "Then here is what you must do."

As he gave the boy directions, his heart raced deliriously, like that of a novitiate skipping his prayers. He explained to the lad how to make egg broth for his little sister and instructed him to add a few eggs to the pottage.

Though their eyes widened in surprise, the tanner's kin never voiced a protest. Garth was a priest, after all. No one questioned the word of a priest.

Watching the eggs go into the pot, Garth felt as sinful as a lad throwing stones at chapel windows. The Abbot would have stripped him of his rank for such an act. But Garth also felt more alive than he had in years. Finally, he was doing some perceptible good. Blessings and prayers could only heal the spirit. These people needed healing for their bodies. And if he could save one soul to serve God on earth, what sin was there in that?

His heart still pulsed with quiet joy as he left the tanner's cottage to see what further service he could render. To his wonder, the sun already declined toward the western hills, painting the green knolls with buttery light. Lady Cynthia would wish to leave soon.

Down the lane, he saw her speaking with a cluster of young women. As he strolled toward them, he overheard her urgent pleas.

"Wormwood most of all," she said. "But in the days ahead, if you can find hellebore, nightshade, and monkshood . . ."

"I've seen nightshade at the far end of the glen," one maid offered.

"And monkshood usually grows near the brook," another said.

A third woman shook her head. "But wormwood . . ."

Remorse stopped him in his tracks. The women of the village, grateful for Cynthia's healing, were offering to replace the precious herbs missing from her garden. Herbs *he'd* allowed to be ruthlessly plucked from it.

Ashamed, he drew the hood of his cloak forward over his face and quietly left her to rejoin her guard. He'd walk home beside them tonight. Tonight, he didn't deserve to share Cynthia's palfrey.

Beyond the window, a fox yipped once, its voice muffled by the night fog. Somewhere in the distance, a wildcat warned off an intruder with a plaintive squall. And then the world grew silent. Cynthia peered out past the sill. Mist made a white corona around the moon and crept between the shutters.

She kicked the coverlet off for the third time. She couldn't decide if she was hot or cold. Every time she snuggled deep into her bed against the chill mist, her thoughts would stray to Garth. To how his fists locked when he was frustrated. How his emerald eyes softened with compassion. The unyielding line of his jaw. The gentle thunder of his voice. The wayward curl that was wont to spiral beneath his ear. The wool-apple-woodruff scent of him. The sinuous curve of his mouth. And the taste of him . . . oh, the taste of him.

She wanted more.

A wisp of a cloud passed before the moon, blowing ragged shadows across her naked skin. She shivered.

The journey home had been naught but torment. Garth declined to ride, plodding beside her instead like a hound home from a fruitless hunt. He trudged silently over the rocky soil as if he did penance for some imagined sin. Yet the only sin he'd committed, as far as Cynthia was concerned, was refusing her the comfort of his arms.

He'd helped her to dismount at the stables, spanning her waist with his broad, strong hands. His shoulders had bunched beneath her fingers as he lifted her down. Her breast had brushed his arm, her thigh sliding along his. He'd placed her between his spread feet, close enough to kiss.

But he'd not kissed her. And in the end, that was only more torture, torture that kept her awake tonight, burning with heat one moment, shuddering with cold the next.

Defiantly, she rose naked from her pallet. The moonlight bleached her body to blue-kissed ivory and tinted her woman's thatch of bright red curls to an icy blonde. The cool vapor caressed her bare flesh, stippling the skin of her arms, tautening her nipples. She welcomed the cold, for it helped to douse the unrequited flames of passion blazing inside her.

Brazenly, she moved to the window and peered out. It was almost as bright as day. Shadows stretched across the sward like ragged cloaks thrown over the silvery grass. No breeze stirred the trees. No owl cracked the silence of the night. It was too brisk for crickets. Her roiling desire felt like a scream against the quiet.

And then she heard a low thunk and a soft, scraping sound from the herb garden. Again, and yet again, in an easy rhythm. Unmindful of her undress, she leaned out to seek a better view. The cool stone pressed against her bare waist.

It was a priest. Garth.

For the space of two heartbeats, sheer lust poured over her loins like hot honey, sharpening her senses, making her fingers curl upon the ledge.

Until she realized what he was doing.

Then her yearning congealed into a cold, bitter knot.

She watched in horror as the brute shoved the spade deep into the soft earth of the garden, her precious herb garden, and wrenched it aside, making the soil well up in a growing mound.

What the devil . . . ?

Hurt, then anger, flashed through her as swiftly as fire through dry rushes. How dare he ransack her garden again!

. Had he not done enough damage already? They were *her* herbs. And it was *her* garden. He had no right to play God, ripping out perfectly healthy plants simply because they offended him. Even the Abbot had not been so audacious.

Grinding her teeth in fury, she wheeled from the ledge and tore her cloak from its peg so fiercely that she rent the shoulder. Cursing, she wrapped it about her and felt along the shadowed side of her pallet for her boots. It was far from decent attire, but she had to hurry. She had to stop the plunderer in the garden before it was completely laid waste.

The wet grass squeaked beneath her as she hastened across the courtyard. The glowing hedges made eery shadows along the ground, and the mist spiraled away from her swift feet.

Then she slowed. She came up behind him. Silently. Seething. Wickedly hoping he would jump ten feet with guilt when she asked him just what in the devil's name he was doing.

But as she rolled the choice words around in her mind, she chanced to notice the seedlings laid out beside him. Wormwood. Monkshood. Hellebore. Her "devil's herbs." She watched in stunned surprise as Garth set the spade aside and eased the wormwood into one of the holes he'd dug. Using his hands, he scooped dirt around the plant, packing it down with a firm touch. He moved on to the monkshood. Then the hellebore.

Sweet Lord. He was replanting them.

Her throat tightened. Her eyes grew watery. All the caustic accusations she'd prepared splintered into meaningless syllables. Her heart slowly filled with a wistful longing.

She wanted this quiet hero.

This man who gladly held the hand of a sick child.

Who spoke God's word as if he'd written it himself.

Who crept to the garden in the middle of the night and used his own two hands to replace her precious plants.

He was her champion.

And they belonged together. She'd known it from the first time they met, among the jasmine, when she'd sensed his goodness, his strength. And nothing could change that. Not the mask of indifference he chose to show her. Not his friar's trappings. Not the fact that he was sworn to chastity.

She flicked her tongue lightly over her bottom lip.

She should go back to bed.

There was no reason to disturb Garth. Besides, now that she saw the true nature of his deed, she was ashamed of her misplaced suspicions.

Aye, she should go.

She watched him as his hands cupped the mound of earth as tenderly as a lover caressing a breast. Her nipples stiffened against the rough wool of her cloak. She closed her eyes against a potent wave of desire.

And backed slowly away.

Garth heard the footstep behind him. He'd known someone was there for some time now. But he wasn't worried. The spade was in arm's reach. When the stalker took another soft step, he spun toward the sound, bringing up the shovel before him in a swift arc that would have impressed his warrior brothers.

"Jesu!"

Garth froze, cataloguing the scene before him in a series of quick flashes. Cynthia. Fear. Wild hair. Stumbling. Bare. Wide eyes. Dark cloak. Pale skin. Bare . . . bare . . .

He averted his eyes and snapped his head down. He lowered the spade, but he couldn't let it go. His fists were clenched too tightly around its handle. His unruly heart raced like a loosed pup, and he could scarcely draw air into his lungs. He dared not look again. And yet, he now understood the terrible quandary of Lot's wife as he fought the urge to lift his eyes to the wonder before him.

He squeezed his eyes shut. Surely it was his lewd imagination, he thought. Lady Cynthia didn't wander the castle grounds in the middle of the night, half-naked. That perfect, creamy, dark-tipped breast peeping from her cloak had been a creation of his own mind. He took a ragged breath and slowly lifted his gaze to her again.

She tightly clasped the front of her cloak.

"I—I . . ." she stuttered. "I . . . didn't mean to disturb you. I only heard the noise and . . ."

She *was* naked beneath that cloak. He knew it. And she knew that he knew it.

"I . . . I couldn't sleep."

He nodded once. He, too, could find no relief in his bed.

The moonlight glowed upon her bright curls. Her breath, quick and shallow, formed tiny mists upon the chill air.

"Th-thank you," she said, "for . . ." She nodded to indicate the herb garden.

"It was the least I could . . ."

"They're truly not devil's herbs," she assured him.

He nodded.

She took a step forward. "You have a kind heart."

He resisted the impulse to raise the spade in defense.

She lowered her eyes, then lifted them languidly to his. "I couldn't sleep because I kept thinking . . . I kept thinking of you," she blurted out recklessly.

His jaw tightened. How could he tell her that she haunted his every waking moment as well? That he'd paced the floor of his quarters for nigh an hour, obsessed by her? That he'd come to the herb garden to free his guilty soul, to relinquish all claims he yearned to demand of her?

He couldn't. Not while the moonlight veiled her in ethereal white. Not while she stood vulnerably bare beneath a single layer of wool.

She took another step toward him. Her lips trembled with her boldness. Her eyes beckoned to him.

"I kept thinking about your eyes," she said breathlessly. "How they're the color of pine in a winter forest."

She advanced slowly. There was nowhere for him to go, not without crushing the herbs he'd just planted.

"And your hands," she murmured, reaching out to graze the back of his white knuckles with a finger. "Like a warrior's, but . . . gentle."

His hands were anything but gentle now where they clasped the shovel in a death grip. She stood close now, close enough for the curls of mist escaping his lips to wreathe her moonlit head. The spade was the last obstruction separating them.

"But your kiss . . . ," she whispered, her eyelids dipping shyly, sensuously.

Cold sweat flecked his forehead. Aye, he remembered.

"So soft," she breathed.

Her mouth was so inviting, so voluptuous. . . .

"So sweet."

Growling in his throat, he cast the shovel aside.

14

Who reached for whom he didn't know. Or care.
One moment, mist and moonlight separated them. The
next, they flowed together like droplets of quicksilver. He
hauled her to him, all cloak and curls and succulent mouth.
And she clung to him as if she feared he'd break away. But,
sweet Jesu—the Pope himself could not have pulled him
from her at this moment.

Her lips were moist and eager. Sweet mulled breath
flowed from between them and into his open mouth. Her soft
mewls of desire taunted his wits, stretched his nerves tauter
than a bowstring. She darted her tongue across his top lip,
and hot lightning snaked through his body. Blood surged
through his veins. He slanted his mouth hungrily against
hers, devouring her with the pent-up passion of four long,
chaste years. She delved her hands into his hair, and his fingers embossed the contours of her back, arching her toward
him.

The mist thickened around them, but all he could feel was
the searing heat of Cynthia. All he could think about was the
supple flesh concealed beneath her cloak, just a single layer
away. Overcome with avarice, never stopping for breath, he
hauled her with him into the concealing shadows of the castle wall.

He was past hope now, past reason. With quaking fingers, he followed the line of her lowest rib forward until his thumbs met at the juncture of her cloak. An inch of her skin lay exposed there, a sliver of satin against the rough wool. Gasping against her mouth, he teased the passage wider. She gave no resistance, thrusting her breasts full against him.

His loins ached. Liquid need engorged him until he feared he would burst. Slowly, he pulled the edges of her cloak back, exposing more silken flesh to his touch. Then he let his fingers climb upward, beneath the wool, till he found the lower curve of her breasts. His breath whistled in between his teeth. He continued the ascent with the backs of his knuckles until he brushed the hardened tips quivering under the cloak.

She sucked in a hard, startled breath, but she voiced no protest, pressing her hips forward against him instead, inflaming his already blazing staff. Driving him mad with desire.

Cynthia shivered, not with the cold, but with sheer animal need, as the pads of Garth's thumbs swept across her sensitive peaks. She could feel his staff harden, crushed recklessly against her belly. She moaned as he ravished her mouth, grazing her teeth and suckling at her tongue. Never had she been kissed like this. Her husband's kisses, loving though they were, had never moved her to such an ecstasy of yearning. The curls between her legs moistened as desire squeezed the juices from her. Every part of her body strained to couple with his, like lightning drawn to lightning.

And then he kissed her neck, the spot just below her ear where her pulse beat wildly. She arced against him, clutching great handfuls of his thick hair, pleading wordlessly for more.

He gave her more, panting heavily against her ear, cupping her breasts, licking ravenously at her throat, nipping her shoulder. And then he parted her cloak to trail kisses across her bosom.

The wet touch of his tongue lapping at her nipple shot an exquisite current of desire through her body. It sizzled through her loins and charged every inch of her skin. He groaned as he suckled, and the sound seemed to echo through her, rasping across her soul like fine silk.

A moment more and he might have touched her warm, secret woman's place, swelling with longing. She might have sought out the firm velvet length of him with a questing hand. A moment more and they might have consummated their passion then and there in the garden, by the smoldering light of the moon.

But piercing the cool silence of the night, a voice suddenly rang across the courtyard.

"M'lady?"

Elspeth!

They separated as quickly as split timber.

The moment vanished.

"Lady Cynthia?" Elspeth picked her way across the dew-bejeweled grass as if she feared to break the shimmering diamonds.

Cynthia snapped her cloak tightly about her neck.

"What is it, El?" Sweet Lord—her voice was little more than a croak.

"Why, whatever are ye doin' out of doors on such a night, m'lady?"

Cynthia wiped her mouth with the back of her hand, erasing any trace of his kiss, and stepped cautiously into the light. Certain the maid saw the flush of desire on her cheek. Heard the frenzied beating of her heart.

"When I didn't find ye in yer bed, well, Roger and I, we looked high and low for ye. What are ye doin', lass?"

Cynthia's gaze flitted over to the spade. "Planting," she improvised.

"Plantin'?"

"Aye." She picked up the spade. "The chaplain and I . . ." She turned to the niche beside the wall where she'd abandoned Garth. But he had disappeared, evaporated like mist. "We . . . we brought back some new herbs from the village. I wanted to be sure to plant them straight away."

Elspeth shook her head. "Well, ye'll come to bed now, lass. The plants'll wait till mornin', and I won't have ye takin' a chill."

Cynthia nodded and scanned the empty shadows of the

castle wall one last time. A part of her was relieved. Garth had escaped undetected. But a part of her was disappointed. And for that part of her, it promised to be a very long night.

Garth sat on his pallet, hanging his head, and ran a shaky hand through his tousled hair.

He couldn't stay. That much was painfully obvious. Cynthia might have extricated herself from the embarrassing situation tonight. She might have given Elspeth a plausible explanation for her presence in the garden in the middle of the night. But there was no excuse for him.

He couldn't fool himself. He knew that if he stayed, it would not be the last time he trysted with Cynthia. Whether it was by some enchantment she'd cast upon him or his own damnably weak will, a compliant woman was as addictive as opium wine. He'd crossed over a line. He'd tasted her. And now he only wanted more.

But he wouldn't do that to her. He wouldn't allow Cynthia to be disgraced. He cared too much for her. It never would work anyway. He was unfit as a man. Sooner or later, she'd discover that.

He blamed himself. This whole awkward situation was his fault, all of it. He was a priest. It was up to him to control his passions. And tonight, he'd failed miserably.

Outside, the moon began its descent. The fog thickened, blurring the line between the treetops and the sky.

He stuffed his few possessions—quills, ink, parchment, books, candles—into his satchel, and looked one last time around the chamber that would be his no more.

With a heavy heart, he stepped into the night. He was leaving Cynthia to fight her battle against the village murrain alone—he knew that—but mayhap it was better this way. The burden of lust would only taint her healing gift and weigh heavily on her soul. In a week, he told himself, he'd forget her. He'd fall back into the comfortable routine of the monastery—praying, copying, teaching. And then Lady Cynthia and Wendeville Castle would recede like a pleasant, brief dream. He told himself the lie and tried to believe it.

•   •   •

The Abbot shivered impatiently in the crofter's cottage. The hovel provided little comfort against the chill of the night. He was eager to return to his hearth at Charing. But his spy had assured him she brought important news, and so he'd endured the cold like a hair shirt.

"He . . . replanted the herbs?"

The young girl's teeth chattered, but she managed a nod in the small pool of light cast by the single candle he held.

"The chaplain?" he repeated, unable to fathom it.

He'd hand picked Garth de Ware for Wendeville because of his humility and his lack of ambition. Surely Garth posed little threat to his own plans. After all, the fool had thrown away his own chance at wealth and power for the seclusion of an impoverished monastery.

"You're certain?" he asked, narrowing his eyes.

"Aye, Father," she said, bobbing her head like a nervous chicken. "And there's . . . somethin' else."

The lass was reluctant to speak. She fidgeted with the edges of her cloak and wouldn't meet his eyes.

Biting back peevishness, he reached out with false tolerance and gently cupped her chin, lifting it. Her skin was frigid to the touch. "Do not be afraid, child. 'Tis God's work you do."

Her chin quaked, and she spoke barely above a whisper. "The chaplain . . . he . . . I saw him . . . with Lady Cynthia."

His fingers tightened on her jaw. Nay. It couldn't be. "Aye?" he goaded her. "Aye?"

"They were . . . kissin'," she breathed. Moisture filled her eyes, whether of shame or lust, he wasn't certain. "He . . . he opened her cloak, and he . . . touched her. . . ." Her hands fluttered awkwardly before her.

He struggled to keep the impatient edge from his voice. "He touched her bosom?"

She ducked her head.

"Go on," he bade her.

"He . . . he kissed her . . . there."

"And?"

She shook her head. "Elspeth came. He ran away." She looked up hopefully, her soul unburdened at last. He could see by the glistening in her eyes that she wanted her reward now. But it would have to wait for another time. Her cold flesh and chattering teeth held no appeal for him tonight. Besides, he had much to think about.

He chewed at his lip. It seemed he'd misjudged the humble friar. It was too early to tell exactly how. But there were two possibilities.

Either the man's flesh was pitifully weak or Garth de Ware was perpetrating a seizure of power more complex than his own.

The Abbot's lip curled in self-mockery. He fought back hysterical laughter.

Garth de Ware was either the ruin of him, or the perpetrator of the most opportune twist of fate he'd ever fallen heir to.

Cynthia's mount plodded along the gray road toward the village, as reluctant as she to brave the morning cold. In the interminable gloom, the world seemed to have no beginning, no end, and her path through it, no purpose.

She wasn't hurt, she told herself, wiping away a tear brought on certainly by the chill, nothing more. Only a fool would be hurt.

Garth had made no promises to her. He hadn't pledged his undying love. He hadn't sworn to forsake all others for her. God's bones—he hadn't even promised to remain at Wendeville. Only a fool would take an impulsive midnight tryst as a sign of something deeper.

She wrapped the reins tightly around one fist. The leather bit into her palm.

Nay, it wasn't hurt.

It was only anger.

Anger at the way he'd left Roger and Elspeth without saying good-bye. Anger at his abandonment of the good people of Wendeville. Anger that he'd forsaken the dead and dying of the village to retreat like a coward to the comfort of his monastery.

She hadn't seen him go, but when she glimpsed his cell, clean and blank as the day he'd arrived, she knew that was where he'd fled. At the monastery he could seclude himself behind safe stone walls and contemplate the error of his ways for months to come. By day, he could bury his nose in some dusty religious tome, and by night, punish himself for feeling the passions of an ordinary man.

And all with nary a thought for those he left behind.

The pervasive fog swirled about her. It had both her eyes watering now. She dabbed at them with the tippet of her sleeve. It wouldn't do to let the villagers see her upset. The infirm depended upon her strength, and for that she must maintain a vibrant countenance, not the visage of melancholy the gloomy day painted upon her.

As her palfrey trudged forward, its steps muffled on the damp road, the thatched cottages of the village emerged one by one through the cloudy veil, like ghosts materializing from another world. She shivered. On such a day, spirits might leave their lifeless bodies and become lost in the mist. On such a day, the villagers needed the comfort of a priest more than ever. She prayed no soul would have to make that journey today, for there was no one to guide them to heaven.

The corners of her mouth turned down bitterly one last time, and she sniffed against the cold. Then she nudged her horse toward the first house, within which, God willing, someone waged victorious battle against the sickness.

It was difficult to tell how many hours she labored. The bulky cloak of fog blanched the sun's beacon to a vague gray haze. The day dragged lethargically on, filled with hacking coughs and trembling sweats and poor souls bent in half with pain. Nearly every household had been ravaged in some way by the dread disease. It had spread its destructive fire with frightening speed, as swiftly as a brand touched to thatch. Thank God, it had at last almost burned out.

But if it left the village, if somehow it spread . . .

The thought was overwhelming. The terror of her dream returned to hound her. Not enough herbs to treat the sick. Not enough time to reach them all. Not enough strength. Already she felt her power wane, the flow of energy less each time she laid hands on another victim. What would she do if the demands upon her increased?

The darkening hue of the ashen sky served as the only indication that day's end drew near. Like the fog, the sickness hung stubbornly over the village. Of the victims she had treated, many had improved. But several had grown worse, as she'd sensed they would.

There was naught more she could do.

Wearily pulling herself onto the saddle, her bag of medicines grown fearfully light, she had at least one thing to be thankful for. In answer to her prayers, no one had died.

Cynthia thought about a warm bath all the way home. One to leach from her bones the mist seeping relentlessly into them. A nice, long, soothing bath scented with rosemary or angelica.

The moment she set foot in the great hall, she knew it was not to be. Elspeth rushed at her, flapping her arms like a distraught hen.

"Oh, m'lady, somethin' terrible's happened!"

"Now, Elspeth," Roger scolded, striding forward to take Cynthia's cloak. "Let Lady Cynthia at least warm herself by the fire."

"What is it?" she asked, unable to contain her curiosity, as Roger guided her by the elbow toward the crackling tinder.

"It's Father Garth, m'lady!" Elspeth cried.

"Oh." Cynthia let the air sigh out of her chest as she sank onto a chair before the hearth. "I know. He left last night. He's likely gone back to the monastery. We shall have to fetch another—"

"Aye, he has, but m'lady—"

"A messenger came from the monastery," Roger interrupted, knitting his gray brows. "Father Garth is . . . not well."

Faint alarm registered in her breast. She searched Roger's eyes. "What do you mean, 'not well'?"

"He has the sickness, m'lady!" Elspeth burst out. "The sickness from the village!"

Dread insinuated itself like odious, curling smoke into her thoughts. She stared, unseeing, into the flames.

"He's asked for ye," Elspeth whispered.

Garth. He'd walked all the way to the monastery in the chill damp of night, probably already suffering from fever. Such exposure might have weakened him, left him more susceptible to the murrain's attack, unable to effectively battle it.

Then a darker, more sinister thought followed. If Garth carried the disease . . .

"Sweet Jesu!"

He'd communicate it to the prior, his novitiates, and eventually all the monks. Despite the blazing fire thawing her bones, she shuddered.

Already she sensed the sickness encircling the monastery like a grim cloud raining death.

15

SOMEONE WAS SHAKING THE BED. GARTH COULDN'T wake up enough to make them stop. He heard voices, but the low, somber murmurs were indistinguishable, as if a thick blanket enveloped him, separating him from the rest of the world. And yet he was cold, colder than he'd ever been. Cold to the marrow of his bones.

He drifted like a snowflake at the will of the winter wind, now floating toward the surface of awareness, now delving toward the frozen wasteland of oblivion. How long he wafted over the endless, icy landscapes, he didn't know. Time had no meaning.

Once, his eyes fluttered open for just an instant, and he was aware of a vaguely familiar, comforting, parchment-colored expanse flickering above his head. And once, a man's cool, chubby fingers rested upon his forehead, soothing him even as they chilled his shivering flesh. But before he could grasp and hold the recognizable images, he was plunged back into alien vistas of fathomless snow.

A moment, or hours, or days later, the sharp nick of a blade in his arm spurred him from his uneasy slumber. His eyes opened to narrow slits. On the inner side of his elbow, blood welled from a small cut and dripped slowly into a pewter bowl. He drew a shallow, shuddering breath. He had to stop the blood. Stanch it with something. Bind the wound. But he was too weak to move. Currents of panic rose around him, and the waters of unconsciousness closed over his head again.

When he awoke, his arm was bandaged with linen. The limb looked pale and foreign. He couldn't move it. A rhythmic rasping rattled his ears, his own labored breathing. Every inch of his body ached. Still frozen with cold, he was too feeble even to shiver.

He catalogued his surroundings with his eyes alone, his eyeballs clicking as they jerked dryly about the room. It was his cell at the monastery. The plaster overhead glinted in the candlelight. His cloak dangled from the peg on the wall. Sweet smoke drifted from a spiced candle burning at the foot of the bed. A heavy tapestry from the prior's office hung at the window, blocking out the light. If indeed there was light. He had no idea what the hour was. All he could remember was stumbling onto the steps of the monastery sometime in the dark hours before dawn, drenched with drizzle, shaking with cold, and weak as a fledgling bird.

He tried to recall more. Why had he been traveling in the middle of the night? Where had he gone? Why did he feel as if someone had beaten him with a mace? But his head began to throb with the effort of thought. Closing his eyes, he returned to the peace of oblivion.

The dreams began sometime soon after. Pleasant dreams and troubling ones.

Fragments of fond remembrances. Romping across a summer meadow with his brothers. Studying Latin in the checkered shade of the willow. Sitting by the fire, listening to the old knights of his father's castle recount heroic deeds.

Then came memories he wished he could bury forever. Mariana's bed. His own pathetic staff lolling upon his stomach, unable to rise. Tears of rage and humiliation burning behind his eyes as Mariana voiced her scorn. The shattering sound of her laughter as she sent him from her sight.

And then finally, new dreams washed over the old, like paint on plaster, obscuring the deep-seated cracks and imperfections. Jasmine scented these dreams, and the hum of bees ran through them. Dreams of luminous blue eyes and fragrant herbs, of copper-bright curls and the honeyed taste of summer. Dreams of the most beautiful woman in the world, walking toward him, her arms outstretched. Cynthia . . .

But then a terrible shadow cut across the dream. A black chasm opened up between the two of them, spreading like the devil's smile, growing wider, separating them. Cynthia reached for him, her eyes wide with desperation. She screamed his name. He stretched his arm forward, but the farther he reached, the more distant she became.

"Nay!" he cried out. His chest burned with longing. "Nay!"

"Hold him still, Andrew," a nearby voice murmured.

"I'm trying, Father."

"Nay!" Garth yelled hoarsely.

"Stephen, help him. I've got to get this down him."

"Cynthia!" he wailed. "Cynthia!"

"Cynthia, Father? Who—?"

"Later, Stephen. Hold him steady now."

Cynthia shrank away from his sight until she was a tiny bright spot across the dark abyss, no bigger than a bee's stinger, lost between his fingers. His lungs ached with grief.

Someone clutched at his shoulders, restraining him. A noxious odor assaulted his nose. He jerked away.

"Stephen!"

"I'm trying, Father. But he seems to . . ."

A hand anchored his jaw, pulling his teeth apart. Something cold and vile gurgled into his mouth. Poison! His throat spasmed, and he gagged the liquid back out. Wildly, he flailed his good arm about, hoping to knock his assailants back. He contacted flesh. Then something shattered on the stones with a brittle crash.

"Garth! Can you hear me? Are you awake?"

He lifted his lids the merest fraction of an inch, just enough to make out the worried face of the prior hovering over him.

"You must swallow this concoction, Brother Garth." He turned to the novitiate beside him. "Bring me another vial, Andrew. Quickly."

Garth looked at the ugly green splashes staining the prior's cassock where the first vial of God-knew-what had spilled. He looked at the fat bandage binding his arm where he'd been bled. God's wounds—he might die from whatever it was he had, but he'd not do it with a belly full of poison and a body full of holes.

With the dregs of his strength, he snagged the front of the prior's cassock and with inborn de Ware command, yanked him down till they were nose to nose.

"Get me Cynthia Wendeville," he demanded, the words scraping painfully across his raw throat like quicklime. "Now."

"All right," the prior answered, his Adam's apple bobbing nervously. "All right, then."

But already Garth was drifting back toward his private world of illusions.

Cynthia bit her lower lip as she paused before the door to Garth's cell. After a long day in the village, she hadn't much healing left in her. She silently prayed for strength. But more than that, she prayed for emotional fortitude. It would devastate her, she knew, to see Garth wasted by disease, no matter that he'd abandoned her. It would be torture to lay hands upon him and feel his weakness. Mayhap she could help him. But what if it wasn't to be? What if he was fated not to live, but to . . .

She clamped her lips together. She wouldn't think of that. He needed her. He'd asked for her. And she'd do everything in her power to save him.

Squaring her shoulders, she entered the cell.

The first thing she did was calmly empty it of the half dozen monks who stood gaping at her. Women were normally not admitted to monasteries, but she didn't have time to argue with them. They endangered their own health every moment they lingered. Pushing back her sleeves and authoritatively dropping her bag onto the pallet, she informed the prior she needed to work in peace.

Only when the door closed behind him did she let her mask of cool detachment slip. She rushed to Garth's side, peering anxiously into his face.

Dear God—by the candlelight, his skin appeared as pale and transparent as vellum. Beneath damp tangles of hair, his brow was troubled, creasing now in a furrow of suffering. His breath came shallow and strained, scarcely budging the wool coverlet doubled over his chest. He shivered faintly, as if the marrow of his bones were made of ice. As she watched him, his eyelids rippled, and his lips moved over silent syllables of the language of dreams.

She closed her eyes. The gift was weak within her, weary with use. Still, praying for one last glimmer of her exhausted talent, just enough for Garth, she began rubbing her hands together.

His temples were hot where she placed her palms upon them, yet he trembled as if he slept in snow. A faint vibration tickled her fingertips, and she gratefully felt the golden glow expanding, connecting her energies to his. Then she waited for a sign. The name of an herb. A vision of the specific combination of extracts that would heal his particular ills.

When the vision swirled and resolved to crystal clarity, she snatched her hands back. But it was too late. She'd seen it. The all too familiar black demon still slithered across her mind, breathing poisonous fog to wither everything in its path.

"Nay," she wheezed.

The black snake. Death.

"Nay."

Garth couldn't die. He was young and fit. His entire life stretched out before him.

It couldn't be true. And yet, she'd never been wrong.

Garth de Ware was destined to perish.

"Nay," she said again, twisting her fingers, as if repeating the word would somehow drive destiny away.

He couldn't die. Couldn't. He was too precious to die. Too extraordinary. It wasn't fair. The poor man had never truly lived. Never sworn his eternal love to a bride. Never bounced a child, his own flesh and blood, on his knee. Never known the deep satisfaction of gazing across land that belonged to him.

Tears of dismay filled her eyes even as her chest heaved with angry breath. She doubled her fists.

He couldn't die. By St. Peter's ballocks, she wouldn't let him.

She clamped her jaw and ran a shaky hand through her hair. There was no walking away. Not while he needed her. Not while he yet breathed.

She sighed raggedly. For Garth to have any hope of survival, she'd have to joust with death itself.

From the depths of his dream, Garth groaned. The ache of spent desire rested low in his belly. But Mariana, her green eyes full of smoke, her hair splayed like splinters of charred wood against his skin, still smoldered with longing.

"Take me. Take me again," she pleaded.

He wanted to. Lord, he wanted to. Mariana was devilishly beautiful. Her writhing body shone with sweat, accentuating each supple curve and alluring hollow. Her breasts heaved dramatically with every breath, her hard, red nipples balancing like ripe cherries atop the snowy globes. The tangle of ebony curls between her legs was matted, soaked with her juices, yet the dark pink petals of her womanhood swelled for him again. His milky essence painted her breasts and belly and thighs. And still she wanted more.

She deserved more. He wanted to give her more.

But he couldn't.

Five times he had risen for her, joined with her, made her moan and scream with ecstasy as they rode over the brink of lust together. Another half dozen times he'd pleasured her with hands and tongue until he thought she'd surely swoon with exhaustion. And now *he* was exhausted. She'd depleted him. His weary flag refused to rise even once more. Jesu— he'd hardly the strength to hoist a flag of surrender.

"What have you done to me, woman?" he murmured with a smile, slurring the words.

"Done? I've only begun," she purred, bisecting his chest with a sharp fingernail.

This time his groan was half a chuckle. He was drunk with exhaustion. "You've worn me out."

"Nonsense," she breathed, dragging her thigh sensuously over his.

"Drained me dry."

She pouted prettily and traced circles in the damp hair

below his navel. "I'd wager your brothers would not tire so easily," she mewled in disappointment.

He rose to the bait at once. "My brothers?" He stopped her fingers in his.

She shrugged and gave a small sigh. "But then, you aren't quite like your brothers, er, half-brothers, are you?" Cruelty overlaid her sweet words like a sheer, bitter veil as she patronizingly patted his limp ballocks. "Not quite the man that Holden and Duncan are."

She slunk from the bed then, brushing past him like a sultry current of air blowing through a chill day, then moving on.

If a man had spoken the insult, he would've slammed him up against the wall faster than a cat pouncing on a mouse. No one compared him unfavorably with his brothers. And since he'd earned his spurs, no one dared call him less than a man.

But Mariana was a lady. She cared for him. Whatever she said, she said out of love and concern, or pity. He was sure of it. If Mariana believed him inferior to other men, then mayhap it was so.

Suddenly, he grew painfully aware of his nakedness, of the shrunken member slumbering in its dark nest. It took all his will not to cover it with his hands, to hide the despicable thing from her sight. Shame scorched his face, burning him with a hotter fire than lust ever had, a fire that would never be extinguished.

Yet even as he watched the trailing hem of her scarlet robe slither out the door and heard the brittle jangle of her departing laughter, from the edges of sleep came refreshing solace. Someone stroked his fevered cheek with a wet cloth, gently blowing mint-scented breath across his skin to cool him. The painful dream melted like chips of ice. His tension eased as the furrow between his brows was wiped gently away.

Briefly, he raised his sleep-heavy lids, just enough to peep through his lashes.

Tousled orange curls. Strong, graceful hands. Eyes darkened in concern and compassion.

Cynthia.

Relief swept through him.

Cynthia. Not that lust-filled dragon wench stealing

through his dreams, but a real woman, kind and genuine. He sighed. With that sweet comfort, he closed his lids and sank deeper into sleep, past the land of dreams.

Cynthia held her breath. Had Garth wakened? Or was it only a figment of her desperate imagination? After two days of watching over him, grabbing what rest she could in short, fitful naps in the chair the prior had brought, she wasn't sure.

Those two days, Garth had smoldered like a slow-burning log, alternately sweating and shivering, breathing with the shallow gasps of a child. He'd tossed weakly on his pallet, his sleep plagued by upsetting dreams, and he'd been unable to keep down even the weakest broth with eggs she'd smuggled in. There wasn't a part of him she didn't know intimately now, from the rough stubble of his unshaved chin and the glossy scar traversing his breast to the fine line of hair dividing his belly and the carved hollows of his lean buttocks. But none of his features, not even his man's staff that occasionally, inexplicably decided to rouse, could distract her from the overpowering dread that she was going to lose him.

She dropped the cloth into the basin of water and ran a tired hand through her sticky hair. No healing flowed through her hands now. She was too exhausted. Now she relied on sheer instinct.

She leaned back against the table and watched him. As absurd as it seemed, she couldn't stop the feeling that she was partly to blame for his condition. She curled her hands in frustration, catching splinters of wood under her nails.

If only she'd stayed in her room that night . . .

If only she'd resisted her desires, hadn't pushed him so far . . .

He might not have trudged all night in the damp, killing fog to reach the monastery, weakening his resistance to the murrain.

She turned her back to him, unable to face her guilt. Vials and packets of extracts and herbs covered the table before her. Two days ago, they'd been effectual cures, the reliable tools of her trade. Today, they seemed like the counterfeit oils and ointments of a gypsy merchant.

Behind her, Garth's breathing grew ragged. She feared it

would become much worse. Then coughing would set in. And eventually difficulty drawing air into his lungs. Finally . . .

She couldn't think about it. Since that first night, she'd not called upon her powers. She wouldn't do it now. She didn't want to face despair.

She eyed the medicines on the table again. Somewhere in that vast array of rainbow-colored bottles, there hid a cure. She had to find it.

Garth's dreams possessed such accurate memory when it came to painful details.

Slats of black hair obscured Mariana's smoldering eyes, but diluted none of her scorn.

"Marriage?" She rocked backward onto her bread-soft buttocks, gripping Garth's trembling thighs between her own. "Why would I want to marry you when I can have you anytime I want?" She coiled a lock of his hair around her finger.

"Because . . ." Because he loved her. Utterly. Desperately. Devotedly. But he couldn't tell her that. Not while derision tainted her voice. "Because it's the proper thing."

"And do you always do the proper thing, Garth?" Grinning, she reached behind her back and gave his ballocks a tweak.

"Mariana . . ."

"Aye?" She slid back and forth against him, ready for another bout.

"Mariana," he said, grasping her knees to still her. "Not now. I wish to speak with you."

"Speak!" She scowled, ruining her finely-painted features. "Speak! All you ever want to do is speak!"

"But Mariana . . ."

Diplomacy was useless now. She was riled. And when she was riled, her temper exploded quicker than a thundertube.

"What kind of beast are you?" she fired, dragging herself off of him. "Other men would give their right arm to lie with me!" She snatched her vermilion gown from the peg. "Yet here I stay—ready, willing, begging for your affections!" She struggled into the surcoat. "And you! You want to talk!" The dress scraped over her hips and pooled at her feet like blood. "Do you know what I think? I think you have nothing left to give me!" She ran her long nails briskly through the tangles of her hair. "You say you want to marry me. Well, I've waited months for you to mature, to grow into the lover they claim is the de Ware legacy, and I have yet to see it." She stuffed her feet into her slippers. "How can you call yourself a de Ware? How can you call yourself a man?"

An unshed agony of tears burned Garth's throat. His chest felt heavy, as if he were burdened by ten coats of chain mail.

His vulnerability must have shown on his face, for Mariana's next words were laced with pity.

"I cannot marry you, Garthie. No woman should have to live so . . ." She glanced at the bed. "Unfulfilled." Whirling her matching red cloak about her shoulders, she gave him one last, long, appraising look. Then she added with a gentle sigh, "Mayhap you were right in choosing the church after all. You should have no trouble pleasing that bride."

And then she was gone forever.

Beneath his ponderous ribs, his crushed heart knifed diagonally against his lungs. Pain and shame and despair balled into a knot in his belly. For an awful eternity, he was unable to draw breath.

Then, when he did, when he knew he'd not die mercifully of a broken heart, the air rasped across his torn throat in a horrible, inhuman sob.

"Mariana!" he cried. "Don't leave me!" His own voice sounded foreign to his ears, like the wailing of a tortured prisoner. "Mariana!"

"Garth!"

From the mists of sleep, Mariana's voice sounded strange. "Garth!"

The colors of his boyhood room faded as he was pulled away by the voice. The pain in his chest increased.

"Garth!"

Someone was tugging at him, making him sit up. He didn't want to. It hurt too much.

"Garth, you must help me."

The pungent scent of mint roused him from the vestiges of his dream. He involuntarily inched upward to accommodate the voice's command. And was instantly sorry. The movement triggered a series of deep, chest-cleaving coughs that brought tears to his eyes.

When the barrage finally subsided, he was left with no strength and a wheeze that grated against his windpipe every time he breathed. It was so excruciating, he almost wished he were back in the agony of his dream. Almost.

Then he peered at his tormenter. Cynthia stood over him, wafting the steam from some minty concoction toward him.

She looked like she'd bargained with the devil. And lost. Dark smudges ringed her eyes. Her features were pinched, her skin so translucent that the freckles stood out like bloodstains on linen. In short, she looked like he felt.

And then he noticed the tears on her cheeks. When he would have asked her about them, swallowing against the pain of wetting his throat to speak, she brushed the back of her hand across her face, wiping them away.

He drew in three more tortuous breaths. His heart pounded sluggishly in his throat and temples. His belly felt empty, besieged, as if underminers had collapsed the wall of his stomach. They must have beaten him as well, for every bone in his body throbbed.

And then he realized why she wept.

She'd used her sight. She'd seen his fate.

He was going to die. She'd felt it, sensed it with her magic.

His heart staggered. She knew.

He swallowed once more, wincing against the pain. His voice was little more than a rasp. "I'm dying, aren't I?"

She glanced anxiously at him. "Are you awake now?"

He closed his mouth and swallowed again. "Am I . . . dying?"

Her tongue flicked nervously across her lip. She set the basin of steaming herbs aside and busied herself wiping her hands on a linen towel.

Damn the wench, he thought.

With every last ounce of his strength, he seized her by the wrist and pulled her near, forcing her palm against his forehead, as he'd seen her do to the sick so many times. "Am I?" he wheezed.

Her fingers curled defensively, and her chin quivered. She looked away.

"Cynthia . . . please . . . answer me."

This time she clamped her jaw tight, as if she fought and won some inner struggle. She looked at him, directly at him, her eyes wild and fierce. "Nay," she answered. "Nay, you are not dying!"

She lied. He knew she lied. And, God forgive him, he loved her for it.

16

THE MONASTERY BELL TOLLED ITS MIDNIGHT ADMONI-
tion. Cynthia's eyes fluttered open in panic. Lord, how
long had she dozed? The last thing she remembered was
kneeling to pray. Judging from the stump of the guttering
candle, that had been at least an hour ago. She sat up, rubbing
the bed linen wrinkles from her cheek, and peered anxiously
into Garth's wan face.

He still breathed, but just barely. As the bell chimed, she
bent near to count the feeble breaths whistling through his
pain-clenched teeth. God—his gasps were so shallow, so far
apart. He wasn't taking in enough air to sustain a sparrow.
Her weary eyes filled with frustrated tears.

"Nay," she mewed. Her voice was so raw with despair she
hardly recognized it. She took his slack hand in her two and
massaged it. "Oh, please, nay. I didn't mean to fall asleep.
It's just so hard to . . ." She bit her trembling lip. "I didn't
mean to leave you. Please don't die. Please don't . . ."

But Garth surrendered to the formidable foe slowly
squeezing the life from him. In the next moment, he ceased
breathing.

Cynthia felt the life leave her as well. A horrible crushing
weight compressed her chest, and for a long moment she
could draw no breath.

He couldn't be dead. He couldn't. It wasn't possible.

The room swam around her.

Garth couldn't be dead.

The light dimmed as she felt the tug of sweet unconsciousness, blessed oblivion.

And then her lungs scraped in a harsh, deep, painful breath, and she was dragged back to consciousness, back to tortuous reality, like a drowning man cast ashore. And instead of grief, this lungful of air was rife with anger.

"Nay!" she groaned, her voice shaking with ire. "Nay! You cannot die! Do you hear me?" She shook his lifeless form. "You cannot!" Tears blinded her, but she continued to rail at him pitilessly. "Your family needs you, damn your soul! The monastery needs you! Wendeville needs you! I . . . oh, God." She choked on the words. Grief once again threatened to claim her as she realized what she must do.

Though it tore at her already tattered spirit, she quickly bowed her head over fiercely clasped hands and took a terrible vow over his ravaged body. Tears streamed down her cheeks, and her heart broke in two as she murmured the words.

"Please, God, let him live. Give me the strength to do this one last healing, and I'll call upon my gift no more. Let him live, and I promise I won't try to . . . change him. I promise . . ." Her voice broke. "I promise I'll return him to the church. I'll give him back to you. Completely. Forever."

Garth felt his body floating in dark, calm waters. Memories of his boyhood pond in summer drifted over him as the waves closed above his head, blocking out the sun and leaving him pleasantly cool. Somewhere deep within, he knew he should break the surface, needed to, but it was so peaceful here, surrendering all care to the welcoming arms of the deep. The light dimmed above, the sun growing fainter and fainter until it was but a tiny white point, and then that, too, winked out.

Then something disturbed his rest, something merciless and insistent. It pulled roughly at him, wrenching him from serenity back up through the cold currents, into the screaming sunlight. A jagged breath rasped across his throat into his starving lungs. Lord, it hurt. His eyelids would only creak open halfway, and his tongue was thick and sour. His ribs ached, his belly was sunken with hunger, and his pulse beat with a dull throb at the back of his head. He wondered what army had marched over him. Just the thought of moving pained him.

His only source of comfort was the gentle hand resting atop his forehead. From that point of contact, a soft energy suffused him, soothing him, radiating outward to bring him ease. For a fleeting moment, as weak as he felt, he wondered if it was the touch of the angel of death. But nay, this was no cold bone claw. It was a hand of flesh, warm and supple.

With great effort, he strained his eyelids open to look upon his benefactor.

It was an angel after all. Pale and haggard, aye, but an angel nonetheless. Lady Cynthia. Her tangle of hair sprawled carelessly over her shoulders. Her forehead was etched with despair, her closed eyes limned with purple shadows. Her lips parted over the silent words of a prayer. As he watched, a silver tear stole from the corner of her eye and streaked down her cheek.

Ah, nay—he couldn't bear to see her cry. Not over him. In all the long, exhausting hours spent battling the disease in the village, she'd shed so few tears. Not when she lost a child. Or when an old friend slipped away. Not when the villagers drained her of even the energy to stand. Nay, he couldn't let her weep over him.

He sluggishly lifted his arm—by the saints, it was as heavy as a Scots claymore—and reached a shaky hand toward her face. Resting his fingers on her cheek, he caught her tear on a trembling fingertip.

Her eyes flew wide. She jerked her hand from his forehead. A hundred emotions flashed across her countenance. Shock. Gratitude. Disbelief. She searched his face, her eyes red-rimmed and bleary with fatigue. A fresh tear welled in one of them.

"Are you . . . ," she whispered, the hope naked in her gaze.

His throat felt like a church bell gone to rust. He knew he'd never push a word past it. But he could probably manage a smile. His lips were parchment dry, but he slowly stretched one corner up in a reassuring grin for her.

Which only made her begin to sob in earnest.

He started to pull his arm back, dismayed by the havoc he'd unwittingly wrought. But she clutched at his hand, holding it tightly inside both her own. He watched in wonder as she hailed tear-laced kisses upon his fingers. And as battered and weak and hungry as he was, he still felt a wave of marvelous warmth envelop his body, removing all pain and care, leaving room for only one all-embracing, powerful emotion. An emotion long buried in the fertile soil of his boyhood. An emotion that refused to lay dormant, but was destined to break through the crust of repression, to blossom.

It was love.

He loved Cynthia.

Everything about her.

Her compassion. Her innocence. Her fire. The gleam in her eyes when she planned mischief. The wistfulness of her smile as she gazed at her garden. Her quicksilver temper. Her nurturing patience. The flowery scent of her hair. The healing touch of her hands. The honey taste of her lips . . .

He remembered now, though it seemed ages past. The herb garden. Kissing her. Her welcoming arms. Her sweet breast, bare in the moonlight. Soft. Innocent. He swallowed hard as the memory washed over him like a wave.

Affection must have shown in his eyes. Cynthia stilled, and her own eyes softened as if in answer. Tears clung to her lashes like fragile drops of ice. No breath stirred them. For one aching, bittersweet moment, gazing nakedly into each other's eyes, into each other's hearts, they shared their desire. For an instant, a warm presence seemed to unite them in a marriage of nature.

Then the joy in her face darkened, as if a shadow had fallen across her. She pulled back, distancing herself from him. Her eyes filled with despair. In the single beat of a heart, she grew as elusive as mist. She'd not meet his eyes, and all at once there were a hundred things to do with her hands. She rearranged the vials of medicine atop the night table.

"You must be famished," she said, her voice cracking like brittle glass.

He was, but somehow that didn't seem so important any-more.

"You'll have to start out slowly," she said, half to herself, wringing out a linen rag over a basin of water. "Barley water." She hung the rag over the clothing peg. "A posset of almonds."

"Cynthia." Even to his own ears, the word sounded like a studded mace scraping across chain mail, and hurt worse, but Garth had to know what was wrong.

She wiped away the tears that continued forming in her eyes. "Bits of bread."

"Cynthia."

She sniffled and turned her back. "I'll fetch the prior. He can tend to you now." She swept up her satchel and began re-placing the medicine bottles. "You should recover fully within a sennight."

He frowned. She might have proclaimed him fit for the grave, for all the sorrow that colored her words.

"Cynthia."

"I must go home now. To my life," she said, stifling a whimper, jamming the last of her herbs into the satchel. Her next words were more sob than speech. "And leave you to yours."

He scowled. What did she mean? He had no life without her.

"Nay!" he protested, cursing the feebleness that left him unable to block her path to the door.

Without a backward glance, Cynthia flew from his cell, leaving no evidence of her visit save the faint scent of her womanly skin and the hollow ache in his heart. An ache that pained him more than all his other ills together.

Cynthia wept all the way home, great tearing sobs that felt as if they ripped her very soul from her. By the time she rode through the gates of Wendeville, she was so exhausted, so empty, so bereft, she couldn't even answer Elspeth's anxious questions. Refusing the posset of almonds the maid handed her, she trudged up the steps to her chamber and slept for nearly an entire day.

When she finally awoke, it was to the sound of splashing

water and the scent of violets. The sun lit her chamber in ripe afternoon shades of russet and rose.

"Are ye with us now?" Elspeth asked, drying her hands on her apron and hovering near to chatter away like a squirrel. "Ye must have been worn out, m'lady. At first, we thought perhaps the chaplain had succumbed, so sorrowful was yer countenance last eve." Without ceremony, Elspeth whipped back the coverlet and proceeded to undress her. "But then a prior came, askin' after ye and bringin' a cask of fine monastery wine to thank ye fer savin' Father Garth's life."

Cynthia shivered as El peeled off her sweat-stained underdress and handed her a linen cloth for modesty. She tangled a hand in her own matted hair. How long had it been since she'd combed it? She ran her tongue across her teeth. Her mouth felt as dry as dust. As she staggered, still half-asleep, to the bath, her belly growled with hunger.

Elspeth must have heard it. "We'll get ye fed proper when ye're cleaned up."

The warm water helped to revive her body, but did nothing for her spirits. Even Elspeth's gentle prodding couldn't unearth the source of Cynthia's melancholy.

She supposed she should be rejoicing. She'd won, after all. She'd single-handedly vanquished almost certain despair, looked death in the eye and beat it back from the door.

But at what price?

"How fare the villagers?" she asked.

"Not a one lost." Elspeth beamed, continuing to scrub at Cynthia's back. "A few are still weak as lambs, but they'll be up and about in no time."

Cynthia closed her eyes and breathed a prayer of thanks for that.

"In sooth, m'lady," El confided, sluicing a bucket of warm, clean water over Cynthia's head to rinse out the soap, "I trow the lot of 'em might be shoveled over now if it weren't for yer healin'."

Cynthia bit her lip. That was what she most feared. She'd taken that oath to save Garth in the name of God, but it seemed now like a pact with the devil. How in heaven's name could she keep it? How could she ever stand by in silence, knowing she possessed such a gift, and watch others suffer?

"El, I've done a foolish thing."

Elspeth stopped her ministrations and circled to stand before her in askance.

"I've made a reckless promise." A violet petal floated beside her on the water's surface, and she pressed her finger over it until it sank and drowned. Then she told Elspeth all about Garth's brush with death, her vow to use her gift no more, his miraculous recovery.

She didn't dare tell her about the other part of the bargain. Elspeth wouldn't understand. The maid thought of Garth as a priest, no more. She didn't know about the man inside, begging to be free.

"Don't ye fret now, lass," Elspeth said, patting her hand, but unable to conceal a small frown of worry. "The Lord works in strange ways." She bundled Cynthia's hair in a linen towel and gave it a twist at the top. "Ye know, ye've given more of yerself than most do in a lifetime. Perhaps the Lord's just givin' ye a rest. 'Tis time others did for *ye,* m'lady." She helped her from the bath and wrapped another towel about her. "And m'lady, if I may speak my mind?"

Cynthia gave her a helpless smile. Since when did Elspeth ever ask to speak her mind?

She led Cynthia to a padded bench and sat beside her. "Wendeville is a rich estate with grand holdings. Ye cannot leave it lie forever like a helpless doveling for all the greedy falcons circling about. Ye must get an heir eventually. Ye *know* that, lass. And ye must choose a good father for that heir."

Cynthia said nothing. For once, she listened.

"I know it's not long yer John has been in the tomb." She paused to cross herself. "But I know he'd want this, too. He'd not like to see his castle fall to ruin for want of an heir."

Cynthia swallowed and looked out the narrow window, where the last soft, hazy sunlight of the day kissed the rolling hills a fond good-night.

Elspeth was right. The promise John had extracted from her, to wed again for love, had been more than a gesture of magnanimity. John had wanted his legacy to continue, even if he didn't survive to see it.

Once before, Cynthia had sacrificed her own selfish desires to please her father, her sisters, her king. Perhaps such was the lot of a noblewoman. She was merely a pawn to be surrendered for the sake of those with greater need.

She wiped at her cheek with the linen square, unsure whether she dried a rogue droplet of water or a stray tear.

Perhaps she *should* find a lord for Wendeville. She was no longer of use to the castle folk as a healer. The least she could do was marry a kind and decent and fair overlord to ensure their future.

She swabbed up another drop she knew was a tear this time. It wouldn't do to let Elspeth see her weep. Weeping over such things was childish. Besides, her tears would only bewilder Elspeth. El would never understand, when she'd gone to such great pains to introduce Cynthia to every marriageable man in England, that the only man Cynthia was interested in, the only one who touched her heart and consumed her soul, was the one she could never have.

Garth would be damned if he'd take a sennight to heal from the murrain. He was, after all, of hale de Ware stock. After three days of the prior's coddling him like stained glass, he was ready to tear down the walls of his hospitable prison, stone by stone.

But healing from his wounded heart . . .

He'd heard nothing from Cynthia since she'd fled his cell, as if when she was through with his sickness, she was through with him as well. And yet, in sooth, she'd done no more than follow what he'd preached to her all along. She'd repeated his wisdom plainly. The monastery was his home. Wendeville was hers. He belonged in this world. She belonged in another.

Why then, when she'd finally accepted the truth, did every fiber of his being cry out in denial? Why could he not believe his own words? And why could he not drive her from his thoughts?

Fine particles of dust sifted down through the sunbeam in the scriptorium, illuminating the half-finished parchment. Garth dipped his quill again into the ebony ink, then paused, his fingers tightening as he stared at the word he'd scribed across the page of Scripture.

Cynthia.

He sighed, vexed at his distraction. No matter how neat the penmanship, *Cynthia* did not belong in the middle of the Psalms. He tossed the quill down in frustration. It made a stain on the page like a squashed spider.

"Something amiss?"

Garth scrabbled hastily at the parchment, crumpling it in his fist before Prior Thomas could see the mistake. How long had the stealthy old man been standing there?

"I . . . I need a new quill," he invented. "This one is split."

The prior picked up the quill, examining its point. "Hmm." He eyed the parchment, wrinkled beneath Garth's hand. Then he circled the scriptorium desk and set the quill down upon the edge.

"Brother Garth." He steepled his stumpy fingers against his pursed lip. "Your body has healed well and quickly, with God's blessing."

"Aye." Garth's smile felt forced.

"But . . ." He clapped his solid hand atop Garth's. "A hale body does not make a man whole." Garth tightened his grip on the parchment. "Your mind is yet troubled, Brother Garth, is it not?"

"Troubled?"

To his alarm, Prior Thomas gently pried the ball of parchment from him. Then he continued speaking, gesturing with the damned thing. "Aye. Troubled. Tormented. Restless."

Garth cleared his throat. "A priest's mind is . . . is ever restless while there is . . . sin in the world."

Silence reigned for a moment. Then the prior chuckled, tossing the unopened parchment back onto the desk. "Sin? Or Cynthia?"

For an instant, Garth was mortified. He clenched his fists, prepared to protest.

"Now lad, 'tis no use trying to deceive this old fox," Prior Thomas assured him with a wink.

Garth challenged the prior's gaze. But Thomas's eyes were full of empathy, not scorn. The man was genuinely trying to help. Garth forced his hackles down, surrendering. He ran his fingers wearily through his hair.

"It's hopeless, Father," he said softly, resting his forehead on his palms. "I cannot banish her from my mind. I pray. I fast. I immerse myself in this . . ." He picked up the wad of parchment, stared at it. "And still she haunts me."

The prior nodded. "Like the other one?"

He frowned. "The other?" Mariana. He meant Mariana. Sultry, scheming Mariana who roused him with the wiles of a harlot. "Nay. Nothing like her. Mariana was cruel. Cynthia is . . ." There were no words to describe her, at least none he could repeat to the prior, nothing to relay the wholeness of spirit, the rightness he felt with her. "Cynthia is not."

The prior smiled dryly. "High praise indeed for the woman who saved your life."

Garth's mind seized the alibi faster than a hound snatching a morsel of meat. "Aye. Mayhap that's it. It's merely gratitude."

"Gratitude?" The prior chuckled. "Nay, I think not. I administered a bit of medicine to you myself, but 'twas never my name you cried out in your fever."

Garth let out a long breath and rubbed at his temples, where a dull throbbing had begun. "Surely God has abandoned me. And yet I have done everything in my power to succumb to His will. Why does He not guide me in this?"

The prior sighed and waddled slowly before the desk, musing. "Perhaps He does." He tapped his bottom lip thoughtfully. "Brother Garth, let me speak plainly." He laced his fingers together over his round belly. "The crops are planted. The monastery stores are ample. I have two novitiates drooling over your desk like pups, eager to practice their letters. And in light of the quantity of broken quills and wasted parchment I've seen of late, I must say I'm tempted to let them."

Garth straightened defensively. "I can pay for—"

"Nay, nay, 'tis not my point," the prior said, waving away his offer. "Besides, your father has endowed us with enough silver for a mountain of parchment and a sea of ink. Nay, the marrow of it is that God seems to be guiding you most deliberately." He paused expectantly.

Garth frowned.

"Your work with Lady Cynthia is obviously not finished," Thomas explained, "in God's eyes."

Garth pressed the wrinkles from his brow.

"You're not needed at the monastery, Garth," the prior gently confided. "But Wendeville continues to lack a chaplain."

"Then find another." Garth frowned again. "I cannot work beside her, feeling . . . what I feel."

The prior took his hand in a surprisingly firm grip until Garth raised his eyes. "You cannot stay here, my son, feeling what you feel."

Garth bit the inside of his cheek. He wondered how it was possible to feel hope and dread at the same time. His heart raced at the prospect of seeing Cynthia again, but apprehension paralyzed his limbs. He vacillated in indecision.

"Garth, I've given Brother Andrew your cell."

"What?" He blinked.

"I've promised him that when you are fully healed—"

"You're banishing me from the monastery?" Garth asked, incredulous.

"Nay, not banishing." The prior scowled, patting his hand. "Pushing you . . . from the nest."

Garth was outraged. In sooth, Prior Thomas was tossing him out like a bothersome drunk from an alehouse. And yet, in his heart, he realized that the old man was right. Garth was clearly useless at the monastery. He couldn't even scribe two consecutive verses properly. Not while he was haunted by a pair of sapphire eyes.

Still, he couldn't imagine how things would be any better at Wendeville.

"Do not brood, Garth. God will guide you," the prior said, clapping him on the shoulder, "in the manner He has all along."

Garth smiled glumly. That was what he most feared.

By day's end, Garth stood before the doors of the great hall of Wendeville, holding his breath. At worst, he expected a chilly reception from the castle denizens. After all, he had, in effect, deserted them, and in the midst of Lent, in the midst of sickness. At best, he hoped for forgiveness in the form of a subdued but polite welcome. He never anticipated the desperation in Roger's eyes as the steward swung the door wide.

The man looked absolutely stricken. Dark shadows bruised the flesh beneath his eyes, and the grim turn of his mouth had aged him a decade beyond his years.

"Roger?" He dropped his satchel to the stones. "What is it? What's wrong?"

Roger wrung his hands together as his weary eyes filled with tears. An eery prickling coursed up Garth's spine, and his pulse beat unnaturally loud in his ears.

"What's happened, Roger?"

Roger fretted at the sleeve of his surcoat. "I fear I have bad tidings."

Garth's heart kicked a sudden macabre jig against his ribs. Bad tidings.

Elspeth came scurrying up behind Roger, she, too, bleary-eyed and as worn as pauper's linen.

"'Tis Lady Cynthia," she blurted, half-sobbing into her apron.

A sharp pain cut across Garth's breast. He staggered, catching himself on the frame of the door.

Roger reached out to steady him.

How it happened, he didn't know, but in the next moment Garth found himself with his fists clenched in the steward's surcoat, hauling the poor man within inches of his scowling face.

"Nay!" he growled.

Roger's eyes widened, and his mouth opened and closed twice, like a hooked trout's, before Garth realized what he was doing.

"Stop!" Elspeth cried.

He instantly released Roger, aghast at his own behavior.

"What . . . ," he began, choking on the words. "What has happened?"

Mercifully, Roger wasted no time restoring his composure. His garments still askew, he said, "She has the sickness. She may be . . . dying."

Garth's heart stabbed sideways through his constricted chest. His lip quivered. His eyes moistened. But not with sorrow. With rage. Rage that God would dare let the dread sickness darken Cynthia's threshold. Cynthia, who comforted the dying and brought new babes into the world. Who selflessly battled the devil's worst diseases, championing those with no strength to fight. Whose life lay yet unbloomed before her. Rage burned inside him until his skin crackled with it.

"Take me to her," he ground out. "Now."

It was Cynthia who needed a champion now. She had fought for everyone else. Lord, she'd fought for *him,* saved his life. He owed her as much. By the saints—*God* owed her as much.

With dread for a companion, he raced up the steps to her chamber, armed with naught but his wits, his will, and a love that, he hoped to God, could conquer anything.

The Abbot listened with feigned patience as Mary tearfully blurted out her confession. Garth de Ware had returned to Wendeville. He'd been there two days already, threatening mayhem and wreaking havoc, according to Mary. Her whimpers disturbed the flame of the single candle he held, making shadows dance up the soot-darkened walls of the cottage like bats taking flight at twilight.

"Brother Garth went mad as a bull, Father! I had no choice but to fetch the herbs for him! I swear it! And when I refused to bring him the eggs, it bein' Lent and all, he . . ." She broke off with a sob, running grimy fingers under her nose. They came away slick. The Abbot curled his lip in distaste. "He told me I'd swing from the gallows if Lady Cynthia died."

Died? Here was a surprise. "She's that ill?"

"Aye, Father. She's tossed with the fever for five days now. And Brother Garth, he's never left her side. Won't let anyone go near her either, except her maid and me. And now she lies still as death." Mary's brow fretted itself into an ugly contortion of suffering, and fresh tears coursed down her face. "Oh, Father! God will forgive me, will He not? I *had* to fetch the herbs!" She grabbed two fistfuls of his cassock. He grimaced, remembering the condition of her hands. "I *had* to!"

"I will intervene on your behalf," he said, more to shut her up than to give her solace.

It worked. She was reduced to raining tears and kisses upon the hem of his cassock.

He rapped his knuckle pensively against his teeth. Was Lady Cynthia dying? Even more significantly, was her death being hastened? Mayhap he hadn't given Father Garth enough credit. Mayhap the sly chaplain wasn't without selfish motives after all. Mary had seen their sordid encounter in the garden. Could it be that the crafty monk had insinuated himself into Cynthia's good graces with the intent of eliminating her?

Some of those devil's herbs he'd bade Mary fetch were poison. Did Garth intend, as soon as his inheritance was secure, to quietly finish Cynthia off with some deadly elixir?

The Abbot sighed unhappily. It niggled at him that he'd so misjudged Garth de Ware. Usually he could spot men of his own ilk, men of power and ambition, as readily as ink spilled on vellum. He'd missed this one.

What if Garth did succeed in eliminating the last remaining heir to Wendeville? In sooth, it would cast less suspicion on the Abbot's own person were another to see to Cynthia's disposal. And in the end, Garth would still lose. The Abbot had played the game much longer. He had the tools to destroy Garth de Ware, to strip the cassock right off his back.

He had the list of devil's herbs.

He had proof that the strictures of Lent had been disobeyed.

And he had a witness, who even now groveled at his feet, to the chaplain's midnight indiscretion with Lady Cynthia.

Oh aye, one way or another, both Cynthia Wendeville and Garth de Ware would pay the price for their sins.

Righteousness welled in him like a font, turning the dismal hovel suddenly bright with promise. Even his usually critical gaze, as he stared down at the wretch worshiping his garments, grew more charitable. Mary seemed not so pathetic now. The fat tears glistened like polished jewels on her pale cheek, and her hair wound sinuously over her quaking shoulders. In sooth, she seemed almost holy. Her hands clasped the edge of his cassock to her bosom as if it were a relic. Murmurs of prayer fell from her reddened, sob-swollen lips.

The poor child was suffering. She needed him. Needed his forgiveness. His blessing. His offering.

He hardened at once.

Garth ran a shaky hand through his grimy hair. His eyes felt as gritty and raw as salted mussels. He stank of sweat and worry. His belly whimpered with hunger, but he couldn't eat. Spots of color fluttered before him like moths, reminding him of the sleep he'd neglected too long. He scrubbed at his eyes, temporarily vanquishing the flitting lights. But he knew they'd be back. Just like the gloom that visited him between bouts of hope.

For three days and nights, he'd stayed with her. Watching her. Fighting for her as she hovered on the brink of death. In all that time, he'd never voiced a single prayer, not because he lacked faith, but because he knew he would have just as willingly called upon the devil as God to save Cynthia if he thought it would work.

Already he'd violated Lent. Already he'd used herbs known to be Lucifer's own. And a hundred times he'd touched her intimately—bathing her fevered skin, changing her soiled garments, brushing her hair back from her pale cheek. Nay, God would not listen to his sinner's pleas now.

And yet he was desperate.

He reached out for Cynthia's wrist. Beneath his fingers, her pulse was weak and slow, and her skin was clammy. He held his palm before her lips. Her breath made only the faintest stirring there. He swallowed hard, fighting off the despair that threatened to envelop him.

It was not just.

He should be dying, not Cynthia.

Who was he? An empty vessel adrift on a nameless sea. Half a man who was good for neither church nor husband. But Cynthia—Cynthia was full of life and love and purpose. She brought the omnipotence of God to men's hearts more powerfully than any of his own hollow sermons ever would.

It was a travesty. She'd drained herself to save him, and now she lay dying.

His mouth twisted bitterly. On the table beside Cynthia's bed, shriveled leaves and shredded bark lay in neat piles on a wooden platter. They were the weapons he'd meticulously prepared, mimicking as best he could Cynthia's own, to fight off the demon attacking her. He'd believed they could save her, as they had the villagers. But now they seemed mere impotent weeds and chaff. Without Cynthia's touch, without her healing gift to empower them, the herbs were useless.

Frustration fed the fury growing inside him, mocking him, tormenting him until it exploded in a storm of pain. Snarling a curse, he swept his arm violently across the tabletop, knocking aside the tray and scattering the herbs into the rushes. Futile tears stood in his eyes, blurring his vision, and the need to sob out the injustice of it all wrenched at his chest.

But in the end, the only words he could speak were ones that had become as familiar to him as his own name. Broken, he clenched his eyes shut and surrendered to his fearsome God. With tears of fatigue streaming down his cheeks, he fell to his knees before Cynthia, clasped his fists together, and prayed for the Lord's mercy upon her.

Over and over he said the words until, eventually, his fervent prayers diminished, becoming syllables murmured mindlessly as spots floated again before his eyes. Exhaustion overcame him. Three sleepless nights caught up with him and hauled him into the muddy waters of slumber.

One hour might have passed, or ten. He wasn't certain. But some soft sound awakened him. He lifted his head from the wool coverlet and, for a moment, couldn't remember where he was. His eyes were swollen, and his cheeks felt stiff from the salty tracks of his tears.

"Garth?"

He came wide awake in an instant. He'd know that dulcet voice anywhere.

"Cynthia?" he croaked.

She looked as feeble as a new-hatched dove, her neck wavering as she strained to lift her head. But she was breathing. And her color had returned. She was alive. Praise God, she was alive!

"Cynthia!"

His first impulse was to crush her in an embrace of pure

euphoria. He longed to cover her face with kisses of celebration, to pick her up and whirl her about the chamber.

But, stepping near the bed, stretching out a hand, gazing into her faintly shimmering eyes, he saw her for once more clearly than he ever had before.

This was a woman who deserved the best of life. God had wrenched her from the grasp of jealous death so that she might dwell a bit longer among the living, sharing her gift, fulfilling her dreams. Who was *he* to dull the bright light of her spirit? To stain the precious years she had left with regret and disappointment? Cynthia deserved far better. She deserved more than what Mariana had proved him—half a man.

As she stared expectantly at him, her beautiful cornflower eyes full of hope, shining with gratitude, soft with affection, his heart sank to his stomach.

It would kill him, he knew, to deny his feelings. It would break her heart as well. And yet, it was the only right thing to do.

He looked away, unable to bear the mild confusion and pain he knew would enter her eyes. He withdrew his extended hand, closing it into an impartial fist. And he hardened his heart against the flood of emotion that threatened to unman him and make him forget his good intentions.

"Are you . . ." He cleared his throat. "Do you feel better?"

Her silence forced him to meet her gaze again. She looked hurt, puzzled.

"You . . ." Her voice creaked like an iron hinge in need of oil.

She struggled to sit upright. He couldn't stand by and watch her futile attempts. Steeling his emotions, he vaulted forward, cradling her in the crook of his arm and bolstering her with several pillows. Then he reached for his hip flask of watered wine, uncorked it with his teeth, and raised it to her lips. She covered his hand with her own two and drank greedily. Surely it was unwise to drink so much at once, but he couldn't deny her. He let her drink her fill.

After several gulps, she pushed the flask aside and wiped a shaky hand across her lips. Then she raised her eyes to his.

"You stayed with me."

It sounded like an accusation. He slipped his arm from around her, corking the flask and dropping his gaze.

"How long?" she asked.

"Not long," he lied, putting the flask away.

"Long enough to grow this," she said, reaching up to stroke his stubbled chin.

Her fingers burned like hot embers against his face. He turned his cheek aside.

"Please . . . ," he whispered.

He felt her eyes on him, searching his face a long while before she turned her head to look despondently toward the window.

"How many days have I been ill?"

"Five . . . six." He picked up the wooden platter from the floor and set it on the table, squaring it up with the edge. He had to get away from Cynthia. Now. Before he forgot his intent and begged for her touch again. "I'll fetch Elspeth. She'll be relieved that you're well."

"And are you?" She still gazed out the window, and her words seemed more thought than speech.

"Am I . . . ?"

"Relieved?"

More than you can possibly imagine, he thought. He answered evasively instead. "Of course. It's always a blessing to see the work of God's hand—"

"It wasn't *God's* hand that healed me." She turned toward him, and there was such desperation in her eyes that he couldn't bear it.

He bit the inside of his cheek, avoiding her piercing gaze. "I fear you blaspheme, my lady."

Before he could halt her, she clasped his hand in her two. "It's *this* hand I remember between bouts of sleep, holding mine, smoothing my brow, stroking my cheek, healing me." Her voice was rough, and she blushed as if the words came from her against her will. Then she lifted his trapped hand to place a quick and reckless kiss along his knuckles.

His heart fluttered. He wanted her kiss. Her soft breath was a sweet caress across the back of his fingers.

"Then you must forget this hand," he whispered harshly, reluctantly pulling away, knowing he crushed her. "It has been an instrument of God's will, no more. And that is all it will ever be."

He made the sign of the cross and walked stiffly toward the door, feeling the pain he'd inflicted all the way. Before he left, he turned to her once more. "It's all *I* will ever be."

17

THE SICKNESS IN THE VILLAGE INDEED FOUNDERED AND died, and the air filled with the sweet scents of nature's renewal. The sun coaxed tender shoots of grass up from the earth, and tightly curled leaves and buds tipped the dark branches with vivid green. By Easter, everyone, peasant and noble alike, was eager to crowd into the great hall of Wendeville for an enormous feast. Cynthia hired mummers to perform a St. George play, and Father Garth, promising loyal service to the castle henceforth, blessed the colorful pace eggs, as was his duty, for the men and women to exchange.

The days passed in subdued harmony while the garden erupted in a slow explosion of color. But for Cynthia, the blooms brought little joy. They were only a bright reminder of how dull her own life had become.

Elspeth continued to bring candidates for Cynthia's hand, and while she tried to greet them civilly, none of them seemed of adequate intellect or appropriate demeanor to take on the responsibility of Wendeville. Certainly none of them even remotely stirred her emotions, and while it wasn't necessarily a prerequisite for marriage, if she wanted an heir, she had to at least be willing to bed Wendeville's lord.

The situation seemed hopeless, and having Garth nearby did nothing to remedy that. She compared every man to him.

This lord's eyes were not as bright. That lord's smile was not as bewitching. This gentleman's touch was not nearly as warm, that gentleman's not nearly as firm.

But at last, on a brilliant morn in late April, when tufted clouds frolicked like lambs across the jewel-blue sky, he came.

His name was Philip.

He was perfect. Not too handsome, not too plain. Not overly extravagant, but far from miserly. Fair-minded. Polite. Humble.

She didn't love him. Far from it. But he was acceptable as lord for Wendeville. She could see he would be good for the people. Roger liked him. Elspeth liked him. The castle folk liked him. Everyone would be glad of a wedding between the two of them.

Everyone but Garth. Garth hated Philip at once. And just as instantly prayed for forgiveness. There was no real reason to hate the man. He was perfect for Wendeville, perfect for Cynthia. It was only that ugly beast, jealousy, that perched upon Garth's shoulder.

It had no license to do so. Not while Garth was a priest. Not after he had separated himself so neatly and thoroughly from Cynthia's affections.

It had not been easy, but since that blessed day when God had seen fit to save her life, Garth had dedicated himself wholly, devotedly to his religious duty.

He made frequent visits to the town now. He knew the villagers by name and considered each soul his solemn responsibility. He'd even arranged, with the permission of Wendeville's groom, to send palfreys each Sabbath to transport the elderly to Mass at the chapel.

He helped with the distribution of alms and trenchers and worn clothing to the poor, and even spent odd hours scrubbing plaster and polishing the stained glass of the chapel until it shone with heavenly luster.

The children of the keep he taught to read, and even the falconer, who had no real use for letters, but who'd come to him with a longing so sincere he couldn't refuse to school him. He tended to the infirm, prayed for the destitute, blessed two newborn babes, and gave the old castle brewster last rites.

And through it all, he managed to keep apart from Lady Cynthia. She even obliged him by respecting his chosen detachment from her. Once he'd explained, once he'd made clear to her that her life had been bargained for upon his faith, she seemed to understand. She no longer summoned him to the garden or teased him at supper or wore the scent of jasmine in his presence.

Only when he passed one of the fragrant sprays of white and yellow blooms Cynthia cut and placed about the castle did a faint but persistent longing pierce his heart. Only when the scent of flowers wafted through his thoughts did he feel strangely bereft.

And if he sensed empathy in her, if she, too, seemed particularly wistful in idle moments, he told himself it was the loss of her husband that made her so, or a feminine longing for a child, or the simple restlessness of spring. It would have tortured him too much to hope she felt the same pangs as he.

And as it turned out, he was mistaken about her melancholy. In sooth, she wasted no time at all finding a new lord for Wendeville.

Elspeth, with her usual stubborn persistence, had continued to inflict eligible noblemen upon the castle, and, for a while, Cynthia had discarded them as arbitrarily as a fisherman throwing back too small catch.

It would have been a lie to say her actions disappointed Garth. In his eyes, none of the men had seemed good enough for Cynthia Wendeville.

But then Sir Philip de Laval arrived.

He wasn't nearly as flamboyant and engaging as Lord William had been, but then the man would never eclipse Cynthia's light. Garth could see in his forthright gaze that Sir Philip was a good man. *His* spirit wasn't troubled by doubt. *He* wasn't plagued by moral dilemmas. He was simply a decent, God-fearing, honorable man.

Apparently Cynthia thought so, too. Within days, she'd accepted his informal proposal of marriage.

It was probably for the best. She did look peaceful

strolling the courtyard on his arm. The smiles they exchanged at supper were fond, and the way Philip's face glowed with quiet pleasure when she entered a room, Garth knew he'd treat her well.

And in the occasional moments when envy surfaced amongst his thoughts, Garth pressed it down like an autumn apple, filtering the bitter seeds from the sweet cider. If his throat closed when he thought about having to be the one to seal their eventual bond of marriage, he reminded himself that Cynthia deserved so much more than he, Garth, could give her.

Thus it was that on days like today, the first of May, when all Wendeville was agog with feasting and merrymaking and festivity, Garth welcomed the chaos to which the castle was reduced, for he scarcely had time to dwell on such troubling matters of the heart.

In sooth, his own exuberance amazed him as he stood at the edge of the wooden palisade constructed for the great May Day tournament. In the lists, Wendeville's finest warriors kicked up swirling clouds of dust, battling afoot in the melee, wielding blunted swords and shouting aspersions against their foes.

Garth's heart pounded, and he felt his own shoulders tense as he watched the knights whirl and slash at their opponents. Of course, in his opinion, none of them were fit to polish the armor of his magnificent brothers. Duncan and Holden could have taken on the entire Wendeville fighting force without a scratch, he was sure. But that didn't curb his enjoyment of the spectacle, and before he knew it, he was yelling out insults and encouragement along with the rest of the crowd.

It was a friendly melee. When it was over, the victors held out their hands to their fallen foes and clapped them on the back for a battle well played. Blunt blades were used in the sword duels. The jousting, as well, was done with coroneled lances. Which was why the accident came as such a shock.

Garth had taken a cup of wine from a passing maidservant and was eyeing the pennons of the visiting knights to see how many he recognized when a collective gasp from the crowd drew his attention. He turned his gaze at once to the field of the lists. One of the jousters had fallen, which was nothing surprising, but he lay silent where he fell for a long while. Too long. And when the helm was pulled from his head, it was obvious the unconscious knight was but a lad.

Garth swore under his breath. Aye, his brothers had both done their share of filching armor as boys and fighting in tournaments for which they had neither permission nor experience to participate. But then, they were destined to be the finest knights in England. This boy was clearly . . . a boy.

The men on the field had removed his breastplate and were slapping at his cheeks now, trying to rouse the lad, to no avail. Lord, if they didn't hurry . . .

Garth dropped his cup to the ground, heedless of the wine that trickled onto the sod. He hoisted up his cassock and leaped over the palisade on one arm, charging forward as soon as his feet hit the ground.

Cynthia gathered her skirts and lunged forward without thought. A lad lay unconscious on the field. She had to help him.

She heard some vague sound of protest as she left. Philip, no doubt, concerned for her safety. But she rushed off anyway, half-conscious that her betrothed dogged her every step.

"Back away!" she snapped at the knights as she flung herself to the ground beside the fallen jouster. "Give me room to work."

Behind her, Philip gasped. "Cynthia! Surely you're not going to . . ." he began, likely appalled by the sight of his bride squatting like a peasant in the dust.

"Let her be." Cynthia's ear caught on the soft, deep voice above her. It was Garth. And in that instant, as he stood so close that his cassock rippled against her surcoat, an unexpected breath of desire blew past her like wind from a warm and faraway land.

"But she cannot . . ." Philip sputtered.

"Let her be." Garth spoke quietly, but with enough force to silence Philip. Then he caught her gaze. "Will he live? Can you save him?"

Gazing into his solemn green eyes, she was transported back to the monastery. She'd asked that very same thing as Garth lay languishing in his cell. She'd seen his death. But she'd not accepted it. And she'd bargained with . . .

Dear God! She couldn't do this. She couldn't use her powers. She'd made a vow. . . .

"Cynthia!" Garth barked, demanding her gaze. "Can you save him?"

Philip intervened. "Chaplain, I must protest—"

"If you can save him, you must," Garth told her.

Cynthia caught her lip under her teeth. She'd made a promise . . . but surely God couldn't mean for the boy to die. What was she to do?

She stared up at Garth and saw the answer in his steady, calming gaze. He didn't judge her. He didn't question the source of her power. If she could save him . . . she must. She must.

Though she feared the damning watch of God upon her, she closed her eyes and began rubbing her palms together.

She heard Philip protest behind her. "What the devil?"

Garth whispered, "Not the devil. It's God's work."

She'd not used her gift in weeks, and it returned reluctantly, but with such strength that she felt scarcely able to control its power. Bolts of current seemed to shoot up her arms and through her legs, skewering her between earth and sky like lightning. Her skin crawled with prickles of fire. Quivering with trepidation, she stretched forth her hands and placed them lightly upon the lad's forehead.

An image clapped into her brain like the flashes of a night storm, swift and sharp and clear. But it seemed so strange, so perverse. . . .

She frowned and opened her eyes, snatching her hands back. The image made no sense.

Wetting her lips, she closed her eyes and tried again, placing just the tips of her fingers upon the boy's temples. There it was again. The same aberrant picture. It couldn't possibly be right. And yet what choice did she have? The lad grew paler by the moment, his skin cooling even as she wrestled with her thoughts.

•   •   •

Garth's heart raced. If Cynthia didn't make quick work of it, if she couldn't decipher the cure soon . . .

Suddenly she emitted a small moan of frustration or confusion. Then she inclined her head toward the lad's. For a moment, it appeared as if she intended to kiss him.

Philip cursed. "What in the name of—"

Garth again intervened, blocking Philip with his arm. "Wait."

But even Garth's faith was tested as her lips fell upon the boy's mouth in a most improperly intimate fashion. She blew out a long breath of air, and the lad's cheeks puffed out like a frog's. The surrounding knights began to mumble amongst themselves as if wondering what to make of this strange perversion. Again she exhaled into the boy's mouth.

"What wickedness is this?" Philip demanded, incensed. "Come away from him now, Cynthia." He reached forward to grab her arm.

She shook it off, and he gaped in astonishment.

"Leave her be," Garth said.

"I will not stand by and let . . ."

Suddenly a rasping breath pierced the air, and Garth saw the boy's chest rise. Relief and wonder filled him. She'd done it. She'd saved the lad. Literally blown the breath of life back into him. He caught her gaze, and such profound joy shone in her eyes that he longed to embrace her in sheer triumph.

But it wasn't his place now. He was a priest. And Philip, Cynthia's betrothed, still scowled at his side.

A great cheer went up, echoing into the stands, and the boy struggled up on his elbows, dazed, embarrassed, but thankfully alive.

Abruptly the back of Garth's arm was caught in a sharp pinch.

"How dare you endorse this . . . this work of the devil," Philip hissed. "Have you no care for Lady Cynthia's soul?"

Not waiting for a reply, Philip let him go and wrenched Cynthia up violently by the arm. "And you," he muttered under his breath. "That boy should be dead. How could you interfere with the will of God?"

Before he knew what he was doing, Garth, incensed by

the man's rough treatment of Cynthia, seized him by the shoulders and spun him around. "Lay a heavy hand on her again," he bit out, "and I'll chop it off."

Those who heard him gasped. They were not the words of a humble chaplain.

Philip blinked several times, astonished as much by Garth's threat as by his own rash behavior. Then he continued more gently and with great concern, "My lady, prithee excuse my . . . severity. I'm certain God will forgive you for your ignorance, but if you are to be my wife, you must promise me you'll not work that . . . that witchery again."

Garth still reeled from the heady rush of violence pumping in his blood. He bit the inside of his cheek, stifling the words that came to his lips when he beheld the pain and bewilderment on Cynthia's face. But she made no objection. Though it must break her heart to do so, she merely swallowed back her tears and nodded in acquiescence.

The rest of the day was spoiled for him then. Cynthia had performed a miracle, and the man she was to marry had scorned her for it. Garth wondered how Philip could live with himself, knowing he rejected the very essence of all that Cynthia embraced. It was a tragedy, and there was nothing he could do to resolve it.

The rest of the afternoon he kept his emotions carefully concealed, doing his best to be a good chaplain to the celebrants at Wendeville. He blessed their meal, found napping places for those who'd drunk too liberally, and even chuckled good-naturedly at the heathen antics of some of the castle folk, gently guiding them back toward a spiritual bent. He tried to keep up a joyous countenance.

But it was evident later, after the revelry had died down, when the keep echoed with the soft snores of the well-fed, while he restlessly wandered the corridors and the hall and the courtyard, where the musky spring air was ripe with sultry promise, that none of it changed the way he felt.

Lord, he still loved her.

The profile of the rising moon, low in the purple sky, glowed golden, dusting the leaves of the trees rising above the garden wall. A subtle breeze made the branches shiver in the dark with shimmering radiance. Crickets played lusty music for their mates, and in the distance, an owl hooted softly.

Garth clenched his fists once, all but paralyzed before the privy garden, silently cursing the cunning wanderlust that had brought him to this place.

For the gate was ajar.

And that could mean only one thing at this late hour.

Cynthia was there.

Through the crack in the door, he saw the light filtering down over the shifting branches onto a narrow slice of the path, but little else. A gust of warm wind came up behind him, brushing over his cassock and past him, shoving the gate open another inch, goading him forward.

He shouldn't go in.

He should turn around, return to his quarters, and try once again to seize elusive sleep.

Nay, he shouldn't even think of it. Not when he'd kept his emotions so well reined in. Not when he'd managed to restore a semblance of cordiality with Cynthia without letting her glimpse the molten fire boiling beneath his surface.

He couldn't destroy that accomplishment. He was committed to Wendeville now. It was a long road the two of them might travel together. If he couldn't ever fully express the depth of feeling he had for her, then he must learn to live with that. He must settle for being a platonic companion to her.

And so, tonight, he should leave her be.

She probably wished to be alone anyway. God knew *he* needed to be alone. Too many things could happen if they were alone together on a sultry evening like this one.

He shouldn't.

And yet his feet carried him forward, toward the inviting gap in the garden wall.

Slowly the gate swung inward under his hand. It creaked low, widening the wedge of light. A few pale apple blossoms fluttered to the ground, glowing softly in the refined light.

And then he saw her.

She sat on the sod bench between the deep shadows of the willow, bathed in moonlight. Her sorrowful face was turned toward him, as if she'd been weeping and waiting for him forever.

He held his breath, wanting naught but to look at her. God—she was beautiful, more stunning than the stars. How he longed to hold this moment for all eternity. He stood absolutely quiet, certain that breathing, speaking, moving might destroy the fragile bond that mere gazing forged.

Yet, however he yearned for her, he was also her friend and her priest. So against his better instincts, his feet propelled him forward. He pressed the gate closed behind him, slumping back against it, knowing as he did that he sealed his fate as well.

There was no turning back.

A whiff of cursed jasmine beckoned him. Taking a deep surrendering breath, he walked toward her. Shadows of branches snaked over his cassock like Eden's serpent, as if in warning. And yet, he could no more resist the temptation to go to her than Adam could resist Eve.

She waited for him, her hands clasped patiently in her lap, till he stood but an arm's length away. Her eyes shone translucent and trusting and deeply melancholy as they searched his face, the colandered moonlight glazing them to a pewter sheen. Shadows of leaves played across her parted lips. Once, he thought with a twinge of yearning, he had tasted those lips. They were sweet and warm and yielding.

He wouldn't think about it.

"My lady, you should be abed."

"Should I have let the boy die?" Her eyes filled with tears. "Is that what troubles you?"

How fragile she looked, like a newborn fawn, unsure where to step. He wanted to curse Philip for planting such doubt into her head.

"Mayhap it *was* God's will," she said brokenly.

He seized her by the shoulders, forcing her gaze to his. "God gave you that gift. It's a wondrous thing. He meant for you to use it. Never doubt that."

"But Philip—"

"To hell with Philip!" She flinched at his words, and he could have bitten his tongue. "Forgive me. It's not my place to . . . judge. But Philip would deny you your powers. However well-meaning he is, he will not accept your gift."

A lone tear wound its way down her cheek. "I do not love him." Her voice was but a whisper. "I never did. I only wanted to please Roger and Elspeth and John and the people of Wendeville. But I do not love him."

Garth blew out a long and shaky breath.

"And I fear I will dishonor him if I wed him while . . ."

A tendril of hair blew softly across her face. Without thinking, he reached down and brushed the silky strand back from her cheek, tucking it behind her ear. "While . . . ?"

She caught his wrist gently, like a child trapping a sparrow. She closed her eyes and pressed his hand against the warm column of her neck.

Despite her serene countenance, he could feel her pulse beating wildly against his palm. A rush of pleasure shot through him at the heat of her touch, so long imagined, so long denied.

"While my heart belongs to another," she murmured.

His heart careened recklessly against his ribs. He should pull back, he knew. She was a lady, and he . . . But he'd known that when he stepped across the threshold. It was too late now. Desire tugged at him like the tenacious undercurrent of the sea.

"It's you I love," she whispered. "You know it's you." She turned her head slightly, and he felt her moist breath upon his hand. She placed a tender kiss in his palm, then another, and another. He watched in wonder, breathless, as she worshiped his fingers one by one, her own breath fluttery and uncertain, her eyes squeezed as if in delicious torment.

"We mustn't," he said, his voice quaking violently.

And then she tucked the tip of his finger inside her mouth. A change like lightning seared his loins as her tongue caressed him, suckling gently. His legs weakened, and he sucked a sigh hard between his teeth. A roaring grew inside his head, like a feral lion demanding release.

"Nay," he growled.

He'd fought that lusting animal before and won, just barely. But it had grown since then into a snarling, raging beast, blotting out the quiet voice of reason.

He was powerless to resist.

With a groan, he sank to his knees before her. Furrowing both hands into her hair, he surged forward to claim her mouth.

Her gasp of pleasure fueled his passion. He answered her with hungry grunts, nipping at her parted lips. His hands moved over her with a will of their own, finding every part of her soft and warm and supple.

He kissed his way toward the shelter of her neck, a starving man who'd dreamt often of this feast, and she eagerly bared her throat to him. He whispered wordlessly against her ear, and she shivered in his arms, clutching feverishly at the front of his cassock. With deft fingers, he threw back her cloak and loosened her surcoat.

His groin tautened with need as he reached tenderly inside her underdress and found the precious curve of her breast. It was like velvet, its tip puckered into a tiny rosebud. He freed her from the dress's confines and let his mouth take suckle at the sweet flesh.

She moaned in encouragement, and then her hands moved down over the woolen folds of his cassock. He gasped as she discovered what she sought through the wool, fully erect, throbbing with a burden of seed. And at last, the pressure of her fingers against him shocked him to reason.

"Nay!" he cried suddenly, pushing away from her, stumbling back against the punishing stones of the garden wall, one hand holding his cassock closed, the other across his sinning mouth.

Cynthia staggered, trying to catch her breath. Her gown hung off one shoulder, her breast bare to the breeze. But, reeling from the heady drink of passion, she was past care.

Aye, she belonged to another. Aye, she broke her sacred oath to God, for she longed to have Garth for her own, whatever the consequences. She'd pay them, even if it meant the damnation of her soul, if he would only hold her in his arms again. Kiss her. Admit his love.

But he slouched against the wall, clutching his cassock to him as if it were a talisman. His face was a study of suffering. His eyes blazed. With anguish. With desire. And something more.

Victory.

He thought he'd won the battle over his emotions. He thought he could simply withdraw and win.

But she'd come this far. She'd risked telling him the truth, bared her heart to him as well as her body. And she had no intention of giving up the fight.

"What is it you fear?" she whispered, taking a step toward him.

He pulled back, stiffening against the wall.

"Why do you resist what we both desire?" She took another step.

His jaw tensed. He looked as wary as an injured cat cornered by a mastiff.

"You want me," she murmured, moving close enough to catch the compelling scent of vanilla and woodsmoke on his skin. "And God knows I want you."

He squeezed his eyes shut, as if he could block the truth by blinding himself to it.

"You're not a monk anymore. What wrong can there be . . . ?" she said, clasping his forearms lightly.

Cat-quick, he turned his hands to trap her wrists away from him, searing her with a fiery glare.

"Leave me!" he hissed.

"Why?" she demanded. "Why?" She was so close to hurt now, she could taste it. But she had to know. She searched his eyes for the answer. "Is it . . . Mariana?"

"What?" he exploded. "How do you know about . . ."

"You cried out her name before." Tears welled in her eyes, and she felt the prick of a blade at her heart, but she had to discover the truth. "Is it Mariana? Do you love her?"

"Nay." He scowled at her as if she were crazed. "Nay."

"Then why do you turn me away?"

"Leave me," he snarled. "Go to Philip . . . or another. I care not. But I have nothing to give you. I have nothing to give any woman."

His voice was harsh, and his hands were uncompromising on her wrists, but as she gazed into his eyes, she saw something entirely different.

A plea.

A desperate plea.

He wanted her to prove him wrong.

"Nay," she breathed. "That isn't true. You have enough for me. You've always—"

"Nay!" he said, shaking her once. "You don't know. You cannot know."

"Cannot know what?" she persisted. "That you suffer pangs of desire? You tell me I must not refuse the gift that God has given me, and yet you refuse the manhood He has given you. Would you deny that you feel the cravings of any mortal man?"

"But I am not a man!" he exploded, turning with her then and pinning her against the stone wall, his face contorting in anguish. "I am only half a man!"

She didn't know what he meant. But she could see pain in his eyes as profound as the sea. And she wanted nothing more than to ease that pain.

"Then let me make you whole," she whispered.

The tiniest flicker of hope entered his eyes before he lowered his gaze to her lips, focusing there with the savage hunger of a wolf. His tongue flitted quickly over his lower lip, and his nostrils flared.

"Let me make you . . . ," she repeated, but already his mouth had found hers.

He kissed her ravenously, fiercely, as if he feared it might be his last chance. Groaning, he swept his tongue fully across her lips, parting them. She moaned as he released her wrists and tangled his fingers in her hair, tilting her head to gain entrance to her mouth, plunging his tongue inside to mate with hers.

Lord, he was strong, stronger than John had ever been, stronger than Philip would ever be, strong enough that a thrill of something akin to fear coursed up her spine.

Suddenly, her limbs felt worthless, and she grew as limp as a cloth doll. Somehow, she clung to his cassock as he laid siege to her lips, but how she stayed on her feet, she couldn't tell. The place between her legs swelled with yearning, as if it would burst. Once, his thigh brushed against her there, and she gasped with the painful pleasure of it. Vaguely, she grew aware of the pressure against her belly as Garth hardened.

She let her fingers slip down then to scrabble at his belt, but she was too distracted to untangle the knot. She murmured a curse against his mouth.

He untied it himself, his lips never leaving hers, and when he opened his cassock, she let her fingers drift through the crisp curls he revealed. There she discovered, with a hushed gasp of wonder, his hard, warm staff. Lord—he was far larger than John. Almost menacing. With a shiver, she enclosed him gently in her palm. He drew in a rough breath, and his fingers tightened on her shoulders. She closed her eyes and nearly swooned, imagining that silken length inside her.

Then, with a soft cry, she hiked up her skirts, laying her head back upon the stones. He heaved one awe-filled sigh and lifted her up, bracing her against the wall. His well-muscled thighs felt like fire as they spread hers. His breath rasped against her ear, murmuring endearments, begging entrance.

She sighed in answer.

And then he was there, impossibly huge, impossibly hot, poised to penetrate her.

She couldn't wait. Inch by slow inch, she sheathed him herself, reveling in his slow groan as her skin pulled taut and her muscles strained to contain him. Dear God—she feared she might explode. And yet, there was something about the tightness, something about the way he slid against her . . .

"Oh!"

He pressed deeply up into her, and she shuddered with pleasure, her fingers digging into the thick muscle of his chest.

"Oh, God," he growled. "Cynthia."

To her astonishment, tears gathered in her eyes. Sweet Lord—she wanted to stay here forever, joined with this man, filled by him. She wanted to bask in their completeness.

But such was not the way of things with men, she knew from experience with John. This sweet lethargy wouldn't last long. She had to work quickly.

She drew away, biting her lip at the exquisite friction of his flesh gliding against hers. Then, ignoring her selfish desires and that instinctive, languorous rhythm that called to her, she initiated the brisk pattern of motion she knew well.

Garth clenched his teeth against the incredible sensation. It had been four years since he'd been enveloped by warm womanflesh. And yet mating with Mariana had been nothing like this. Cynthia was far softer, sweeter, comforting. By the rood, if she didn't slow down . . .

"Wait," he managed to gasp.

Everything was coming too fast. Too intensely. He'd be spent in another instant, leaving her behind, if she continued bucking like that.

"Wait!"

Using sheer willpower, he stopped her frenzied thrashing, hoisting her in one easy movement from the wall onto the grassy bench carved into the sod. He swooped down upon her, trapping every silky, lissome, soul-wrenching bit of her beneath him. Then he plunged with languid grace into her wet, welcoming haven.

This was where she belonged. Here he was master. Here he could pleasure her at his own pace. As long as he could control his own seething ardor.

"Aye," he sighed, trembling with the restraint of four long years. "Aye."

Cynthia arched up in a tempest of confusion and ecstasy. This was wrong. She was supposed to sit astride *him*. It had always been thus with John. But Garth had her pinned like a cat with a moth. He blinded her, blotting out the moon with his great bulk, so that she could see only him. He smothered her so she could scarcely move. Surely she'd be crushed beneath him.

And yet, it felt so right. She could breathe after all, enough to relish the intoxicating masculine scent of him. And she felt no desire to look upon anything other than his face. His flesh melded to hers like molten steel, and that part of him nesting deep within her . . .

Ah, God—he moved. Slowly. Elegantly. Like a dance. He forced her to feel every inch of him as he withdrew, then pressed inward again, as if boasting of his size. And yet, his hands caught her face with utmost tenderness, his thumb brushing across her lower lip before he bent to steal a kiss.

Crickets chirped lazily in the distance, and the wind soughed through the trees overhead, but all other sounds grew muffled as Garth groaned and murmured against her ear.

Her whole body began to tingle, the way it did when she performed a healing, but the heat centered at the point where their bodies joined and spread inexorably outward like consuming fire. Every stroke was a breath fueling the flame.

There was no room for thought. Only perception. It was like a film of gauze surrounded her, blurring the world, stifling all but the extraordinary sensation building within her. Her nipples ached, and he seemed to read her mind, palming the throbbing buds. Her hips surged upward of their own accord, striving for, for . . . she knew not what. Her head rocked from side to side, and the moans coming from her were foreign to her own ears. Sweet Mary—some delirious demon seemed to possess her, stealing her command, shredding away her gentility like worn linen. Never before had she known such madness, such helplessness, such ecstasy.

And then, rising to a dizzying peak with alarming swiftness, came a moment when nearly everything ceased. No breath stirred her lungs. No word escaped her. No sound penetrated the preternatural silence. Her body seemed to hang in perfect balance between two worlds. But that one spot, the place where their bodies met and merged and danced together, refused to cease. It glowed brighter still, carried beyond the realm of reality, becoming pure spirit and light and sensation.

And then waves of intense pleasure rushed over her like drowning waters, claiming her body, wrenching all will from her. She sobbed out her ecstatic release on the syllable of his name.

Garth followed her almost at once over the precipice. He groaned with a ferocity that was frightening as he plunged again and again within her, marking her with his seed, shuddering afterward like a frisky steed.

Then the ethereal world receded. Slowly, slowly she began to hear the crickets again. Stars glittered between the gray-green branches of the willow. The sod beneath her was damp and fragrant.

Her body, spent and weak as a kitten, felt as if it belonged to someone else. And Garth loomed over her, his flesh still melded to hers, his breath heavy upon her cheek, his male scent strong and virile.

She closed her eyes. Horrified.

She'd done something wrong.

She must have.

Never had she lost control like that. Never had she surrendered so wholly or felt so vulnerable.

What was wrong with her?

She'd completely neglected Garth. She should have helped him find fulfillment. It was her duty. But nay, she'd been so focused on her own thirst that she'd scarcely heeded his. And that focus had proved fatal. She'd had no power whatsoever over her body. Not over her limbs, which flailed and clutched at him like a madwoman. Not over the savage moans and cries she uttered. Not even over the gluttonous, self-indulgent thoughts that led her to forget his needs in favor of her own desires.

He must be appalled.

Jesu—she was like a greedy child.

And she'd paid for it. Oh aye. God had sent her soul to the very edge of death.

Garth wished he could stay there forever, sealed to Cynthia, inhaling the womanly scent of her, watching the shadows of breeze-blown leaves dance across her moonlit skin, listening to the ragged sound of her breathing, feeling her heart beat against his. He wanted to think of nothing but the gentle, tempestuous, serene, wanton woman beneath him. He wanted to fall asleep with her there, cradling her in his arms, protecting her from the night, dreaming of jasmine.

But he'd learned the harsh truth from Mariana. The lovely woman nestled under him was far from satiated. It was but the beginning for her. And since he'd come this far, he owed her the best he could offer. Even if it couldn't be enough.

So he summoned up what strength was left him and willed his flagging staff to stand. He ran the fingertips of one hand down past her curving waist, over a perfectly sculpted hip, through the mat of curls still damp from their love. Gently, he spread the petals below, opening her to stroke the moist bud within.

"Nay!" she hissed.

Reflexively, he drew his hand back. Dear God—what had he done?

"Nay," she whispered.

He searched her face. There was no malice there, no disgust. Only a queer shame that kept her from meeting his eyes.

And suddenly, he was ashamed.

She was unsatisfied. That was it. Just as Mariana had said. He was not man enough.

"I can do more," he said gruffly, the blood rushing to his face. But even now, he could feel his ardor diminishing.

"Nay!" she hastened to say. "Nay. You have done enough already."

His pride threatened to crack, but months of enduring Mariana's barbs had hardened him enough to keep him from foundering altogether. Aye, humiliation stained his cheeks, but it was doubtless concealed by the moonlight. And the tear standing in his eye . . .

He wiped it away as brusquely as he withdrew from her.

The crickets seemed to applaud in mockery as he wrapped his cassock around his wicked body again. The shadows of the garden seemed harsh now against the hand-packed path.

Cynthia looked lost as she gathered her garments about her, like an orphan cast suddenly out of an inn.

"I'm sorry," she muttered, glancing about for her boots.

He could do little more than nod. He was choking on a knot of emotions. Of course she was sorry. Sorry she'd ever set eyes on him.

She found her boots and stood clutching them to her chest. Her chin trembled as she tried not to weep.

In sooth, he couldn't blame her. He was a disappointment. It wasn't her fault. How could a woman truly understand what it was like to be half a—

"I'm sorry," she blurted out tearfully. She turned to flee, but not before he saw the first drop slide down her cheek. "I'm so sorry."

He stared at the ground rather than watch her run from him as if he were cursed. He was sorry, too. He'd known better. From the beginning, he'd known they were from different worlds.

And yet, in a way, he wasn't sorry, not at all. For one shining moment, he'd held heaven in his arms. And if he never shared a woman's bed again, at least he'd always have that.

18

Two weeks past Easter, the Abbot spurred his mount forward, wincing at the ache in his hips from the long ride. He was unaccustomed to riding at all, but it was one advantage that being master of his own castle afforded. He at least had the pick of the scrawny nags stabled in Charing's stalls.

Before him, the precisely cut gray stones of Wendeville rose out of the earth like a brazen salute to the God who'd thought He'd cast man out of a perfect world. But more than that, the splendid castle seemed to mock the Abbot's own battered Charing, where one counted oneself fortunate to find a corner free from drafts on a damp night.

It irked him to have to come here himself, and he swore he'd not do it again until he was ready to confront the Wendeville slut with orders for her execution, until he could claim Wendeville for his own.

But he'd had to come. His plans had taken a nasty turn. Garth hadn't killed the bitch after all. And she hadn't died from whatever disease it was she had. In fact, she'd apparently recovered enough to be courting. According to Mary, Cynthia Wendeville had already as good as promised herself to Sir Philip de Laval, which boded nothing but ill for the Abbot.

So he'd come to the castle to take matters into his own hands again. He'd befriend eager Philip, talk with him, pore over Lady Cynthia's . . . bewitching ways. After all, the devoted couple had known one another but a little over a fortnight. The Abbot knew her so much more intimately. Apparently, Cynthia had even managed to perform one of her healing "miracles" at the Easter tournament with Philip as witness. All the Abbot need do was whisper in sanctimonious Sir Philip's ear what he knew about unscrupulous Cynthia Wendeville and her devil's herbs. He was certain within the space of a few hours, he could convince the gentleman to part company with his tainted betrothed.

Leaving the Abbot that much closer to victory.

He peered up again at the bold pennon flying jauntily above the majestic keep and grimaced at the bitter taste of dread. He was so close, and yet fate seemed ever determined to thwart him. He felt like a hound slavering over a bone that persisted in staying just out of reach.

Elspeth knew something terrible had happened. But proud Cynthia wouldn't speak a word of it. Since Easter, the poor girl had retreated to her chamber, taking her meals there, coming out only for crises that Roger couldn't handle himself. She'd scarcely even spoken to the man she was to marry.

At first, Elspeth wondered if the sickness had left some lasting mark on the lady. Or if perhaps the Easter celebration had been too taxing. Then she worried it was some new malady. But at the heart of it all was fear. Never before had Cynthia retreated so far into herself. Never had she locked Elspeth on the other side of her chamber door. And never had she smelled of strong drink so early in the day.

It was those thoughts that occupied Elspeth as she supervised the laying of the new rushes over the stones of the great hall. And so she was caught completely off her guard when she flung open the outer doors and discovered the Abbot on the threshold, standing there like Death come to collect souls.

"Oh, la!" she shrieked. "Abbot!"

"Elspeth."

She hated the way he said her name, as if it were a Saxon curse.

"I didn't know ye were . . . that is . . . had I known, I . . . ," she muttered, trickling stems of meadowsweet onto the floor. "Why *have* ye come, Abbot?"

"Now, Elspeth." Roger came up behind her, placing undue pressure on her spine as he prodded her out of the way. "Let's see to the Abbot's comforts ere we start questioning him, shall we?"

She stood dumbfounded for a moment until she realized she was being rude. "O' course. O' course. I'll get a cup of ale for ye, Father. Come in." She stood aside and let him in, against her better judgment.

Lord, she thought, her hand trembling as she poured the ale a moment later in the refuge of the buttery, the Abbot couldn't have picked a worse time to come. Lady Cynthia needed strong armor to battle the wretched holy man, and at the present, the poor lass could scarcely dress herself in the morn. What would she do if he brought bad tidings?

Her hands were still shaking when she scurried across the newly laid rushes toward the hearth, where Roger and the Abbot sat conversing.

"I hope the lady's not ill?" the Abbot inquired, his forehead crinkling in a web of false concern.

"Ah, 'twill pass," Roger said, nodding and giving the Abbot a broad wink.

Elspeth had no idea what that wink meant, but she was grateful beyond words to Roger for his guile. She passed cups to the both of them and hovered nearby.

"And your chaplain?" the Abbot asked.

"Father Garth," Elspeth piped in. "He's workin' out well, that one. 'Tis a worthy choice ye made, Abbot."

She hoped she wasn't lying. In sooth, over the last several days, Father Garth had made himself as scarce as a squirrel in January. His Sabbath offering had been an uninspiring sermon on the merits of going on pilgrimage. Even the chaplain himself could barely stay awake for it.

The Abbot glanced at her dismissively, the way he always did, and turned again to Roger.

"I hear congratulations may be in order for your lady. A wedding?"

Elspeth exchanged a quick, panicked glance with Roger,

then cleared her throat. "There is a man come to call, a good gentleman, fine and honorable. O' course, he knows naught's to come of it for a while yet, not till the lady's done her proper grievin' for Lord John, God rest his soul." She hastily crossed herself, more to seek forgiveness for the lie than to bless John.

"Of course." The Abbot mimicked her motion with slow reverence.

Elspeth took a steadying breath. She wondered if the Abbot believed her. Not that it mattered. He wouldn't be performing the ceremony anyway. By the time he learned of the wedding, the deed would be done by Wendeville's own chaplain.

"Any . . . troubles?" the Abbot inquired.

"Troubles?" Roger repeated, taking a swig of ale and screwing his face into a thoughtful frown. "Nay. None that I know of. Unless you count the last rabbit I snared wiggling out of the trap." He guffawed and slopped a little of his ale over the cup.

The Abbot's somber expression never changed. Elspeth wondered how soon they could get rid of him.

"Well," the Abbot said, running a single bony finger around the rim of his untouched cup, " 'tis all I came for. You know, I'll always have a warm spot in my heart for this castle." He looked around the hall, at the tapestries hung from the scrubbed plaster walls. "I'll always think of Wendeville as my home."

Elspeth doubted there *was* a warm spot in the Abbot's heart. And as for Wendeville being his home, was it her imagination, or did covetousness glint in his eyes when he said that?

Fortunately, Roger had more tact than she.

"You'll always have a place here, Father."

The Abbot drained his drink all at once, then sat back, staring into the gentle flames of the low fire as if he never planned to move again.

"Well," Elspeth finally broke in, unable to stand the uneasy silence or the suspense any longer, "will ye be stayin' then for supper?"

" 'Tis a long way home, and I fear my bones are weary

from the ride. If I could burden you for one night . . . I'd like to meet this suitor of Lady Cynthia's."

"Of course," Roger hastily replied.

"My thanks." He handed his empty cup to Elspeth. It was a good thing he didn't bother lifting his eyes to her, else he would have immediately spotted the displeasure on her face.

Garth grimaced as another stone cut into the sole of his boot. If he made many more trips like this to the village, he'd have to buy another pair of shoes. His feet ached from the long walk home.

And yet it was a familiar ache. One he'd earned doing an honest day's work. One he could salve with oil and herbs. Not like the ache that pressed in on his chest, threatening to squeeze his heart till it burst.

That ache would never heal. No matter how many times he trudged to the village to preach to sinners. No matter how many babies he blessed, nor how many marriages he performed. That ache would live with him for the rest of his life. And only time would erode the sharp edges of such pain.

The sun perched on the hills like a giant eye, watching him as he walked briskly up the gravel path toward Wendeville.

He wondered what supper would be. Or if he'd be hungry for it tonight. Most of all, he wondered if *she* would be there.

She hadn't come down to supper once since their unfortunate affair in the garden. Which relieved him immensely. Between her confinement to her room and his trips to the village, supper and Sabbath were the only time they were likely to come face-to-face. And thus far, she'd avoided supper.

He'd considered confining himself to his quarters where he'd be certain of dining in peace. But both of them supping in seclusion? It would have been suspect. It would have endangered Cynthia. And more than anything, he had to protect her from his corruption.

So, his shoulders tight with anxiety, he passed through the massive oak doors of Wendeville, just in time for the late afternoon meal.

Once again, Cynthia had absented herself.

Instead, the Abbot, visiting from Charing, commanded the place of honor at the high table. To Garth's chagrin, he also commanded the company of Wendeville's chaplain.

The Abbot normally didn't frighten Garth. Aye, he was as sober as the grave, and aye, he resembled the skeletal rendering of Death in the monastery Bible. But he was a man of flesh and blood, no matter how little of either he had.

What did unsettle Garth were the questions he was asking. The Abbot may be a mere man, but he was a powerful man. One who could exile and condemn with a mere sweep of his bony arm.

Garth was certain guilt was smudged across his forehead like the ashes of Lent for the Abbot to see. Surely the stain upon his soul lay bare to the Abbot's shrewd eyes. And if the Abbot could sniff out *Garth's* sin . . .

An image of innocent sky-colored eyes and bouncing orange curls flashed through his mind.

Thank God she'd remained in her chamber.

He pushed his platter away and wiped his knife on the large linen napkin, painfully aware of his elevated seat above the castle folk. It was strange to sit there after four years of dining among commoners. It felt as if he were being tried and judged.

"So you're content with your position here, Father Garth?" the Abbot asked quietly, picking idly at his trout.

"Aye," he replied carefully.

"'Tis a . . . splendid keep."

Garth glanced around the hall. Cream-colored candles flickered golden against the white plaster walls. Painted shields and rich, dark tapestries hung between the narrow windows. It *was* splendid. Nearly as splendid as Castle de Ware. But in sooth, since his arrival, he'd paid heed to little but Cynthia's splendor.

"Your quarters are acceptable, I presume?"

"Aye." Garth shifted in his chair. This type of talk made him restless. There was some motive underlying the Abbot's words, but he'd be damned if he could name it.

The Abbot gave a pinched sigh through his nose. "'Twas difficult to leave."

Garth scanned the faces before him, all of whom he could readily identify now. "They are good folk."

The Abbot creaked his head toward Garth and gave him a most curious half-smile, as if Garth were some insect he was trying to identify.

"Good folk. Aye." Then he lifted a tiny morsel of trout to his lips, taking it off the knife with a sucking noise.

Garth glanced at his wine flagon. It was empty. He wished he had a full cup to slug back.

"And how are you coming with that . . ." The Abbot bent near to whisper low. "That vice for which you took the vow of silence?"

Sudden heat flamed across Garth's cheeks. Did the Abbot know? Did he know that he lusted after the lady of the castle? Did he know that he'd slaked that lust between her lovely legs mere days ago?

He dared not look up.

"Well," he replied as evenly as he could. "Very well."

The Abbot studied him a long while. Then he dabbed at his lips with his napkin.

"Aye. Well, 'tis comforting to hear. After all, there is so much more . . . temptation . . . away from the monastery."

Garth held his breath. It would come now. Now the Abbot would close his trap.

"And how do you fare with," the Abbot murmured, "the poor child?"

"The child?"

"Lady Cynthia?"

He nearly blurted out that Lady Cynthia was no child. But at the last moment, he wisely choked back the words.

"Fine."

The Abbot tapped his eating dagger on the edge of his silver platter. "Fine?"

"Aye." He knew he should expand on that, but he could think of nothing to say that wouldn't tighten the noose around his neck.

"Come, come now, Garth," he chided, actually elbowing Garth. "The truth shall set you free." Then he whispered, "The wench is a hopeless heathen, rife with lust and vulgarity, the handmaiden of the devil himself. For years I tried to bring her to the light, but I'm afraid . . . I failed miserably. I had hoped that you might . . . endear yourself to her, show her the error of her ways, instruct the child—"

"She is not a child," Garth hissed, unable to listen to more slander. He instantly regretted his outburst.

"What's this?" the Abbot asked slyly, bending close enough to ruffle Garth's hair with his fishy breath. "Has she tried her provocative wiles on you so soon, Father Garth?"

It took all his fortitude to turn and face the Abbot straight on, to look him steadily in the eyes and speak a lie. But he did it. For Cynthia.

"Nay," he said. "I am a man of God. I've made it abundantly clear to her."

The Abbot's interested stare diminished after that, dimmed perhaps by disappointment. He hoped so. For Cynthia's sake, he hoped so.

The Abbot lowered his eyes to the dissected trout spread across his platter. He'd unconsciously arranged the remains in the shape of a cross, something that had become a habit with him. He arranged his cope and sandals thus at night. And the collection of jewels, gifts of his flock, which he took out from time to time. Mayhap, he thought with satisfaction, he'd arrange Cynthia in such a fashion when he had her executed.

As he knew he would.

Garth's face had assured him of that.

The idiot wore his passions like a banner.

He'd thought it was sheer cunning at first, that Garth had wormed his way into Cynthia's affections for his own profit. But now he could see it wasn't artifice at all. The fool was in love with her.

He popped a piece of sugared fig into his mouth and chewed slowly. Usually he hated sweet things, but tonight was cause for celebration.

Condemning Cynthia on the herbs alone would have been tricky. In sooth, there were many noblewomen who practiced the art of healing, and few could stand too close a scrutiny of their cellar.

But this . . .

Seducing a man of the cloth, enticing him away from God . . .

For this, she would pay.

All he had to do was catch them in the act.

He'd leave Wendeville on the morrow. By the time he was through . . . enlightening Lord Philip, he was sure the godly man would want to pack up and leave as well. Then there would be nothing to stand in the way of their perfidy, the foolish friar and his unholy mistress.

Aye, he'd leave them to their vices. But he wouldn't stray far. And he'd watch them like a hawk.

19

THE ROOM SPUN AS CYNTHIA CLIMBED INTO THE STEAM-
ing tub, her mug of strong ale still clutched in one hand.

"I don't care," she mumbled drunkenly, frowning.

The dizziness was all right. Better by far than the terrible guilt and shame that had tortured her for a fortnight, days spent hiding from Garth and Elspeth and the decent man everyone wanted her to take to husband. Everyone but her. Hell—today, according to Elspeth, she'd even managed to hide from the Abbot himself.

She plopped down into the water and let her head nod forward.

"Piss."

She'd forgotten to take off her linen underdress. It stuck wetly to her like snake's skin.

"Well, I don't care."

She was miserable. For no good reason.

She should be happy. She was healthy. She was rich. Soon she would be wed. The seeds she'd planted were already poking their little green heads up through the soil.

But she felt wretched.

Ale slopped over the side of her mug into the bath, and she quickly righted the cup, then looked for a place to set it. There was none. She scowled.

"Mary!"

The tapestry on the wall swayed as she watched it, and she closed her eyes to stop the nauseating motion. She really shouldn't be drinking so much, she supposed. Drinking spoiled her gift of healing. Of course, the man she was to marry had forbidden her to heal anyway, so she supposed it shouldn't matter. But ale gave her a horrible headache the next day. And it ruined her authority over the servants. Why, it had taken her more than an hour just to get the water for her bath.

She slugged back the rest of the cup.

"Mary!"

"Did you want somethin', m'lady?"

Cynthia narrowed her eyes at the bug-eyed face peering around the door. It wasn't Mary.

"Elspeth!" She saluted her maid with the cup. Then she frowned. She couldn't quite remember what it was she wanted. Ah, well, she decided, it was good just to see Elspeth's friendly face.

"Oh, m'lady," Elspeth said, clucking her tongue. She shut the door behind her.

"Where's Mary?"

"I sent her to the hall to make excuses to your guests," she said, bustling forward. "Can't very well let them see ye like this, can I?" She shook her head. "Oh, m'lady, ye've got yerself well sotted now."

"Aye," she agreed, grinning wide. "Well and truly."

"Come now, m'lady," Elspeth said more gently, plucking the mug from her hand. " 'Tis time we had a chat. What's this about? For a week ye've moped about like a harlot sent to convent. And now, ye're so sotted ye can barely . . . "

Cynthia snickered once, then threw back her head and let out a long laugh.

"M'lady!"

"A harlot?" she guffawed, smacking one hand across the surface of the water. "Sent to convent? Forsooth, Elspeth?"

But as funny as it sounded for a moment, the thought suddenly made her horribly sad as well. Even as her laughter rang off the walls, tears welled in her eyes.

"A harlot sent to convent," she repeated ruefully. Bless Elspeth—the maid didn't know how close to the truth she was.

Cynthia closed her eyes and sank down into the soothing water, letting it close over her neck, her mouth, her nose.

"M'lady!"

Elspeth hauled her up by the neck of her gown. Cynthia gasped, choking on the water, and slapped at the maid's hands.

"Talk to me, m'lady," Elspeth said in a voice that brooked no argument.

Cynthia swallowed. She didn't want to talk. "First I need another drink."

"Pah! Ye need another drink like the Abbot needs another cock."

Cynthia hiccoughed. A bemused smile slid across her face.

"Now tell me what's amiss," Elspeth commanded.

Cynthia drew circles on the surface of the water with a fingertip. "God," she said. "He's punishing me."

"Punishin' ye? God?"

"Aye. He nearly seized my soul the other night," she murmured, shivering. Her body could still recall the awful thrill of passion that consumed her as she hovered at the precipice of death.

"What do ye mean, m'lady?"

Cynthia licked her lips. Suddenly they felt very dry. "I mean . . . " She glanced down at the wet, transparent pocket of fabric draped between her legs. Her woman's curls looked as innocent as ever, despite her sin and her tumultuous brush with immortality. "I bedded a man."

Elspeth's hand flew to her mouth, but she uttered not a word.

"It was . . . it was . . . wonderful." She smiled. Her ears buzzed as she recalled the heat of Garth's arms about her, his warm flesh melding with hers.

Then she thought better of it. "Nay. Nay. It was terrible." She screwed up her face. It took her a moment to recall why it was so terrible. Then she remembered. "I couldn't breathe. I couldn't speak. I couldn't think. The devil put awful moans in my throat, and God . . . "

She frowned. Elspeth was making some strange noise. She peered at the maid beneath heavy-lidded eyes.

Damn her!

Elspeth was snickering behind her hand. Her shoulders shook with suppressed mirth. If she hadn't been drunk, Cynthia would have kicked the impertinent maid all the way to the door. As it was, she settled for calling her names.

"Why, you cursed old bag of bones," she said, her speech slurred by the ale. "What's so funny about . . . about thrashing like a beheaded chicken and . . . "

Elspeth cackled, beside herself. "Oh, m'lady, stop! Stop!"

Cynthia crossed her arms over her chest and waited for Elspeth's laughter to cease.

"M'lady," Elspeth finally managed to gasp out. "Is that all? Is that what's troublin' ye?"

"Isn't it enough?"

Elspeth stood over her and held out a hand. "Give me yer gown, m'lady. We've got some talkin' to do, and ye might as well have a good bath while the water's warm."

Elspeth did have some talking to do. She told Cynthia things that made her eyes widen and her ears burn. She spoke of men and nature and the way of the world, things she said Cynthia's mother had apparently neglected to tell her. She spoke until the water grew tepid. But Cynthia listened to every word, too chagrined to argue. And by the time Elspeth was done with her sermon, hope had taken root in Cynthia's heart.

"But with John . . . ," she began as Elspeth finished toweling her off.

"John was an old fool," Elspeth said bluntly. "'Twasn't his fault. But he knew naught of pleasurin' a woman. A young man, though, like Lord Philip? There's a fine one to ruffle yer skirts."

Cynthia giggled. Ruffle her skirts. Garth certainly did that. Joy blossomed suddenly inside her. Garth obviously knew how to pleasure her. So there was nothing wrong after all.

She thanked Elspeth with a squeeze that made the maid squeal in protest, then allowed herself to be tucked into bed. When Elspeth leaned over to kiss her forehead and inquired in a whisper, "Do ye love him then, m'lady? Do ye love Philip?" she pretended she was asleep.

As soon as she heard the door bump shut, Cynthia opened her eyes. She was too relieved and too excited to sleep. She must tell Garth. She must heal the senseless rift between them. And she must do it now, before he suffered through one more night of disillusionment. Aye, she'd slip on her silkiest gown, steal through the hall, and go to him in his chambers. She'd repair everything.

The scent of ale roused Garth from sleep. That and the harsh whisper slicing through the night.

"Garth!"

He threw back the coverlet and reached for the sword that wasn't, and never had been, under his pillow.

"It's me!" Cynthia whispered loudly, sending another puff of ale-laced breath wafting in his direction.

"Cynthia?" he whispered back, his heart pounding. What was she doing in his room?

"It's all right," she breathed. "Everything is all right."

"What . . . ?" His head spun. If he was going to make any sense of this, he'd have to get up and light a candle. "Wait."

He groped his way to the hearth and stirred the banked coals, all the while wondering if he was completely mad to let Cynthia remain in his chamber. For the love of God, the Abbot himself lodged in the castle this eve.

He lit the blackened wick of a candle on a glowing log, and it sputtered to life. Then he turned to face her.

Aye, he decided, he was indeed completely mad.

Her hair cascaded wild and loose and damp about her. One shoulder of her sleek, flimsy gown hung askew, low enough to reveal the cleft of her arm and part of her breast. Her feet were bare, and her toes clutched playfully at the rushes. She was obviously besotted. She swayed unsteadily, her eyelids drooping lasciviously as she stared at him. He nearly groaned when she winked and gave him an intoxicatingly sultry smile.

He fumbled the candle into the holder at the foot of his bed.

"You're drunk." At least that explained her imprudent

presence here. But his cursed body didn't know the difference. Blood surged to his loins as if he might indeed bed the reeling woman before him. "Go back to your chamber."

"Nay," she said, rushing forward.

He held his breath.

"Nay," she insisted. "You don't understand. It's all right now." She pressed her palms flat upon his chest and gazed up into his eyes. She smelled clean, wonderful. "It's perfect."

He had no idea what she was babbling about, and he suspected neither did she.

Sometime soon he would need to breathe. "Go now, Cynthia. Go."

"But . . . " She looked dismayed for an instant. Then sudden inspiration sparked in her eyes. "Kiss me!"

His gaze dropped involuntarily down to her mouth, that wide, sensuous mouth that probably tasted of fine ale.

"Nay, my lady."

"Then I shall kiss you."

It would have been unforgivable to jerk away from her then. Particularly when she looked so naive and vulnerable, weaving on her feet. It would have hurt her. At least, that's what he told himself. But he should have. He should have recoiled as if from fire. Instead, he let her raise her mouth to his.

Her lips tasted like autumn, with the harvest done, and the smells of cut wheat and ripe apples filling the air, when pine boughs crackled on evening fires and tankards of golden ale warmed the belly. He could no more refuse that taste than a starving man could refuse a loaf of bread. And once lost in that intoxicating nectar, he could do naught else but drink deeper.

She was warm from the bath. Her damp hair smelled of spice. He wove one hand into the fragrant mass as he plundered her mouth. The other hand slid along her spine, catching in the delicate fabric of her gown, slipping it across her satiny skin.

Somewhere in the back of his mind a voice protested, telling him he was making a mistake, telling him he should stop now before he made a fool of himself. But he ignored it. It sounded too much like Mariana's scolding. And at present, the voice of passion spoke louder than the voice of reason. It spoke like thunder in his ears.

Cynthia wriggled closer, locking her arms about his neck, devouring him as if he were a Christmas feast. She moaned against his lips, wordlessly begging for more.

And, God help him, he obliged.

He plunged his tongue deep into her mouth, savoring the sweet, warm recesses with the desperation of a condemned man at his last meal. Desire rushed through his veins like strong poison, leaching out all sense, compelling him to taste her, to embrace her. Compelling him, aye, to take her.

Still ravaging her mouth, he wrested out of his cassock. She, too, pulled free of her garment, tearing the neck of the frail thing. It slid sinuously over her curves and pooled at her feet. And then there was nothing between them.

Tongues of fire lapped at him as she kissed his neck, his shoulder, his chest, seeking and finding his mouth again. He endured the torture of her nipples grazing him, her unbound hair rasping across his skin, the sizzling of his blood as she danced just out of reach. And then he could endure no more.

He hauled her up against him, hard, forging her flesh to his like iron to steel. He swept her onto the bed. His bed. Where he'd spent too many long, guilty nights dreaming of this very thing, this soul-searing union he'd never hoped to relive.

Yet here she was, beneath him, writhing, gasping, twisting her head back and forth across the furs as if she were tortured by some demon of yearning.

He knew how she felt. The blood pounded in his loins and sang through his body like a siren's call, driving him mad. Mad enough to cover her hot flesh with his own. Mad enough to rest his lust-heavy weight atop her. To part the swollen petals of her womanhood and plunge into the welcome harbor of her womb.

It was heaven. God forgive him, it was heaven.

Whorls of sensation circled Cynthia, leaving her dizzy and breathless. She was drunk, aye, but this euphoria had naught to do with ale. Garth was everywhere—above her, around her, inside her—and it was where he belonged. She felt possessed by him, as if their two souls were somehow forged together.

Then he moved, and it was much finer than she remembered, that slow, relentless tide he forced her to. Her loins prickled with need, and he soothed that need with each stroke. She wrapped her legs about him, wanting him closer, and she could feel the muscles of his buttocks flex and release. Her hands wandered over his massive shoulders, down his tensed back, and that delicious thrill of fear coursed through her once more.

She was losing control again. She could feel it coming as surely as the sun came up over the hills. Moans came to her lips unbidden. Her hips undulated to their own rhythms, striving upward against him. She held on for dear life. But this time, as she teetered on the narrow ledge of fulfillment, she felt no panic.

Perhaps it was the ale. Perhaps it was Elspeth's words.

This time, she let the flood carry her away, past care, past reason. She gasped, arching impossibly beneath him as he, too, drove with bold abandon deep within her. For one glorious moment, they were one, soaring high above the earth like a solitary flaming angel. Then they plunged downward, clasped together, rocking with tremors as old as time, to extinguish their passion in a tranquil sea.

Cynthia drifted on that sea like a ship without a wheel. She couldn't cease smiling. Her whole body glowed the way it did when she stood too close to the fire. But she didn't want to move away from this fire. Nay, she wanted to lie here beneath Garth forever.

The last thing Garth wanted to do was move. He was drained, physically and mentally. Cynthia would want more. For a woman, Mariana had told him, once was never enough. But lying quiet, he could float aimlessly, oblivious to the guilt threatening to press down upon him, oblivious to the demands surely to come from Cynthia, demands he wasn't sure he could answer.

And yet, affection did what neither guilt nor demands could.

He *longed* to fulfill her again.

He longed to satiate her completely.

At least he had to try.

His poor staff had no strength to rise again. He knew that. There was no help for it. But what it couldn't achieve, a skilled hand could accomplish.

Separating from her no more than an inch, he snaked his fingers down over her flat belly toward the damp curls mingling with his. Carefully, gently, he parted the folds of her womanhood and ran one slick finger over the tiny bud hidden there.

"Nay," she groaned, wincing, halting his hand.

He hesitated. Was he hurting her? Or did she protest, like Mariana frequently had, as a game? Again, he slipped his finger over the sensitive nubbin.

"Nay, Garth. Please." She jerked beneath him, then squeezed her thighs together.

A deluge of fears fell around him: He hadn't pleased her. She regretted her actions. He was but half a man. She couldn't endure his touch.

But the truth was *she* had come to *him*. She had sought him out. Why? Why, if there were more capable men available, if she'd been unsatisfied by him before, would she have sought him out again?

"Do you not wish . . . more?" he asked, all his fears perched on his shoulder, waiting for her answer.

"More?" She laughed. But it wasn't the jeer of ridicule Mariana had perfected. Cynthia's laugh was capricious, full of delight and relief. "Oh, Garth, more?" She squirmed away from his hand, giggling. "More and I shall die, truly. More and it will be the end of me. They shall have to pry my cold bones from around yours. Nay, I could not endure more, or I should die of pleasure!"

A fierce love swept through him then that had nothing to do with the remnant of fire in his loins.

"You're . . . satisfied?" he breathed, scarcely able to believe it.

She answered him with a giddy sigh, locking her fingers about his neck and smiling up into his waiting eyes. "I told you it was perfect."

He searched her face. She spoke in sooth. And her words

acted upon him like a keystone dislodged from a dam, releasing a rush of long-checked emotions all at once. His throat jammed on an unmanly sob, and he dared not speak or breathe. Instead, he gathered her in his arms and hugged her so tightly for so long she squealed in protest.

He didn't remember loosening his hold. Or slipping from her. Or rolling to her side to keep from crushing her. He thought he was too agitated for slumber. He was wrong. Within a moment, he was sleeping more deeply than he had in days.

It was a surprise then when, sometime near the hour of Matins, he snorted awake to discover the candle sputtering and Cynthia slung like a heavy cloak over his body.

"Cynthia!" he hissed, shaking her shoulder.

She mumbled incoherently.

"Cynthia! You must get up!" He rattled her again, harder this time. "Come! It's late!"

She murmured again and snuggled closer.

"Nay, Cynthia!"

He cursed under his breath. How could he have been so stupid as to fall asleep? He'd compromised both of them. He had to get Cynthia back to her chamber.

Briskly he disentangled himself from her and shrugged into his cassock, raking his hair back into some semblance of order. Then he stared down at the angel lying on his bed, and he had to smile. She looked like the victim of a shipwreck, cast ashore by a haphazard wave. Her hair spread across the pillow like seaweed, and her skin glowed in the fading light with pearly luminescence. He stood there long enough to commit her features to memory, for in days to come, when they passed in the great hall or at chapel or by the garden, he wanted to remember her like this.

Then he bent to scoop her from the pallet. He was never sure she came fully awake at all, even when he slipped the gown over her head. He half-carried, half-dragged her through the field of dozing bodies that populated the great hall, knowing the Abbot would be sequestered in the lord's chambers and praying the servants were still abed as well. Cynthia slogged up the steps to her chamber on his arm, and he tucked her hastily into her bed.

He silently congratulated himself as he picked his way back to his quarters. It wouldn't happen again, this clandestine midnight meeting between lovers. It was far too dangerous for both of them. They still lived in two different worlds. She had her betrothed, and he had his church. Nay, Cynthia had given him back his manhood. He'd have a sweet memory to sustain him. And, with any luck, she wouldn't remember a thing.

Unfortunately, he counted too much on three things. On the amnesiac properties of ale. That, once tasted, he could possibly resist Cynthia's bounty. And that they hadn't been caught.

20

Elspeth recoiled into the shadows at the bottom of the stairwell. She clapped a hand over her mouth to stop the squeak that was wont to come out. She even clenched her eyes tightly for a moment, hoping that when she reopened them, what she'd seen would prove to be a trick of the moonlight.

But nay, as sure as she knew the back of her own wrinkled hand, that was Father Garth carrying Lady Cynthia up to her bedchamber. She sank against the cold stone wall, suddenly feeling all of her sixty-three years.

Mayhap, she reasoned desperately, willing her heart to quit its crazed jig, things weren't as they appeared. Mayhap Cynthia had gone to him to confess her sins and then . . . fallen asleep, or . . . or the Father had found her dozing in the buttery, where they'd both chanced to fetch a midnight bite. Perchance she'd fallen down the stairs and . . .

But nay. Garth wasn't in any hurry with her. If anything, his step was heavy with stealth. And his face, where the wall sconce lit it up for an instant, was filled with such warmth and affection for his burden that there could be no mistake.

Garth was Cynthia's lover. Not Philip.

It pinched at Elspeth's old heart to think of it. Aye, Garth was comely and kind and generous. He came from a fine family. He was young and hale. He'd never given her cause to question his loyalty. And the two of them together, well, they made a handsome pair with their strong features and their formidable height. What children they'd—

She gave her head a hard shake.

The man was a priest.

Peering up where the two had just disappeared into Cynthia's chamber, Elspeth crept out and made her furtive way toward the steward's quarters. If anyone knew what to do in such a coil, it was Roger.

He awoke most rudely, nearly lopping her head off with an outward flailed hand when she waggled his shoulder.

"Watch yer fist!" she hissed. "Ye old fool! 'Tis me. Me. Elspeth!"

"What the devil?"

"Keep yer voice down. I must speak with ye."

"Then light a candle," he groused, "so I can at least be assured 'tis you and not some other harpy come to torment my sleep."

She snatched up a candle stub and lit the wick from the banked fire at the foot of his bed. By the time she returned, Roger was sitting up, the covers pulled up to his neck, his hair askew, and his expression cross.

"What's this about?"

"Ah, Roger, I hardly know where to begin." But apparently she did, for the story spilled out of her with little difficulty. She told him about Cynthia's melancholy, blushing as she skated over the subject of their conversation in the bath, and recounted what she'd seen in the great hall. "'Tis a tragedy, Roger. What shall we do?"

Roger sat silent for a long while, his gray eyes thoughtful, his mouth stern.

"Nothing," he finally said, flouncing over to go back to sleep.

"What!" Elspeth exploded, wrenching him back over. "How dare ye . . . have ye no . . . what do ye mean, *nothing*?"

"I mean nothing," he said. "I mean you've done enough already. You've taught her all she needs to know. She's a grown woman, not a child."

"But she can't lie with the chaplain!" Elspeth screamed under her breath.

"And why not?"

"Because . . . because . . . he lived in a monastery. His vows . . ."

"He's not a monk anymore, Elspeth. He's a chaplain. It's not entirely uncommon for a chaplain to take a wife."

"A wife, aye, but a concubine? Our Cynthia?"

Roger scowled. "I'm sure he'll do the right thing." He yanked the coverlet back around his shoulders dismissively. "Besides, Garth de Ware is a far better man than those weasels you've been digging up from God-knows-where."

Her mouth dropped open of its own accord.

"Lord Philip is a decent, God-fearin'—"

"Did you not hear? Lord Philip's apparently so God-fearing he's let the Abbot convince him to go on pilgrimage instead of marrying."

"What?" she gasped. "You mean . . ."

"He leaves on the morrow." Roger snorted. "As for the rest of the motley prospects, you know none of them have been good enough for our Cynthia," he accused. "I'm surprised at you, Elspeth."

She clapped her mouth shut again and planted her fists on her hips. "Well, I don't see *ye* bringin' any gentlemen by."

Roger snorted. "I'd be well pleased to call a man as forthright as Garth de Ware lord and master of Wendeville. And I'm just as glad that Cynthia has the good judgment to think so, too."

Whatever answer Elspeth sought in waking Roger, it was certainly not this.

"Then ye'll do nothin'? Not even protect her from the gossips? From the Abbot?"

Roger eyed her from beneath his bushy brows, suddenly serious. "Do you think the Abbot knows?"

"I pray to God he doesn't," she said. "But if we don't watch out for her, for them . . ."

Roger nodded. "The Abbot will be on his way come sunrise. Until then, I suggest you watch her through the night."

Elspeth pursed her lips. It wasn't exactly the response she'd hoped for, but it would serve. If the lass couldn't govern her heart, at least she had two friends who would guard her reputation.

After Lord Philip's hasty departure with the Abbot, Garth's attempts at chastity succeeded about as well as a fish's attempts at flight.

The very next night Cynthia cornered him in the herb cellar and had her way with him. He blamed himself, claiming a momentary lapse of judgment on his part.

The night after that she lured him to the stables, and in a moment of weakness, he acceded to her lusty wishes.

The following afternoon, she surprised him at his bath, and since he was already disrobed . . .

By the fourth night, he abandoned all excuse and accepted the fact that if it was Cynthia's will that he revel in her, then there wasn't a blessed thing he could do to prevent it.

It was the beginning of the most magical summer Garth could remember. For nigh a dozen glorious weeks, Cynthia filled his life with more color and joy than all her beds of flowers, delighting him, surprising him, fulfilling him. No corner of the keep was safe from their passion—the buttery, the dovecote, the dungeon. And if he preached chastity on Sunday and trysted with Cynthia the rest of the week, it was his own private sin for which he'd pay.

Later.

For now he wanted to wring every last drop of bliss from what bit of summer remained.

But they had to be cautious. There were those, including the Abbot and the king, who might judge them harshly, those who believed solely in marriages of diplomatic convenience for such women as Lady Cynthia, and those who held to the practice of chastity without compromise for men of the cloth.

So they followed unspoken rules. They never met where they might be discovered. They displayed no public affection, not even a hand given in comfort. And they shared no confidences. With anyone. Above all else, Garth and Cynthia cared for their vassals. If they thought for one moment their actions might do harm to the people of Wendeville . . .

It was a hell's ransom to pay for heaven. But he had no choice. If they revealed their love, the uncompromising

Abbot would have Garth exiled from the church, and if that came to pass, what kind of future could he offer Cynthia? He'd not fool himself. He had spent the good part of his life in preparation for the priesthood. What did he know of commanding a castle? Nay, if he were cast from his faith, there was nowhere else for him to turn.

And yet the alternative was just as unthinkable. If they kept their hearts secret, he knew that one day the impatient king would choose a suitable husband for Cynthia himself, a man to further Edward's own political interests. And that would be the day Garth's soul shriveled.

He clenched his fists, wishing he could tear asunder the images of the impossible future before them.

He visually measured the sun's ascent above his sill. Nearly an hour since she'd left for her bathing pool. Probably enough time. But he couldn't be too careful.

Sometimes, though he was no longer held to a vow of chastity and though he kept his faith, what he and Cynthia did felt like sin. If they were caught . . .

He didn't want to think about it.

Still, he felt a twinge of trepidation as he glanced through the window toward the wood and the overgrown deer trail that marked the path to the pool.

She swore the place was private, that everyone knew it, and no one dared encroach on her summer bath. But that didn't change the fact that the two of them would be out of doors, together, in broad sunlight, for the first time.

He'd tried to persuade her to stay with him in his chamber. But she'd pleaded with him relentlessly, flashing the smile that turned his knees to custard. He'd punished her with a growl and a fierce kiss, hauling her over his thigh and onto the pallet, pinning her there. A thrill of pure animal lust had shivered every muscle in his body as he gazed at her. But she remained adamant.

He could have changed her mind in an instant—both of them knew it—with one strategic brush of his lips, one caress of his hand.

But he hadn't.

And now he feared that fate would realize it had left them too long alone.

• • •

Cynthia shivered in spite of the strong midday sun as the water sluiced over her naked shoulders. It was a glorious day. At the north end of the wide pool, the stream babbled over the smooth pebbles and dove several feet, spreading with a gurgling sigh. The pool was clear as glass, so deep that the bottom was a green blur. Bits of sunlight flashed on the waves like winking jewels as the water circled and was siphoned once again at the opposite end into a rushing brook.

She wondered what was taking Garth so long. Sometimes his sense of propriety annoyed her. What they did—was it so wrong? Surely nothing so heavenly could be evil in God's eyes. True, Garth was a man of the cloth. He had taken certain vows. But he was no longer a monk. Chaplains sometimes married. Certainly this was not so different. As for her, why should the king care who she wed? She was hardly a virgin. She couldn't have cared less about rumors that might tarnish her reputation.

She tipped her head back, drenching her hair in the cold current that swirled around her. It was so peaceful here. She'd made the lovely spot her own domain. No one ever intruded upon her. In sooth, the only other visitors she had were birds, squirrels, frogs, an occasional fox that skittishly drank at the pool's edge, and fish that nibbled at her toes. It was a perfect haven.

And the perfect place to tell Garth the happy news.

She smiled and rubbed her palm over the slight swelling of her belly. In sooth, it was scarcely noticeable. But she was certain that sometime after the new year, she and Garth would be blessed by their own child.

It had been sheer torture to keep it from Elspeth, to pretend to endure her monthly courses at the usual time when she'd missed three. But she wanted to tell Garth first.

She wasn't sure how he'd respond.

Over the last three months, she'd seen him blossom into an expressive, passionate, vivacious man. She'd heard him laugh long and loud, near fainted at his whispered words of desire, harkened to the music of their joined souls when nary a word was spoken between them.

She'd learned all there was to know about Garth de Ware

and his family. She smiled now, recalling the tales he'd told her of his illustrious brothers. Holden de Ware was a ferocious warrior, unmatched in combat, a man who had garnered the confidence of the king with his skill in battle and his keen sense of diplomacy. That diplomacy had earned him his wife, Cambria Gavin, laird in her own right of a Scots clan. According to Garth, Holden's mail-clad wife was as sly and savage a fighter as her husband. Of course, Cynthia had to admit, that appraisal may have been tainted by the fact that Cambria had once outwitted Garth.

Garth's oldest brother, Duncan, was as kindhearted as Holden was fierce. Castle de Ware was nigh overrun with recipients of Duncan's charity. Orphans and half-wits were drawn to him like iron fillings to a lodestone. And yet he'd had to exercise considerable charm to win the heart of Linet de Montfort. She was a Flemish woolmaker, a member of the guild, competent and independent, sure she had no use for a husband. Apparently, Duncan convinced her otherwise aboard, of all things, a sea reiver's ship.

Aye, they sounded charming. And she looked forward to meeting them . . . if Garth would have her. It was the one thing of which she was unsure. Garth seemed to care for her now, but when he learned of the child . . .

Everything could change in an instant. He could slam that great helm closed over his emotions again. He'd certainly had enough practice.

Still, she had to take the risk. Before anyone else found out. And hopefully, bathing in the refreshing waters of this special place, with the sun beaming down and birds warbling from the bushes, Garth would take the news well. Hopefully, he'd be pleased.

A rustling came from the nearby willows. She grinned and twirled in the water toward the sound.

"Garth?" she ventured.

No answer.

"Garth," she said. "You can come out. It's safe."

The branches parted.

It wasn't Garth.

A portentous cold lump settled in Cynthia's stomach as she looked into her maidservant's wide and culpable eyes.

"Mary?" Her voice quavered. That would never do. It would establish her guilt at once. Nay, she had to take charge. "Mary!" she scolded. "Return to the castle at once! This is my private domain! What the devil are you doing here?"

The branches parted further. Mary wasn't alone. The lump in Cynthia's belly congealed into a block of ice as she stared into familiar, cruel, hard features. The Abbot.

"*I* commanded her to bring me to you."

For a long, painful moment, she felt as paralyzed as a deer caught in an open meadow.

Then the brush surrounding the pool rattled, and four burly scarlet-clad knights emerged. At the Abbot's command, they sloshed forward through the current toward her. She gasped, trying to shield herself from their greedy eyes with her hands, but still they came. She panicked, turning in the water, looking for escape. Finally, one knight clenched her arm in a steel gauntlet, dragging her forcibly forward.

"Nay," she protested. "You're hurting . . ."

Her words fell on deaf ears. Leather and mail scraped against her bare skin as the four brutes hauled her roughly from the water, ignoring her pleas. And to add insult, all the while they struggled with their slippery prize, the Abbot loudly intoned some absurdity about herbs and witchery.

She shrieked in outrage, heat suffusing her face, as they set her naked upon the bank. While she stood, drenched, shivering, one of the men pressed a curved dagger to her throat. Another pinioned her arms behind her back, thrusting her breasts forward like an offering to the horrible man who continued to drone on and on about her supposed crimes, brandishing a silver cross and licking his lips like a wolf about to devour a rabbit.

And then he uttered something that struck terror into her soul.

". . . proof that she bears the child of Lucifer himself."

All too soon, before she could understand, one of the men clapped irons on her wrists.

"What is the meaning of—" she cried, earning a quick prick from the knife at her chin.

Panicked, she glanced at Mary. Surely she could find empathy there. But Mary only stared at the ground, guiltily worrying her knuckles.

"You," she breathed. It was Mary's doing. Somehow Mary had divined her secret. And she'd divulged it to the Abbot.

"Gag her," the Abbot ordered, pointing one bony finger. "I won't have the witch casting some demon's spell upon you good men while you do God's work."

They stuffed linen between her teeth to silence her. It was hardly necessary. She doubted she had the power to speak. Not with such fear and confusion rattling her mind.

What had the Abbot said? That she was a witch? Dear God—did he truly believe that? And if he did, did he have the power to do anything about it? The church reigned supreme in spiritual matters, aye, but surely the word of one man could not . . . Sweet Jesu—what would he do with her? What would he do with Garth? And what, for the love of Christ, would he do with her child?

She closed her eyes, hardly noticing the slap of branches against her arms as she stumbled barefoot along the leafy path.

This wasn't happening. It *couldn't* be.

Garth cursed mentally as he rounded the stairwell to the great hall. He'd hoped to steal from the castle to Cynthia's bathing pool with little ado. But the place was brimming with people.

Only as his boot scraped the rushes of the last step did he notice the odd commotion in the midst of the hall.

A handful of brawny knights in the scarlet surcoats of Charing muscled their way forward, hauling some burden he couldn't make out. Probably a thief, he mused, or a poacher on Wendeville lands. As the men swaggered toward the center of the hall, the castle folk made way for them, gasping and falling back like an ocean wave around a formidable ship.

He frowned.

"M'lady!" Elspeth shrieked suddenly from across the hall.

The sound was like a needle driven through Garth's heart.

"Lady Cynthia!" Roger groaned from the dais, staring, then tearing his eyes away from the knights' burden. "Blessed Jesu!"

Fear catapulted Garth from the stairwell. He strode on wooden legs through the crowd of servants, dread a bitter taste on his tongue. *Please, God, don't let her be . . .* he prayed wildly, unable to even consider the possibility. *Please don't let her be . . .*

His heart in his throat, he broke through the crowd and spun to face the knights.

For one brief moment, relief filled him like sweet nectar. Praise Mary, Cynthia was alive. Breathless, a little bloody, but alive. Thank God the knights had found her in time.

But his relief turned quickly to rage. Satan's ballocks—she was completely naked! Not one of the men who saw fit to call themselves knights had offered her a cloak.

He opened his mouth to launch a scathing rebuke when Cynthia caught his eye. Her face was filled with despair. Not shame. Not outrage. But despair.

Suddenly he realized the truth. These men were not her rescuers. They were her captors. And worse, behind them, looking on with morbid satisfaction, stood the Abbot.

He should have felt fear, but outrage took command. Garth drew himself up to his full height.

"Abbot!" he snapped, unmindful of the stir his dominating voice caused. "What is the meaning of this?"

The Abbot started visibly but recovered quickly enough. "I fear I bring unfortunate news."

Before he could elaborate, Garth jostled a serving girl beside him. "Your cloak," he demanded.

She sheepishly surrendered the careworn garment.

The Abbot took in a sharp breath. "Oh, I'd not stand too close, Father Garth," he warned, relishing every syllable. "You see, your lady, I'm afraid, is a servant of Satan."

The servants gasped collectively, backing a pace further, then began to murmur speculatively among themselves.

"What?" Garth asked, incredulous. "What nonsense is this?"

He sneered and stepped forward to drape the cloak about Cynthia's shoulders. The poor thing shivered with cold and fear. Her lips trembled. Her skin was pale as vellum, and her hair hung in long mahogany strands that did little to conceal the puckered tips of her breasts. He clenched his jaw in ill-suppressed anger. Her hip and one thigh were badly abraded, and her cheek bore a small cut, clearly the marks of rough handling by the armored brutes. God, how he wished for a blade.

"I warn you," the Abbot intoned. "This woman is a witch. You approach her at your own peril."

"That is absurd! Lady Cynthia is no more a witch—"

"I should warn you also," said the Abbot, holding up a subduing palm, "that *your* faith, Father Garth, must be held up to the light."

"My faith?" What was the Abbot spewing now? Cynthia stood, wet, terrified, quaking before him. What did his faith have to do with . . .

"Surely you could recognize the signs of possession. You are a man of God, after all." The Abbot lifted his bony shoulders and let out a whispery sigh of feigned regret. "And yet you did nothing. She used the devil's herbs, and you turned a blind eye. She led others to break the covenant of Lent, and you looked aside. And now—"

"This woman has saved countless lives. Who gives you the authority to condemn her?" Garth demanded. But already his heart beat madly in his temples. Jesu—if the Abbot knew about the herbs . . .

"The Lord God," the Abbot announced dramatically, "gives me the authority. Would you challenge His will?"

At a nod from the Abbot, three of the scarlet knights drew their swords. The crowd scattered back with muffled shrieks.

Garth wasn't afraid. He was enraged. In sooth, had he a sword and had he spent the last four years in a tiltyard instead of a monastery, he was sure he could best a whole army of knights, so angry was he.

But he had neither. And it would serve Cynthia ill to spill his blood across the rushes. Then she would be left without a champion. Nay, he would use his wits, not the blade.

"You would send three warriors against an unarmed priest?" he scoffed. Then he turned toward the people, the servants and nobles who had flourished under Cynthia's care. "Do you believe these charges?" he asked. "Do you believe that this woman . . ." He gestured to her, and the hopelessness in her eyes made his voice crack. "This woman who has stitched your wounds and set your bones, this woman who has salved your cuts and birthed your babes, do you believe she could possibly be a witch?"

For a long moment, a quiet guilt settled over the castle folk. Surely they wouldn't betray Cynthia. Surely they owed her more than that.

Then the Abbot broke the silence with cool confidence. "Does anyone here know of the existence of Lady Cynthia's lover?"

The crowd looked uncertainly about. Garth scowled. What did that have to do with . . .

"Nay? Then how is it," the Abbot mused, "that she carries a babe in her belly?"

The room rustled. Garth fired a glance at Cynthia, but her eyes were trained on the floor.

"Who," the Abbot continued, "but the mistress of the devil could carry a babe in her belly without the benefit of a lover?"

A babe? Garth scarcely heard the mutters of surprise around him. A babe? *His* babe. Joy swelled his heart for one brief moment before it faded like a falling star against a black night.

He locked eyes with Cynthia. Worry etched her features. But not for herself. For him. Because she knew what he would do. What he *must* do.

He stretched himself to his full height. His whole being trembled with the enormity of what he was about to say. It would ruin him. It would stain his family name. Worst of all, it would exile him from the church that had given him some small measure of solace and peace. And yet, hadn't he known it would come to this? From the first time he and Cynthia lay together, the possibility had been there. And with each passing week, that possibility turned into a probability. He couldn't lie and say he'd never considered the consequences. Oh aye, he'd never let those consequences surface, but in his heart of hearts, he knew very well what he was doing. And probably, that this day would ultimately come.

In a strange way, its coming gave him a sense of relief. The decision was made for him now. His cassock felt like an old snakeskin, ready to be shed.

He raised a hand for silence from the castle folk. "I declare before all assembled here," he announced, "that I, Garth de Ware, am the father of Lady Cynthia's child."

Elspeth bit back a sob, and Roger could not have looked prouder were Garth his own son. But Garth was certain they didn't believe him. They likely assumed he sacrificed himself for Cynthia's sake. For one triumphant moment, the Abbot looked very anxious indeed.

Then Cynthia issued a feeble protest. "Nay."

Garth looked at her in surprise. Cynthia was shaking her head, her face as cold and unyielding as stone.

"Nay. He is not the father."

Garth frowned. What in the name of God . . . ?

"He is not the father of my babe."

His heart twisted in pain. It was some foul jest. How could she utter those words? How could she betray him? Of course the babe was his. She'd lain with no other. He knew that, *knew* it. Knew it as well as he knew the color of her . . .

Eyes. They shone softly toward him, two translucent gems of blue, in silent entreaty. Then he realized the truth. She denied him for love's sake. She knew he would be ostracized from the church if he admitted to siring a bastard. She was protecting him.

The idea that she would sacrifice so much for him left a choking lump in his chest. His eyes watered as he gazed into her loving regard.

In all his searching, all the hours spent in prayer, all the days copying the holy Scripture, all the weeks and months and years of enduring the poverty of the flesh to aspire to heaven, he had never even come close.

This, he decided, was heaven.

Not some black-haired wench twisting and writhing under his hips. Not the sweet plainsong of holy men echoing through a monastery. Not even carefree summer days spent frolicking in grassy meadows. Nay, heaven was the love of the most precious woman on earth.

Despite lips that trembled with emotion, he spoke with more conviction than he'd ever put into a sermon. "Whether the babe is mine or no, I do lay claim to it. And to the woman you so unjustly condemn."

The crowd's murmurs rose to a dull roar.

The Abbot licked his thin lips, his beady eyes darting about, then raised both arms. "Silence! Silence!"

Garth furrowed his brow. "And if it's the only way . . ." He clasped the wooden cross about his neck, jerking it downward to break the chain, and let it drop to the ground. "I renounce my priestly vows to do so."

The bystanders gasped as a single being, and it took far longer this time to hush their amazed chatter.

Garth stood tall. He was free at last. Now he could rescue his lady. Now his life could begin.

The Abbot made a face that looked as if he'd been chewing green oranges. Then his eyes gentled unexpectedly, and he gave Garth a perfidious smile of pity.

"I fear, good people," he said, interlacing his fingers piously before him, "that Father Garth has been bewitched by your mistress. We must pray for him. Perhaps, once temptation is removed from his path and he is no longer under the witch's influence, he will recover his holiness." He indicated with a bony arm the direction of the dungeon. "Take her below!"

"Nay!" Garth exploded as two guards dragged Cynthia toward the dungeon stairs. "She is innocent! You cannot—"

"You poor, poor man," the Abbot announced, shaking his head sadly. "She has obviously ensorcelled you. I shall pray for your soul," he promised.

"Nay!" Garth yelled, hurtling wildly after her. "Nay!"

The remaining two guards seized him by the arms and wrenched him backward. He struggled with all his might to escape their hold, but he was no match for the armored giants. The last thing he saw was Cynthia's pale bare foot quivering as she stepped down the first stair toward the dungeon. Then someone drove a mailed fist into his cheek, exploding stars across his vision that faded to leave a deep black canopy.

"There, that's a lad."

Droplets sprinkled Garth's forehead. He flinched.

"Comin' around now, are ye?"

He opened his eyes. Elspeth's lined face wavered above him.

"Clouted ye good, he did. Ye've been sleepin' most o' the day."

He sat up instantly. That couldn't be right. It seemed as if he'd just watched Cynthia being dragged off.

"Here, have a care," Elspeth chided, bracing his shoulders. "Ye'll be wobbly as a new foal for a bit."

He *was* dizzy. The last time he'd been cuffed that hard, it was for scribing Latin exercises over his brother Duncan's love letters, and that was nigh seven years ago. He shook his head to clear the cobwebs.

"I must go to her."

"Nay, ye'll be doin' no such thing."

"She needs my help."

"She'll be fine . . . for the moment. The last thing she needs is for ye to get yerself locked up with her. Ye can't help her from the confines of the dungeon."

He ran the fingers of both hands through his hair. Elspeth was right, of course. But he couldn't bear to think about his beloved Cynthia shivering somewhere in the dank bowels of the castle while he sat . . .

Where was he? A row of waxed cheeses hung from the low ceiling. Glazed earthen jars winked in the candlelight from beneath shelves of warped wood, where various cloth-wrapped bundles and bottles crowded together.

Elspeth answered his unasked question. "Ye're in the buttery. Roger thought 'twould be best to keep ye from beneath the Abbot's nose for a bit. For yer own good."

"I will not hide here like a frightened rabbit while—"

"Ye'll only endanger Lady Cynthia and yer child if ye—"

"My . . ." He snapped his eyes toward her. "Then you believe . . ."

"What?" Elspeth said with a rueful snicker. "That the child is yers? Well, after all the tumblin' the two of ye've done in half the chambers of the castle, whose else would it be?"

To his chagrin, Garth blushed. "I never meant to . . ."

Elspeth tugged the cassock up around his shoulders in a motherly fashion. "Aye, lad, truth to tell, ye never had a prayer, priest or no. Once Cynthia makes her mind up about a thing . . . well, ye'd have to swim harder than a salmon upstream to resist her will, that one." She patted his hand. It felt strangely comforting. Then she clamped her lips together tightly. Her eyes watered. "But now she's in the hands o' the devil, God save her, and, will or no, she'll not wish to drag ye into that hell. She'll deny the babe is yers till they tie her to the stake and . . ." Her voice cut off with a choking sob.

Garth slammed a fist against the wall. Flakes of plaster fluttered to the hard-packed dirt floor.

"I have to go to her," he muttered between his teeth, scrambling to his feet. "I have to go."

"Please," Elspeth begged, bunching his cassock in desperate fingers. "Ye mustn't. Aye, ye're her only hope now. But ye've got to find another way."

He took her by the shoulders and looked back and forth between her two brown, tear-bright eyes, his mind running quickly over ideas like a pen scribbling on parchment.

"The Abbot cannot sacrifice an innocent babe," he said. "The church forbids it. The mark of the devil must be proved. The child must be born." He ran a hand across his mouth. "So we have . . ."

"Six months, mayhap seven."

He gazed pensively over her head, past the jars and bottles, past the cheeses, past the peeling plaster of the buttery walls, to a place in his mind's eye that had grown dusty with disuse.

It was time to swipe away the cobwebs now. Time to don the faded surcoat and rusty mail of the youth who once knew how to wield a sword. Time to rub oil into the squeaky hinges of the war machine.

"Bring me parchment, ink, and quill," he said, surprised by the authority of his own voice. "And a trusty servant who can ride like the wind. Nay, three servants."

Elspeth nodded and hurried to do his bidding, wringing her hands and casting one hopeful glance backward before she left him in the buttery alone.

He ran a hand over his cheek, wincing as he found the tender place where the knight had doled him the blow. For four years, he'd turned the other cheek. It was time now to fight.

Holden would be amazed to hear from him. But he'd come. Garth knew he would. And, with God's grace, in time. If there was one thing in this world he could depend on, it was his brother's love of a good battle.

21

CYNTHIA SCRATCHED A MARK INTO THE DANK STONE wall with a fragment of beef bone. She'd salvaged the tool from her first supper in the dungeon. Two months ago, according to her tally.

So it was October, then. The time for sowing peas and beans, for transplanting leeks and spreading cinders under the cabbages.

She sniffed back the drip that seemed to be her constant companion since she'd taken up lodgings in this damp place. There was so much she missed—the changing of the seasons, birdsong, her garden.

Most of all, she missed Garth. And at first, she'd tried not to think about him.

Instead, she focused on the babe growing inside her. Her belly was as round as a plumped goose now. It amazed her that the child continued to thrive, heedless of the lack of fresh air and sunlight and proper care. She supposed babes were as stubborn and hardy as weeds, able to grow in the most infertile soil. But she longed to give this babe the healthy start it deserved. Her aching back and idle muscles and pale skin yearned to feel the restoring touch of nature.

She supposed she should be thankful. Wendeville's dungeon wasn't so awful. Aye, it was dank and dark. Moss sprouted from every crack between the stones. An occasional rat would poke its twitching whiskers into her cell, then, finding no supper, scamper off. And it was cold all the time. But she was given a chamber pot, which was emptied regularly, food that was filling, if not always savory, and a rough wool blanket thick enough to thwart all but the most persistent mists. She kept the cell as clean as possible with what few makeshift tools and rags she squirreled away. Things could be worse.

She'd even befriended her guard, a thick-headed lummox by the name of Rolf. He was a giant of a man, but simple of thought and sweet of manner, once he was cut off from the pack of his companions. She'd discovered so one morn, weeks past, while forcing down her usual breakfast of lumpy, tepid porridge. She noticed the big man scowling and rubbing at his temple, and asked him about it. The rest followed as naturally as the night the day.

Poor Rolf suffered from constant aches of the head, she learned. So she taught him how to relieve the pain by preparing willow bark tea and rue wine. After a time, she earned his trust. Eventually, he even allowed her to reach through the iron bars to lay a healing hand aside his temple.

After that, her porridge was not so tepid, and Rolf usually pulled a crumbling fruit coffin or a syrupy sweetmeat from his pouch to go with it. He even managed to sneak in a bucket of warm water several times so she could wash her face.

But best of all, he supplied her with news. News about the castle folk. News about the Abbot. And most recently, news from Garth.

She'd had to stifle sobs of gratitude when Rolf slipped the first scrap of parchment through the bars of her prison.

It came from a good man, he'd said, a man who lived in the village and took care of the old and the sick. The good man had promised to remember Rolf in his prayers. He'd asked Rolf to deliver the message to the lady in the dungeon and not to tell a soul.

Cynthia's fingers trembled as she took the parchment from his great paw, and her eyes blurred when she recognized the flawless script and the name set with a modest flourish at the bottom. Garth.

According to the missive, the wheels of rescue had been set in motion. He could not be more specific, lest the parchment find its way into enemy hands, but he felt this guard could be trusted to carry their correspondence.

From then on, every few days she received word from Garth and scratched a reply on the back of his parchment with a piece of charcoal Rolf brought her. His notes were full of longing, but they also spoke of hope. She learned that Garth had cast aside his cassock, but he'd never ceased doing the Lord's work. He toiled alongside the villagers now, safe from the scrutiny of the Abbot.

As for the Abbot, he busied himself gathering men about him—from what she could surmise, a band of overgrown dullards and religious fanatics, men he'd recruited into his personal army at Charing. Each day, more scarlet-surcoated knights slowly trickled in to usurp the chambers of Wendeville's nobility. For what cataclysmic battle he prepared, she didn't know. Surely the Abbot didn't need an entire army to slay one woman. And yet they continued to arrive.

She also learned that the Abbot was forbidden to execute her until her babe was born. He may believe she carried the devil's spawn, but until irrefutable proof was obtained, church doctrine prevented him from laying a hand on the innocent child.

Cynthia stroked her swelling abdomen as it twitched now with subtle movements. About three more months. It would pass in the blink of an eye, she knew. And then, if Garth's rescue somehow failed, since none could gainsay the edict of the almighty Abbot, he'd have his will. Cynthia would burn at the stake for a witch.

Unwelcome tears flooded her eyes. Despair descended upon her as suddenly as a June squall. Her chest hitched, and a sob fell from her lips ere she could stop it. She clapped a fist against her mouth and struggled to cease her weeping, cursing the emotions which, of late, seemed wont to overwhelm her without warning.

Surely Garth would save her. And even if he couldn't, the babe would survive, she told herself, dabbing furiously at her eyes with a corner of her surcoat. Elspeth and Roger would see to that. As for her, if all else failed, if she was to be executed, she intended to go to her death painlessly. When they came for her, she'd beg Rolf to fetch her opium wine. With any luck, she'd be half-dead long before the flames licked her flesh.

Then she chided herself for her doubt. Garth would save her. He'd promised her as much. There was naught to cry over.

Heavy footfalls sounded outside the door.

"M'lady!" Rolf's familiar voice huffed through the iron grate.

It would distress Rolf to see her thus, so she wiped away the last vestiges of her tears, then stood by the small barred window. "Rolf? What is it?"

"There's men comin'. An army. Big, big army! Half a day's ride out." His blond-bearded face was florid with agitation. Beads of sweat dotted his forehead.

"More of the Abbot's men?"

"Nay, nay, nay, nay," he said, shaking his great head like a plowhorse. "A diff'rent army."

Cynthia's heart stilled. Then it fluttered with an emotion she'd almost forgotten. Hope. She clutched at the bars. "Who?"

Rolf's face screwed up in frustration and self-loathing. He didn't know or couldn't remember.

"It's all right." Cynthia's fingers flexed with schooled patience on the bars. "What standard do they carry? What color is their flag?"

Rolf squinched his eyes shut and chewed on his lip. "Green!" he said explosively. "Green. Green." He nodded. "And black!" he added as an afterthought.

Green and black. Could it be?

"Big animal. Mean animal," Rolf muttered.

"A wolf?" she asked breathlessly.

"Aye!" He nodded vigorously. "A wolf. A wolf. The wolf of . . . of . . ."

"The wolf of de Ware?"

"Aye, that's it!" He grinned hugely. "The wolf of de Ware.

And there's hundreds of 'em. Hundreds and hundreds and . . ."

Cynthia stopped listening and turned from the door. Her eyes filled again, this time with joy. Garth had sent for his brothers! He'd done it. He'd come to her rescue.

"I have to go now, m'lady," Rolf said. "The Abbot's makin' a terrible fuss."

For the first time in weeks, Cynthia smiled. "No doubt. No doubt he is. Thank you, Rolf. Thank you for everything."

He grinned sheepishly and trudged off.

Cynthia leaned back upon the cold iron door. The torch in the hall flickered, making her shadow dance a merry jig of celebration across the damp stones of her cell.

They might survive—the babe and her.

Hope lightened her heart.

She wished that she'd asked Rolf more. What were the Abbot's orders to his men? How were the castle folk taking the news? And where was Garth? But then, she supposed she'd learn in time. For now, it was enough to know that the knights of de Ware came to rescue her. Hundreds and hundreds of them.

The babe wiggled inside her as if sharing her delight, and she laughed aloud, though the sound was almost like a sob.

"Soon," she said, soothing the infant with long gentle strokes, "we shall be free of this place." She glanced at the dripping walls, the broken floor, the cracked chamber pot. It truly was a wretched place, no matter how she'd tried to plaster over it in her mind. And in a few hours at best, a few days at most, she'd walk through that sagging door, never to return again.

"The first thing I intend to do is stretch out on the sod of the garden," she said, half to the babe, half to herself. "Just soak up the sun's warmth. I want to smell the ripening apples and hear the cuckoo's call. And I want to run my fingers through the fallen leaves. Gold, orange, yellow, crimson." She closed her eyes, imagining it.

The sound of Rolf's clumsy tread returning broke through her thoughts. His face appeared at the door, disturbed, his mouth working nervously. He said not a word, but there was no mistaking the apology in his eyes. There were two guards with him. An icy trickle of fear ran down her neck.

"What do you want?" she croaked.

"Back off, Rolf!" the second guard ordered. "Give me room." He rattled a key in the lock of the door.

"What . . ." she began again, swallowing the words involuntarily.

The door screeched open, and the guard grabbed her by the elbow. As ludicrous as it was, she resisted, strangely reluctant to step from the cell that had been her home for so many weeks.

"Come along now, witch," the guard said, half-dragging her. "It's time for a bonfire."

His laughter was lost on her as her feet scraped over the rough stones. She rolled her eyes wildly, searching for some word, some gesture that would make them put her back in the cell. But it was hopeless. The tears she saw standing in Rolf's eyes distressed her all the more. And the last horrifying thought she had as they hauled her up into the blinding daylight of the great hall was that she'd never have the chance to take her opium.

"Chaplain!"

Garth looked up from the pile of split timber. The villagers still called him chaplain, though he kept his wooden cross inside his tunic and hadn't delivered a sermon or spoken a prayer since the Abbot's arrival.

"Chaplain!"

The familiar bear of a man atop his huge warhorse galloped toward him from the hill above the village, his scarlet tabard flapping about him like a giant hawk trying to carry him off. Garth brought the ax down one last time, wedging it into the thick oak stump, then wiped callused hands on his nubby linen tunic. Stinging sweat dripped into his eye as he squinted toward the sun to watch the man's approach.

Every few days, Rolf came to deliver messages. It was the only way Garth kept from going mad, living here out of harm's way in the leatherworker's cottage. Even so, he suffered the anguish of hell, knowing Cynthia languished in a cold, dank dungeon.

God, he yearned to see her, to watch the babe, *his* babe, swell her belly. He craved her smell, her taste, her touch. He'd neither slept nor eaten properly for weeks, stretched to the limit upon the rack of waiting, and he'd distracted himself from that agony by strengthening his body for the battle to come. For hours on end, he split wood, drove oxen, built fences, practiced with a sword—anything to keep his mind off Cynthia's horrible torment.

Almost three months had passed since he'd penned the letter to his brother. Surely it had reached Holden by now. He'd sent three riders along to guarantee its delivery. Certainly the message—a cryptic invitation to Garth's wedding requesting the full force of his army—would send Holden bolting for his steed. Aye, any day now, his brother would gallop up to the walls of Wendeville with his entourage. His fierce, heavily armed entourage.

A large plume of dust rose as Rolf's steed closed the distance with reckless speed. Garth shielded his eyes.

"Chaplain!" came a broken cry. "Chaplain!"

Garth frowned. Tears streamed down Rolf's florid cheeks. Something must be wrong. Garth hurtled forward to catch the reins of the horse.

"Chaplain!" Rolf sobbed. "Ye got to come!" He slipped gracelessly from the saddle and would have fallen if Garth hadn't caught him.

"What is it, Rolf?"

The poor man could barely speak around his gasping and sobbing. "The wolfs . . . the wolfs are comin' . . . for the . . . for the lady."

A sudden rush of sweet air filled Garth's chest. The wolves? Holden had come. He'd come at last. Garth gave Rolf's shoulder a hearty thump. "That's a good thing, Rolf. The wolves are our friends."

"Nay," Rolf insisted, bending forward with his hands on his knees to catch his breath. "They're too far away. The Abbot . . . the Abbot wants to . . ." He lifted his head and looked perplexedly up at Garth. "He wants to . . . set her on fire. He's buildin' sticks to set the lady on fire."

Garth's heart stopped. "Now?"

Rolf nodded vigorously.

Horror sucked the breath from Garth's lungs. He staggered.

"Ye got to save her," Rolf begged, clawing at his tunic. "Ye got to . . ."

Garth's body took over while his mind reeled in shock. In one fluid movement, he mounted Rolf's horse and wheeled the steed about. He hadn't ridden at such a pace since he was a boy, but the skill came as readily to him now as the words of the Lord's Prayer. Mile after mile, driven by the fuel of rage, man and horse chewed up the road, spitting out pebbles and dust behind them. By the time Wendeville's towers broke the horizon, the poor horse's sides were heaving as it wheezed through its frothy mouth.

But the loyal palfrey galloped all the way up the long hill to the castle, past the barbican, and through the courtyard gate, stopping only when Garth tugged back on the reins to avoid the milling throng of humanity.

The courtyard overflowed with people—nobles, servants, peasants, merchants, and more scarlet-clad, mounted knights than he expected. Except for the merchants, who enthusiastically hawked their wares as if they'd gathered for a spring fair, a strange hush reigned over the crowd. Women talked behind their hands, and men shuffled their feet uncomfortably.

Was he too late? Was she gone? His heart pounded against his chest. His eyes raced over the courtyard and lit on a single blackened pole pointing at the sky like an accusing finger. But the crowd was too thick with mounted knights to make out what lay at its base.

He pressed his mount forward, pushing between two quarreling boys, skirting by a pastry vendor, nudging aside a pushy wool merchant with a huge wagonload of fabric.

At last, he saw Cynthia. She was bound fast to the pole with heavy cord, her skin as pale as alabaster where it kissed the dark wood. The bones of her face stood prominent now, and her hair, dulled by filth, lay matted to her head, making her look frail, helpless. The cool October wind fluttered the edges of her grimy linen shift, causing her to shudder, and exposed in indecent relief the burgeoning swell of her belly.

Bitter rage filled his mouth, rage so deep he could find no

words for it. He kicked his mount, intent on charging the gallows and freeing Cynthia. But the horse was hemmed in. Garth's knee was clutched by someone in the close quarters, but he ignored it, trying desperately to maneuver the steed forward. Now someone tugged insistently on his tunic, demanding his attention. He cursed and pulled hard on the reins, frustrated to nigh madness. Standing in the stirrups, he swatted away the arm that continued to grab at him. He'd considered dismounting altogether when someone made that decision for him, dragging him out of the saddle and onto the sod on his hindquarters. Shaking his dazed head, he prepared to lambast his attacker. But when he saw who towered over him above swirling burgundy velvet skirts, all he could manage was a stunned gasp.

"Do you want to save the lady or no?" she snapped, her eyes glittering.

Though her voice crackled with familiar sarcasm, he'd never heard sweeter words.

Despite the feast of fresh air, Cynthia could inhale only a thread of it between her compressed lips. Her betraying knees wobbled beneath her. It was only hunger, she tried to convince herself. And yet her belly roiled at the thought of food. She shivered. From the cold, she thought, though clammy sweat beaded her forehead. But it wasn't fear. Never fear. After all, had she not faced death a hundred times? There was naught to fear. Death brought peace, an end to suffering. So why did the tall, black-shrouded executioner looming over her with a pitched brand snatch the very air from her lungs?

Red-clad soldiers stacked tinder haphazardly at her feet. Someone jerked at her bonds to check the knots. Then the Abbot himself stepped up onto a tall wooden crate serving as a makeshift platform. He looked uncharacteristically slovenly, as if he'd just come from his bed. His robes were askew, his meager black hair combed in haste. He seemed harried and nervous, as if he were all too aware of the sin he was about to commit and in a hurry to put it behind him. He tugged the hood of his cassock closer about his scrawny neck and held a pasty hand up for silence.

"In the name of God," he announced self-righteously, "I condemn this woman"—he pointed an accusing finger—"to burn as a witch. . . ."

Faces swam before Cynthia . . . Elspeth, Jeanne, Mary . . . friends, foes, strangers.

"The proofs being these three," the Abbot droned on. "That she used herbs to cure which are commonly known as the devil's. That she used enchantments to coerce others to break the covenant of Lent. And that she bears the seed of Satan, having no earthly father to lay claim to her infant."

A bold voice split the air. "As I have said all along, I lay claim to her infant!"

Cynthia's vision cleared instantly at the familiar sound, and hope shot straight into her heart. The crowd parted, and a muscular man made his way brazenly up to the Abbot. Cynthia held her breath. Was it Garth?

"I am the father."

It couldn't be. This man had the shoulders of an ox and legs like two young oaks. He wore the rough tunic and leggings of a peasant, and his skin was bronzed by the sun. And yet . . .

He turned to her then, enveloping her in his forest green gaze, a gaze filled with such love and promise that she nearly collapsed into relieved tears.

"Father Garth," the Abbot intoned. "I had hoped your separation from this woman's evil influences would make you see the error of your ways. But alas, I fear 'tis not so." He clucked his tongue. "You see," he announced, "how the witch has driven poor Garth to insanity and godlessness. There is no hope for him, except . . ." The Abbot's eyes sparked with sudden inspiration. "Except that the purifying fire might refine his soul as well."

The Abbot nodded to the executioner. The immense hooded figure snagged Garth about the arm in an iron grip and wrested him up the pile of kindling to the stake.

"Nay!" Cynthia screamed, her hopes killed as quickly as they'd been born.

"What the devil?" Garth cried. "Unhand me! What you do is blasphemy!"

"We shall all pray for you," the Abbot promised.

"Nay!" Garth shouted, grappling with all his strength against the brute lugging him to his death. "You will burn in hell for this, Abbot! You are murdering an innocent! Your soul will be damned for eternity!"

But Cynthia saw the truth of the matter. No matter how Garth proclaimed his innocence, her innocence, the babe's innocence, no matter if he shouted till his voice grew hoarse and the flames licked at his feet, the Abbot had no intention of releasing either of them. Not even the will of the people, some of whom stood weeping and moaning, some shouting in horrified protest, could alter the wretched man's intentions. For whatever ungodly reason, the Abbot wanted them both gone, and no force on earth would sway him from his purpose.

"Your soul will rot, Abbot!" Garth snarled, throwing his head back like a wild wolf.

It was the executioner who finally silenced him. The big man gave Garth's shoulder a rough shake and hissed, "Quiet! Look to your lady, man! Lend her your strength."

Garth stopped struggling and looked into Cynthia's face. She tried to stop the tears, but they spilled over like a rain-swollen brook. Garth quieted.

"I'm sorry," she whispered as he mounted the platform beside her.

"Nay," he murmured. "Do not be. I've come to rescue you."

Rescue her? How could he rescue her now? He was about to be burned at the stake beside her. Or perhaps, she thought, fresh tears blinding her, he meant her spiritual rescue. He sacrificed himself to save her soul.

"It's all my fault," she choked out.

"Nay," he repeated fiercely. "Never think that. Never. I don't regret a moment of what we've done. Do you hear me? Not a moment. I don't want to live without you. I . . . I *couldn't* live without you."

The executioner bound him to the opposite side of the stake. Then Garth reached behind him to catch her hand.

"It won't be long now," he assured her.

As Garth's warm fingers closed around hers, Cynthia felt the sharp, icy terror of the moment slowly drain out of her.

Her pummeling heart still beat violently against her ribs, but its pace slackened.

It was too late to have regrets, to agonize over what might have been. He couldn't save her now. He could only be with her. But it was enough to have the strength of his comforting hand as the consuming fire claimed their bodies.

Through bleary eyes, Cynthia took in all the details surrounding her with a curious detachment. Time slowed. Every movement, every smell, every sound came to her now with crystal clarity.

Below her, a horse stamped its hoof, crushing a tiny daisy in the courtyard grass.

Beyond the crowd, a chicken squawked and flapped ineffectual wings as a hound snapped at it through a hole in the wattle fence.

Two little girls at the fore fought over a cloth doll.

Mothers with babes she'd birthed sobbed in loud protest, pressing futilely against the restraining wall of scarlet knights.

Behind the row of guards, Elspeth buried her hitching head in her hands.

The aroma of pork pastries wafted past.

Heads she'd once laved with healing elixirs wagged in impotent grief.

Nearby, a wool merchant wrested her cart brazenly past the guards, undaunted by the spectacle about to take place, extolling the virtues of her broadcloth and worsted. Cynthia noted wistfully that, like herself, the woman was also large with child.

Below, the executioner's brand blossomed into flame, and the odor of curing pitch curled sweet and heavy into her nostrils.

Images flashed by more quickly.

A beautiful dark-haired wench in burgundy skirts flirted saucily with one of the guards.

A hawk wheeled high overhead, screeching.

Black smoke blew across Cynthia's field of vision as the brand was brought aloft.

The merchant called out, "Worsted! Fine worsted!"

A wave of heat suddenly made Cynthia nauseous.

The flirting wench gave the guard a coy wink.

Cynthia could almost taste the ash as the burning torch swung by.

"Broadcloth!"

Icy fear made a cold sweat break out over Cynthia's brow. She clutched in panic at Garth's hand. He gave her palm a long, slow, steady, calming squeeze.

"It will be over in a moment," he whispered roughly. "And then, I swear, nothing will keep us apart."

Cynthia bit her lip. "I . . . we'll . . . love you forever."

The dry tinder snapped and popped as it ignited. She coughed as the first acrid smoke rose. Holding tight to Garth's hand, she willed herself not to scream.

22

BELOW CYNTHIA, THE WOOL MERCHANT'S WAGON rolled slowly forward. She frowned as it steered perilously close to the fire. Jesu, if the woman didn't take care . . .

The stack of cloth in the wagon shifted, writhing as if it were alive. At first she thought it was a trick of the fire. But the fabric continued to undulate. She blinked back the impossible sight. Yet before her eyes, the wool bulged upward like a foaling mare's belly, billowing out, then falling away at last to deliver its contents. She gasped, inhaling a lungful of acrid smoke. Up sprang a knight in full armor wielding two enormous swords. He struggled to his feet in the midst of the cart, kicking the bundles of cloth aside.

With a great cry, the man slashed toward her with both swords. Cynthia thought for an instant that he meant to slay her outright. She closed her eyes, but didn't flinch. It would be a blow of mercy, after all. But his blades came down instead on the binding ropes, and at once she found herself untethered. So abruptly that she nearly tumbled onto the cracking tinder below.

In the blink of an eye, Garth, cut free as well, scooped her into his arms. Then, without a backward glance, he tossed her over the smoldering kindling. It was none other than the executioner who saved her from a fiery death. He caught her in his massive arms to set her down safely upon the ground. While her mind was still dazed, he tossed back his hood, revealing a handsome, swarthy face, an overlong mane of gleaming black hair, and blue eyes that sparkled as he grinned.

Before she could gasp in surprise, the pregnant wool merchant appeared at her side, her eyes narrowed in concern. "Are you all right?" she asked, cradling Cynthia's belly as tenderly and familiarly as if she'd known her all her life.

Cynthia could do little more than nod.

The knight who'd sprung from the cloth wagon now tossed Garth one of his two swords. To her chagrin, the weapon looked as natural in the chaplain's hands as the Bible. Garth leaped from the pyre, scorching his tunic as he just cleared the flames burning high now.

"Come." As the wool merchant urged her toward the haven of the castle wall, Cynthia caught a glimpse of the pretty, dark-haired wench still flirting with the guard. As she watched, to her amazement, the lady whipped a silver sword from beneath her skirts and, without blinking, savagely attacked the former object of her affections. The man drew his dagger, scarcely able to defend himself from the woman's fierce blows.

"Never mind her," the cloth merchant said, tugging Cynthia by the wrist. "She's just showing off."

At last out of the press, Cynthia stared in wonder at the turmoil taking place around her. Here and there, what had appeared to be crippled beggars shrugged off their ragged cloaks to reveal coats of mail and gleaming swords. They hauled the scarlet guardsmen from their mounts, leaving a fray of confused, walleyed horses rearing in the close confines of the courtyard. The peasants scattered from the trampling hooves, dropping staffs and aleskins in their haste to escape. The fire blazed on, high now against the shimmering towers of Wendeville.

In the midst of the melee, Cynthia spotted Garth. In his smudged and tattered tunic, his teeth bared in a ferocious grimace, he looked nothing like a man of the cloth. He'd become a warrior. He slashed right and left, pummeling shields, nicking mail, wounding flesh. He spun and lunged as intuitively as if he'd been born to the blade, moving with the grace and power of a wolf on the hunt.

And while the tumult grew around her, Cynthia noticed that a great green wave poured slowly in through the gates—men mounted in such tight formation that their horses rode flank to flank. The wool merchant saw them, too.

"It's fortunate my husband arrived early, though he had a devil of a time finding Garth. You see, Holden's been at Wendeville for nigh a sennight now with his spies," she confided, "secretly planning your rescue. The fighting should be over soon enough now that the de Ware armies have come." She winced as the dark-haired wench spun past to sink her sword into an unfortunate victim's thigh.

Holden. Garth's brother. Cynthia frowned. Then the dark-haired warrior wench must be . . . "Cambria," she murmured.

The wool merchant smiled. "The one and only."

"And you're . . . Linet?"

The poor woman had no time to answer. Her green eyes widened in alarm as the executioner's blade whizzed over their heads, missing them by inches.

"Sorry, my ladies!" the man called as he pursued a terrified guard.

"I'm Linet, and that," the wool merchant said, "is my reckless husband."

"Duncan?"

"You may call him Dolt, if you like," she said with a frown of mock severity. "He's in rare form today." She clucked her tongue. "It seems to me he lit the pyre a little too soon, did he not? You could have been scorched." She leaned forward conspiratorially. "I told him Holden should have played the executioner. He has the more suitable temperament for it. But nay, Duncan just had to have the villain's role. He simply adores that ebony worsted cloak." She shook her head. "Men."

Cynthia's head was spinning. She frowned, trying to understand. "Holden . . . was the man in your cart."

"Aye, and if he slashed any of my swatches with those great blades of his, there'll be the devil to pay."

Cynthia felt overwhelmed. As much chaos riddled her

brain as filled the courtyard. Moments before, she'd been prepared to die. Now she chatted with Garth's kin as if they'd been friends forever. Her executioner had become her savior, and her gentle chaplain had become her sword-wielding hero.

The de Ware knights filled half the courtyard now. Few had bothered to lower a lance or raise a blade. Their sheer numbers were enough to intimidate most of the scarlet knights, who readily surrendered their weapons, kneeling for mercy on the sod.

Cynthia searched among the confusion until she spotted Garth. He had ceased fighting, but his chest still heaved with unleashed strength. It was a side of him she'd never beheld. With his snapping eyes and a bloodied sword gleaming in his fist, he looked like an avenging saint.

"Go on," Linet said, nudging her forward. "'Tis safe enough now. Go to him."

She wanted nothing more. Leaving Linet behind, she picked her way through the crush of people, one arm shielding her belly. She was halfway to Garth when he swiveled his head to look at her. His shoulders dropped, and his face lit up with a strange mixture of emotions—relief, wonder, perplexity . . . but mostly sheer adoration.

She felt as if she were made of pure light, so well did his look warm her. All the weeks spent in darkness vanished. All her fears dissolved like water into the soil. His regard felt like a protective cloak wrapped around her, her and their babe.

She'd taken another step toward him when a scarlet sleeve reached out to snag her. Startled, she flinched.

"M'lady. Oh, m'lady." It was Rolf. He held tight to her arm, sniffling, his fleshy face blubbering and grinning all at the same time. "When they lit the . . . I thought . . . but then the ex'cutioner . . . oh, m'lady, I knew ye'd . . ."

Rolf strangled on his words as Garth's forearm wrapped around his throat, choking off his air. His eyes bulged in terror.

Garth spoke between his teeth. "Unhand her. I'll slay you where you stand if you don't take your—"

"Nay!" Cynthia screamed. "It's Rolf, Garth, it's Rolf!"

She shivered. She'd never heard such cold venom in

Garth's voice. His eyes, as hard as emeralds, frightened her. But he at last loosened his grip slightly, and she rested a soothing palm on his tense forearm.

"I'm sorry. I didn't . . ." Garth released Rolf, and the big knight stumbled aside, none the worse for wear. Garth then gave a shuddering sigh and let the sword drop from his fingers as if it burned him. He shook his head at his uncharacteristic display of brute force. "I'm sorry. I . . ." he began, combing a hand through his disheveled hair.

There was naught to forgive, but Cynthia could endure mere words no more. She rushed into Garth's embrace with all the grace of a suckling lamb, eager for the nourishment he provided her soul. His arms closed about her tentatively, and he gasped as her protruding belly mashed against him. But she needed this, and if the babe had survived nearly three months of watery pottage and dank filth and the near fatal kiss of fire, surely it could survive a jostling by its father.

She pressed closer, and at last Garth returned the hug, clasping her about the shoulders and back and head as if to assure himself that she was real. She burrowed her head against his chest.

His clothing smelled of smoke. Perhaps Linet was right, she thought with a smile. Duncan had set the fire a bit too soon. But none of that mattered now. Garth was here, safe, and she wanted naught more than to snuggle against him for the rest of her life.

She scarcely noticed when the cheer arose around them. Garth returned the encouraging calls with a smile and a wave. Then Elspeth came forward. Her face looked like a disease-mottled red rose from weeping, but it was clear she'd have none of Cynthia's pity.

"Ye come inside now, lass," she ordered. "Ye've no business out here among the bloodshed. Ye need to give that babe rest."

Cynthia shook her head apologetically. "I've spent almost three months in that castle, Elspeth. There's naught I want more right now than to feel the sun's light and the wind's breath."

Elspeth's chin quivered, but she nodded brusquely.

"Garth!" Duncan called. "Are you going to introduce your

lady love to me?" He whirled his black cloak dramatically over one shoulder and waggled his eyebrows. "Or is your head so dazed you cannot remember your manners?"

"If it's dazed," Garth replied sourly, "it's only from that too close brush with death."

"Ha! If it weren't for me, oh so holy Father," Duncan fired back, "you'd be roasting in hell even now!"

Cynthia swooned a little, weary with shock and disturbed by the vivid image his words conjured.

Linet jabbed Duncan in the stomach. "Mind your tongue, Duncan," she muttered. "Can't you see she's in a delicate condition?"

Cynthia had to smile at that. No one had ever used the word *delicate* to describe her. But Linet's chiding worked. Duncan had the grace to look abashed.

Holden marched forward then, a mahogany-haired, more serious version of his brother, his helm stashed under his arm, his sword at the ready, a forbidding scowl furrowing his brow. But the eyes that met hers were calm and steady, affording her a high level of respect. "The Abbot's guard are under control now," he told her. "What would you have me do with them?"

Cynthia blinked as he awaited her command. The man was speaking to *her*. She chewed her lip. God's wounds—how would she know what to do with prisoners of battle? Wendeville had never been under siege before. And besides, unlike his sword-wielding wife, she knew naught of warfare.

Before she could frame a lame reply, Cambria came to her side, a smudge of someone else's blood painting her cheek.

"I'd gather them in the great hall to secure their fealty," she confided, her voice arching over the words with a slight Scots lilt. "They appear to be misfits and half-wits, most of them, fairly harmless. And who knows? Mayhap if they see your caring ways with your own servants, they'll come to love you and follow you in time."

Cynthia nodded. It was a sage suggestion. "Aye. Thank you."

Holden left at once to begin moving the prisoners.

"Now. I have just one more question," Cambria said when

her husband had gone. "Where, my lords and ladies, has the Abbot gone?"

Cynthia's breath flew quickly from her parted mouth. "He's . . . he's gone?" Her voice came out on a thin thread of sound.

Garth rested a solid hand aside her neck, pulling her toward him. "As long as I have breath in my body," he said, his voice rough with emotion, "I swear that man will not touch you again. I care not if he is priest or cardinal or Pope. He will not touch you."

The determination in Garth's eyes made her believe him. She could trust him. He would protect her. She let out a slow sigh and nodded.

Cambria, however, wasn't so convinced. She gave Garth a quick appraising glance from head to toe, probably remembering that castle she'd once taken out from under his nose.

"We'll find him," she said, "within the hour."

Eventually, the fiery pyre dwindled into a mass of gray coals, its glowing crimson heart beating out the last of its life.

The de Ware force operated like a well-crafted loom. Holden and his knights rounded up prisoners while their squires stabled the horses. Pages collected discarded weapons, wiping them clean with rags before stacking them in a neat pile. Linet directed two women in the repairing of the damaged wattle fence around the chickens while Garth tended the wounds of one of Cambria's unfortunate victims. Duncan gathered a pack of distressed, sniffling children and kept them occupied, regaling them with some clever tale.

Cynthia surveyed the damage to the courtyard. Her herbs were crushed beyond saving, plowed under by horse hoof and cart wheel. The fire had scorched the sod. And what was left of her grass had been trampled into a muddy mess.

But the seasons would turn again. The ground could be repaired. By next spring, a whole new garden would grow up to replace . . .

Someone was sobbing.

She let her gaze drift along the castle wall. There, deep beneath the shadows of the dovecote's eave, Mary sat upon her knees, rocking back and forth, crying as if her heart would break.

Slowly, Cynthia ambled over, dodging knights and pages packing weapons. A foul smell arose as she neared, and she could see something black writhing on Mary's lap, some injured animal or . . .

"Oh, m'lady," Mary wailed. "Forgive me, m'lady, and forgive him, I beg ye." Her young face was ugly with weeping. "Please forgive him."

"Who, Mary?" Cynthia asked gently, coming closer despite the stench.

Mary glanced down at her lap.

Sweet Lord!

The Abbot, the sleeve of his cassock slick with fresh vomit, writhed in agony. He groaned, gripping his stomach as if he would tear it out. Cynthia dropped down beside him.

All her fears, all her hatred were forgotten in that instant. A man was suffering. She had to help him.

"What happened?" she asked, brushing her shift aside.

"I didn't mean . . ." Mary wailed.

She took Mary by the shoulders and shook her once. "Tell me what happened."

Mary blinked her eyes. "I couldn't let him do it, m'lady. Don't you see? 'Tis a mortal sin to kill an innocent babe. I couldn't let the Abbot's soul burn in the eternal fires of hell. I couldn't!"

Cynthia glanced at the Abbot. His skin was a sickly shade, and blisters swelled and distorted his mouth. Poison. "What did you use, Mary? What did you give him?"

"Hellebore. I gave him black hellebore." She laced her fingers over her face and began to cry again in earnest.

Cynthia slowly began to rub her palms together, though the sinking in her heart told her it was futile. Black hellebore was a powerful poison with no cure.

Footsteps approached behind her.

"Mother of God!" It was Garth. "What's happened to him? What . . ." Then, realizing Cynthia's intent, he grabbed her abruptly by the arm. "Nay. Nay, Cynthia. You owe him naught. Stay away from him. Stay away from the devil."

She ignored him, focusing on the heat growing between her hands.

"He tried to slay you," Garth reasoned. "Jesu—he tried to kill our unborn child! How can you . . ."

"How can I not, Garth?" she answered without looking up. "Just as you are a man of God, I am a healer."

He fell silent then, and as she worked she heard others gather behind her, but none uttered a word. She laid a hand upon the Abbot's clammy brow and closed her eyes. He made small mewling sounds as the poison seeped into his veins. For a long time, she waited while the priest twisted in pain. As she suspected, it was too late to save him. But it wasn't too late to relieve his agony.

"Fetch me my opium wine from the cellar. Hurry!" she directed to no one in particular. Someone sped to do her bidding. To the Abbot, she said, "The pain will be over soon. The opium will ease your suffering." She stroked his head gently with one hand and laid the flat of her other palm upon his cramping belly. Warmth filled her, stronger than she'd ever felt before, and she directed the energy toward the Abbot, moving it in soothing waves over his stomach. Gradually his grimace relaxed, and his breathing, though shallow and rapid, was at least devoid of moaning. His onyx-dark gaze was puzzled as he raised it to her.

"I was . . . wrong, my child," he croaked, lifting one skeletal hand to lock onto her arm. "You're . . . not . . . a witch . . . at all." His eyes grew distant for a moment, as if they glimpsed the world beyond. Then he looked at her one final time. "You're . . . an . . . angel."

Garth knelt beside her. He retrieved his once discarded wooden cross from inside his tunic and clutched it in one hand. With the other, he made the sign of blessing over the Abbot. He peeled the dying man's hand from Cynthia's arm and held it in his own, against the cross. Then, in a voice ringing with faith, he began the sacred words of the last rites.

By the time Linet and Cambria arrived with the opium wine, the Abbot was already gone, and they were startled to find their husbands uncharacteristically silent and solemn, staring in awe at Cynthia as if she'd performed a miracle.

23

CYNTHIA TOOK A DEEP BREATH OF THE LAST OF THE October air. The leaves twirled and twisted on the gray branches of the canopy overhead, like ladies dancing in gowns of lemon and apricot and cerise. A few, caught by an unexpected puff of wind, swirled loose to flutter to the ground, flickering in the pale sunlight on their way. The scent of ripe apples permeated the brisk air, mixing with the odors of smoke and mulch to mull the wine of the autumn breeze.

They waited for her within the privy garden, just past the gate—her betrothed, the priest, the few witnesses. But impulsively, Cynthia kicked off her boots and allowed the nurturing energy of the earth to seep up through the soles of her bare feet. She closed her eyes, letting the sun burnish her thoughts to a golden hue.

At long last, she took Roger the steward's arm, giving it an affectionate squeeze, and they walked slowly forward through the gate, along the leafy path toward the man she was about to marry.

It was an intimate wedding, here in the lush quiet of the garden. The feast afterward, of course, would be enormous. The retinues of both de Ware brothers, her own castle folk, and the nearby villagers were invited to partake of a sennight's worth of festivities, including, at Cambria's insistence, a grand tournament. Elspeth had slaved for days organizing the great event. And Linet had wielded her creative authority, ordering the attire for the bride and groom with a practiced hand.

But the wedding ceremony itself was of Cynthia's design.

Beneath the leafless peach tree, Prior Thomas from the monastery, Bible in hand, beamed at her. Near him, Elspeth blubbered into a linen kerchief. And on either side of the path, Garth's closest kin stood, their faces a sweet blend of encouragement and acceptance.

Cynthia, however, only had eyes for Garth.

He wore a surcoat of rich, deep gray velvet overlaid with a fir green tabard that perfectly matched the smoky hue of his eyes. Around his neck hung the wooden cross proclaiming him a man of God. But it was the first time since he was a boy that Cynthia had seen him attired in clothing befitting the son of a noble. The silver link belt slung low on his hips caught the folds of fabric in a manner that accentuated his bold, lean figure, tripping her heart and turning her knees to pudding.

Cynthia swallowed hard. Were it not for the half dozen witnesses present, she might well have thrown herself at him, so intense was the wave of desire that washed over her as her handsome hero captured her gaze with his own.

She nervously fingered the soft material of the gown Linet had made up for her. It was of her finest Italian blue, Linet had said, claiming it set off Cynthia's eyes like two pale sapphires set in a summer sky. At the moment, Cynthia didn't care if it glowed with starlight. She didn't plan to be wearing it long after the ceremony was over.

As if scolding her for impure thoughts, the babe inside her suddenly aimed a hearty kick at her ribs. She gasped, then giggled as five faces showed instant concern. How sweet it was, she decided, to garner such affection from those who'd shortly be her kin. Why, she'd known them less than a fortnight, and already they looked after her like a baby sister. Linet fussed over her clothing as if Cynthia were a queen. Duncan flattered her mercilessly with odes to her virtues. Holden stood guard over her like a mastiff. And Cambria taught her the history of her own Gavin clan, of which she insisted Cynthia would soon be a part. Cynthia couldn't be happier.

Roger guided her to her betrothed, and Garth held a beringed hand out to her. She glanced at the insignia. It was the Wolf of de Ware. It was right that he wore it, she thought. It would remind him that though he also wore the cross of peace, the warrior wolf was always within him.

He took her hand, and Prior Thomas began the solemn rite of marriage. The moment seemed enchanted as the words fell from his lips in an elegant rhythm, their magic echoed even more powerfully by the man beside her. Even as Garth spoke, the sun peeped from behind a silvery cloud, spraying its rays through the bare limbs of the tree and down over his head like the halo of a saint in a cathedral painting. She sighed. How magnificent Garth was—beautiful and honorable and noble—and how lucky she was to have him.

She hugged his forearm and stepped a pace closer.

Suddenly, something wiggled beneath her bare foot. She shifted her weight. It wiggled again. Nay, she thought, holding her breath. It couldn't be. Not in October.

She didn't mean to scream. It was just such a surprise. And such an unpleasant one when she'd been drifting along on such lovely thoughts.

Of course, once *she* screamed, Elspeth shrieked in turn. Garth's eyes narrowed dangerously, and the poor prior backed away in alarm. Cynthia heard three swords unsheathe behind her. But all she could do was hop about on one foot, trying very hard not to curse as the pain of the bee sting throbbed under her toe and even harder not to laugh as she beheld the de Wares—Duncan, Holden, and Cambria—with swords drawn to fight the insect foe.

Decorum was eventually restored. As the prior dabbed at his brow, Garth used his dagger to gently dislodge the barb, murmuring with a smile that the task seemed all too oddly familiar. Elspeth's heart resumed its normal pace under the calming ministrations of Roger the steward. The de Ware swords returned to their sheaths, and the prior to his post.

Later she'd apply a poultice of lemon balm and mint to the swelling. But for now, she wanted to continue with the ceremony. The clouds had thickened ominously, and she could smell rain in the air. Besides, Garth's palm cupping her bare foot had done little to assuage the desire surging through her veins. Her body was unmistakably eager to consummate the marriage.

She spoke her vows sincerely but hastily, halting just once when the babe again pressed a sharp heel against her rib. She was over halfway through them when she heard the breeze begin to rise lazily through the boughs of the willow. She supposed that was why she didn't notice the other sound earlier—the soft wheeze coming from behind her.

But there was no overlooking the quick, furious whisper that came moments later. That was followed by a long sigh, then a quicker, more furious whisper. Soon there were whispers from all sides and something that sounded suspiciously like a curse. Finally, she couldn't ignore them anymore. She stopped mid-sentence and wheeled around.

Everyone was gathered about Linet. Her face was strained and as white as birch bark, and she staggered against Duncan.

"What the devil?" Garth said.

"Dear God!" Cynthia cried, picking up her skirts and rushing to Linet's side. "It's the babe, isn't it?"

"Oh . . . Cynthia . . . ," Linet puffed, "I'm . . . sorry."

Cynthia waved away her words. There was neither reason nor time for apology. By the looks of her, Linet might well deliver her babe ere she could get inside the keep.

"Duncan!" she ordered, snapping into action. "Spread your cloak on the grass here. Help her lie down."

"On the grass?"

"Aye! There's no time! Holden and Cambria! Fetch hot water from the kitchen! And Elspeth . . ."

"I've got it," the trusty maid called, already on her way. "Primrose, yarrow, and raspberry tea. I'll bring them all. Roger, come along to fetch linens!"

Cynthia briskly rubbed her hands together and crouched beside Linet, laid out now upon the sod. She smiled at the huffing woman in reassurance.

"It's your second child, aye?"

Linet nodded vigorously.

"Then we'd best hurry."

A first babe nearly always took half the night, but a second . . . there was no telling how quickly it would come. Cynthia blew a loose strand of hair from her eyes and glanced at the sky. Lord—she was so ill-equipped outside, and the heavens looked ripe to loose their burden any moment. It was ludicrous. She needed a bolster and linens and hot water. And a midwife. It took more than one person to properly deliver a babe. But there was no time.

She peered tensely around her. Who could help her? Prior Thomas was scarcely a candidate. He stood frozen to the trunk of the peach tree, mortified. Duncan was already busy comforting his laboring wife. She'd sent the others on errands. That left only Garth.

She looked at him, a silent plea in her eyes. Bless his heart, he came to her rescue at once.

"What can I do?" he asked gravely, resting a hand on her shoulder.

"I'll need a midwife," she said.

"Where? From the castle? The village?"

"Nay, there's no time. I need *you* to be the midwife."

His hand tightened on her shoulder, and his eyes widened for an instant in fear. Then he sighed, clamped his lips together, and nodded. "All right." He knelt beside her and pushed up his sleeves. "What shall I do?"

Heat glowed between her palms now. "Look beneath her skirts. See if the babe is coming." She was too busy laying her hand on Linet's damp forehead to see the glower Duncan gave his little brother as Garth hesitantly complied.

"There *is* . . . something . . . ," Garth said, wrinkling his brow.

Linet moaned.

"Don't worry, Linet," Duncan muttered. "After this is over, I'll beat Garth purple for his impertinence."

Cynthia closed her eyes, ignoring Duncan's grousing. Almost at once she received a brilliant picture . . . a healthy girl infant, a smiling mother—but no herbs. She frowned. She should at least see primrose. She took a deep breath and relaxed her mind. Nothing. Not a single leaf. She pursed her lips in frustration. Why would there be no . . .

"Something . . . ," Garth continued, at a loss to describe what he saw.

"Lord!" Cynthia exclaimed, popping her eyes open as it suddenly became clear. "The babe's crowned already, hasn't she?" She lunged past Duncan to see for herself. Sure enough, a patch of fuzzy black the size of a crest medallion appeared. There'd be no *time* for herbs. "All right, Duncan, help her to sit up and push with the next . . ."

Linet groaned. Sweat stood upon her fair brow, and she screwed up her features in a grimace of determination.

"That's it," Cynthia encouraged. "Squeeze Duncan's hand. Push hard. Garth, what's going on?"

"It's . . . it's coming out. Nay, it's going back in. I can't . . ."

Linet panted as the wave passed.

"All right, in a moment, we'll try again," Cynthia said.

She glanced at Duncan. He'd turned as pale as snow, but he clutched Linet's hand with true de Ware fortitude.

Linet sucked in a few deep breaths, then bore down again. The cords of her neck stood out in relief as she pushed with all her might.

"That's it!" Garth said. "That's it! I can see it! I can see . . . Damn! Lost again."

"Breathe slowly," Cynthia told Linet. "You're working very hard. You must rest between." She carefully unpinned the veil about Linet's head and pressed it into Duncan's hand. "You can use this to mop her brow."

"But . . ." Linet puffed. "That's . . . silk from . . ."

Duncan swabbed the cloth across her forehead. "I don't care if it's the Golden Fleece," he muttered anxiously.

"Of course . . . *you* don't. You didn't have to . . . bargain for it with . . ." Linet's indignant retort was interrupted by the wave of another contraction.

"One long push now," Cynthia said, laying a healing palm upon Linet's furrowed brow.

"I see it," Garth said as Linet groaned with strain. "It's increasing. Aye. It's large as a plum now. And now an apple. Aye . . . aye . . . nay." He looked up apologetically. "It's slipped back in."

Linet pounded a discouraged fist on the ground and slumped back against Duncan's chest.

"It's all right," Cynthia told her. "You rest now." She chewed at her lip. She'd seen this before, when the head of the infant was too large for the mother. Linet was strong. She was pushing with far more power than most. It would weary her soon. But she was getting nowhere. Too long a delay might harm the infant. And, to add more fodder to the fire of her troubles, the first fat drops of rain began to pelt the ground.

"Let's try something," she decided, rubbing her hands together and placing them atop Linet's belly. "Garth, get ready."

"Ready?"

"To catch."

Cynthia caught a glimpse of terror on Garth's face just before Linet gulped in a quick breath, then squeezed hard. As she pushed, Cynthia laid the full weight of her arms over the top of the bulging mound and pressed down.

"Aye!" Garth cheered. "Aye! It's coming now. I can see the brow! And the nose! And . . . Jesu!"

"What?" Duncan snapped. "What's wrong, damn you?"

Garth suddenly dove between Linet's legs.

"I'll break every bone . . . ," Duncan threatened, his voice cracking with fear.

"Got him!" Garth cried in victory. But his look of triumph soon turned to wondrous horror as he held the bloody, squirming, squalling bit of humanity.

Cynthia rocked back on her heels and winked at Linet, who lay breathless but smiling in relief against Duncan's chest. "Men," she said, shaking her head. "*Him* indeed." Then she whispered, "It's a girl."

She tore a sizable swatch from her own wedding gown, ignoring Linet's weak protests, and, taking the tiny girl from Garth, swaddled her appropriately in Linet's "finest Italian blue."

By the time she cut the cord and delivered the afterbirth, a veritable deluge pounded the sod. Duncan and Garth, on speaking terms again as they tried to outbrag each other regarding their part in the delivery, shielded their women and helped carry Linet to shelter. Once inside, Elspeth made raspberry tea for the new mother. Roger comforted the shaken prior and sent him on his way.

It wasn't till much later, with Linet tucked comfortably into bed beside her new babe, when the skies cleared and the harvest moon shone golden through Cynthia's window, upon the marriage bed she shared with Garth, that Cynthia realized they'd forgotten something.

"Garth," she crooned, slipping one bare leg over him and running a finger along the sensuous swell of his shoulder.

"Aye, my love." He arched against her thigh, nuzzling her hair. It felt divine.

"Do you remember," she said, slightly distracted, "what happened at the wedding?"

His lips curved into an irresistible smile. She had to kiss it. And then she had to kiss him again. Sweet Mary—he tasted like mulberry wine.

Chuckling, he lapped at her mouth with a delicate tongue, taunting her, enticing her, until she could stand no more. Completely forgetting her piece of news, she threw her arms around his neck and clambered atop him. Heedless of her own sinful abandon, she kissed his forehead, his eyelids, the bridge of his nose, settling again on his delicious mouth. Her low-slung belly brushed his, and he stroked her softly there, lingering awhile before he cupped the heavy weight of her breasts. She gasped. Her breasts prickled as his fingers grazed the distended nipples.

He laved her tongue languorously with his own, making deep, primitive sounds in his throat as she rocked against his warm, naked flesh.

Just as she thought she would burst with need of him, he lifted her hips and settled her down slowly onto his lap, filling her sweetly.

Their dance was subdued now. Her girth allowed only gentle movement and soothing rhythm. But it was exhilarating beyond belief to feel Garth's sweet restraint, to watch the ecstasy crease his features as he mastered his own release. And it was empowering to ride astride him, setting the cadence, choosing the tide, quivering with rapture as her body edged closer to the precipice.

This time, she leaped over the edge first. A hundred tremors shook her on the wondrous journey down. She cried out his name, squeezing him between her thighs, clutching at his broad shoulders. Her hair shivered over her breasts, which tingled almost painfully. And then she was floating.

He followed her almost at once, thrashing his head across the pillow, bucking against her like an untamed stallion, groaning as if he endured unimaginable torture. And then he, too, was still.

She continued to straddle him, too exhausted to move, yet almost asleep sitting up.

"Now," he inquired silkily, grinning, "what were you saying about the wedding?"

She peered at him through nearly closed lids. It was hard to remember anything in the presence of that captivating crooked smile. "Oh, it's naught that cannot wait," she said, slipping languorously aside to snuggle against him.

They had a lifetime ahead of them—mellow autumns, cozy winters, vibrant springs, sultry summers. Their love was firmly rooted in fertile soil now. The stock was strong and hardy. And the growing season had just begun. Contentment, the warmth of Garth beside her, and the soft rhythm of their mingling breath lulled her to sleep.

Epilogue

"IT WON'T BE LONG NOW, M'LADY," ELSPETH SAID, SWAB-bing Cynthia's brow with primrose water.

"Breathe," Jeanne the midwife bade her with irritating calm. "That's it. Slow and steady."

"Get," Cynthia ground out. "Father. Paul."

"As you can see," Jeanne continued, ignoring her temper to lecture the eight maidens gathered around her heaving belly in various states of interest and disgust, "it's helpful to have at least two individuals attending the birth. One stands here," she said, moving to the foot of the pallet, "to monitor the progress of the birth . . ."

"Bring . . . Garth," Cynthia panted.

"And one here," Elspeth added, indicating herself, "to comfort the laboring . . ."

"El!"

"Aye?" Her eyes were suddenly sweet and concerned.

Cynthia let out a breath of self-disgust. She shouldn't be impatient with the woman. Elspeth was so excited to have a new charge on the way. She couldn't help it if her enthusiasm was occasionally annoying.

Still, Cynthia *was* in labor. It was painful and, though she'd delivered dozens of other women's babes, having her own was strangely frightening.

"Please . . . get them."

Elspeth frowned and bent near, whispering as if to a child, "But, m'lady, a birthin's not a proper sight for a husband." Then she frowned. "And why do ye want Father Paul?"

Jeanne turned to the maids and explained. "Sometimes at this stage of the birth, the mother gets confused and—"

"Listen!" Quickly, before the rising wave of pain could incapacitate her, she hauled Elspeth to her by the front of her surcoat. El dropped her rag, and the maidens stared in surprise as Cynthia spat out her demands. "I need Father Paul. And Garth. Now!"

Elspeth's perplexed face blurred as the dull ache in Cynthia's back sharpened, forcing her attention to her labor again.

Elspeth tapped the shoulders of two of the maids. "Go to the chapel. They're likely there, both of 'em, prayin'."

They scurried off to do her bidding.

The pain surged to a peak, then fell away slowly, like the swell of the sea. Cynthia shut her eyes and focused, trying to envision her fate, willing the familiar images to come, but it was useless. The door that usually swung open for others as easily as a wattle gate was closed upon her own destiny.

"Is she all right?" whispered one of the maids.

"She'll be fine," Elspeth murmured, though Cynthia could hear doubt in the maid's voice.

She opened her eyes, silently cursing herself for letting things wait so long. She should have taken care of the matter the night Linet had her babe. But at the time, the household had been in a tumult, and then Garth had distracted her with that divine body of his. After that, she'd shared three months of utter bliss with him—cuddling away the long winter evenings, planning the Christmas feast, working together to convert the spare chambers of Wendeville into a magnificent teaching infirmary—and somehow the whole issue had slipped her mind.

She glanced at the young women gathered around her. It was little wonder the infirmary had occupied her thoughts so completely. The place was nothing short of wondrous. And these maidens were a testament to the miracles that occurred daily. None of them had witnessed childbirth before. But with Jeanne the midwife's help, they would learn today how to deliver and care for a newborn.

Garth and Cynthia had turned Wendeville into a refuge, a place of hope for the spirit and the body. Since they'd opened their doors, they'd managed to restore the faith and the health of nearly every patient admitted, as well as providing trained physicians for Charing and the village. Of course, Garth was too busy now with secular duties to devote himself as fully to the chapel, but he'd found a good chaplain for Wendeville in Father Paul. Though Garth was never seen without his sword, he still wore his wooden crucifix as a constant reminder of his faith.

Another seizure claimed Cynthia. This time, all her panting did nothing to assuage the pain. She dug her fingers into the pallet while Elspeth stroked the hair back from her tossing head.

But it, too, passed, and she heard El speaking softly to the maids. "It's helpful," she said, "to remain quiet and calm while she's laborin'." Then she took Cynthia's hand and bent to whisper frantically against her ear. "Dear God, m'lady, why do ye call for the chaplain? Have ye foreseen yer death?"

"Nay," she said with an incredulous laugh. But her levity was interrupted by the onslaught of another contraction. She squeezed El's hand and huffed out shallow puffs of air. An irresistible urge to push overwhelmed her. But it wasn't yet time. She refused to birth this babe until the chaplain came. Until Garth stood by her side. She held back, breathing faster until the desire passed.

There was little time between pains now. Scarcely did one wave subside when another began. If the Father was delayed . . .

"You must watch for the head to crown," Jeanne explained to the women.

The maids peered solemnly between her legs, as if they looked for the arrival of the Holy Grail. If she hadn't been so consumed with pain, Cynthia would have laughed.

Just as she thought she might succumb to the need to push, the two maids returned with their quarry. Garth was as white as vellum. But Father Paul seemed only bemused, betraying his surprise with but a lift of one white brow. "You called for me?"

"Why did you call for the chaplain?" Garth demanded, his voice weak with fear, pushing his way past the women to come to her side. "Are you . . . is the babe . . . ?"

A wave of incapacitating pain prevented her speech.

"Nay, Cynthia," Garth pleaded, the terror naked in his eyes.

"It's not . . ." Cynthia gasped, clutching at the chaplain's sleeve. "'S'all right . . . don't . . . ah . . ."

She couldn't resist the desire to push this time. It was stronger than anything she'd ever felt. She bore down, clenching her fists, holding her breath.

"I see it!" a maid yelled excitedly. "The babe is coming!"

Cynthia sucked in a fast gulp of air and seized a fistful of the chaplain's cassock.

"Hurry!" she panted. "Before the babe is born!" She groaned with the need to bear down.

Garth sank to his knees beside her. Anxiety creased his features as he clung desperately to her arm. "Sweet Jesu, Cynthia!"

"For the love of God," she gasped at the chaplain. "Marry us! Marry us quick!"

"What!" Garth exploded.

"We . . . never . . ."

It was the most difficult thing she'd ever done, spitting out the words of the marriage rites as labor pains exerted their control over her body. But somehow she did it. And somehow Garth managed to gasp out his own part of the covenant.

By a narrow miracle, their babe was born not a by-blow, but the legitimate heir to Wendeville.

Little Lord Arthur, with gray-green eyes and a tuft of hair the color of marigolds. With a gift for healing and a talent with the quill. His grandfather le Wyte's stubbornness and his grandmother de Ware's wiles. The noble, healthy, squalling son of Lady Cynthia and Lord Garth de Ware. The beginning of a litter of pups that would become the next generation of the Knights of de Ware.